THE LAST
CONFESSION
OF AUTUMN
CASTERLY

Also by Meredith Tate

Freedom Trials
Missing Pieces
The Red Labyrinth

THE LAST CONFESSION OF AUTUMN CASTERLY

MEREDITH TATE

putnam

G. P. Putnam's Sons

G. P. Putnam's Sons
An imprint of Penguin Random House LLC, New York

Copyright © 2020 by Meredith Tate
Penguin supports copyright. Copyright fuels creativity, encourages diverse
voices, promotes free speech, and creates a vibrant culture. Thank you for buying
an authorized edition of this book and for complying with copyright laws
by not reproducing, scanning, or distributing any part of it in any form without
permission. You are supporting writers and allowing Penguin to
continue to publish books for every reader.

G. P. Putnam's Sons is a registered trademark of Penguin Random House LLC.

Visit us online at penguinrandomhouse.com

Library of Congress Cataloging-in-Publication Data
Names: Tate, Meredith, author.
Title: The last confession of Autumn Casterly / Meredith Tate.
Description: New York: G. P. Putnam's Sons, [2020]
Summary: When Autumn Casterly goes missing after a drug deal gone wrong,
her estranged younger sister, Ivy, searches for her, uncovering dark secrets along the way.
Identifiers: LCCN 2019005506 (print) | LCCN 2019008912 (ebook)
ISBN 9781984813503 (eBook) | ISBN 9781984813497 (hardcover)
Subjects: | CYAC: Missing persons—Fiction. | Sisters—Fiction.
Secrets—Fiction. | Concord (N.H.)—Fiction.
Classification: LCC PZ7.1.T3837 (ebook)
LCC PZ7.1.T3837 Las 2020 (print) | DDC [Fic]—dc23
LC record available at https://lccn.loc.gov/2019005506

Printed in the United States of America

ISBN 9781984813497

1 3 5 7 9 10 8 6 4 2

Design by Dana Li
Text set in Janson MT Pro

To my parents, Paul and Jessica
And to my husband, Vincent

To my beautiful hometown of Concord, NH

And especially,
To all the survivors who are
shut down
gaslighted
silenced
slut-shamed
blamed
and called liars,
I see you. I believe you.
You deserve the world.
This one's for you.

THURSDAY

AUTUMN

On a scale of one to ten, my desire to talk to the cops who've spent the last twenty minutes digging through my locker is a raging negative fifty. And yet, here I am.

I breathe out a heavy sigh, watching them examine every single book, binder, and random thing in there.

The shorter cop holds up a baggie full of nuts. "What's this?"

"Honey-roasted peanuts. Very scary stuff." If I had known I'd be yanked out of fifth period, I wouldn't have blown two hours of my life writing that Faulkner paper last night. But everyone thinks their time is more valuable than mine—it comes with the territory of being a teenage girl.

"What's this dusting on them?"

I lean against the row of lockers behind me. "The honey-roasted part." If they were coated in cocaine, does he really think I'd look him in the eyes and say, *They're coated in cocaine?* "Otherwise I would've just said 'peanuts.'"

This is Kaitlyn Kennedy's fault. Each second I stand here, the anger inside me simmers hotter. It's pretty much at a full-blown boil right now. Kaitlyn's lucky she's not here. She won't be so lucky later.

I survey the pile of my crap they've dumped onto the common-room floor. "Can I go back to class now?"

"We're almost done." The other cop, who looks like a less-hot clone of Rob Gronkowski, yanks the spare box of tampons out of my backpack. To my horror, he opens it. He literally opens my tampons and starts taking them out, one by one, right in the middle of the common room.

"Seriously?"

"We're just doing our job, Ms. Casterly." The short cop pulls out one of the tampons and sniffs it, and I pretty much want to melt into the carpet. What the hell? If they're going to sniff my stuff for drugs, at least bring a drug-sniffing dog for me to pet.

Principal Greenwich hovers nearby, his caterpillar eyebrows low over his eyes. "Autumn, why is it that whenever there's a hint of trouble in this school, all roads seem to lead back to you?"

"I didn't do anything, Mr. Greenwich. There's nothing in my locker but books and trash. And tampons." I'm not lying. I'd never keep my stash in my locker for this very reason.

But it doesn't matter if they find anything or not. The principal has already pegged me as a criminal. I'm one of the "bad kids," and labels come with assumptions. They assume the bad kids are always monsters, and the good ones never are.

A couple of doe-eyed freshmen whisper to each other as they pass, not even trying to hide their stares. Probably excited to tell their friends they witnessed Autumn Casterly getting her ass handed to her by the cops. One of them looks like she might try and talk to me, but I glower and they walk faster.

"You're probably one of the only senior girls whose locker isn't loaded with selfies and pictures of giant groups of girls making duckfaces." The cop chuckles, thrilled by his own joke. Ah yes, we've got a real comedian here. Nothing is funnier than belittling teen girls. But I can't help feeling like there was a hidden question in his statement—*Don't you have any friends?* I grind my shoe into the dirty carpet.

Not-Rob-Gronkowski grins, holding up a photo of my dog, Pumpernickel. "Who's this?"

Literally none of your business. "My dog."

"He a miniature schnauzer?"

"Yep."

"Cute. My sister has one, they're great."

Five minutes ago he made fun of my Proud Vegetarian magnet, so I'm pretty pissed he thinks he has the right to compliment my dog right now. I can almost see the amusement on his face that the school delinquent has a well-loved pet. As if the fact that I deal pills means I should be surrounded by vape pens and switchblades and maybe something *really* illegal, like a mountain of Kinder Eggs. But I love my dog. Loving animals is so much less complicated than loving humans.

"Aw. This you?" He holds up another photo, crinkled at the edges. It's my mom and me sitting on the tire swing at Merrill Park when I was six. Back when we lived on the east side of town.

Something catches in my throat. My mom's been dead for almost seven years, and I thought I'd be able to handle these things better by now. Everyone told me it would get easier—five stages of grief and all that stuff—but it hasn't yet.

I look away. "Yep."

The cops finish their prying and declare my locker officially drug-free. They don't offer to help put back my stuff they've so generously left strewn in the middle of the room. I force a smile as they leave, mentally shoving both middle fingers up their asses. The funny thing is, if they searched my bedroom, they'd have enough evidence to lock me away for a couple of years. I suppose that's what would happen if the system actually worked.

"Thanks for your cooperation, Autumn." The principal says it like I had a choice. He nods as I start shoving books into my locker. "You can go back to class when you've finished up." No apology for ruining my day, of course.

I throw my things inside a little harder than necessary, the metal clanging in my ears. My face gets hot when the bell rings and a flood of people burst into the common room.

They send smiles and waves my way. Everyone wants to say they're Autumn Casterly's BFF. But none of them give two shits about me—they just want me to sell to them.

The moment they think I'm out of earshot, words get tossed between them in hushed whispers. *Bitch. Slut. Liar.* They'd never say it to my face, but my hearing is good. Too good. I stuff everything into my locker faster.

Maybe if I was weaker, their words would pierce me. My mom used to say that we should be like ducks, letting gossip and insults flow off our backs like drops of water rolling down oily feathers. But I'm not a duck.

I'm a predator.

With each book and binder that I cram back into my locker, I repeat one promise in my head over and over: Kaitlyn Kennedy's getting her ass kicked after school.

IVY

Kevin is taking forever to make his move. His leg jitters against the chair leg beside me. Our Ticket to Ride Europe game board takes up half the table. Every time his knee jiggles, it knocks some of the train pieces off their spaces.

"Hey, Marino, you planning to draw cards this year?" Alexa asks.

A pink tinge spreads across Kevin's cheeks. "I'm thinking."

Alexa's long, glittery fingernails click impatiently against the tabletop.

We started the Nerd Herd Club last year, trying to make it a thing. It's still just the six of us. Our meetings usually start with someone geeking out over Final Fantasy and end with an argument about *Star Wars* (Han shot first, I don't give a shit what Jason says). We've recently delved into the wonderful world of board games—which is why we're meeting in the gross cafeteria today, because the librarian accused us of being too rowdy. I mean, I wouldn't call us *rowdy*, I'd say we have a spirited sense of competition.

"Okay, I'm gonna build," Kevin says after an eternity.

"Finally," Jason mutters.

Kevin lays four blue train pieces onto the board, connecting Edinburgh and London.

"Asshole!" Alexa fake-punches him in the arm. "I was gonna do that."

The janitor swishes a dirty mop over the tiled floor. He looks less than thrilled to see us here after school.

I nudge Kevin. "Let's meet at your place tomorrow. I feel like we've outworn our welcome in the cafeteria."

"My mom's renovating our kitchen."

"Better than this." Alexa flicks a lock of purple hair behind her ear.

"She says no visitors until it's finished."

Alexa's girlfriend, Sophie, finishes polishing her glasses and pushes them up the bridge of her nose. "Isn't there a rule that school clubs have to meet at school to count?"

Jason lays a few tracks on the board. "I don't think hanging out every day counts as a club anymore."

"It's a stupid rule anyway." Alexa rolls her eyes at him. "Seriously? I was *just* about to build there."

"Can we go to your house?" I ask Alexa.

"Nope. My parents haven't seen this one since we officially started dating." She affectionately nudges Sophie. "And I'd rather avoid the third degree. You know my dad would have the 'what are your intentions with my daughter' talk with her."

I snort. "Oh please. You're the one doing all the corrupting in this relationship."

"It's true." Sophie grins. "But you have to let them see me before homecoming."

"You going to homecoming, Ivy?" Jason asks. "You should go with me. As friends. So we don't look like losers."

"I think it's too late for that," I say. "But sure." I'm a little relieved. Me and Jason have been going to dances as best-friend dates since freshman year, and I always worry he's going to get a girlfriend and ditch me. Then I'll be that person hanging out by the bathroom during slow songs.

Alexa huffs. "What if she'd wanted to go with a real date?"

My heart sinks. "He is a real date. Friends count." I draw two, doing a happy dance at the wild card. "Unless Patrick Perkins wants to move back to Concord and sweep me off my feet."

Jason laughs. "Your lover."

Patrick Perkins has been an inside joke ever since I told the group about him. I was so smitten with that kid back in fifth grade. We were besties. Seriously, he snuck two pints of Ben and Jerry's out of his parents' freezer for me the day I got my first period and wanted to die. That kid was the shit. Then his parents got a divorce and he moved away. It sucked. But now it's kind of funny.

A couple upperclassmen stroll through the cafeteria in workout clothes, making a beeline for the snack machine. "Wassup, dungeon masters?" one of the guys yells. They practically fall over themselves laughing. I don't really get what's so funny; we're playing board games, ha-ha?

Kevin slinks down in his seat, his cheeks turning pink again. He's not great with standing up for himself when jerks show up. The rest of us protectively slide closer to him.

"We're not playing D and D today," Alexa says coolly. "But I'll let you know next time we do. We've been looking for someone to play the troll."

"You can be *my* dungeon master," the other guy says, popping quarters into the machine.

I'll never understand why douchebags always hit on Alexa. First of all, she's been dating Sophie for, like, five months now, and they're always holding hands and stuff in the hallway. Second, she's got a big *"I like my coffee like I like my men. I don't drink coffee."—Ellen DeGeneres* button on her messenger bag. And lastly, she's deathly allergic to assholes.

"Great! Here's my dungeon key." She sticks up her middle finger. "Get your snacks and go away."

"This machine's been ransacked. You sure your friend didn't eat them all?" The way the guy says *friend* is ambiguous, but I know he's talking about me.

"Hey." Jason jumps to his feet. Sophie puts her hand on his elbow to calm him down.

"Wow, food jokes about the fat girl," I shout as they stride out of the cafeteria. "How original." Seriously, every time someone makes a crack about my weight, they think they're saying something revolutionary. As if I had no idea I was fat until they pointed it out.

"Sorry, Ivy." Jason settles back into his seat. "Those guys are pricks."

"The tall one sits behind me in chem," Alexa adds. "Judging by his score on our last quiz, methinks he should spend less time being a dick and more time actually, you know, opening a book."

I grin. "A radical concept. What were we talking about before that rude interruption?"

"Where to meet tomorrow." Kevin blinks at his train tracks, which are spread victoriously across the entire map of Europe on the game board. "Also, I just completed my long route."

The rest of us groan. Half the time I think Kevin is hustling us, because he acts so innocent but then kicks our asses at almost every game.

"Total annihilation," Jason says.

"What about your place, Ivy?" Sophie asks. "Can we meet there?"

I shudder. "Nope. Never. I live with Satan."

Jason snickers.

"Is your sister really that bad?" Sophie asks. "I don't think I've ever actually met the infamous Autumn Casterly."

"You're lucky. She should probably be in juvie," I mumble. Last year, I found this pamphlet on how to protect yourself from a snarling dog threatening to bite. You're supposed to avoid eye contact, back away slowly, and speak in a calm tone when absolutely necessary; that's kind of what living with Autumn is like.

"I wouldn't mind hanging out with your sister." Jason winks, laying down a couple tracks.

"Jason Daly-Cruz, do you have the hots for Autumn?" Alexa wiggles her eyebrows.

Jason grins. He thinks it's hilarious to joke about dating Autumn.

"No." I draw a card. "No chance in hell." Kinda sucks when your sister is the pretty one and you have to listen to everyone talk about her constantly. I wouldn't be surprised if Jason did have a crush on Autumn. If not, he's probably the only hetero guy in our whole school who doesn't. Rumor has it she only goes out with college guys, though, and rumors are about as close as I get to actual details about her life.

Deciphering Autumn's rumor mill is like playing two truths and a lie, but in this version of the game, there could be one truth, or two, or three, or zero, and I'd never know which. In the past week, I've heard that Autumn (1) blew off AP Euro to smoke weed in the teachers' lot, (2) was responsible for Carly Quince's ankle brace, and (3) sold painkillers to one of the school secretaries. All I know is, she vanishes constantly, and I don't even want to know whose bed she's sleeping in when she doesn't come home.

With her reputation, I wouldn't think guys would fall at her feet like they do, but Autumn's beauty is like the rush of the ocean in a hurricane. From far away, she's mystifying and beautiful, like waves crashing on a stormy shore. However, the closer you get, the wilder and more dangerous she becomes, capable of pulling you under until you drown.

"Not meeting at my house, and you're not getting near my sister," I tell Jason. Basically, Autumn would eat him alive, spit out his bones, and pick her teeth with them. Some of these board games require six people, so I need him to not be human floss.

"Okay, I have to ask." Alexa leans toward me, lowering her voice to a whisper only we can hear. "Did you ever get confirmation if that rumor about her is true?"

"You're going to have to be more specific."

"About, you know." She smiles deviously. "Her and your step-brother?"

Jason and Kevin huddle closer to me to hear. Ugh. I thought everyone would have dropped this by now. That dirty little secret people felt the need to constantly ask me about back in seventh grade. My friends thought it was *hysterical* at the time.

"What, that she slept with Chris? I guess." I shrug. "I don't keep tabs on what or who she's doing." I mean, it's not really a secret around here. I was only in middle school at the time, but it got through the grapevine pretty quickly, and everything at home got super uncomfortable afterward, so I'm guessing it's true. It kind of skeeves me out. She couldn't have picked anyone else?

Time for a subject change.

"Jason, how about we go to your place for the next meeting?" I ask. "I haven't hugged your mom in, like, a week." Jason's house is really cool. They have a game room with a foosball table.

"I think you like my parents more than you like me."

"That's accurate. But it doesn't answer my question."

He thinks for a moment. "Maybe. My brother might have people coming over tomorrow, though. I have to check." The funny thing about Jason and his brother is, in photos they look nothing alike; Micah is a clone of their blond Irish father, while Jason's the spitting image of their dark-haired Filipino mother. But when Jason and Micah are standing side by side, the resemblance is uncanny. They could pass as fraternal twins, even though they're five years apart.

Sophie takes her turn, drawing two cards. "We can go to my place."

"Sold!" I slap down my train tracks, accidentally knocking a few pieces off the board. Last time we met at Sophie's place, her dad made us say grace before eating our Taco Bell takeout. But Sophie's house is always full of these awesome strawberry cookies from her grandparents in Seoul, and it's way better than camping out in the cafeteria after hours.

"Hello, everyone." Coach Crespo strolls through the cafeteria, giving us a jolly wave. A whistle hangs from a lanyard around his neck. It bounces against his crimson Concord Football windbreaker with every step.

Jason and Sophie snicker.

"Hey, Coach." Alexa smirks. "What're you up to?"

"On my way to a meeting with Ms. Bratten."

"I'm sure you are," Sophie mutters under her breath. Jason snorts.

"Gotta get the field hockey team in fighting shape this year."

Jason buries his face in his elbow, half a second away from bursting, while Kevin and Alexa are grinning like six-year-olds on Christmas morning. In other news, I'd like to submit an application for some less embarrassing friends.

"You kids enjoy your game." Coach Crespo heads into the hallway, his footsteps fading into nothing.

The table erupts in laughter.

I shake my head. "Could you guys be any more obvious?"

"Creepo's on the prowl," Jason says. "Hide your daughters."

Alexa snorts. "More like hide your mothers."

Coach Crespo—more commonly known as Coach Creepo—has quite the reputation. And I'm not just referring to the line of trophies outside the gym. Apparently the female coaches will only go into his office in pairs. And back in March, someone left an anonymous note under the principal's door, swearing Creepo was peeping on girls in the workout room, but nothing came of it. Last year, someone Photoshopped his yearbook pic into a meme that said variations of *Who wants to see my bat?* It made the rounds on Tumblr for three months. He was my stepbrother's coach back in the day, and he was creepy then, too.

It's pretty messed up, and I don't think it's funny. I want to tell them to stop laughing about it. I open my mouth, but my jaw just kind of hangs open.

There's a big part at the end of *Harry Potter and the Sorcerer's Stone* where Dumbledore gives Neville points to Gryffindor for standing up to his friends because it's just as hard as standing up to his enemies. I like to think I'm more of a Ginny than a Neville, but I felt that scene so hard.

I take a deep breath. "Hey, guys?" I peep, barely louder than a whisper.

"Your turn, Ivy," Jason says, having not heard me.

I close my mouth and draw a card. I would not get points for Hufflepuff today.

"Where the hell is Ahmed?" Alexa checks her phone. "He's my ride home, and he's missed the whole game." She barely finishes her sentence before our sixth member strolls into the cafeteria. "Jeez, he's like the Babadook—you say his name, and *poof!* He appears."

"Ha-ha. You're *hilarious.*" Ahmed groans when he sees our game board. "Ticket to Ride again?"

"Well, if you'd been on time, you could've had a say in what we picked," Alexa says. "But alas."

"We're almost done anyway," I say. "Kevin's kicking our asses."

Ahmed sets his backpack on the floor and takes a seat beside Sophie. "I wasn't trying to be late. I was showing this new kid how to put money on his ID card. I actually invited him to join us, if that's okay."

"It's not a seven-person game," Jason says. He's always so over-protective of our little club.

I take a swig from my bottle of Cherry Coke. "It's fine. The more the merrier."

"He'll fit right in, I promise—he's got a BB-8 backpack."

"Sweet," I say.

"One of us, one of us," Alexa chants.

Ahmed waves. "Here he is!"

I look up right as the newcomer walks in and nearly choke on my drink.

"Whoa." The guy grins and runs a hand through his light hair. "Hey, Ivy. Long time no see."

There, standing right in front of me, is a several-years-older Patrick Perkins.

AUTUMN

I lean against the locker room door, sliding on my rings—two on each finger. Field hockey practice ended a while ago, and players are slowly trickling out, their hair cemented to their foreheads with sweat.

No one snitches on me.

Scratch that. Some people do. But no one snitches on me twice.

A criminal record would ruin everything. Not even the worst college wants a drug dealer, no matter how good their SAT scores are. Last year, I found out Amanda Carlson told our pre-calc substitute that I had pot in my backpack. The sub didn't do anything—I'm 90 percent sure he was high himself—but it scared the shit out of me; if anyone had checked my bag, they would've learned Amanda was telling the truth, and I would've been suspended. It was a good lesson for me and Amanda, though. I haven't carried drugs to school since, and Amanda's brand-new Hyundai got an introduction to my house key.

"You sure she's still in there?" Jaclyn asks. She's wearing bright red lipstick today, which is too severe against her pale skin and platinum-blond hair.

"She's there." I throw on a coat of gloss and smack my lips together. "She always showers after every practice." Before Kaitlyn, I don't think anyone had used those nasty gym showers since, like, the eighties. "But she won't do it when her team's still around. I know Kaitlyn—she won't even change in the same room as them." Back in the day, when everyone went to sleepovers together, the rest of us put on our pj's in the main room, but Kaitlyn would go into the bathroom and shut the door. You never know when tidbits like that will come in handy.

Abby lazily flicks her lighter, watching the flame burst up and shrink back down. "How do you know it was *her*, though? It could've been—"

She stops abruptly as another field hockey player saunters out of the locker room. The poor girl's eyes widen when she sees us. She's short and scrawny, probably a freshman, but everyone knows who I am. Hell, even kids at the community college know who I am—maybe even at the middle school, too. I can see conflict crossing the freshman's face. Should she be a hero and warn Kaitlyn? Or get the hell out of here while she still can? I arch a brow, inviting a challenge. The girl scurries away, her eyes glued to the floor.

I continue. "Cops were at my locker with Principal Greenwich." Three hours later, I'm still pissed about it.

Abby snorts. "So? You don't keep your shit there. Anyone could've tipped them off."

"My *locker*, Abby." I roll my eyes. "If it was Sarah Solomon, the cops would've been at my car. If it was Derek, they'd be checking my cubby in the bio lab. But they were at my locker, and that has Kaitlyn's paw prints all over it." The best way to learn who you can trust? Plant some fake seeds. See which ones sprout.

"Let's make this quick," Abby says. "I don't wanna be late to meet the guys."

"They can wait." It's a stretch; our supplier and his guys will probably get bored and leave if we don't show up on time. But this needs to be done first.

A sophomore strolls past—I don't remember her name. I think she's on cheer squad or something. Her eyes light up when she sees me. "Hey, Autumn!"

I nod, not bothering to wipe the bored look off my face.

"You going to the football game against Central next weekend?" She's grinning so wide, it's like she's storing acorns for winter.

"Nope." I hate football. "Not my thing. Sorry."

Her face falls. "Oh." The girl hovers a moment, shuffling her feet. I pretend to check my phone, hoping she'll leave.

That's a funny thing about being popular; everyone wants to say they know you, even tangentially. I can picture this sophomore expecting me to say I was going to the game like everyone else. Then at the game she'd tell all her friends that I told her I'd be there, like we're friends or something. Last year, this super-annoying girl, Lily Howell, loaned me a pen in physics when mine ran out of ink; after class, I overheard her telling her friends that she didn't have an extra pen because she *loaned it to Autumn Casterly.*

They taught us the trickle-down theory in economics. Our teacher drew a tree on the board, each branch with a bird on it. As the bird on the top got the most fruit, it started dropping fruit for the birds on the lower branches, and the birds on the bottom got the least. This kid Brad, who is always a giant shit to everyone, said, "So the bird at the top poops, and it lands on the heads of the little birds below it?" He was being a smartass, but he had a point. I don't want to be the bird with shit on my head. I want to be on the top branch, deciding who gets the fruit.

"So I'll see you guys later?" the girl says.

I position my body slightly to the right, facing Abby and Jaclyn with my back to the girl. She gets the message and keeps walking.

When her footsteps fade, I press my ear to the door. The rushing shower water mingles with Kaitlyn's muffled singing voice. She thinks she's alone. This will be good.

Holding my finger to my lips, I slink through the locker room door. Jaclyn and Abby follow, their footsteps not as stealthy as mine. Steam clouds the room, hot and foggy against the mirrors. A pair of jeans and a button-down shirt are neatly folded on the bench, waiting for Kaitlyn to get out of the shower.

Abby gently pushes them to the floor. "Oops."

Jaclyn snickers into her hand. They're loving this.

I take a moment to adjust the tiny silver hoops in my ears in the bathroom mirror. It crosses my mind to remove them in case things get physical, but I don't. They look cute on me. Besides, I'm the one with the upper hand here.

A balled-up sock lies abandoned on the floor. I kick it into the corner and approach the showers.

The water cuts off with a squeak.

Kaitlyn slides the shower curtain open, a towel wrapped around her body. She sucks in a sharp breath, nearly stumbling over herself when she sees us.

I grin. "Hey there."

She tries to run, but Abby and Jaclyn have already grabbed her arms and pinned her to the wall. Kaitlyn's practically got muscles growing on her muscles, but my girls are tougher. A scream rockets from her mouth.

Oh, for fuck's sake.

My girls grit their teeth but don't relinquish their grip on Kaitlyn's arms.

"Would you shut the hell up?" Jaclyn snaps.

The scream echoes around the hot room. No one will hear her unless they're creeping around the basement after hours, but I don't take chances. I pluck the dirty sock off the floor and cram it into Kaitlyn's mouth.

I step back and smile. "There. Much better."

Abby smirks. "You're awfully quiet now. Too bad you couldn't have kept that mouth shut around the cops, huh?"

Fear flashes across Kaitlyn's face. She makes muffled sounds behind the gag, like a sick animal or something. Probably begging. Why do they always beg? If you need to beg for mercy, it's too late—mercy's not coming.

Kaitlyn's panicked eyes flick between me and the girls pinning her. But karma's a bitch, and I've got no sympathy for snitches.

"You know, I liked you, Kaitlyn." I step closer to her. "Trusted you. Considered you a valuable customer, like I value all my customers."

She blinks back tears, mumbling something that sounds suspiciously like *Please, Autumn.*

I wag my finger at her. "I'd have thought the captain of our varsity field hockey team—seventeenth in the nation, am I right?—would have more stones than this. Woman up, please. You're making yourself look bad."

Jaclyn and Abby cackle.

"Now, what should I do with you?" I tap my chin, pretending to ponder. "Would suck to play the championships next month with a broken arm, huh?"

She whimpers.

"Nah." I shake my head. "I've got school pride. Can't let you get your asses kicked by Central . . . *again.*"

I really should win an Oscar for dragging this out so much.

"Now, if you can promise to stay quiet—not that anyone's coming to save you, anyway—I'll take this out." I lazily point at the gag in her mouth.

Kaitlyn nods enthusiastically and I remove the wet sock, tossing the gross thing far away.

"I'm a forgiving person." I anchor a hand on my hip. "But you ratted me out. That's not cool."

"Not even a little bit," Jaclyn adds. She's got several inches on Kaitlyn.

"I didn't tell the cops anything!"

I tsk at her. "Kaitlyn, Kaitlyn. You know I know when you're lying, right?"

"I swear it wasn't me. I wouldn't tell the police—why would I?"

"Then you told someone who *did* tell the cops. You're not supposed to tell *anyone* about me, no matter what."

She blinks. "Don't you want new customers?"

"I have plenty of customers. You know my rules. If you want to refer someone, you give me their name and *I'll* get in touch with *them* if I trust them. You don't just go waving my name around like a fucking flag." I swear, information leaks through this school faster than a damn sieve. "Because shit like that is why the police spent an hour searching my locker today."

"I didn't mean to." Kaitlyn's voice shakes. "I swear. Someone asked me where to get Ativan, and I told them to talk to you—that you keep a stash in your locker. I didn't know she'd tell."

"Oh? And who would this *someone* be?"

She hesitates.

I sigh. "Guess she wants to rock a cast for a while."

"No! No. Okay. It was Hailey Waters."

I'm taken aback. Hailey's literally the last person I'd expect to be sniffing around for pills. That girl is like a walking billboard for the Catholic Church. I've never even spoken to her, and for good reason. Still, no one's perfect, and Little Miss Hailey probably has dirt like anyone else. If I find out she's the reason those cops were sniffing my tampons, that dirt might accidentally find its way onto the morning announcements.

Abby laughs. "No way."

"I swear. She must have told someone."

"I'm not surprised," Jaclyn says. "I'd get high too if I had to be in marching band." She nods at me. "Doesn't your sister play an instrument? Bet she knows Hailey."

I think for a moment. My useless sister, Ivy, could come in handy for once. Between her and the merry band of losers she hangs out with, someone's got to know Hailey well enough to have insider information. But it seems risky dragging her into this. She'd tell our dad in half a second.

"No. I'll find out on my own." I always do. Another valuable lesson my mom taught me before she died: don't depend on anyone but yourself. "As for this one . . ." I nod at Kaitlyn, who cringes. My friends tighten their grip on her arms.

"I told you what you wanted!"

"Yes, you did." I twist the heavy rings on my fingers. "But it's not enough." I swing my fist like I'm about to punch her, but stop an inch short of breaking her nose; she winces and closes her eyes. Fake-outs are very effective—they spread fear without leaving marks. I lower my voice to a whisper and get right up next to her ear. "Don't mess up again."

On cue, Jaclyn and Abby rip the towel off her. Before she can cover up, I've already snapped a photo. I flip my phone around so Kaitlyn can see a clear shot of her tits. "If you do, not only am I going to break your face, but this picture is gonna make the rounds all over Twitter. Reddit. My entire email address book. Every number in my phone. Instagram, until they flag it. The bulletin board in Panera." I count off the locations on my fingers. "Your church on Green Street."

I learned this tactic last year. This girl Kasey Muller was talking shit behind my back, so we snuck a photo of her drinking beer at a party. Her parents are super strict and would've grounded her forever if they knew she drank. I told Kasey I'd make sure her parents saw the picture if she didn't cut it out. Never had trouble from her again, and then her family moved to Maine. Oh well.

My girls shove Kaitlyn away. When no one's looking, I covertly delete the photo. I'm a bitch, but I'm not a monster.

She throws her clothes on, her face flushed pink, and practically bowls through us to get to the door. Her shirt buttons aren't even and I'm pretty sure her fly is only half zipped. That's good—it means she's more afraid of me than of being seen half undressed at school. Jaclyn and Abby laugh.

A pang of guilt thrums to life inside me, but I swat it away. I know this looks bad, but Kaitlyn had it coming. They always do. It's not like I actually *want* to hurt anyone or take joy in it or something. But if I get caught dealing, they'll throw me in prison and I can't let that happen.

"Pleasure doing business with you, Kait." I smile. "See you around."

Kaitlyn pauses, one foot out the door, like she's contemplating whether getting in the last word is worth being in deeper shit with my girls and me. She takes a breath, her eyes burning with hatred. "This'll come back to bite you one day, Autumn Casterly. Someday you won't have your minions with you and you'll be all alone.

You just wait. You'll never see it coming, and then you'll be sorry."

"Kait. Honey. Two things to know about me." I hold up my index finger. "One, I don't give two shits about your threats. And two?" I raise another finger. "I'm never sorry."

Jaclyn and Abby's laughter drowns out whatever Kaitlyn says next. But from the way her lips move, I catch it anyway, the moment before she plows out the door.

"You will be."

AUTUMN

I drop Jaclyn and Abby at Dunkin' to get us fuel while I stop at home for cash. There are too many Kaitlyn Kennedys at school to risk leaving money lying around there.

I pull into Dad's ugly cracked driveway and climb out. My ancient Civic reeks of pot. I used to Febreze it after every ride so Dad wouldn't get suspicious, but I stopped caring last year. If he doesn't give a shit, why should I?

I grab the wad of mail stuffed into our metal mailbox. The screen door slams behind me with a reverberating crash. Pumpernickel runs over to me, his claws clicking against the tile. I don't know if dogs can smile, but I swear, he always looks like he has the biggest grin on his face every time I come home. It's the only reason I come home, to be honest.

I scratch his ears, keeping my back to the wall. "Hey, boy. You have a good day?"

He wiggles in response. A hint of a smile twitches on my face.

It quickly vanishes.

A *Maury* rerun blares from the TV, and the scent of cigarette smoke permeates the room. Growling snores rip from the couch. Kathy's feet dangle off the armrest, sporting chipped pink nail polish. Our musty old afghan is wrapped around her like a cocoon. My mouth tightens.

"Kathy!" I slap the back of the sofa. "Get up."

My stepmother startles awake so suddenly, she nearly knocks over the mug she'd left balancing between the cushions. "Oh. Sorry. Hi, Autumn."

"Were you smoking in here?"

I already know the answer; wisps of smoke curl from a fresh butt in the ashtray on the coffee table. I *hate* the smell of cigarette smoke. Maybe Dad and Ivy let her get away with this shit, but not me. If she had lit the house on fire and killed Pumpernickel, I would have murdered her.

"I just needed one."

"You fell asleep with a lit cigarette in the ashtray." I slap the pile of mail onto the coffee table. "Go outside if you have to do that."

"It's not always easy to go outside, honey. It's very cold out there now."

"Well, here's an easy solution: move out." The wooden crucifix hanging on the wall glares down at us. If Jesus is real, he's totally judging me. I'm going straight to hell for this, but I can't even make myself care. And Dad is nowhere to be found—big surprise.

"I know you smoke in your bedroom, Autumn. And I know it's not tobacco."

"You wanna know the difference?" I slam my finger on the TV power button, right before a paternity-test reveal that Kathy will now never see. "This is *my* father's house. You're a freeloader. No pay, no say." It's not entirely true. Kathy got some money six years ago, before we met her, when her father died and left her eighty-five thousand dollars. She's milked that money as long as humanly possible, and still forks over a couple hundred bucks a month for rent and stuff. But it's not enough to make me care. I grab a can of seltzer off the counter and stomp upstairs.

I slam my bedroom door and lean against it. I hate this—I hate her. Every time I see her, it's like a demon takes over my body, flooding me with rage. Sometimes I worry I'll freak out and punch her.

Punching Kathy doesn't scare me. What scares me is, I don't know if I'd be able to stop.

I press my hands to my forehead, fighting back the urge to scream. Through my half-closed eyes, I can make out the tattoo scrawled across my left wrist. *It goes on*, says the brushy black script, from a Robert Frost quote: "In three words, I can sum up everything I've learned about life. It goes on." The tattoo does its job; it calms me down. I take a deep breath.

Something in the hall jingles, and I open the door. Pumpernickel takes a seat in my doorway, looking up at me in silent question.

"I'm okay, buddy." I scoop him up and carry him to my bed. It's not actually a bed—it's an air mattress covered in sheets. We're not too poor for beds or anything. I just sleep better on a plain old air mattress, when I sleep here at all. I threw out my old bed when we moved, along with most of my other junk.

My bedroom looks like it belongs to a fifteen-year-old goth boy. That's because it probably did. When we moved into this shithole, I didn't do a damn thing to the existing room. Some little emo jackass wanted to paint the walls gray and obscure the broken blinds with black curtains? Fine. Chunks of gray paint are chipped off at four corner points, as if the person ripped their posters off the wall in a fit of rage and didn't bother fixing the damage. Dad told me to cover them with my own posters, but I didn't care enough.

I keep a wad of cash and a stash of pills in the bottom of a tampon box in my closet. Ironic, I know. But it's the best hiding place. Dad will never look there, Kathy doesn't give a shit, and Ivy knows I'll kill her if she comes into my room.

I take the fifty I earned at school today out of my back pocket and add it to my existing cash wad. $7,052 total. It'd be a lot more if I didn't owe Liam a giant cut after every sale or have to split my share with Abby and Jac. I also do one of those monthly sponsor-a-panda things, which I probably shouldn't spend cash on when I'm trying to save, but they're pandas, and they're endangered, and they send me a free calendar every December. Still, I'm nearing $10K. It's good money, but not enough. I'll need to pay college tuition, and for textbooks, and rent, and whatever it costs to move out of state. When graduation rolls around, I'll get the hell out of here forever. Eight months to go.

Sometimes the way people at school talk about college makes me mad. Oh, your mommy and daddy are paying, no loans required? How nice that must be for you. Meanwhile, my "mommy" is dead and my "daddy" can barely afford his own living expenses, let alone mine when I move out. So if selling pills gets me out of this house, then I don't give a shit.

Under my pillow I find the buck knife I stole from Target last year. I slide it into the front pocket of my black hoodie. The guys would never screw me over, since I'm Liam's best customer, but I always take precautions.

My phone buzzes—Liam. You wanna make a few thousand bucks tonight?

Typical Liam, sending me cryptic texts.

Me: How?

Liam: Remember when I worked at the corner store? My buddy just told me their new security code. They stock the ATM every Thursday night. $$$

I read his text over and over.

Burglary is some serious shit. When I was thirteen, I started shoplifting—little things Dad couldn't afford, like a heavy-duty phone case and a set of AirPods after I lost mine. Sometimes I got new clothes. I even stole a pair of sunglasses for Ivy when she was going on a school trip to the beach and kept bitching about not having any. I didn't tell her they were from me; I just left them in her drawer. It's kind of thrilling, stuffing something in my pocket and walking out of the store with it. I never really needed the shit I stole—I just *wanted* it. But I really, *really* need this money.

Still, my fingers hesitate over my phone screen. Breaking in after dark to crack open an ATM would mean serious jail time if we're caught.

But it's fine. The corner store is an easy target; they get hit all the time. Plus, if Liam knows the alarm code, that's easy money. I need to get over it and just do it.

Me: Fine, but if you want my help I want twenty extra of whatever you've got. For free.

He replies within seconds. V and K this week. You can have ten.

Valium and Klonopin. Not a bad haul.

Me: Deal.

The second after I hit Send, I delete the texts; I know people joke about CIA agents watching our phones, but I can't be too careful.

I store my gloves in the sweatshirt pocket with my knife. Skinny jeans, black hoodie, black boots, a tiny bar in my septum piercing. I look like a punk, but not a criminal. I tuck a lock of short brown hair behind my ear. There's still a streak of platinum blond in the front, but I need to re-dye it soon. Long sleeves hide the tattoo on my arms, and my piercing may be a little conspicuous, but it's small. I run my fingers through my hair, throw on some silver liquid eyeliner and black mascara, then dab some sparkly shit on my cheeks. Funky makeup gives me confidence sometimes, and right now, confidence is what I need.

Before I leave, I always give Pumpernickel a squeeze and a kiss. When I go out, there's always a tiny chance that I won't come back. People assume that I'll end up dead in a gutter someday, and part of me thinks they're not wrong. I guess it's better than a jail cell.

Pumpernickel's the only one who'd miss me anyway. Hell, he's probably the only one who'd even know I was gone.

Kathy's eyes are glued to some trash on MTV. When I enter the living room, her hand immediately retracts from the cigarette on the table she was obviously planning to light.

I clench my jaw. "I'm going out."

"Where are you going, honey?"

Every time she calls me *honey*, I want to slap her. "None of your business."

"Your father will ask."

I plow out the door before she can get another word in. She doesn't come after me. I fight off the sinking feeling in my stomach, forcing myself to believe I don't care.

IVY

Jason's SUV takes a wide turn out of the school parking lot. Some indie band I don't recognize booms from the speakers. His car always smells like four-day-old McDonald's. I don't dare peek over the seat behind me to see what's lurking in the back.

We head down to Main Street, the old brick buildings and tiny storefronts sailing past us. Every five seconds, Jason slams on the brakes for a pedestrian crosswalk and we all lurch forward.

I can't stop staring at Patrick. It's super awkward, because we're in the back seat together. Jason reluctantly agreed to drive Patrick home once he realized the new kid lives three streets down from him. He would've looked like a megadouche to say no, and I would've killed him basically.

My fingers drum against my thighs. Patrick's got his arm draped over his BB-8 backpack, which is sitting in the middle seat like a fifth passenger, separating us. His blond hair has gotten so long now, it's the perfect length for me to imagine brushing my fingers through it.

"So, what was Baltimore like?" Sophie asks from the front. She always claims shotgun and this is the first time in history I didn't complain about being relegated to the back.

Patrick shrugs. "It was fine. Good food. We went to DC a lot."

"What's DC like?"

Patrick starts talking about monuments and cherry blossoms and museums, and in the rearview I can see Jason rolling his eyes.

Sophie cranes her neck to the back seat, giving me a *Why the hell are you staring at him like a creep instead of talking to him like a normal person* look.

I try to communicate *Because this is weird as hell and I honestly thought I'd never see him again and he has a little bit of stubble on his face now and it's so cute and you know I turn into an idiot around hot guys, remember the Aaron Dunlap incident?* with my eyes. I don't think the whole message gets through.

I'm busy making hand gestures at Sophie when I realize Patrick stopped talking and is now returning my stare.

I blink at him. "What?"

"Oh, I just asked what you've been up to the past four years."

I feel like I shouldn't be this awkward. Why am I always so awkward? "Not much. Nerd Herd stuff mostly. I'm in band, too. I play the trumpet but I suck at it. Mr. Warner gave me a solo for the spring pops concert, but I think he only did it because he hates me."

"Living the dream," Jason says. I kick the back of his seat.

"What's this Nerd Herd stuff?" Patrick asks.

"It's our club . . . ish. Group." Sophie ponders, tugging at her chin-length black hair. "Gang?" She's going to get a crick in her neck from twisting toward the back seat for so long.

"We play board games and video games and talk about geeky stuff," I say. "Sometimes, when we're bored, we film parody videos on our phones and post them on YouTube. It's not as exclusive as you'd think. We do occasionally talk to other people—if they make it through the hazing."

I said it as a joke, but by Patrick's expression, he took it seriously. "That's . . . cool."

"You have a girlfriend back in Baltimore?" Sophie asks.

What the hell? I pretty much want to rip open the car door and barrel-roll outside, because I'm guessing I have a better chance of surviving that than this conversation.

Patrick shifts in his seat. "No, nothing like that."

Sophie very obviously wiggles her eyebrows at me and I want to shrivel up and die. Thankfully, Pat changes the conversation topic.

"You guys ever do cons?"

Sophie laughs. "Well, we epic failed at one last April."

"I maintain it was a valiant effort," I add. Last year, Kevin's mom drove all of us down to Boston Comic Con in her minivan. We had wanted to go as the Avengers—*Infinity War*-style, so we could fake-fight on the judging stage and be badass. We even planned to do a mock "Thanos snap" and throw fake ashes all over the stage. Six main Avengers, six of us, works perfectly, right? Jason went out to get a set of Avengers action figures for costume inspiration, but he couldn't find Black Widow anywhere—and Alexa was practically born to play Black Widow, maybe even more than ScarJo. All the toy packs were just the five dudes. So in boycott, we decided to all go as lesser-known Avengers instead. I went as Ant-Man. I swear, Ant-Man is the most underrated Marvel hero. "Let's just say, the judges didn't recognize our creative costumes."

"Low-budget costumes," Sophie corrects.

"Hey!" I pretend to look affronted. "They were innovative."

"Would've helped if we'd had an Iron Man and a Cap," Jason says.

Sophie nods. "And a Hulk. You can't *not* recognize a big, green, snarling Hulk."

"Next year," I say. "We'll plan better."

"That's cool. I dressed as Lee Adama for Baltimore Comic-Con last year," Patrick says. "I didn't enter the judging, but they probably wouldn't have recognized me, either." The fact that he cosplays *Battlestar Galactica* characters literally melts my insides.

"You'd need someone to play Starbuck for that to work." Sophie winks at me. "Hey, Ivy, you'd make a great Starbuck."

I shoot her the deadest deadpan I can muster. Could she be any more obvious than to suggest I play Lee Adama's sort-of girlfriend? "I don't look anything like Starbuck, Soph. I'm not skinny, blond, a viper pilot, or covered in tattoos."

"You could pull it off," Patrick says. He smiles at me, then quickly looks away.

Before I have a chance to overthink that statement, Jason pulls into my dad's driveway and jerks the car into Park. "Okay, freeloader, get out."

"So kind." I blow him a kiss. He pretends to be disgusted and swat it away.

"Oh, is this your new place?" Patrick asks. "I remember your house on Profile, with the massive garage."

"Yep. We've been here a couple years now." I'm always a little self-conscious about this house. The lawn looks like a jungle starter kit, there's a mini Grand Canyon in the driveway, and I'm well aware that it's half the size of our previous home. We tried to keep the old house after Mom died, but without her income, it wasn't happening. There was this really bad patch when Dad took a second job, and I'm pretty sure I only saw him for forty minutes a week. Sucked when I had to bring home that band permission form in middle school asking for a hundred bucks to go to Six Flags. I almost didn't give it to him, but I caved when he heard about it from Alexa's parents. I didn't even want to go on that trip; I don't like roller coasters and I can't comfortably fit in many ride seats anyway. But everyone was going, and no one else had complained about the cost, so I let Dad write me the check. I still feel bad about it.

Dad never admitted it, but I think part of him didn't want to stay in that house anyway. Every room and stair and corner was tainted by Mom's passing. Even though she'd been dead for several years when we finally sold it, I could see the relief on Dad's face when we drove out of that driveway for the last time. Still, it was a way nicer house than this one. Patrick is probably super judging me for it right now.

I hate when other people think I don't notice things about my own life. Like when you go to someone's house and it stinks, but they've lived there so long they can't smell it, so you don't know if they realize how bad it is. Or when people point out I'm fat like it's breaking news to me. So I try to state the obvious as much as possible. "Dad needs to mow, it looks like shit. It's pretty small, too. I miss the old place." I don't really miss the old place. But it feels like something I should say.

"It's great," Patrick says. I can tell he's just being nice.

I grab my bag off the floor, stalling. "Hey, can I get your number?" I keep my eyes down. "So we can catch up."

"Sure! Here, give me yours, too." Patrick hands me his phone and I put my number in. Two seconds later, a text pops up on my screen: This is Patrick Perkins's number followed by a bunch of animal emojis. I add him into my contacts as P-Squared; that was his nickname back in the day.

Jason rolls his eyes. "I gotta get home, can you do that later?"

Sophie slaps his leg, giving him a look.

I climb out of the car and wave as Jason drives away. Within seconds, I'm texting Sophie.

Did Patrick say anything about me after I left?

I stare at the screen as three little dots appear. I want to grab her through the phone and tell her to type faster.

I'm so focused, I don't see my sister until I almost walk right into her car. Autumn's leaning against her Civic, smoking a joint. Right there in broad daylight. Where the hell is Dad? I already know the answer; he's working at the auto shop until eight thirty tonight.

"Hey, Autumn," I mumble, dodging away from her.

She rubs the end of her joint against the driveway and leaves it on the ground, grabbing an open can of seltzer off the roof of her car. "Ivy! Wait."

I stop dead. I don't remember the last time Autumn called me by my name. Usually she just grunts and walks past me when we're home. At school she acts like I don't exist. I mean, the only seniors who usually talk to lowly sophomore me are other band kids, but it kind of sucks when your own sister can't spare a wave when she passes you in the hall. Alexa's sister Charlotte Snapchats her from college in New York. They FaceTime every Tuesday and they're already planning stuff for when Charlotte's home for their Christmas-Hanukkah festivities. Alexa told Charlotte about losing her virginity before she told any of us. Sometimes I wish I could swap my sister for someone like her.

Once upon a time, me and Autumn would sneak out of our bedrooms at night to steal snacks from the fridge and watch movies on her iPad, one earbud for each of us, until Mom or Dad caught us and sent us back to bed. She was the first person I told about my crush on Patrick, back in the day. Then everything changed. Autumn was always there for me, until she wasn't.

Which is why it's unnerving that she's talking to me today. I fidget with my bag straps as Autumn jogs up beside me.

I can't stop staring at her hands. They're so pale and dainty for having so much figurative blood on them. She's wearing like eight thousand rings, and her black nail polish is chipping. I wonder how many pills passed through those fingers. A can of raspberry-lime seltzer is clutched in her left hand and she's using her right to fiddle with the aluminum tab. My sister is incapable of drinking anything from a can without ripping those tabs off. Why can't I stop looking at her hands?

Her fingers push the tab back and forth, back and forth.

"Do you know where I can find Hailey Waters?" she asks. It would be an innocent enough question, if I didn't know my sister.

Hailey Waters sits behind me in band. She plays the trombone, is really awesome at winging her eyeliner, and loaned me her bio notes last year when I had mono. Right now, she's probably at her boyfriend's place, or hanging out with the soccer girls at White Park, or at the indie movie theater where she works. God, I hope she's not mixed up in Autumn's bullshit.

"Nope." I blink. "Never heard of her."

Snap. The tab flicks off the can and tumbles to the grass, where Autumn leaves it.

She narrows her eyes at me and takes a solid swig of seltzer before climbing into her car. It's a used Civic Dad got her from an impound auction a couple years ago, but it's still more than anything I'll ever get.

"Where are you going?" I don't know why I ask. I don't really want to know.

"To church to confess my sins. To a food drive to help the less fortunate. To receive an award for good citizenship." Her tone grows increasingly sarcastic with each additional option. "Pick the one that makes you happiest and get the fuck out of my way."

I step off the driveway just in time to avoid getting run over as she guns it, disappearing down the street.

My phone does a classic Wookiee growl, alerting me to a new text. But I'm still staring at the empty road.

I'm not sure why, but I'm struck with a bad feeling.

Autumn

Liam has a misdemeanor on his record for shoplifting, but he's never been to jail. Which is ironic, since he lives down the street from the New Hampshire federal prison. It's the kind of house where visitors joke that they shouldn't pick up hitchhikers on their way home, but the proximity's never bothered Liam. Some people assume we're dating, but I wouldn't touch him with a ten-foot pole. He's more like my stoner older brother who I want to punch in the face half the time.

My girls and I park on the dirt driveway and walk to the back of the house. *House* is a generous term—it's more like a crappy duplex one hurricane away from crumbling into dust. Laughter and deep voices get louder the closer we get to the bonfire roaring in the small backyard. I bury my left hand in my sweatshirt pocket, taking comfort when my fingers graze my familiar knife.

The first thing I notice is, there are *way* too many people here.

I immediately size everyone up. I don't recognize most of them, but they're all older than us. Two guys I've never seen before sit on lawn chairs in front of the fire, one of them vaping and the other clenching a bong between his legs. A girl with a flannel button-down and ripped jean shorts lies on a blanket with her head in Liam's roommate's lap. Fucking Liam, he was *not* supposed to have this many people here tonight. My fingers tighten around the half-drunk can of seltzer still clutched in my right hand.

Liam's friends run the gamut from harmless potheads to downright sketchballs who'll probably be in prison at least once before they're twenty-five. A handful of them *have* already been in jail—this one guy, Derek Foster, got nailed for two DUIs last year and proudly made his mugshot his Facebook profile picture. Then there's Collin Jameson, who doesn't need to buy weed because he grows his own and calls himself a "skilled botanist." Concord's finest.

Abby's thumbs dance across her iPhone. Jaclyn folds her arms and yawns. Both girls are so at ease, it makes me feel stupid for being uptight. But I don't take my hand off the knife.

The middle-aged couple who rent the other apartment in Liam's duplex sit at a card table on the porch with a couple of beers and cigarettes. They give me a lazy wave. When I first met Liam, I asked if his neighbors cared about all the underage drinking and smoking on their property. Then I learned that the sweet older couple were the ones providing the stuff.

A girl saunters over in an NHTI hoodie, double-fisting a beer and an iced coffee. "Are you Autumn Casterly?"

I shift in place, mildly uncomfortable. "Yup." If Liam doesn't come outside in the next five seconds, I'm leaving.

"Didn't you break some guy's fingers behind the Irving station last year?"

Tyler Fenton. We didn't break his fingers, but we did threaten him with pliers. He owed me sixty bucks and thought I'd forget. I never forget.

"No, that wasn't me."

Jaclyn cocks her head at me, silently questioning why I denied our takedown of Tyler Fenton. I glare icicles at her, reminding her to keep her mouth shut around strangers.

"Do you guys go to the Tech?" Abby asks, pointing at the girl's sweatshirt. She's a master subject-changer. "I've thought about applying there if I don't get into Keene."

It's such a lie. Abby doesn't give a shit about school.

The girl busts out a giggle that would never come from a sober person. "Fuck no." She touches the NHTI logo. "This is my sister's. I'm a bagger at Market Basket."

"Oh cool. I've thought about applying there."

Abby and Jaclyn keep her busy while I hunt down my supplier.

Liam isn't hard to find. I see him the moment he steps outside, with a bag of Tostitos in one hand and a giant lighter in the other. He drops the chip bag into a girl's lap and hands the lighter to another guy, picking up a box of half-eaten pizza.

Liam's only nineteen, a year and a half older than me, but he's been living on his own since he dropped out of high school. We met a couple years ago, at the local library of all places. Dad's printer died and I needed to print something for school; Liam was there using one of the computers. Go figure.

Tonight, a navy-blue sweatshirt hood covers his short red hair and already-receding hairline. He used to have a thick red beard, too, but shaved it off because it made him a bazillion times more recognizable. Also, his friends kept making lumberjack jokes.

"Autumn. Hey." He opens the pizza box. "You want a slice?"

The smell of pepperoni makes my stomach roll. I look away. "No. Put that somewhere, I have to talk to you."

He stuffs a slice of pepperoni into his mouth and sets the box on the grass beside one of his friends.

"Inside. Now." I grab his hand and practically drag him onto the porch and through the door. A stack of dirty dishes on the counter wobbles, threatening to crash onto the tile, when I slam the screen behind me. "You're not supposed to have other people here when I come to buy. That was our deal."

"They're harmless." He waves it off. "They're just hanging out."

"Yeah, harmless until they snap a picture of me in this outfit right before we bust an ATM." Anxiety prickles to life inside me, and I swallow it down. I can't lose my cool. I need this money.

He checks the time on his phone. "Store's open for another hour. We gotta wait until after eleven."

"Are you sure they didn't change the code?"

"Autumn, baby." He wraps his arm around my shoulders. That's how I know he's about to switch into condescension mode. The jackass. "It's fine. I promise. You can't say no to that much cash."

He's right. I can't.

"Fine." I thrust a wad of bills at him. "Get me my stuff while we wait."

Liam disappears into the depths of the house. His place is so bizarre. He's got this hollow sculpture by the door he loves to call his "art"; meanwhile it's tacky as hell and looks like a giant urn.

I hover in the foyer, peeking around the corner into the living room. A couple of girls are spiking apple cider with Captain Morgan and mixing it in a couple of old Dunkin' cups, probably so they can drink them in the car without getting pulled over. As if that trick hasn't been done a zillion times before. Between that and all the drugs, it's like the embodiment of a New England stereotype in here. I half expect a cow to come wandering out of Liam's bathroom. I *hate* townies. Mostly because I'm probably doomed to become one.

Sometimes I wonder what my life would've been like if I'd grown up in a place like Boston or New York. I'm a big fish in a tiny pond here, and sometimes that pond feels cramped. I can't leave the house without wondering who I'm going to run into, because there are only so many places in this town for people to go.

I can't wait to move out—as far from Kathy and my fucking family as possible. Preferably another state. I fantasize about that a lot. I'm going to give a final one-finger salute to Kathy. My dad won't get a goodbye; he's ignored me for so long, the least I can do is return the favor. Ivy too. She'll probably throw a party when I leave. Good riddance to all of them. I slug back the last sip of seltzer and toss my empty can into the urn sculpture for Liam to find later.

Abby wanders into the room, her brown hair now sitting in a messy bun on top of her head, with that drunk girl tailing behind. "There you are. I was looking for you."

"Just waiting for our stuff," I mutter, keeping my eyes on the people sitting at the other end of the room.

"Look." Abby nudges her head toward the window. Outside, Jaclyn is laughing in the arms of some loser with a cig hanging off his lips. "Do you think Jac's going to have sex with him?"

I wouldn't be surprised. Jac's a serial offender of boning the grossest guys she can find. She could do way better than this loser.

I don't get the big deal about sex. Then again, it's not like I have loads of experience; I've only done it once, and I was drunk.

I asked Jaclyn about it last year, in the car on the way back from school. She'd never really brought up her sex life before, and asking about it felt weird, but I was overcome with curiosity.

I turned down the volume on the radio. "You like sex, right?" I asked her, keeping my voice casual.

Jac shrugged. "Yeah. Of course. I mean, who doesn't?" When I didn't respond, she added, "Why? Don't you?"

"I don't know. What's there to like about it?"

She laughed. "Um. Is that a serious question?"

"Yes, Jaclyn, for fuck's sake." I bristled.

"Wait . . . You're not a virgin, right? Didn't you lose your virginity to, um . . . you know. Chris?"

It felt like being slapped. I had never told Jaclyn and Abby about that incident, but obviously they'd heard about it. Everyone had. I slowly cruised to a stop at a red light. "Yeah. I guess." A squirrely feeling came over me. I hated the phrase "lose your virginity." This whole conversation was getting way too personal, and suddenly I regretted bringing it up.

"Do you . . . want to talk about it?" she asked.

"No." I hit the gas and turned the radio back up. "Forget I said anything."

I never brought it up again.

And now Abby's question is veering dangerously close to that territory.

I shrug. "Maybe. Who knows? Why do you care?"

"I've heard that girl Jaclyn gets around, if you know what I mean," the drunk girl says. "She's such a slut."

I almost burst out a laugh. Jaclyn sleeps around and is called a slut, I've had sex once and am called a slut, and hell, Abby's a virgin but sometimes wears low-cut shirts and I've heard the word used to describe her, too. As if this drunk girl has some sort of moral superiority because she hasn't met the arbitrary measurement of sex to constitute sluttiness. "How about you mind your own business and stop worrying about who other people are fucking?"

"Jeez. Okay." The girl gives me a look and slinks away. I cross my arms, trying to tame my pulse that's threatening to rocket out of my skin. This day needs to end soon. I wish I was in my car, or back in my room, or literally anywhere else.

By the time eleven o'clock rolls around, I've got a grocery bag full of pill canisters stuffed into my sweatshirt pouch. Most of Liam's friends—or customers, or whatever they are—have gone home or passed out. Jaclyn called her mom to inform her she was sleeping at Abby's house, then promptly left with the guy she'd been hanging out with.

"Can we go soon?" Abby whispers in my ear. "My mom won't get off my ass that it's after curfew."

Guilt gnaws through me. Me and Liam have become masters at shoplifting together, and now we're planning a full-on burglary, but I've never told Abby or Jaclyn that I steal. I'm not sure why. As far as they know, I hang out at Liam's house alone sometimes because we're hooking up.

It hits me that I've spent the past three years hanging out with people who still don't know a thing about me. If I got stung by a bee, Abby and Jac would probably watch me die, because they've got no clue I'm allergic and have to keep an EpiPen in my purse. Whatever. I used to care about stuff like that, but now it seems juvenile. Friends are a waste of time.

I hesitate. "Yeah. I'm sleeping at Liam's tonight. But we'll drop you off first."

She gives me a halfhearted thumbs-up, midyawn.

I climb into the front seat of Liam's beat-up old Camry and buckle my seat belt. Abby gets in the back. The light from her iPhone illuminates the dark car as we drive. I bite my thumbnail, scraping off the black nail polish. My insides feel jittery, like I've drunk too much caffeine. I'm not sure why I'm suddenly so uncomfortable. Maybe it's all the people at Liam's house.

Liam's fingers tap against the steering wheel, the only noise breaking through the silence. He's got a brown knit cap hiding his head and a maroon scarf wrapped around his neck and chin, like he's bundled for a blizzard rather than disguising himself for a break-in. I tuck my hood over my hair to obscure my face, suddenly feeling a little too exposed. Liam said they don't have cameras. That there's no way we'll get caught. But the more I think about it, the less I believe it.

"Have fun." Abby winks at me when we drop her off.

I stall. I should tell her where we're going, see if she wants to help. It's stupid to hide this from her and Jaclyn. I'm not ashamed. But it would mean an extra pocket to split the cash with, and I can't afford it.

"See you tomorrow," I say instead. "Let's see if we can get rid of some of this shit." I slap the bulge in my sweatshirt pocket, and the pills rattle in their canisters.

"Please, Ryan Philips has been after me all week. We can pawn off half a bottle on just him during lunch."

I nod, watching her disappear into her parents' apartment building. "Let's get this done," I mutter. Liam guns it, and we take off into town.

Streetlights blaze past, shining onto empty sidewalks. All the storefronts and old houses are sleepy and dark. We turn down a deserted street, cruising past White Park. I used to do all my deals there, in the parking lot or up by the sledding hill. It got too risky when cops started patrolling every night.

We stop at a red light, and out of nowhere, Liam turns to me. "Do you believe in God?"

I blink. "Are you high?"

"Nah, man. It's a serious question."

I roll my eyes, leaning into the window. Liam does this a lot. He'll get all existential right before we're about to steal shit. It's super annoying. "No."

"Not even heaven?"

"Especially not heaven." I glare out the window. "Can we focus on the job, please?"

"Where do you think you'll go when you die?"

"A hole in the ground? I don't fucking know."

"I can't believe that. There has to be somewhere we go, some higher power or something."

"You can believe what you want," I say. "But do it on your own time."

"You just don't want to believe in anything. You're too cynical sometimes, Autumn."

He's wrong about that. I wish I did still believe in God. "Can you just drive the car? Where's all this religious bullshit coming from?"

"Don't you want to believe there's more than this?" He gestures around the car. "That when you die, there's a next step? There's . . . something?"

I do wish that. Then I wouldn't have to picture my mother decaying in the frozen ground. How comforting it would be to believe there's a happy place for good people, and all the bad people will get what they deserve. Sometimes I think that's a flaw we all have; we assume truly evil people will always get what's coming to them, in this life or the next. But good *and* bad people meet the same fate: ashes.

"I don't know." I press the heels of my palms into my eyes. My pulse ticks under my skin like an overly jittery second hand on a clock. "Can you just . . . stop talking for a minute?" This conversation— this whole day—is going on too long. "I need to take something. You have any Ativan?"

"Glove compartment."

Technically I have a whole pouch full of pills in my hoodie, but

I know Liam has a private stash. We're only a few blocks from the store now, and I need to calm down. It'll take a few minutes to kick in, but a couple of these should do the trick. I pop open the glove compartment, and sure enough, there's like eight thousand containers and envelopes.

"You've got a damn Walgreens in here," I mumble, pawing through his stash.

"Don't take too many. I gotta sell those."

I fish out the first bottle. Liam's slapped masking tape on each one and hand-scrawled a coded label across it in Sharpie. It's a good thing he's honest, because these little white pills could be Tic Tacs or poison for all I know.

X—Xanax—too strong for tonight.

P—Percocet—not what I want right now.

I keep digging and pull out a crisp white envelope. Scribbled across the front is a big red *R*. "What's *R*?"

"Rohypnol," he replies without skipping a beat, like he's telling me the weather.

The car shrinks, suddenly too small and too hot. My blood turns to ice, freezing me in place.

What the actual fuck?

Liam wouldn't have this. He couldn't.

A cold, creeping fear snakes through me.

Why *wouldn't* he have this? Was I that naïve to think Liam was anything other than the scumbag he appears to be?

"What the hell is wrong with you?" I shove the envelope in his face.

Liam swerves. "Shit, Autumn, I'm driving!"

"You asshole." I shouldn't yell at him, deep down I know I shouldn't—he could have a gun, we're all alone—but I can't stop the words from flying out. "Why the *fuck* do you have roofies in your car?"

"Calm down." He snatches for the envelope, but I yank it away. "I don't use them, I just sell them. Okay?"

"How would that make it okay? If you've got roofies, you're trash."

"C'mon, Autumn, don't lump me in with those guys. I'd never drug anyone."

"Who buys them? Who are your customers?"

"I can't tell you, you know that."

"So, you're not *one of those guys*, but you cover up for them so they can get away with it." I snort. "You're a scumbag."

"I'm not the one using them." He enunciates the words too clearly, like I'm a fucking toddler. "I'd never do that. I just sell them."

Just sell them.

I can barely breathe. My eyes fog with tears as I ram my head back into the seat. I crumple the envelope in my fist. "Let me out."

"That stuff cost me money, Autumn. If you destroy them, you better be paying for them."

"Pull over and let me out."

"Stop freaking out. We're almost there."

"I don't want anything to do with you."

"Fine, bitch." He jerks the car to the side of the road. "I don't need this shit. I'll do it myself. You can walk home."

I jump out of the car so fast, I nearly trip over myself. I'm going to be sick.

Liam flips me off, and I slam both middle fingers against his passenger window. He shouts something as he drives away, but my piercing scream drowns it out.

I fist my hands in my hair and scream until I can't scream

anymore. I kick a stop sign. I stomp back and forth across the deserted side street.

Liam. I hate Liam. I hope he gets caught at the corner store and rots in prison.

I could call the cops right now. Get his sorry ass arrested.

I pull out my phone, Google the local police department, and dial. It starts ringing. Venom runs thicker than blood through my veins. If I could smash Liam's head into the concrete, I'd do it.

"Concord PD."

I take a breath. My mouth opens, then closes.

Holy shit. What am I doing?

I slam my thumb onto the red button and hang up.

A blanket of star-filled black sky covers me. In the distance, crickets and peepers fill the night with an orchestra that calms my nerves. I close my eyes and take a few deep breaths. It has to be after midnight by now. I am alone, with no one in sight. Alone is always better.

I start the long walk back across town to Liam's house to get my car, my footsteps against the pavement the only noise breaking through the still night air.

IVY

I should probably be in bed right now. Okay, scratch that. I'm technically *in* bed. What I'm not doing is sleeping.

You're going to hate Mr. Bennett's algebra class, I type back to Patrick on my phone while balancing my laptop on my knees. He gives pop quizzes all the time and is just generally unpleasant.

I think for a moment. Also, he smells like boiled cabbage.

Patrick responds with an eye-roll emoji. What about English 10 with MacDougall?

I type back, If you can suffer through picking apart every detail of Walden, I think you'll be fine. She's nice and brings cookies for finals.

Sweet. A thumbs-up emoji. What about Mr. Connolly? I have him for Econ.

He's the best, I respond. Everyone loves him!

My laptop warms my legs through my green-and-white-spotted pajama pants. Some trashy MTV rerun plays on my tiny TV on the dresser, but I've barely glanced at it. I'm too focused on other things—like stalking Patrick on Instagram on my laptop while simultaneously texting with him and pretending I'm not doing the former.

My internet creeping has taught me that Patrick is pretty much the same guy he was four years ago. He still eats string cheese improperly (biting right into it, like a monster) and still worships the Bruins. But now he seems to have an interesting pet.

I open my group chat with Alexa and Sophie. They're both probably asleep and will wake up to a zillion messages from me, but they'll deal; this is important. `Patrick has a big snake`, I type. `He posted like eight zillion pictures of it on Insta`. I think of Alexa's dirty mind and quickly add, `Like, a literal snake. The reptile. A ball python. It lives in a tank in his bedroom`.

It's a pretty cool pet, but not something I'd expect Patrick to have. In one selfie, the snake is draped over Patrick's neck. In another shot, the snake sunbathes under a heat lamp in a giant tank while a hand dangles a dead mouse over it. `Dinnertime for Chester`, reads the caption. Well, that's gross.

His most recent photo is of a towering oak tree, its leaves varying shades of red and orange. He didn't even need a filter to capture the radiance of the colors. `#TBT—took this when we lived in NH last time`, reads the caption. `Thought I'd post now that we moved back—ready for fall! #fallfun #NH #NewEngland #BackHome`

His New Hampshire pride makes me smile. I'm already contemplating ways to convince him to come to the haunted corn maze in Gilford with the Nerd Herd this year. Okay, yes, I always scream and freak out when the chainsaw guy pops up, but this time I'll have a reason to latch onto Patrick's arm.

I can't stop looking at this photo. It's such a refreshing change from Autumn's Instagram. I used to creep on her pictures, before she made her page private. It was always stuff like "F this place" and "I hate Concord" and "What kind of a shitty city has a mall that looks like a ghost town?" with middle-finger selfies, flipping off places I love.

Autumn used to like Concord, back when Mom was alive. Afterward, it was like the town went from being a seat belt, a comforting dose of protection, to a straitjacket, intent on keeping her back and trapping her here forever. She started pushing back, fighting its hold on her. We'd drive down Loudon Road and she'd point out all the chain restaurants—the same ones we ate in occasionally, growing up—with an eye roll, as if she'd outgrown it all. She stopped wanting to go apple picking in the fall and refused to come to Midnight Merriment with Dad and me at Christmas, even though we went caroling there as kids. Each insult felt like she was dragging *me* rather than our town. I know I shouldn't feel rejected by it, but I do.

Concord's practically stitched into my DNA. I love the old brick storefronts downtown, and swimming at the docks, and yes, even the deserted mall; it has character. I don't *want* to leave. And I know Autumn counts that among my flaws.

I take a sip of my formerly hot—now lukewarm—cocoa, and frown. My Tolkien mug left a giant ring on my side table. I rub at it with my finger, but it doesn't come off. Well, crap. This IKEA table has always been sort of rickety, mostly because I insisted on putting it together myself when I was twelve, but I still feel bad.

I say good night to Patrick, type an apology to Sophie and Alexa for all the spam, and head downstairs for paper towels.

Kathy sits in the kitchen in her bathrobe, swirling a spoon in a mug of tea and reading something on her phone. A wisp of smoke curls from a fresh butt in the ashtray. My nose crinkles at the smell. "Oh, hello, Miss Ivy." She gives me a guilty smile, quickly grinding the cigarette further into the tray. "I didn't know you were awake."

"Yeah. I was just watching TV." I grab a fistful of paper towels, frowning at the cigarette. Kathy's not supposed to smoke in the house. "Why're you up?"

"I was talking to your brother. He sends his love."

I hate when Kathy calls Chris my brother. Technically he's my stepbrother, but even that intimacy feels weird—especially after that whole gross Autumn-Chris rumor I'm constantly subjected to at school. We're Facebook friends, but otherwise I haven't talked to him since he left for college two years ago. He sent me a request to list him as my brother, and I've ignored it. It's stewing in my request box along with the Russian roulette of messages from strangers who are trying to either add me on Pokémon Go or send me dick pics.

I rinse my mug in the sink. "Oh, how's he doing?"

"Would you believe it, he's starting quarterback this year." She scrolls through her phone, then shows me a picture of Chris in his football jersey.

"Nice."

"Yeah. The coach told him he's got a real shot of making it to the NFL." She keeps her eyes on her screen. "I always knew he could do it, if he put his mind to it and got a scholarship. We just need the right people to see him play, and all the big scouts seem to watch the Spartan games."

"Cool." I feel like she's talking more to herself than to me. "He coming home for Thanksgiving this year?" I already know the answer.

Her smile sinks. "No, he's going to his father's in Ohio again. Maybe for Christmas."

I know she's just saying it to make herself feel better. Chris won't come for Christmas. Things got really awkward after whatever happened between him and Autumn. When he left for college, he never came back. Which is totally fine with me, to be honest.

"Sometimes I wish he hadn't gone to school so far away," she says. "Driving distance would've been nice. But he's got to be where the opportunities are."

I tear at the edges of the paper towels. "Yeah. That must be tough."

"I don't know." She gives a sad smile to the table. "I just miss him. Your father . . . well, he works such long hours."

I shuffle my feet. I don't want to have this conversation right now. It's late and I don't know what to say. "Okay, well. I've gotta go to bed. Good night."

"Good night, honey."

I speed-walk to the stairs, using my phone as a flashlight, and almost trip over Pumpernickel. He stands, his wide eyes shining up at me in the darkness. "Creepy," I say, giving him a scratch. I always feel bad when he camps out near the door at night. I know he's waiting for Autumn to come home, and she rarely does.

"You miss your mommy?" I crouch and pet him. "She'll be back." Eventually.

My phone buzzes—Jason. Of course. Who else would text me at one in the morning? You still awake?

I type back, Technically. What's up?

I can't sleep. Entertain me.

I can't either, I reply. I was just talking to Kathy and drinking hot chocolate. I take a seat on the stairs, scratching Pumpernickel's head with one hand and typing with the other. And you can entertain ME, bitch.

The first time I met Jason was freshman year at the band camp cookout. Every year, on the last night of band camp, we do a mock field show for the families, followed by a barbecue. I was standing in line to get a burger, and still way too shy to talk to any of the upperclassmen.

This sophomore guy with floppy dark hair stood in front of me, loading up his already loaded paper plates. I remember thinking, Why does he need *two* plates of food? Of course, now that I know Jason, I realize he's just a huge pig anytime there's free food.

He made a grab for the last hot dog, but then whirled around toward me. "Hey, did you want this?"

It took me a second to realize he was talking to me. "Oh no, go for it. I'm more of a burger girl."

"Cool. Thanks." He piled it on top of his deviled eggs, which made me want to vomit. "You play trumpet, right? I'm Jason, saxophone." That's the funny thing about band kids—you're always defined by your instrument. He maneuvered his paper plates trying to shake my hand, which I automatically thought was weird; I couldn't remember the last time someone who wasn't my dad's age introduced themselves with a handshake. But I was still a loser freshman who didn't know any upperclassmen in band, so I put on my widest, cheesiest smile.

"I'm Ivy."

"Whoa, that's a cool name." His eyes lit up. "Like Ivysaur, the Pokémon. Or Poison Ivy, the Batman villain."

I grinned at him. "Can I just say how awesome it is that your first instinct wasn't to compare me to the plant?" I leaned into the table, making my best attempt at being smooth, but ended up sticking my sleeve into the bowl of potato salad.

And that was how I met my best friend. This was followed by, like, eleven months of writing bad poetry about him in my pink notebook, but I'd rather not think about that.

`Fine. Watch this.` He sends me a YouTube link.

I click on it and watch some guy fend off an attacking Canada goose with a briefcase. Immediately I reply with another link, a guy on a skateboard showing off, then spectacularly wiping out (he's okay at the end, I swear). Jason responds with a *BuzzFeed* article—"21 Things Only People from New Hampshire Will Appreciate."

`Specifically #17,` he says.

I scroll through, landing on the one he referred to: *Riding the Boston Tea Party ride at Canobie Lake Park.* I chuckle, remembering the epic prank I played on Jason last summer. He'd never been to Canobie, and therefore didn't know that flume ride has a ridiculous splash radius notorious for drenching spectators. I positioned him carefully, then ran away at the last second, leaving him soaked to the bone for the rest of the day. Of course, he felt the need to envelop me in a bear hug immediately after. Ass.

Jase and I go back and forth for a while, sending funny videos and links. At some point, Kathy scoots past me to head to bed. I should follow her lead, but I'm wide awake. Soon, I'm laughing hysterically, I've forgotten all about Kathy's drama, and it's after two.

`Shit, it's 2 AM,` I type.

He quickly responds with an *it all happened so fast* meme.

I'm about to say good night when the front door swings open. My sister stands framed in the moonlight like a serial killer and scares the ever-living shit out of me. I can't help it; I scream.

Within seconds, the hall light flips on and Dad comes barreling down the stairs. "Ivy? Are you okay?"

"Ivy, honey?" Kathy hobbles up behind him. "What's wrong?"

For a second, the four of us freeze. Dad swallows, his hands flexed at his sides as if facing a wild animal. I know that look; it's saying, *My hooligan daughter was out after curfew again, but if I say anything, she'll freak out at us.* Kathy's jaw tightens, and I can tell she sees it, too.

"Autumn," Dad says gently, "are you okay?"

"I'm fine," she snaps, sounding anything but fine.

"Sorry, Autumn." I keep my voice low and steady. "You startled me, that's all."

"Whatever." She slams the door. "I'm going to bed." She scoops up Pumpernickel and roughly elbows past me.

"Autumn, honey, are you okay?" Kathy asks as Autumn stampedes past her. "Do you want to talk about it?"

"I'd rather die." Within seconds, her bedroom door slams. Dad's shoulders tighten.

"I'm really sorry I woke you guys up," I whisper. "I swear, I was just sitting here. She scared me."

Dad hesitates. I can see on his face that he wants to check on Autumn—or even reprimand her for coming home so late—but he's too worn out. "It's late. I'm going back to bed." He disappears into the dark hallway, barely giving me or Kathy another glance.

Kathy gives me a sympathetic smile, then follows.

I head upstairs but pause outside Autumn's room. Against my better judgment, I press my ear to the door, straining for the tiniest sound. I should check on her, make sure she's okay. I raise my hand to knock, but it just hovers there. I shuffle my feet. Why am I such a coward? Ugh. Hovering outside her doorway brings back memories of when Autumn first stopped speaking to me. It was like in *Frozen* when Anna knocks on Elsa's door every morning, but her sister just tells her to go away; only, in this version, the "go aways" included lots of swearing at me, and Autumn never wanted to build a snowman.

Finally, I tiptoe back to my own room.

I wonder if Dad and Kathy saw what I did when I looked at Autumn. I wonder if they saw the tears in her eyes.

FRIDAY

AUTUMN

For the second time this week, there are cops at my locker. Two officers I've never met stand together, a man and a woman, talking to the principal. I stiffen, wondering if I should make a run for it. No—I didn't burglarize the corner store last night, and I don't have any drugs on me.

I slip out of my sweatshirt and adjust my tight purple T-shirt. I feel like people always get weirdly suspicious of kids in hoodies, and I don't want to give them any reason to think I'm up to something. My silver paw-print charm necklace dangles against my chest. I'm glad I wore it today. Charm necklaces are cute and girly, not something a criminal would wear. And I mean, who would be suspicious of a girl wearing a puppy necklace? They don't need to know I stole it from Claire's.

"Can I help you?" I ask the police, trying to keep my voice light and bubbly.

"Hi, you must be Autumn." The policewoman's tone is sweet as honey. "I'm Officer O'Riley."

I shake her hand without averting my eyes. They want me to choke. That's not happening. "Hi." I drop my bag in my locker, opening it wide so they can see the lack of drugs inside. "I have to go. I'll be late for Spanish."

Officer O'Riley mutters something to the other cop, but they don't move.

Jaclyn and Abby peek out from behind a row of lockers. Jaclyn holds out her hands as if asking me what to do. I subtly shake my head, and they get the message and slink away.

"Can we talk to you for a minute in the principal's office?" the male cop asks.

This isn't good. "Okay."

I follow the principal and Officer O'Riley. The male officer stays a few steps behind me, as if worried I'll bolt. I swallow, trying to reassure myself that this is fine. They don't have anything. I'm too careful.

My stomach sours the moment we enter the room. I rub my upper arm, struck with déjà vu. I hate this office.

The principal pulls out a wooden chair for me and takes the comfy rolling one for himself. The male officer stands by the door, while O'Riley leans casually against the desk.

"I have a Spanish quiz today." It's a lie. Our teacher is on maternity leave, so we've had a sub all month. He doesn't do anything except show us movies in Spanish. I've slept through most of them. "If I don't show up, I'll get a zero."

The principal raises his brows. "Ms. Casterly, are you referring to Señora Albright's class?"

Shit. He knows.

"We just wanted to ask a few questions," O'Riley says. "I'm sure your teacher will let you take the quiz late."

"I'm only seventeen. You can't talk to me without my dad's permission." It's another lie; I turned eighteen two weeks ago. But no one expects a senior to be eighteen by September, and I doubt they'll look it up, so I go with it.

She arches a brow. "We would only need your father's permission if we took you into custody."

Message received. My mouth thins to a tight line, but I nod.

"The corner store on South Main had another break-in last night. The thief used the store's security code to enter the building and then emptied the register. They also seem to have attempted to break the ATM with a crowbar, but failed."

I pick at my fingernails, laboring to keep from full-on fidgeting. I'm not guilty. I shouldn't act like I am.

"It's happened before, but this time the store had a camera." My heart jumps. "We're trying to find a lead on the perp's identity."

"I was home last night."

"Well, we're asking you because someone called the station last night around midnight and hung up. We traced the call this morning to see if it was related to the burglary and it led back to your number, a block from the store, right around the time of the break-in."

"Must've pocket-dialed. Sorry."

She gives me an inquisitive look. "I thought you were home last night?"

"I was. I took a walk."

"You walked all the way downtown? In the middle of the night?" She thumbs through some papers. "According to our records, you live on Church Street—several miles away."

I shrug. "Couldn't sleep."

The cops exchange glances.

Principal Greenwich scrubs a hand down his face. "Autumn, I hear your name floating around this school a lot, from teachers and students alike. I don't know what's going on with you, but please. Just cooperate."

Someone knocks, startling everyone in the room. Mr. Browne, the guidance counselor, strolls inside. I relax a little. Of all the teachers they could've sent, he's the least objectionable. He's kind of a cornball, but Mr. Browne's always been nice to me—even after our last meeting, when I flipped out after he suggested I see a therapist.

"Hello, Autumn. May I join you?" Mr. Browne asks. The principal gestures to the chair next to me, and Mr. Browne promptly takes a seat. "I heard there was some trouble downtown last night."

"I don't know. I just heard about it for the first time." I blink innocently at him.

"Listen, Autumn." Mr. Browne lowers his voice. "I'm on your side here."

"We all are," adds O'Riley.

I bristle. Like hell you are.

"If you're in some kind of trouble, we can help you. We *want* to help you."

Lies. I've heard that before, but I know exactly how this works. People like me are guilty until proven innocent. I want to shake him and shout at them to stop lying. But I keep it together and nod instead.

"You're a bright girl," he continues. "Brighter than you let on. If you keep it up, you'll graduate on time in June."

I nod again and scratch the tattoo on my wrist.

"The last time we talked, you mentioned you're considering going to college out of state to be a veterinarian. Remember?"

I want to punch him. That is *my* business, not relevant to all the people in this room. Everyone's looking at me, watching me, waiting for me to fuck up. I nod again.

"I want to help you get there. We all do. We want you to stay out of trouble and achieve all the wonderful things you're capable of."

I'm scratching my tattoo so hard, skin is flaking off. "I already told you, I don't know anything about it. Can I go to class now?"

Mr. Browne sighs. "Autumn . . ."

"The store owner caught this image on his security feed." The cop passes me a sheet of paper. My heart pounds like a drum. The black-and-white picture is grainy, but there's good ol' giraffe-neck Liam, brazenly tearing open the register like he owns the place. Even with the hat pulled low over his ears and the scarf covering everything but his eyes, it's obvious—at least to me. What an arrogant piece of shit.

"Autumn?" Mr. Browne rests his hand on my arm. "Are you all right?"

I realize I've been clenching my fists around the paper and slowly relax them. I nod.

"Can you tell us who this is?" asks the cop.

My insides turn to stone. I *want* to rat him out and see him thrown into the same prison he drives past every day. But what would happen to me?

Suddenly, I'm back in this same hot room all those years ago, with all those eyes on me. My heart races. The office gets smaller and smaller, and I get dizzier. My vision swims. It feels like I'm going to pass out.

"Autumn?"

"Tell us what happened, Autumn," says Mr. Browne. But his words don't sound like the guidance counselor's voice; they sound like my old soccer coach's.

I close my eyes. My pulse pounds in my ears.

"No." My voice comes out cold and emotionless. "I've never seen him before in my life."

I can't focus all day. I sit through the Spanish movie, a history lecture, and lunch without registering any of it. I don't go to last period calc. I walk right out of the building and across the street to the senior lot, get in my car, and drive to White Park.

Leaning against the car window, I watch the ducks waddle past the pond. An older couple plops down on a bench nearby. Three tiny kids kick a soccer ball back and forth while their mothers chat. I go sit on the swings, gently rocking myself back and forth. A bunch of families and kids walk past me, probably pissed I'm hogging a swing. They're all shouting and laughing and the noise grates my ears. I wish I had a joint. My fingers weave through my purple lanyard, fiddling with the keys on the end.

My phone buzzes—it's Abby, asking where I went. I ignore it, lean my head against the swing chain, and close my eyes.

Mom used to bring Ivy and me to this park when we were kids. Sometimes in the summer we would go in the pool and push each other under the buckets that spill water when they fill up. Mom would watch from the edge, with her feet in the water.

Most parents call their kids things like *sweetheart* and *dear*, but not our mom. She called me "Fall," like the synonym of Autumn. Ivy got it worse—Mom called her "Poison," as in "Poison Ivy." I always thought it was a little corny, but Ivy liked it, and sometimes we'd pretend we were starting a rock band called Poison and Fall. We'd bang sticks against rocks, imagining they were drums.

Then Mom got sick. When other kids were going to shows in Boston and ice-skating with their parents, we sat in hospital waiting rooms. I used to put my headphones on and pretend I couldn't hear

Mom crying when they put the needles in. Cancer is a heartless bastard.

My phone buzzes—Abby again. `Holy shit. I guess Liam got dragged into the police station for questioning??`

Wow, seems they found their suspect even without my help.

I smirk. I don't know whether karma, justice, or plain old luck was involved here, but I'm not complaining.

`Good`, I write back.

`Good?` she replies. `Wtf?`

I consider typing a long response about how Liam's an asshole and he's definitely no friend of mine, but I stop myself. `Long story`, I write back.

`Where are we gonna get our stuff if he goes to prison?` she asks.

I hesitate. What if this is an out? Maybe I could start fresh and get a real job. Go to college with a clean slate.

I scratch my wrist.

Or maybe I'll find a new dealer.

I don't reply to Abby.

I lose track of time, and before I know it, the sun is setting. The kids and families are moving on. Car doors slam in the distance, accompanied by the sounds of children whining.

My phone buzzes again. I roll my eyes, expecting it to be Jaclyn or Abby checking up on me, but an unknown number flashes across my screen.

`I need some cake, know any good bakeries?`

That's the code I've taught my customers to send when they want to buy. But I've never seen this number before. I type back, `Who is this?`

I watch the screen, waiting.

I need cake, they repeat.

I scowl. It's either a prank, a setup, or a new customer who I'm going to slap in the face for being coy. This is why I have rules for new referrals. I'm about to lay into them when another message pops up.

Can't say my name here.

Well then I can't help you, I write back.

Please, they say. I'm feeling really sad and want chocolate cream pie.

They want Benzos.

Better see a psychiatrist for that, I reply, adding the middle-finger emoji.

I'll pay you $500.

Fuck. That's good money. And without Liam's supplies, it could be the last cash I get for a while.

When?

I'm downtown now, he texts, how about the vacant lot on Storrs St?

I've done deals there before. Maybe this guy has, too.

Fine. Meet me there in 20 mins. If you're late, I'm leaving.

They don't reply. I consider texting Jaclyn and Abby, but they'll never make it to Storrs in twenty minutes. Jaclyn lives in the boonies and Abby's probably pissed at me for ignoring her. It crosses my mind to stop back home for my knife, but it's out of the way. I'll stay in my car if things look suspicious, and I won't even bring pills with me now.

The last drop of sunlight fades behind the trees as I pull out of the park. My purple and green Mardi Gras beads hanging from the rearview sway when I take a sharp turn, narrowly missing the curb.

I pull into the abandoned lot five minutes early, and a guy is already standing in the middle. No other cars, no other people. So far, so good.

The fall chill prickles goose bumps down my arms. I slip into the spare hoodie I keep in my back seat. A couple of twitchy streetlights illuminate the lot. Grass and weeds protrude through the cracked pavement and a dilapidated building sits to the side, right by the rusty old train tracks. Rocks crunch beneath my feet as I approach the stranger. I keep the purple lanyard wrapped around my wrist with my car keys positioned between my fingers, just in case.

"Autumn?" He grins, holding out his hand. "Hey. I'm Nick."

I nod, sizing him up. Could be a fake name, in which case he's smart; could be his real name, in which case he's too naïve to do business with me. He's about my age, with a pathetic attempt at facial hair, crooked teeth, jeans, a hoodie, and a black knit cap covering his hair. No visible weapons, no visible wires. "How'd you get my number?"

"My cousin knew a guy who gave it to me."

I narrow my eyes. "You wanna try that again?"

"Sorry." He gives me an apologetic smile. "I'd say more, but I don't know you yet. Gotta protect myself, you know?"

I guess that's fair, but he's going to give me a name before I give him pills, and whoever spread my information is getting a beatdown. "Fine." I bury my hands back in my pocket. "How much do you want? Did you bring cash?"

"Here, let me grab my money. I was right down the street, so I've been here awhile." He points to the abandoned building. "I was in there while I waited for you. My buddies come here to smoke sometimes."

I follow him toward the old building. I've done a handful of deals in the lot, but never actually checked out this place. Cracked concrete walls make up the sides, with pieces of rusty metal hanging off the roof. A crappy piece of plywood is pushed aside in what looks like the doorway. Darkness hangs heavily beyond it. This could potentially be a good place to handle customers in the future, if there isn't an army of rats already camping inside. "What is this place?"

"Not sure. Some sort of warehouse?" Nick disappears through the dark doorway. "C'mon, right in here. Just gotta grab my backpack." His voice and footsteps echo in the empty building, fading into nothing.

I hesitate outside the doorway. Suddenly I'm regretting not going back for my knife. "Where'd you go?" I squint, but can't see past the darkened entryway. "Nick?"

Something smashes into my head. My vision blurs. I stumble, but a hand slaps over my mouth and blocks the scream. Someone shoves me into the building.

My brain goes into freak-out mode. I writhe and kick but another set of hands has already pinned my arms to my sides.

I scream into the hand, biting frantically at the flesh, but someone stuffs a piece of cloth into my mouth. "Not so brave now, are you?"

My heart races. I know what usually happens to girls in these situations. They throw me to the ground, slamming me into the cold concrete so hard my vision blurs.

I shout for help, but it comes out muffled and incoherent.

A foot sinks into my stomach, shooting pain through my core. Someone rips my hands up and binds my wrists with something cold and sharp. I struggle and fight but fists and feet plow into me, crushing the wind from my lungs. A muffled, strangled scream tries to escape my throat.

"Big bad Autumn Casterly."

"No one will miss you."

"Fuck her up."

I curl into myself, but the blows keep coming. Warm blood stains my tongue and seeps onto my face. Another foot slams into my side with a sickening crack. My eyes fog with water.

I shouldn't have come here.

I'm in over my head.

I'm going to die.

For half a second, I go numb. A flash of something bursts across my vision. A face, in the distance. It's familiar, but I can't see who or what it is. In an instant, it's gone.

Pain pulses through every inch of my body. I can't move. Someone shines a flashlight into my eyes. Five. There are five people standing around me, their silhouettes blurry and warped.

The last thing I see is someone's booted foot, smashing down into my face.

Then there's nothing.

Ivy

Friday nights always make me feel like a huge fail. Usually we have pep band, but there's no football game tonight. According to the CW, weekends are for keggers and hookups (or saving the world, if you're Kara from *Supergirl* or that guy from *The Flash*). I mean, maybe that's how my sister spends her weekends. Personally, I've never been invited to a kegger and I don't have anyone to hook up with, so Nerd Herd Movie Night is where it's at.

"C'mon, just pick something." Alexa's tone screams *at the end of my rope*, and she doesn't try to hide it. "I swear, we're all gonna drop dead before you make a decision."

A pink tinge spreads across Kevin's freckled cheeks. "I'm thinking."

Usually we pick the cheesiest-looking movie so we have something to make fun of. Sometimes we find gems.

"Okay, let's go over your choices." I pluck a handful of DVDs from Walmart's five-dollar bin, then dramatically present them, one by one. "First, we have the cinematic masterpiece known as *Paul Blart: Mall Cop*."

"I've seen it already," Sophie says. I give her the *shut up shut up shut up or we'll never get out of here* look.

"Next is the 2015 Oscar sensation *Birdman*." I toss the DVD back into the bin. "Which I'm sure would be a barrel of laughs."

Jason groans. "Can we just watch *Lord of the Rings* again?"

I ignore him. "Finally, we have *Princess of Frost, Ice, and Snow*, which is the generic *Frozen* rip-off you never knew you needed."

Ahmed takes the case, with a smiling blond cartoon ice princess on the front, and shakes his head. "I mean, they're not even trying to hide it."

"Okay, those are your choices." I hold them up to Kevin. "And the winner is . . ."

Sophie and Alexa start a drumroll on the side of the bin.

"Ooh." Kevin fishes into the bin and pulls out *Tomb Raider*. "Found it."

"That . . . was not one of our finalists." Alexa rips the DVD out of his hands. "But whatever, Angelina's hot, and I'd like to actually watch a movie this century, so let's go with it."

"You know, next week is my turn to pick," Sophie says, entwining her fingers with Alexa's. "And I'm picking horror again—last time was fun."

My stomach drops.

Oh, for the love . . .

Sophie, Alexa, and Ahmed start bickering about what the best classic horror movie is, oblivious to how uncomfortable I am now. I glue my eyes to the floor, the ceiling, the toy aisle, looking literally anywhere that isn't at Jason. He's doing the same thing, suddenly fixated on the iPad cases. We both swore we'd never bring up "the incident" again, but it keeps popping up because our friends are idiots.

The last time Sophie chose the movie, it was summer. She forced us into *The Conjuring 2*. I don't do horror movies, no matter how cheesy. No, thank you. I don't like nightmares.

So Jason and I sat in Sophie's bedroom playing Trouble while everyone else stayed downstairs. Even though we kept getting distracted by Sophie's awesome manga collection, we still finished the game way before the movie ended.

We were bored, and feeling like assholes, so we decided to play a prank. We crept outside and hid in the bushes under the living room window. Everyone sat on the couch inside, their backs to us. When the movie reached a nerve-racking, pulse-pounding point of tension, we jumped up and banged on the window. I swear, I've never heard Alexa scream that loud.

They locked us outside in retribution. Jase and I were laughing so hard, I could barely breathe. I don't really know what changed. One minute we were standing there, laughing together, and the next minute it happened.

"You should kiss me," I said. I almost couldn't believe the words flying out of my mouth. I'd liked Jason for months and vowed never to tell him, but there I was, asking for a kiss.

And just like that, Jason's lips were on mine. My heart was beating so hard, I could give the band kids on the drumline a run for their money. Everything inside me lit up, so warm and tingly. It felt like an eternity, but it was literally only two seconds before I noticed he'd stopped kissing me back.

"Shit." He threaded his fingers behind his head. "I can't do this." And he walked away. I think he went back to Sophie's balcony and sat in a lawn chair, because apparently being alone was more desirable than being with me.

A pit formed in my chest. I watched his retreating back, every shitty feeling swirling into a tornado inside me. What had happened? Did I suck at kissing that badly? My only prior experience had been with Brandon Myers last fall. We were on the band bus and Maura Williams dared me. It wasn't the fireworks show Disney had led me to believe. I spent all four seconds thinking that

Brandon's tongue shoving its way into my mouth kind of reminded me of a slithering eel. I remember thinking, Huh, so that's what it's like—and then wondering if there was something wrong with me for not liking it more.

But Jason had kissed a million girls before, and gone farther with some of them. So what was wrong with *me*?

A nagging thought wouldn't stop jabbing me in the brain— Maybe the other girls were prettier and skinnier, like Autumn. Suddenly, Jason's constant jokes about liking my sister felt a little too close to home. The worst question practically bowled me over—Did I just ruin our friendship?

The rest of the night was pretty bad. One of those things where something big happens and no one wants to acknowledge it, so it gets twice as awkward because everyone pretends it never happened. I brushed it off because I couldn't tell him the truth—that I'd had a huge crush on him for the past year, and for a split second, I could've exploded in joy because I'd thought maybe, just maybe, he liked me back.

"I'll go grab some candy," I say quickly.

Jason nods. "I'll come, too."

Well, that's . . . not what I had in mind.

"Get me Reese's Pieces," Ahmed shouts, loud enough to make everyone in the aisle look at him.

"I want Junior Mints," adds Alexa.

Sophie's eyes light up. "Oooh. I'll share yours."

"Excuse me. Says who?" Alexa scoffs. "She'll take her own."

"Can I have Mike and Ike's?" Kevin asks. "I can't have—"

"You can't have stuff with peanuts in it." I salute him. "We got you."

Jason and I amble down the aisles to the ninety-nine-cent candy row. He doesn't say anything as we walk. Instead of bathing in the uncomfortable silence, I text Patrick to ask what kind of candy he wants. Patrick's return couldn't have fallen at a better time. Having him back in my life is exactly what I need.

Jason's eyes flick over to me, but he doesn't say anything.

We grab our friends' candy orders and start picking out boxes for ourselves. Jason grabs a king-size Snickers.

"Hmm." I peruse the selection. "I feel like Raisinets."

"That's funny. You don't look like Raisinets." He grabs the box off the shelf.

I roll my eyes. "Yes, Jason the jokester, ladies and gentlemen."

My phone buzzes with a response from Patrick. Twizzlers? I'll pay you back!!

Me: Red or black? There is only one correct answer.

Patrick: Red. Black licorice is gross.

I grin. That's another point for Patrick.

Jason clears his throat. "Um. So. Maybe we should talk about August."

"Don't worry about it." I force a smile and start walking away.

"No, seriously." He catches up to me. "I'm sorry. I was being weird."

"That's you every day." I fake-push him, slaloming around him like a pro.

"Come on." He steps in front of me, blocking my path. "We never talked about it, and I feel like I never . . . explained."

"Nope. Shhhh . . ." I put my finger to his lips. "We don't speak of it. That incident is Voldemort."

"Voldemort?"

"Incident that must not be named." I shove past him, my heart racing a million miles a minute. We are not having this conversation. I'm not about to lose my best friend because he wants to get all *let's talk about it* on me. I can already picture him saying he likes me as a friend, but *not like that*, blah blah blah. I don't need that right now. I've buried that crush in the deepest pit inside me, never to be unearthed again. That's where it belongs. Patrick is back in my life now, and Jason is my friend. That's it.

"Ivy! Come on. Two seconds. Just hear me out."

My face burns hotter than the fires of Mordor. "Seriously, it's no big deal." I could melt into a puddle on the floor. "Let's just drop it."

"Ivy..."

We round the corner.

Alexa, Ahmed, Sophie, and Kevin are all lying down in the middle of the toy aisle, their arms sprawled out above them. Random shoppers give them dirty looks, which go ignored. Sophie makes an exaggerated gagging noise. I want to hug her for the much-needed distraction.

I raise my brows. "Am I supposed to start clapping?"

"This is what happens when you take eight bajillion years to get candy," Alexa says in a monotone from the floor. "People die."

Jason rolls his eyes, then continues walking straight at Ahmed, pretending to step on his face.

"Let's buy this stuff and get out of here," I say as my loser-but-lifesaver friends get to their feet. "I'm pretty sure we've pissed off half the store."

Jason tries to catch my eye as we head to the checkout, but I don't let him. Instead, I pick up my phone and tell Patrick we're on our way.

SATURDAY

AUTUMN

The morning sunlight pierces my closed eyelids. I groan, roll off my air mattress half asleep, and slam onto the hardwood floor.

That wakes me up. I jolt upward, my heart thudding.

My gaze frantically bounces around the gray walls, chipping paint, blue sheets.

My room.

I slap my hand over my heart, catching my breath. Holy shit. A dream.

I catch a glimpse of myself in the mirror—still wearing my jeans and hoodie from yesterday, hair's a mess, eyeliner's clumpy under my eyes, but I'm fully intact. My clothes are exactly as I left them. No blood. No broken bones. I'm alive.

I sink back to the mattress and rest my forehead in my hands. That was the worst nightmare I've ever had in my life.

I don't even remember coming home and going to bed. How many pills did I take? Fuck, I've never gotten so high that I've forgotten how I got home. I went to the park, I know that. Then a guy texted me. That must've been where the dream started. The memory of the abandoned warehouse floods my brain, and my whole body starts shaking.

I wrap my arms around myself. It wasn't real. I'm fine.

Instinctively, I reach down for Pumpernickel, but he's not curled in a ball at the foot of my bed. That's weird.

Voices from downstairs capture my attention. I exhale a heavy breath. I'm so relieved to be here that my first reaction to Kathy's scratchy voice isn't even to tell her to fuck off. I just want breakfast.

I plow out of my bedroom and into the hall.

"... didn't come home again last night." It's Kathy.

I take the stairs two at a time, quickly turning to the right when I reach the bottom, and head into the kitchen.

Dad rubs his forehead, a wisp of steam curling from the coffee mug in front of him. "I don't know what to do anymore."

"I just hope she's okay. It's nerve-racking when she vanishes like this."

Nice alligator tears, Kathy. You don't give a shit about me.

"Shove it, Kathy." I stroll into the kitchen. "You'd love it if I never came home. Don't lie."

Kathy unpeels a banana in her bathrobe, her eyes fixed straight ahead. "She's a teenager. Sometimes I wonder if we should follow her. Or call the school." She takes a bite. *"Something."*

"Ignoring me?" I open the fridge and survey my breakfast options. "Real mature."

Dad raises his hands, palms out. "If you want to follow her, that's up to you."

"The girl needs help. Remember when she cut all her hair off a few years ago? Normal kids don't do that, Steve. Don't you care about her well-being?"

"Of course I do. She's my daughter."

I raise my voice. "What's going on?"

She doesn't flinch.

"Okay, this is weirding me out." I go to grab an orange from the bottom shelf, but my hand comes up empty. Like my fingers closed around air rather than a piece of fruit. The orange still lies on the bottom shelf of the fridge. *What the actual fuck?*

"It's practically once a week now. This has got to stop. She's too young to be running off who knows where all night."

"She's a legal adult," Dad says. "What am I supposed to do? Handcuff her to the couch?"

"She's a kid, Steve." Kathy pushes herself up and opens the cabinets. She rummages in the pantry and grabs Pumpernickel's dog chow. "That poor dog has been waiting on the stairs for her all night." She pours a cup of food into his blue ceramic dish. I painted Pumpernickel's name across it in yellow letters when I was eleven.

"If this is some sort of prank—some stupid lesson or something—it's not funny," I say.

Kathy places the food bowl on the tile. "Pumpernickel! Breakfast!" Rattling tags get louder as Pumpernickel scurries into the kitchen, his tail quivering slightly.

"Hey, boy." I bend over and reach out my arms. "I missed you."

My dog keeps walking toward me—then right through me.

I jump back, my heart racing. *What the ever-loving fuck?!*

Pumpernickel starts munching his breakfast, oblivious to the fact that I'm standing right here.

I hold my hands up; they're solid—at least, they look solid.

"Dad?" No response. I shake his shoulders. "Dad!" He stares ahead, dazed. "Come on!" Tears burn behind my eyes. "Kathy!" I shove her as hard as I can, but it does nothing. She doesn't even cringe. "Listen to me! Fuck!" I whirl around and kick the trash can; my foot goes straight through the plastic. The trash can stands upright, unperturbed, still full.

I flare my hands out. "What's happening to me?"

The warehouse. Those guys.

I slap a hand over my mouth.

It was real.

They killed me. They murdered me.

I'm dead.

I'm dead.

I press my hands into my eyes and squeeze them shut.

The air grows cold and violent, like a hurricane's sweeping me off my feet. Everything changes.

Bitter cold seeps through my hoodie from the hard surface under my back. My head feels light—disoriented, dizzy—but it's almost like I'm . . . lying down?

The stench of mildew floats around me. My dry tongue searches my mouth, overwhelmed by the metallic taste of blood. It feels overfull, like I swallowed a bag of cotton balls.

I try to open my eyelids, but a layer of crust cements them shut. I manage to force them open a sliver, and it feels like I'm rubbing glass shards into them. A groan escapes my swollen lips. Some light seeps in, but it's dim. Thick rope binds my hands together, biting into my flesh.

Where am I?

I inhale a shallow, rattling breath and searing pain slices through my chest. I wince, trying to raise my bound hands, but someone tied a rope around my arms and torso, strapping them down. My legs are like anchors, pinned to the floor. A jolt of pain shoots through my side; I clench my jaw to block the yelp.

I'm alive.

Tears of joy fill my eyes. I survived. My heart's still beating. My body's still working—barely, but working. I'm so overwhelmed that I barely feel the pain in my ribs. I'm here. I'm alive. I still have time.

Something soft fills my mouth—a towel? They gagged me.

I can barely make out the light glinting off a metal chain, wrapped through the wooden door, presumably leading to a padlock outside.

Agony weighing down on me like a two-ton barbell, I force my body to roll toward the door. Pain splinters through me when my left side hits the wooden floor beneath me. I pry my hand off the cold ground and stretch my mangled fingers, my arms screaming, but the rope holds me in place. My eyes cloud with water.

How long can I survive like this?

I close my eyes.

I open my eyes.

I'm back in my kitchen with Dad, Kathy, and Pumpernickel— back in this uninjured body no one can see or hear.

"I'm alive," I whisper. They don't move. I fist my hands into my short hair.

I'm *barely* alive.

Those guys abandoned me there.

"You have to find me." I get right in my dad's face. "You have to go to the warehouse and save me."

Kathy takes a seat at the table and lights a cig. Dad glances at her from the corner of his eye, as if contemplating telling her off. Instead, he gets to his feet and leaves the room without another word.

"Dad. Please!" I call after him. He doesn't stop or turn around. "Kathy. Listen to me." Kathy browses the news on her phone. "Fuck!"

I'm going to die. And no one will even know.

I race upstairs and into my bedroom. Phone. I need to find my phone.

I grasp at my dresser handle to rip open the drawer, but my

fingers close around nothing. I bury my face in my hands—it doesn't matter anyway, because I left the phone in my car, back at the terrible warehouse. I never should have gone there. Why? Why did I respond to that text? I *knew* something was off.

My mind races, running through everyone who could've done this. Where do I even begin? Liam. It had to be Liam. But he didn't do it alone; there were at least five people in the warehouse. He has so many shady friends, I don't even know where to start.

I hold my fist to my mouth as my body convulses with sobs. This is the end. No one's coming to help me. I'm powerless. A shell.

I think back to our bio lesson about dehydration freshman year. People can last three days without water. That's all I've got.

In three days, I'll be dead.

A fresh sob chokes in my throat.

My shell of a body is broken. I probably won't even last that long.

What the hell *am* I? I'm a ghost. A spirit. A . . . something.

Why am I even here?

"Ivy, sweetie, you up?" A few knocks echo down the hall. Dad stands outside my sister's door with his jacket on.

"Five more minutes," her sleepy voice replies. "It's Saturday."

"I'm going to run downtown to the farmers market before my shift starts. I get out at six tonight. Kathy's here if you need anything." He clomps back down the stairs.

Ivy.

"Ivy!" I barrel down the hall and try to stop when I see her closed bedroom door, but my body plows straight through it like it's air. I catch my breath, swallowing back the fear. This is so screwed up.

"Ivy! Ivy. Please wake up." I pound my fist against the doorframe even though it doesn't make a sound. "Ivy! Come on!"

Her sleeping figure stirs under her yellow comforter. She rolls over, her back facing me.

"Ivy." I stand at the foot of her bed. "Ivy. Please. You're my last hope. Ivy. Ivy." Desperation claws at my voice. "Ivy!" I kick her bedpost. "Ivy!"

Ivy shoots up, her eyes wide and frantic. "Autumn?"

Ivy

I sit up in bed and catch my breath, glancing around my empty room.

That was trippy. Of all the nightmares I've had about Autumn, most entail her screaming at *me*; this time, she was screaming for help.

I yawn, still blinking off that weird dream, and check my phone. Twenty-two texts. Jeez, what could be so important at ten on a Saturday morning?

Aha. They were actually sent at 2:00 a.m. Much more understandable.

Jason: okay, I finally caved and started watching Game of Thrones—you completed your mission to convert me, congratulations

Jason: no spoilers or you're dead to me

Jason: omg if these wolves die I'm shutting it off

Jason: this Joffrey kid is a prick.

I laugh reading through all his ridiculous reactions and predictions. At 3:55 a.m., I have one final message.

Jason: Okay I have to work in, like, five hours, so I'm going to bed. Text when you wake up—I need to know the deal with these dragon eggs.

I smirk, typing back.

Me: You're, like, five years too late for the no-spoilers request.

Me: If you want any hope of staying pure, avoid all
the show hashtags—Twitter, Tumblr, Insta, EVERYWHERE!

Me: Better yet, just avoid social media altogether.
It's really your only hope.

Me: Oh, and now I have some leverage. If you piss me
off, I'm telling you who dies next. You're welcome.

I'm searching Giphy for an appropriately sassy GIF to send him when a chill skirts down my arms.

I remember this episode of *20/20* about twins who swore they could communicate telepathically. One sister would think of a color, and in another room, the other sister would pick the right color on a card. Autumn and I aren't twins, and we don't even communicate the normal way, but I can't fight the feeling something's wrong with her.

Which is stupid. She's fine.

A general sense of unease washes over me. Dammit.

I throw my sheets off and climb out of bed, annoyed with myself. "Autumn?" I step into the hall, bracing myself to get screamed at for waking her up. "You okay?"

This is ridiculous. There's something seriously wrong with me.

I raise my hand to knock on her door. Autumn's never actually hit me; she shoves me out of the way sometimes, but that's it. Still, I don't doubt for a second she would if I woke her up *and* came into her room—double whammy.

Preemptively cringing, I knock. No answer. I press my ear to her door, straining to hear. Silence.

Against my better judgment, I push it open, cringing again when the hinges squeak. My sister's mattress lies empty on the floor, a nest of sheets hanging off the end.

I relax a little.

I guess it's not so unusual.

The worried feeling settles deep in my core, like it's slowly turning all my organs to stone.

Why can't I let this go? I'm being paranoid for no reason.

I'm too lazy to put my contacts in, so I grab my glasses and trudge downstairs. "Kathy?" I call as my feet hit the bottom step. "Have you seen Autumn?"

My stepmom glances up at me from the living room couch, pointing to the phone glued to her ear. "Yes, honey. All right. I'm gonna stream the game—I'll be rooting for you!" Three versions of Chris's face beam at me from the bookshelf: a two-year-old with a face covered in frosting; a teen in his graduation cap; and finally, a college freshman wearing a Michigan State football jersey. "I miss you, too." The grad picture makes him look like a brown-haired Justin Bieber. "Autumn, Ivy, and Steve send their love. Bye, baby." She hangs up and sets her phone on the coffee table. "Sorry about that, honey, your brother called. What's wrong?"

I realize I'm unintentionally glaring at her. I definitely *don't* send Chris my love. Why does she have to say that? And for the eight bajillionth time, he's *not* my brother.

"Have you seen Autumn?"

Kathy's smile droops. "Not today, honey, no. I don't think she came home last night."

"I'm a little worried about her."

"I know. I worry about her, too." She purses her lips and pats the cushion beside her. I reluctantly take a seat. "Do you want to talk about it?"

"I . . . I'm getting a weird feeling. Like something deep down is telling me she's in trouble."

"I wouldn't worry too much. Autumn's been doing this for years now. Sometimes I think she just does it because she hates me." Kathy looks away.

She's probably hoping I'll reassure her that Autumn doesn't *really* hate her, but I have no poker face, and that's a lie. I've always wondered why Autumn hates Kathy so much. I mean, yeah, for a while it was weird seeing Dad with another woman. But I like knowing he has someone. I wish Autumn felt that way, too.

"Don't worry." Kathy presses a hand to my cheek. Her wedding band is cold against my skin. "She always turns up."

"But what if she doesn't this time?"

"She will, honey. I promise."

"I think we should look for her." The words sound silly as I say them—if I had a nickel for every time Autumn vanished overnight, we could've afforded to stay in our old house—but I can't stop myself. "Something's wrong."

"If she's not home by tonight, we'll call the police. Okay?" Her tone is patronizing as hell. She's not taking me seriously. I'm not even sure I'm taking myself seriously.

"Okay."

The feeling intensifies as I stand—it wants me to keep pressing, keep insisting. But I fight it off. I'm overreacting because I had a ridiculous dream. That's it.

"Hey, Ivy?" Kathy pushes to her feet. "I was thinking about our discussion a couple nights ago."

I blink at her. "Oh yeah?"

"You asked if Chris would be home for Thanksgiving and Christmas." She smiles, a hopeful look in her eyes. "I think it would be great to invite him."

I kind of stare at her for a minute. That wasn't what I had in mind. And technically, I only asked about Thanksgiving.

"We've barely seen him since he started college," Kathy continues. "It would be nice to have the whole family together. Don't you agree?"

No. He's not my family. "I guess."

When Dad and Kathy first got married, we used to go to Kathy's sister's house for Christmas Eve. They did the classic Italian thing with all the fish. I loved it. We haven't seen them in a few years. Kathy's never mentioned why, but I think there was some sort of disagreement about their parents' money. But that's the only part I miss about those holidays. Not Chris.

"He would probably feel more . . . welcome . . . if the invite came from your father. You know? Since it's his house?"

I shrug. "I guess."

"Do you think you could talk to your dad about it?"

"Can't you talk to him?"

Kathy sighs. "I don't know. Things have been . . . tense . . . between Chris and Autumn for a few years now . . ."

I suppress a gag. "Yeah, I know all about it."

"You do?" Her eyebrows shoot up.

I mean, the whole town does. "Yeah. These things get around." My mind races to come up with a subject-changer, but Kathy is too quick.

"It was a long time ago," she says, "but I think your father is still . . . uncomfortable . . . knowing what happened. I know—*I know*—it wasn't the best decision for either of them. You can't just sleep with your stepsibling and not expect fallout."

I'm literally forcing myself not to vomit. I wish Kathy would save this talk for her therapist or something, because I'm really grossed out right now.

I nod. "Yeah."

"But it's been three years, and I don't think it's fair that Chris can't come home once in a while. People make mistakes under the influence of alcohol," she continues. "That's why you shouldn't drink until you're twenty-one."

I'm not sure why she's telling me this. It's like she feels the need to mother me or something. Meanwhile, there's one Casterly child who probably needs the alcohol lecture, and she's not here. "Yep. I know."

"But you're Steve's little girl, and he'd do anything for you. I think if you ask him about Chris, he'll let him come. We can have another family Christmas, like we used to."

I scratch the back of my neck, wondering if Kathy can smell a lie. "All right. I'll talk to him." I'm out of the living room before she can say anything else.

I kinda hoped I'd never be subjected to another one of Kathy's fake "look how happy we are together" family portraits in front of the tree. Smiling in a photo doesn't make happiness real, even if we're wearing matching pajamas and slippers. Christmas pj's were always a Casterly family tradition. I'm not going to lie, the Christmas after Dad and Kathy's wedding, it kinda stung seeing my stepmom and Chris unwrap their own pj's and slippers from Dad, just in time for the annual family portrait. It was like Kathy was literally trying to step into Mom's shoes. I didn't say anything, though, because Dad was super excited about it.

Autumn took it worse. She disappeared and didn't even open her gifts. She came back that night, having dodged our Christmas afternoon tradition of watching *Prancer* and drinking cocoa.

Autumn.

"Stop it," I whisper to myself. "Autumn's fine."

I go into the kitchen for some breakfast—okay, *breakfast* is a generous term when it's closer to lunchtime—and fire up the Keurig. Dad bought the French vanilla K-cups from Dunkin' that I love—score.

I rest my hand on my hip.

It's funny, I've seen the same photos, cards, and announcements on our fridge for years and still read them every time. I glance over the Spartans Football calendar, the postcard Kathy's nephew sent us from Puerto Rico last summer, a Save-the-Date for a second cousin's wedding that was clearly a grab for a gift.

My eyes stop on a photo of Autumn and me in our soccer uniforms when we were little kids. Autumn's got her arm wrapped around my shoulders. We both have the biggest grins—hers with braces and mine with a terrible overbite they thankfully fixed.

I sucked at soccer but made my parents sign me up anyway, because apparently my desire to humiliate myself started at a young age. I always got scared when someone kicked the ball at me; I'd freeze in the middle of the field and hide my face. Unsurprisingly, Autumn was super aggressive on the field and scored half the goals for her team every season. Everyone assumed she'd end up on varsity, but she quit playing her freshman year.

I pull out my phone and dial Autumn's number, holding it to my ear with my shoulder as I prep the coffeemaker. It rings, and rings, and rings, and . . .

"Hey. It's Autumn. Leave a message and I might call back. If you've got a craving, don't tell me here. Ciao." I hang up at the long beep, then stare at my phone.

What the hell is wrong with me? When Autumn comes home tonight, I'm going to feel so stupid.

I start humming an Ariana Grande song to change my mind when my phone buzzes—Jason.

You expect me to stay off Facebook while I watch ALL EIGHT SEASONS?!

I type back, Better watch quickly, punk. I offer my

services as a watching buddy if you want to laugh at me for covering my eyes during the bloody parts (so, basically, every scene).

Good, he says. You can warn me when those parts are coming.

I grin. There's something satisfying about watching something you love with someone who's never seen it before. Especially Jason, since his reactions are always perfect. When I made him watch *Serenity*, he screamed the F-word so loudly at the leaf-on-the-wind scene that his mom came running out of the shower in her towel to check on us. Classic.

I grab my Tolkien mug out of the dishwasher, waiting for the water to heat up.

Me: I could use a distraction today. What are you up to?

Work, Jason responds, with a crying emoji. Stop by if you want a free bagel!

Free bagels are tempting, especially since Jase gives me extra cream cheese even without my asking. That's one thing I love about having him for a best friend—he knows literally everything about me. Well, except for all those awful poems in my pink notebook. If he found those, I would probably die.

I'm about to respond, when a message from Patrick pops up.

Hey, Ivy! How's it going? Want to get lunch later? He sends a second text with a bunch of food emojis. My heart jumps. I'm half excited, half curious if he knows the double meaning behind the eggplant emoji he just peppered across my screen.

Wait.

A jumpy, happy feeling skitters inside me.

Did he just ask me out?

No guy has ever asked me out before. I mean, Jase and I get food and see movies and stuff a lot, but they're not, like, *dates*.

But wait. Is *this* a date? Or is Patrick just being nice?

Play it cool. Don't even think the D-word—*any* D-word.

Yeah sure! I type. Where did you have in mind?

This is awesome. I'll put my contacts in, take a shower, and maybe break out that Sephora eye shadow palette Alexa got me for my birthday last year. I mentally go through all the hangers in my closet; I must have something cute somewhere.

I'm so distracted when I grab my drink, hot coffee sloshes over the rim of the mug and splashes all over the counter. Crap. My Tolkien mug is quickly becoming more of a bad luck charm than the One Ring itself. I rush to soak up the mess with a paper towel just as Patrick texts back.

Sorry, never mind. Mom's dragging me to Marshalls to get pants. She says hi btw.

I can't help it—I groan. It's like he pricked my balloon and disappointment came flooding out instead of air.

So close. I was so close to a maybe-sort-of lunch date. I shouldn't be this bitter about a maybe date with a guy I hadn't seen in four years before this week, but I am.

Of course it wouldn't work out. When do girls like me ever get asked out? Never. Guys swarm around people like my sister while girls like me get the "Hey, Ivy, I know you don't have a *real* date, so let's just go to homecoming together as friends" spiel. The "Sorry, Ivy, I can't do this" classic line. In fact, if I ever write an autobiography, that's literally what it will be: line after line of epic fails and guys who like me as a friend.

I huff, slamming the dirty paper towel into the trash.

Last year, I was in the pit band for the school production of *Les*

Mis. I swear, when Éponine was singing about how Marius likes her only as a friend, I felt that deep in my bones. But I was also psyched, because surely they'd end up together in the end, since that always happens in rom-coms. Did they end up together? No. Marius ends up with the hot girl he just met, and Éponine dies. That's my future. I am the eternal Éponine, and the moment a Cosette shows up, everyone forgets I exist.

Aw, bummer! I write back. I miss your mom, tell her I say hi!

Patrick's mom was always nice, but kind of overprotective. When we went trick-or-treating, she'd make us dump our candy out on the floor to check for razors or drugs or something. But if we were shooting hoops in the yard, she'd bring us those squeezable yogurts and pretzels and stuff to snack on. Sometimes Patrick's brother, Will, would come play basketball with us, too, which made me feel super cool, since he was way older than us. Pat's dad was always a dick, though. I'm glad he doesn't live with him anymore.

She says you can come to Marshalls with us if you want lol, Patrick says. Is that weird? She wants to see you.

Okay. I didn't picture going on my first maybe date with a chaperone. But it's better than nothing, and it beats the hell out of sitting around the house paranoid all day.

I startle, suddenly overwhelmed by the urge to go with them—beyond my usual Patrick jitters.

Not weird, I write back. I'm in!

———

The first time I met Patrick was at a community pool party at Rollins Park the summer after third grade. Mom had died six months prior, and we were in that phase of trying to do "normal" family stuff again. The Perkinses had just moved in from Illinois, and Patrick's mom revealed herself as an outsider immediately by calling our town Con-*cord*. My know-it-all nine-year-old ass blurted out, "It's pronounced *conquered*," and everybody laughed. Although Patrick and I quickly became friends, I'm, like, 60 percent sure his mom still thinks I'm a pain in the butt.

Patrick's mom has a different minivan than she did four years ago when they moved away, but there's still a pumpkin spice air freshener dangling from the rearview mirror. The moment I climb into my former usual seat, I'm smacked in the face with the fragrance and feel like I'm eleven again.

"Ivy!" Patrick's mom twists in her seat to hug me, but ends up just patting my knee instead. "How have you been?" A few gray hairs peek out of her dye job.

"I'm good! The usual, I guess." I put on the cheesy grin I reserve for parents and teachers. "I'm in band now—I play trumpet. Only second chair, though. I'm not very good. I spend most of my time playing video games and stuff. But I don't have that awful overbite anymore." Wow, TMI. I snap my mouth shut.

"That's nice." She pulls out of my driveway and gently hits the gas. "You've gotten so big."

My face heats. I know what she means is *You've gotten so old*, but what I hear is *You've gotten so fat*. I wouldn't blame her for noticing. I'm much heavier than I used to be, even beyond the usual preteen growth spurts. But I don't want her to think I don't see it. "I know, I'm fat now."

She gasps like I've said a dirty word. "I didn't mean it like that. You're not fat!"

I squirm in my seat. I hate when people act like *fat* is the absolute worst possible thing I could be. Like, *Oh man, your child's a serial killer? That sucks, but at least they're skinny!*

I don't get why people get so defensive when I call myself *fat*. They always think I'm being self-deprecating or something and try to correct me, but I'm just telling it like it is. I don't think it's bad to be fat.

I shrug. "It's okay."

Patrick shoots me an apologetic look through the mirror on his sun visor.

This conversation is getting a little too personal. Time for some evasive maneuvers. "So, Pat, you never told me why you guys moved back."

"The city got overwhelming. We missed Concord." He grins. "And my brother was still here, so we wanted to be closer to him."

His mom merges onto the highway. "You might've heard, Ivy, but Will's had some tough times."

"Oh no, is he okay?"

"He's just trying to figure stuff out," Patrick says.

"Sometimes I wonder if it was a mistake letting him stay with his dad in Bow while we moved down to Baltimore." She clicks her blinker and cruises off the first exit. "He really wanted to stay with his friends—you know what it's like in high school—so we let him."

"Mom, come on." Patrick slinks down in his seat. "Ivy doesn't need all our baggage."

"No, it's fine," I say. "My sister Autumn's gotten into some bad stuff, too. I can relate."

"I knew back then some of his friends had issues." She keeps going like Patrick and I aren't even there. "But I didn't do anything about it, and I should've. Now he's in all sorts of trouble."

Patrick's face burns redder than the stop sign his mom almost misses. Poor guy. I guess I shouldn't stoke the fire, so I keep my mouth shut.

A car with a Concord High Crew Team bumper sticker zigzags dangerously around us, and Patrick's mom wags her finger at them like she's scolding her kids for not cleaning their room. I sink lower in my seat. Maybe this was a bad idea.

This minivan date is probably nature's way of reminding me I should start saving up for drivers ed. Lots of kids in my grade already signed up for the class, and some even started practice drives with their parents, but I can't afford a car anyway, so I've never given it much thought. Still, I feel pretty pathetic right now.

The skin on my arms prickles, and I glance out the window right as we pass the abandoned lot a block from Marshalls.

And there, all by itself in a desert of weeds and cracked pavement, is Autumn's car.

Autumn

Like I told fuckface Liam, I'm not a religious person. But when recognition crosses Ivy's face and she shouts, "Pull over!" loud enough to make the lady swerve over the double yellow, I want to fall to my knees and thank whatever God in the sky made it happen.

After half a day of shouting at my sister and following at her heel like a puppy, my messages must have finally gotten through her thick skull. I close my eyes, taking in shaky breaths. She's going to find me. It's going to be okay.

The minivan careens to the side of the road, nailing the curb. "Jeez, Mom!" Patrick gloms onto the door, his face drained of all color.

"Are you all right, Ivy?" His equally pasty mother whirls around. "Are you going to throw up?"

Ivy's already ripping the door open and sprinting toward my abandoned Civic.

She's going to find me. It's going to be fine.

"Autumn?" Ivy frames her hands around her eyes and presses her forehead to my car windows, one by one. "Autumn?" She raises her voice. "Are you here?"

"The warehouse!" I'm practically ripping my invisible hair out. "Go. Check the warehouse. I'm right there!" I don't know how this communication works. She doesn't seem to hear me, not really—it's more like she can *sense* me.

"Ivy! Wait!" Patrick jogs after her. "Are you okay? What happened?"

"This . . . this is my sister's car . . ." Ivy forces the words out between heavy breaths. "She's been . . . she's been gone all night."

"Holy shit."

His mom speed-walks toward us, her eyes darting in every direction. "This doesn't look like a safe area."

"Mom, it's Concord, New Hampshire." Patrick points. "Bank of America is, like, right there."

She clutches her purse like we're walking through a back alley in Boston in the middle of the night. I'm used to old people getting anxious around me. Usually I assume it's because of my tattoo, septum piercing, and resting bitch face. But now, in this vacant lot next to the building where I almost died, I can't fight the shivers, either. I'm shaking worse than this pasty-faced mother over here.

Maybe if Ivy finds my phone and reads my texts, she'll figure out that I followed that Nick guy here. Maybe that will get her to check the warehouse.

"Get in my car," I instruct my sister. "Find my phone. Read my texts."

Nothing happens.

I take her hand, desperation dripping from my words. "*Please,* Ivy. Please get into the car. I need you."

As if this draws some invisible connection between us, my message seems to click.

"I need to get into this car." Ivy pounds on the window. She rattles the handle, but it doesn't budge. "Dammit."

The woman grabs her son by the elbow. "Come on. You can't just break into someone's car."

"It's not someone's! It's my sister's!" She points to the Don't Shop, Adopt sticker next to the pole-shaped dent on my bumper. "I know it's hers."

I can see on this woman's face that she doesn't believe her. No. Ivy's so close to finding me. She can't give up.

I scream my fucking lungs out. No one glances at me—not even Ivy.

It's a strange feeling to scream and have no one hear it. At school, I could whisper and heads would turn; now I am a storm barreling across the Atlantic that doesn't rock a single ship. It's a sad, powerless feeling that strikes me with overfamiliarity. I swore I would never be silent again. I swore my voice would always be the loudest in the room. Now they don't even know I'm here.

"When we get inside, we can call your father and tell him about the car," the woman says, like she's talking to a five-year-old. "But it's not safe to be here." She lowers her voice to a whisper. "This is where thugs hang out."

I remember Patrick pretty well. He used to hang out at our house all the time. Of all the pint-size nerds kid-Ivy brought home, he was the least objectionable. But this is the first time I've met his family, and so far, I'm not impressed.

The woman grabs Ivy's arm to lead her away, but my sister seems conflicted.

Panic sets in. "Don't you dare. I'll fucking kill you if you leave." If looks could murder, my eyes would've shot a million daggers into this lady's face by now. "Don't you dare leave, Ivy!" This can't be happening. The warehouse is barely thirty feet away.

She keeps rattling that damn handle. "I can't get in."

"Here. Let me try." Patrick slides a credit card into the crevice between the door and the panel and it's clear he has no idea what the hell he's doing.

"Smash it!" I shout. "I don't care about the glass."

Ivy picks up a small rock and chews her bottom lip, as if contemplating it, but finally lets the rock fall back to the ground.

Fuck. Ivy'll never break the glass. She's too much of a little saint.

Ivy circles my Civic. It's like she thinks the whole thing will spring open like a toaster if she watches it long enough.

My mind races. I need a solution. Something to get her to stay. Anything.

"Ivy, we're going to Marshalls." The mother beckons my sister with her arm. "Come on."

"Go into the warehouse." I focus intently on her. "Find me."

"You coming, Ivy?" Patrick asks.

"Ivy. Warehouse. Now."

"I think . . . I think I should look inside." Ivy points at the abandoned building.

Yes. Excellent. About time.

Patrick looks at her like she suggested running in front of a freight train. "Into that sketchy building?"

"Absolutely not," his mother says. "There are probably homeless people living in there."

"What, like that would automatically make it dangerous?" I snap. "Just go in!"

Ivy squints at the building. "But . . ." She sighs. "Okay. Let's just go." She follows the others back toward the minivan.

I blink in disbelief. No. She can't give up that easy. I'm not going to die because my sister won't stand up for herself.

"Ivy!" I stomp after her. "Ivy, don't go!" Desperation floods my voice. "Come on! Ivy!"

She stops and pulls out her phone. I peek over her shoulder, watching her type a message to some guy named Jason D-C.

What time do you get off work? I have a potentially dangerous mission for us.

She quickly stows the phone back in her pocket, glancing worriedly over her shoulder. I give her a half smile she can't see. Maybe I underestimated my sister after all.

Ivy

The lady in charge of the Marshalls dressing rooms keeps giving Patrick's mom dirty looks. Probably because Mrs. Perkins—I guess I should get used to calling her Ms. Fournier now—is dropping piles of clothes on the table and barking out instructions for different sizes. I kind of want to take a pair of those discarded pants and drape them over my face so no one can see how badly I want to melt into the floor.

I found Autumn's car in the vacant lot on Storrs, I text my dad. He never checks his phone when he's at work, but he'll see it eventually. You should come down here.

My knee bounces against my hand. Patrick's mom has started chiding the lady about the better sale prices at JCPenney, all with a big smile on her face. She reminds me a little of Dolores Umbridge from Harry Potter. If she acquired a bunch of cat photos, she could literally be her doppelgänger.

I've been rotating my phone in my hands for so long, the screen's gotten all sweaty and gross. Maybe I should call the cops. But I don't want to get in trouble, and I definitely don't want my sister to think I tattled on her. It's possible Autumn left her car there and hopped into someone else's. That sounds like something she would do.

My intestines are cramping just thinking about it—or maybe

that's my period. I pull out my pack of birth control and check; still another two weeks on the pink pills. It's definitely nerves.

After an eternity of sitting on the bench outside the dressing room with Patrick's mom while he begrudgingly tries on eight bajillion pants, he picks two pairs of bootcut jeans. I subtly check out his butt when he pops out to show us.

"You should get that other pair, too, Patrick. Your pants are too loose. You're losing too much weight around the waist."

Patrick rolls his eyes. "Mom. It's really fine. I promise I'm not gonna drop dead because my pants are loose." *Sorry,* he mouths at me.

I shrug, covertly checking the time on my phone. I'm starting to hate myself for agreeing to come. I've had two realizations: One, Patrick's mom didn't get the memo that he graduated kindergarten nine years ago. And two, I've never been so grateful to Dad and Kathy for butting out of my business.

"You want to look at any fall clothes, Ivy?" Patrick's mom asks.

I probably wouldn't fit into most of these clothes. The last thing I need is to get stuck in something in the dressing room, and then Umbridge would have to come pry it off me. I'm also broke. "Nah, I'm all set."

Of course, this hot guy from school—Aaron Dunlap of the "Aaron Dunlap incident" himself—happens to be working the register. Which means I'm staying as far away from it as humanly possible. Let's just say last time I spoke to this guy, I had a wipeout that resulted in my jabbing him in the balls with my trumpet.

They pay for the pants while I hang out near the door, pretending to look at purses. I got my current purse at the Sunapee craft show last summer. It has a dragon stitched into the side, and if you pull the tab on the bottom, cloth flames shoot out of his mouth. Best twenty bucks I ever spent.

"With my coupons, we saved seven dollars." Patrick's mom beams. "I might come back later this week and get that other pair. Are you sure you don't want some khakis, too?" She prowls the clearance rack at the exit like a shark smelling blood. "Maybe you should have something a little more formal if you start looking for after-school jobs."

"Mom. I'm fine. We can get other stuff later."

I open the text with my dad to see if he's read it, but the little bar just says Delivered.

"Okay, I need to run a few errands." Patrick's mom pulls a giant notepad out of her purse. "Do you kids want to come, or should I drop you off at home?"

Before Patrick can respond, I get there first. "Actually, my friend Jason is working at the bagel place up the street. Pat, you wanna grab lunch there? Jase can drop us off after."

"Yeah, that sounds good," he says, a little too quickly. I can tell he's just as eager to ditch his mom as I am. Let's see if he's still this excited once he figures out where we're going after.

We say goodbye to Patrick's mom and take the sidewalk up the hill to Main Street.

"Sorry about my mom," he says. "She's gotten a little over-protective."

"A little?" I mutter, then realize I'm being mean. "It's fine. She just cares about you."

"She's been like this with me since Will started getting in trouble."

"That sucks. You and your brother aren't the same person."

"I don't know why she even compares us. I love my brother, but I'm not him."

"I totally get it. My mom—" I stop short. Once, when my mom

was high on morphine after a surgery, she said that Autumn got the pretty genes and I needed to try harder with my appearance. She probably didn't even remember saying it. But I remember. I kick a rock, and it clatters into a storm drain. "Yeah. I get it."

We trudge along in silence until the giant smiling bagel comes into view, hanging over the entrance. I always tell Jason that he has to steal the bagel for me if they ever decide to change their sign. I will totally hang it up in my bedroom.

The bell over the glass door tinkles as we head inside. I inhale deeply, savoring the doughy, garlicky aroma of freshly baked bagels. It's got to be in my top three favorite smells, right up there with Maine beaches and Christmas trees.

Patrick quickly excuses himself to the bathroom, and the second he's gone, Jason emerges from the kitchen.

"Whoa, sexy outfit." I try to wolf-whistle at him in his bagel-making uniform, but it just comes out a gust of air. "How do I get me one of those bagel hats?"

"Get a job here?" Jason darts his eyes toward the kitchen, then back. "Hang on," he mutters, adjusting the white-and-blue apron tied around his neck. "Wait outside."

"Nice to see you, too!" I roll my eyes and push back through the door, making the bell chime again. I swear, Jason better not be in a grumpy mood today. I need his help.

Within seconds, he strolls out, still wearing his apron and hat. "Sorry about that—my boss was up my ass today. You would not believe what Alexa and Sophie did to me."

"Oh no." I slap my hand over my mouth to block the giggles. "Please tell me they got revenge for Operation Trojanscan."

Last month, Jason and I pranked Alexa while she was working at CVS. We brought twenty boxes of condoms up to the register to buy. Then, after she scanned them all, we insisted on returning them—which meant she had to call a manager, over the intercom, to come return twenty boxes of condoms. She swore she'd get even.

"At least, I think it was them. Someone called and ordered fifty raisin bagels under the name Mike Rotch."

I burst out laughing. "Oh man. She got you."

"Picture me calling that order over the microphone for ten minutes."

"I will be eternally sad to have missed seeing this."

"We're gonna need to start plotting revenge. Here." He throws a round paper package at me. "Sesame, extra cream cheese."

"Yes!" I hold it to my nose. "Oh my God." I close my eyes and inhale. "It's still warm."

"Don't let my boss hear you having a foodgasm, jeez. He already thinks I'm the store perv after the whole 'Mike Rotch' thing."

I unwrap the paper, enjoying a deep whiff. "He should take it as a compliment that I love your bagels so much." I take a monstrous bite, exaggerating my reaction just to mess with him. "So. Good."

I open my eyes and Jason's staring at me. We both crack up.

The door tinkles again and Patrick plods outside. "Sorry about that. Hey, man." He nods at Jason. "What's up?"

Jason's smile sinks. "Oh, hey. Sorry. I only brought one bagel. I didn't know you were coming."

"It's okay." I shrug. "He can have half of mine."

"Thanks. I'm starving."

I rip off a chunk of bagel for him.

Jason shuffles his feet. "So, what's this dangerous mission?"

"Okay, so." I swallow a giant bite of bagel. "How do you feel about breaking into cars?"

AUTUMN

I'm about ready to slap someone. And by someone, I mean these two losers my sister insisted on dragging along. We had to walk all the way back to the parking garage for Jason's car, because Mr. Someone Might See Me in This wanted to ditch his ridiculous bagel apron. We then had to make a detour to the candy store, and finally—*finally*—we got into Jason's car and he drove us back to the lot.

Ivy should never have brought these two distractions along, and I'm a little miffed she's not taking this as seriously as she should be.

"Okay, here's her car."

Jason circles my Civic the same way Ivy did earlier. He's got his hand buried in a bag of gummy lobsters from the candy store.

Come *on*.

"I don't think she's been here in a while," he says.

Yeah, no shit, Sherlock. We've established that.

"Go to the warehouse." I cup Ivy's cheeks with my hands and look into her eyes. "Go. Into. The. Warehouse."

"This is going to sound super weird." Ivy unknowingly pulls away from me. She takes a few of Jason's lobsters. "But I really feel like we need to go into that building."

Patrick watches the warehouse like it's a bomb ready to detonate. "It looks like it should be condemned."

Jason glances at him, which Ivy doesn't seem to notice, and puffs out his chest. "I'll go in."

I roll my eyes so hard, I'm surprised they can't see the back of my invisible head.

"I'll stay here and watch the car," Patrick says. "So if it gets dangerous, just shout and I'll call 911." He keeps his eyes glued to the ground, as if we all can't see right through that flimsy excuse.

"Why did you bring these dipshits?" I snap, wishing they could hear me. I follow behind my sister, staying a short distance away.

I didn't realize how badly this ghostly body would betray me. My heart rate speeds faster the closer we get, until it's full-on pounding in my ears. I picture that Nick guy standing here, lying to me. Right outside the rusty metal doorframe, I stop walking and close my eyes.

It'll be over soon.

They're going to find my body, call 911, and everything will be fine.

The weird thing is, the closer we get, the more it looks . . . different. There's no padlock on the door, and I could've sworn I saw one when I went into my body. No chain around the handle, either—it's just that piece of plywood. Maybe I imagined the lock. At least now I won't need to teach Ivy how to pick it.

Ivy steps inside the warehouse first, using her phone as a flashlight. I'm now close to her, my hands hovering at her back. In the daylight, it's a bit brighter. Narrow strips of light seep between the roof boards, shining thin beams onto the dirt beneath our feet. A few lines of illegible graffiti mar the gray concrete walls. The whole thing gives me the eerie feeling that we're on a sunken ship at the bottom of the ocean.

I bob up and down on the balls of my feet. "Okay, shine your light on the ground. I'm here somewhere."

The gravel crunches beneath Ivy's and Jason's shoes, but my footsteps are silent. Like I'm not even here.

Where's my body?

"It smells kinda funky." Jason wrinkles his nose. "Like piss."

I pick up my pace, speed-walking along the length of the wall and into the middle of the room. I've got to be here somewhere. The warehouse isn't that big.

"Do you spend lots of time smelling piss?" Ivy shines her phone around the small square space.

I strain my eyes in the dim light. All I see is dirt.

"What are we looking for, exactly?"

"I don't know." Her light beam traces the edges where the walls meet the ground, illuminating cigarette butts, empty beer cans, and a ratty old blanket balled up in the corner. "A clue. Something."

My pulse races. No. What the hell? Where am I?

This can't be happening.

I can go into my body and call for help. Ivy will hear me then.

I close my eyes and concentrate, thrusting myself back into my mangled body. The familiar cold, hard surface below me feels eerily like a tombstone. I groan, forcing my eyes open. My blurry vision takes a moment to adjust.

Wood. I see wood. A low wooden ceiling. Four wooden walls, boxing me into a space the size of a bathroom.

I suck in a breath, wincing at the throbbing pain that stabs into my ribs. This isn't possible. The warehouse is a cage of concrete.

A rusty metal shelf hangs high over my head; I can barely make out its silhouette. Light creeps in through cracks and spaces between the wooden boards.

Wood. Wood. Everywhere is wood. The smell of dank cedar fills the air, seeping into my pores.

And there, slung through a small hole in the wooden door, the thick-ringed chain locks me in.

A sob chokes in my throat, burning all the way down.

I'm not in the warehouse. They moved me.

Where am I?

Footsteps outside jerk my attention.

"I didn't sign up for this, man," says a deep male voice. "This has gone too far."

"Stop freaking out." Another guy. "It's fine."

I hold my breath, every inch of my broken body alert.

"What if she saw our faces?"

"We'll figure it out. She's not going anywhere anytime soon."

Their footsteps fade. I wasn't abandoned and left for dead—they're holding me hostage. *Somewhere.*

I blink.

Ivy and Jason circle the warehouse, seeking something they'll never find.

"I'm not here." The words escape softer than a whisper. "Ivy, I'm not in here." I blink back tears. "They're going to kill me, and I have no idea who they are or where they're keeping me."

I swallow down a hard lump. She has to find me.

Neither voice sounded like Liam's, but somehow, he has to be involved. Abby said the police were questioning him, and O'Riley had his picture—maybe he thought I snitched. Or maybe he was worried I *would* snitch sometime in the future.

That sick fuck. I hate Liam. He's behind this somehow, and if I see him again, I'll kick him right in the sack.

I'm so focused on Liam—his name, his stupid face—that the second I open my eyes, the scenery around me changes, and there he is.

I've never been inside a county jail, but I recognize it as that immediately.

"You've got five more minutes," barks a guard in a gray uniform.

Liam slumps on a wooden bench in a loose orange jumpsuit. He's got a thick black phone pressed to his ear. "In a holding cell. Yeah . . . I know." Defeat weighs down his words. "They already took my prints . . . Criminal trespass, burglary . . . They had camera footage . . . Yeah, I will . . . They're providing one, I can't afford that shit."

How long has he been in jail? Abby was right—they dragged him down to the station, but that was Friday afternoon, before I got attacked. I steady my quickening breaths.

He has a lot of friends. Connections. People who are shady as hell. Even if it wasn't him, it doesn't mean he wasn't behind it. So who did Liam's dirty work?

Liam's frown is pure misery, and it brings me a tiny speck of joy.

"Enjoying prison, dirtbag?" I ask, even though he can't hear me. But my smugness at Liam's current circumstance is overtaken by a blaring realization: in this body, I can visit anyone I think of.

Okay. I can figure this out. I can find out where I am. I just need to spy on the right people.

I close my eyes and focus on Nick—his name, his face, his shitty wannabe goatee.

Nothing happens.

Anger rages hot inside me. *Fuck.*

I think of my sister, and when I blink, the scenery changes again and I'm back in the warehouse with Ivy and Jason. It hits me— "Nick" must have used a fake name. I try to picture the faces of the other guys but keep coming up empty; I didn't get a good look at them.

A glint on the ground catches my eye. Embedded in the dirt beneath a sneaker print, my purple lanyard lies forgotten, along with the attached keys.

"Ivy!" I grab her hand and tug; of course, she doesn't even feel it. "Ivy! Look!" I point my invisible fingers at the keys.

As if on cue, Ivy turns, her eyes unknowingly following my hand. "Holy shit."

I back up to let her through. Ivy crouches and grabs my lanyard, dusting off the dirt. "These are Autumn's." She cradles it in her palms so Jason can see. I gently brush the keys with my fingertips, savoring the cold metal. It's proof I can still feel.

"Whoa." He flares his hands out. "Okay. So she was definitely here."

"I thought she'd just parked here and switched cars, but . . ." Ivy's brows draw together. "She wouldn't have left her keys." She touches my car key, then my house key, then my CVS rewards card and my key chain of a smiling pig holding an I'm Your Buddy, Not Your Breakfast picket sign, and finally trails her finger up the length of the lanyard.

"If they'd fallen out of her pocket, she would've come back looking for them."

"So how'd they get there?"

"I don't know. Why was she even hanging out here?"

It's a good question. I'm humiliated to admit the answer was that I'm too gullible.

"I didn't wanna go there," Jason says, "but wasn't she . . . dealing? What if she comes here to sell drugs or use them or something?"

"It's possible."

"Maybe she got really high and went to a friend's house and will come back for her keys later. I mean, hasn't it only been a day?"

I'm holding my invisible breath, watching the conviction fade from my sister's eyes.

Ivy fidgets. "Yeah. Technically."

"No," I whisper. "Don't do this."

"I mean, maybe she got high and wandered off," Jason continues. "I don't want to be a douche, but . . . stuff like that happens to people who use drugs all the time."

It's like the fact that I'm a dealer nullifies the fact that I might be in danger. That it's something everyone should expect. A druggie got her head bashed in and left for dead? Just part of the circle of life. Cue *Lion King* music.

"I mean, doesn't she do a lot of weird shit?" Jason keeps going, and I'm stuck listening to it. "She has no self-control, no filter. Like, didn't she sleep with your stepbrother? Who does that?"

I'm thrown off my balance as if ripped by the undertow of a wave and smacked with a memory.

It was something Chris had said to me the morning after the party. I was walking around the house in a hungover haze, trying to make sense of what happened and put a stop to the full-on revolt happening in my stomach. I'd spent the morning scrubbing the remaining eye makeup off my face and gulping water like a fish to stop myself from throwing up. He stopped me in the foyer while I was pulling on my boots.

"So, last night."

I couldn't look at him. The night before felt like a dream. I'd blown off all my friends to go to the party. I'd put my head on Chris's shoulder on his friend's couch. I'd laced my fingers with his. I'd done way too many shots. And now, in the daylight, it all felt so wrong. He was my *stepbrother*, and I'd slept with him, and more than anything in the world I wanted to take it back.

"We probably shouldn't tell anyone what happened," he said. "I mean, your dad would flip if he knew we'd been drinking. And we're technically related now, you know?"

I didn't want to talk about it. I just wanted to pretend it never happened. It was a bad, drunken mistake and I couldn't believe I even did it.

"You just kept looking at me in that way all night, and the way you kept saying my name, it just . . . you were really hot in that outfit. One minute we were heading home, and the next you were all over me." He laughed. My face flushed and I kept my eyes down. Shit, I must've been *so* wasted. How embarrassing. "I guess we both kinda lost control. But we probably shouldn't do it again, you know?"

He was right; people would get the wrong idea. So I just smiled at the floor and nodded.

And now, staring at the asphalt, without words to speak, that powerless feeling returns.

"Please don't give up," I whisper in my sister's ear. "Don't leave me out there to die." I'm begging. My own voice replays in my head, calling me pathetic. *If you need to beg for mercy, it's too late—mercy's not coming.* "Please don't go." I take Ivy's hand, a gesture she can't even feel. "Please, Ivy."

Ivy focuses on my keys. "I'm not leaving until I check her car."

Relief floods through me. If they get into my car, they'll find my phone and read my texts. They'll know about "Nick" luring me here—if that's even his real name. It's a start.

I wait for Jason to protest. Instead, he nods and gestures toward the door. "After you."

The bright sunlight accosts us back outside, and we all shade our eyes. I follow Ivy and Jason back across the vacant lot.

"What are you hoping to find?" Jason asks.

"I'm not sure."

My mind races. I don't leave drugs, or cash, or anything suspicious in my car, and I always text in code. I deleted the burglary messages the second I received them. I spent years perfecting my evidence-free lifestyle; now I'd give anything to have made a mistake.

Patrick leans against my car, tapping his foot against the ground. "Phew. I was worried about you guys. What'd you find?"

"Her keys." Ivy clicks the button, unlocking my car.

Patrick cocks his head. "Are we gonna drive it?"

"No." Ivy rips the door open. "We're searching it."

"What are we looking for?"

Ivy scrunches her mouth to the side. "I'm not sure yet."

"Phone," I shout. "You're looking for my phone!"

The three of them spend a good ten minutes digging through my schoolbooks, old coffee cups, and random crap, while I stand here shouting myself hoarse, screaming the word *"Phone!"*

"I'm going to try calling her again." Ivy puts her phone on speaker, and the boys wait with bated breath.

The muffled sounds of my elevator-music-esque ringtone fill the tiny car. All three of them lean closer, their eyes darting around, seeking the source of the ringing. Ivy clicks open my center console and I exhale a heavy breath. Okay, one step closer.

"Shit," Ivy mutters, fishing my iPhone out of its hiding place. It's probably the first time I've ever heard her swear. She hangs up and the ringing cuts off. Her face grows solemn.

"Check it," Jason says. "Any recent texts? Calls?"

Ivy clicks the home button, and my lock screen pops up.

"Zero-four-zero-two-seven-five," I say.

"I don't know her code."

"Try her birthday?"

I groan as she types in the wrong numbers. Does she really think I'm stupid enough to use my own birthday?

"Zero-four-zero-two-seven-five," I repeat. "Come on."

"Any other dates?" Patrick asks. "Numbers that are significant?"

"Zero-four-zero-two-seven-five!" I'm practically screaming, the words jumbling together. "Zerofourzerotwosevenfive!"

Ivy tilts her head to the side, as if deep in thought. She slowly—deliberately—enters my code. The phone unlocks.

"Jeez, I thought you didn't know her code," Jason says.

"I didn't."

Patrick's mouth hangs open. "How'd you do that?"

"I . . . I don't know."

"Creepy," Jason says. "You work for the NSA or something?"

Ivy gives a weak smile. "It was our mom's birthday. I'm kinda surprised Autumn uses it as her password, though."

"Why?" I ask, even though she can't hear me. When Mom died, Ivy cried for weeks. I didn't. I went to school, hung out with friends, laughed like everything was awesome, even though my insides shriveled like a dead tree. I was determined to show the world that I was still cool, and cool kids didn't cry. Looking back, I was pretty screwed up—but in everyone else's eyes, I was the strong one. I was the brave one. That's the shitty thing about grieving; if you don't look like you're falling apart, they assume you're fine.

Ivy scrolls through my texts. "Why is she talking about cake?" She flaps her arm behind her to get the guys' attention. "Look! She met someone here. A stranger."

Jason peeks over her shoulder. "Holy shit."

"I think we should call the police," Patrick says.

Final-fucking-ly. I want to hug him.

Ivy hesitates. "I . . . don't know."

I throw my head back and breathe deeply. Don't panic. This is it. Once the cops are involved, they'll find me. They have to.

"What do you mean, you don't know?"

"Would you want to be the one who rats out Autumn Casterly?"

"You're her sister, Ivy. It's gotta be you," Jason says.

Ivy's eyes go wide. "She'll kill me." It strikes me how terrified my sister looks—not of my would-be murderers, not of my death—of *me*.

"What if they don't believe me?" She's looking at Jason, but somehow it feels like she's speaking to me.

A stone lands in my stomach. What if they *don't* believe her?

Jason holds up his hand, as if intending to rest it comfortingly on her shoulder. But instead, it drops back to his side. "Look, Ivy. We're here. We won't let them. They'll listen to you."

Ivy looks up, and it seems like she's looking right at me.

"Please, Ivy," I say.

And then, I want to hug her. She calls.

Ivy

The phone rings for a million years. I clench and unclench my hand, my palm wet with sweat. It just keeps ringing and ringing and—

"Concord PD, this is Nancy speaking."

"H-hi. This is Ivy." I mentally slap my forehead; Jason actually slaps his. "My name's Ivy Casterly."

"How can I help you, Ivy?"

"My sister Autumn's missing. I'm at her car." The words stick in my throat. My fingers jitter against my pant leg.

Jason gives my arm a comforting squeeze.

"Her name's Autumn Casterly," I continue. "She's eighteen. She didn't come home last night after school, and today I found her car in an abandoned lot and also found her keys and her phone and I'm worried she's hurt or something."

"Okay, slow down, sweetie. Let me catch all that." I can tell by her tone that she thinks I'm a six-year-old.

"Okay."

"So you'd like to file a missing persons report?"

"Yeah."

"May I ask how old you are?"

Oh God. This is pathetic and I'm so glad she isn't on speaker-phone. "Fifteen."

"Wow, okay. Do you have a parent or guardian who might want to do this instead?"

"Nope. It's just my dad, and he's at work."

"Oh . . . Okay, Ivy, I'm going to ask you some questions, all right?"

For twenty minutes, she grills me. What color is Autumn's hair? What was she last seen wearing? Is she medium build, short, or tall? Does she have any defining birthmarks? Has she ever attempted suicide? Who are her closest friends? Where does she usually go after school?

I hate that I can't answer most of them. Does Autumn have birthmarks? No clue. Maybe I should have paid better attention. Thankfully, I know some things they ask for—like Dad's phone number, which is useless because he never frigging picks it up.

"Has she ever run away before?" the lady asks.

"I mean, kinda?"

She pauses. "Kind of?"

"Well, I mean, she stays out late a lot. Sometimes she goes away overnight and doesn't tell us." I realize that detracts from the severity of the situation and quickly add, "But she always comes home, I swear. This time is different."

"Where does she go when she's gone overnight?"

"To her friends' houses, I think." Sister of the year, right here. "I don't really know, honestly. She doesn't tell us."

"Do you know any of her friends' names?"

This interview is making me look like the worst sister ever. "Um . . . not really."

"Is there anything else about Autumn I should put into the report? Anyone who'd have reason to harm her? Some sort of grudge?"

I bite my lip. If all the Autumn rumors are true, I'd guess there are a *lot* of people who don't like my sister. But where would I even start?

"No. Not really. I don't know." The moment I say it, I regret it. But I swallow down the words in one gulp like they're Jason's gummy lobsters.

"Okay, Ivy. You said you're at the vacant lot on Storrs with her car?"

"Yeah—I mean, yes, ma'am."

"We're going to send a couple officers over to take a peek. We'll give your dad a call first, is that okay?"

I snort. "Good luck reaching him."

"Are they coming this century?" Jason asks from his seat on top of his trunk. His green Converse dangle against the bumper of his gray SUV. "I mean, I wasn't expecting them to come out with sirens blazing, but, like, it's been over an hour."

I sigh. I thought they'd take this more seriously, too. I could kick myself for telling them she disappears a lot. My stomach keeps performing somersaults. I'm starting to regret inhaling that bagel.

I've browsed Tumblr for the past hour, sitting cross-legged on the pavement, and my butt is falling asleep. "Let's give them a few more minutes."

Cars whiz past us on the main road, pulling left into Marshalls or Bank of America.

Patrick leans against Autumn's car, checking his phone. Every few seconds, my eyes coast over to him like the treacherous little traitors they are. I mean, okay. It should be illegal for him to stand like that, his black North Face fleece sleeves pushed up to his elbows. I love the way his brow creases when he reads, like he's concentrating extra hard.

He looks at me, and I quickly find something really interesting on Facebook that I've clearly been studying this whole time. I can feel him watching me. The fact that he's watching me makes me second-guess sitting like a kindergartner. I nonchalantly adjust my body, crossing one leg over the other.

A smile splits Pat's face. "Oh man, you know what I just thought of? Remember Gaseous?"

I burst out laughing. "Oh my God. How could I forget?"

"Did I miss something?" Jason asks.

"You didn't go to elementary school with us, so yes."

In fourth grade, there was this kid named Cassius in our class. Cassius Robert Porter the Fourth, I shit you not. He was kind of a prick—which is expected with a name like that—but he had lots of friends. One day in gym, he farted really loudly, and from then on he was known as Gaseous Cassius, and later just Gaseous. Anytime Pat and I saw a gas station, we speculated that Gaseous was over there, filling up. It was kind of douchey of us, but still funny. I mean, Gaseous himself loved the name and pushed the joke for like two years, farting loudly whenever he could. Then his family moved to North Carolina or something.

"I still think of him whenever I pass an Irving station," Patrick says.

"Wouldn't it be funny if he was there?"

"I would die."

Jason coughs into his elbow, and it's the fakest cough I've ever heard. Attention whore.

I ignore him and excitedly swat Patrick's arm. "Remember when good ol' Gaseous ripped one during that math test and Ms. Gruber threw a fit? And he bowed when she kicked him out of class?"

"Classic Gaseous."

Jason rolls his eyes. "How old are we again?"

I give him a look. This is coming from Jason, king of dick jokes, who tacks "that's what she said" onto literally anything. "Um, apparently younger than you, Gramps."

"You're, like, sophomores, and you're making fart jokes."

Again, coming from Jason, who is always the first one to laugh when someone farts. "I wasn't *making* fart jokes. I was remembering a time someone farted that was funny. Excuse me for living."

Patrick shrugs. "It was just something stupid that happened when we were kids."

"Yeah, *stupid* is the right word," Jason mutters, picking at a loose thread hanging off his bagel shirt. It's nearly impossible to take someone seriously when they have a giant smiling bagel on their T-shirt.

I'm used to Jason's snark, but it bugs me today. He's been a jerk about everything since Pat showed up.

I turn my back on Jason and keep talking to Patrick. "So, do you still have Ivan?" The Perkinses' Jack Russell terrier used to scare the crap out of me when I was little. I'm pretty sure that dog is a demon.

Pat slides his phone into his back pocket. "He's old, and kinda overweight, but yeah."

His mom feeds that dog Kraft Singles every morning, so I'm not surprised.

"I have a ball python now, too," he says. "His name's Chester."

"Whoa, cool." I do my best *this is totally new information for me and I definitely wasn't creeping on your Instagram* impression. "Where'd you get him?"

"He was Will's. When we moved back, he asked if I'd take care of him for a while. I wasn't sure at first, because, like, it's a snake. But Chester's cool. He loves to be held."

"I wanna hold him!"

"You hate snakes," Jason says.

I glare at him. "No I don't."

"Well, come over sometime and you can." Pat grins. "He'll drape over your shoulders."

"That sounds equally terrifying and awesome."

"You won't even watch the basilisk scene in *Chamber of Secrets*."

Is Jason serious right now? "That's because it's a basilisk, dumbass."

"A basilisk is a snake."

"Okay, that's bullshit." I get to my feet. "That's like saying I'm afraid of spiders because Aragog and Shelob are spiders."

"But you *are* afraid of spiders. You make me take them outside in cups for you."

"Excuse me for not wanting to kill them."

"Even that huge gross one in Latin last month. You screamed."

"It was scuttling up my pant leg—you would've screamed, too. Why are you being such a tool?"

He jumps off his car. *"Me?"*

A rusty green Toyota with a growling muffler speeds into the lot and jerks to a halt. We all freeze as the engine cuts off and the door opens.

Autumn

My whole body tightens into a big, solid knot. A teen boy steps out of the passenger side with saggy jeans and a Celtics jersey. The driver's door swings open and a second guy climbs out.

My heart stops.

It's Nick—or whatever his real name is.

He's got ripped jeans and a hoodie, and that same smirk.

It's him. It's really him.

He nods dismissively at my sister, then starts walking toward the abandoned building, chatting with the other kid and casting furtive glances over his shoulder. His voice turns to static in my ears.

I can't look away.

It's a special kind of pain, watching someone who hurt you smiling a big, wide, shit-eating grin. Knowing he got away with it, and seeing that he knows it, too.

Ivy narrows her eyes in their direction, as if my suspicion bled into her. Nick and the other guy pull back the plywood and slip into the warehouse, sliding the makeshift door closed behind them.

I glance at my sister, then back at the building. As if reading my mind, she takes a deep breath and starts tiptoeing after them.

"What the hell are you doing?" Jason whisper-yells.

She swats her hand behind her back and slinks up against the side of the decrepit building.

I sidle up beside Ivy. It's strange being so close to my sister. Probably the closest I've been to her in years.

Ivy presses her finger to her lips as the boys tiptoe over. It strikes me that even though they probably think she's acting ridiculous, they're still trying to help her, and I know it's not for my benefit.

I wish I had friends like that.

I'm taken aback by my own thought.

Jason holds his hands out in a question. "What are you—"

"Shush!" Ivy hisses, flicking her hand through the air. "Shut up!"

Jason grins. "Did you just shush me using a drum major signal?"

Ivy presses her ear to the plywood door. Her face screws up in concentration.

". . . freaked out, man," Nick's voice says from inside. "I don't wanna go to jail."

"No one saw us. It's fine."

"Yeah, easy for you to say—the shit's on *my* phone," Nick says. "I deleted the messages, but you know the government could find that shit."

"It's okay. We didn't leave anything behind."

What were they expecting to find? Strands of my hair? My blood, spattered across the gravel?

"They're talking about me," I say in Ivy's ear.

There's a faint flicking noise, followed by the smell of pot wafting through the thin doorway. Jason wrinkles his nose and bats his hand in front of his face.

"What are they talking about?" Patrick whispers, his lips barely forming the words. "I can barely hear them."

Jason shrugs. "Something shady. C'mon." He beckons with his arm. "Let's get outta here before they see us."

"What if they're connected to Autumn?" Ivy whispers. "We have to stay."

Jason opens his big mouth, presumably to argue, but the plywood door swings open. Ivy, Jason, and Patrick duck around the corner and flatten themselves against the wall right as Nick and his friend clomp outside.

"Anyway, we should leave." Nick's accomplice takes a final puff of his joint before crushing it under his shoe. "Probably a bad idea coming back here anyway, and I've got a shift tonight."

"You still working at the gas station?"

I step out into the open. It's surreal when they don't even spare me a glance. I'm invisible to Nick. Maybe I'm not the first girl he hurt. Maybe I'm one in a thousand, a name he'll forget by next month. The incident that broke me is nothing more than an inconvenience for him.

"Yeah. Living the dream." Not-Nick takes a drag off his cig. "Manager's a prick."

"You're a horrible person," I say, looking Nick right in the eyes.

"You up for hanging out later?" Nick asks.

"Depends when I get off," Not-Nick says. "Maybe. Supposed to meet this girl from OkCupid for coffee or something, I dunno. You?"

"Gotta do some errands. You want a ride to work?" Nick asks.

"Look at me, you piece of shit," I say. Of course, he doesn't. He's just standing here, smiling, while I slowly die somewhere. Frustration wells through me and I shove Nick as hard as I can. He doesn't even stumble.

"Nah, man. I'll walk."

I squeeze my eyes shut to block the tears burning behind them. Nick's friend walks toward Main Street, hands buried in his pockets.

I sneak a glance over my shoulder, where Ivy and the boys are pretending to be really interested in Jason's SUV.

Nick jumps into his car and starts the engine. No. He can't get away. Not before the cops show up. He's right here, and I can't even tell my sister who he is.

"Follow him," I order. "Ivy." I snap my invisible fingers. "Now."

"We have to follow him," Ivy says.

"What about the cops?" Patrick asks. "We can't leave."

Ivy's eyes dart from Nick's car to the warehouse. "We can't lose him. He knows something."

"Come on, Ivy." Jason jumps into his car. "Pat, stay here and wait for the cops."

Patrick nods, a sense of urgency crossing his face.

My sister doesn't hesitate before jumping into the passenger side. "Gun it."

IVY

Jason peels out of the parking lot, his tires screeching against the pavement. I click my seat belt. "Holy shit, dude. Let's not die."

"Do you want to lose him?"

"No, but I don't want to make it wicked obvious that we're stalking him, either."

The green Toyota cruises to a stop at the light. Jason slams on the brakes, and I very nearly smack my head on his dashboard.

"Just FYI, when I get my license, you are officially losing your chauffeur privileges." I nudge him in the side. "I'll be the driver, and you shall be at my mercy, Jason Daly-Cruz."

"Does that mean I won't have to use all my gas money to shuttle you around? And I can put my feet on your dashboard?"

I scoff. "Okay, I did that once."

"Coming home from the beach! I'm still finding sand from your dirty bare feet."

"It's a gift from me to you."

"Well, when you get a shiny new car, I shall bestow the same gift."

I kind of appreciate that he's not acknowledging the obvious: I probably have a better chance of getting struck by lightning in the middle of a date with John Boyega than affording a new car. Or any car, really.

I point to the Toyota. "Do you think he has enough bumper

stickers?" Colorful stickers advertising random stores, restaurants, and slogans cover the entire bumper.

"Imagine being so passionate about"—he squints at the stickers—"AL HAWKE FOR DELAWARE 2012 that you plaster his name on your car forever. What if that guy lost his race for governor or whatever? Then he's still stuck with the sticker."

"At least it'll make the car easier to find in a crowd."

The light turns green and Jason hits the gas—thankfully more gently this time. We follow the Toyota down Storrs Street and up onto Main. Luckily, it's been a relatively straight shot so far, so it's not super obvious we're following him. If he'd taken a bunch of turns, we'd have been screwed.

Jason grins. "Okay, I bet you a bagel he's going to Szechuan Gardens to get sesame noodles. I mean, if he has good taste."

"If he's getting noodles, I think it's only fair we order our own, too. So he won't get suspicious."

"Oh, are you telling me you weren't expecting this adventure to involve noodles? What kind of adventure would that be?"

I can't help smiling. This is one of the things I love about Jason. I can say "Follow that car!" and he will literally jump in and help me follow that car, because he's the best adventure buddy ever.

Okay, wait. I shouldn't have said *love*. It's something I *like* about him. Because I like him. As a friend.

"You know what this reminds me of?" Jason says. "The Domino's car incident."

I laugh. "Pretty sure Sophie's still pissed about that."

Over the summer, Sophie was driving all of us home from the movies in her mom's minivan. We got bored and saw a Domino's Pizza delivery car. Jase, Ahmed, and I insisted we follow it to see who was getting pizza. Sophie complained the entire time, pretty much hating all of us for being so excited about stalking a pizza car. Plot twist—it went straight back to Domino's. We got a pizza, because of course we did. I know it sounds silly, but this is Concord, New Hampshire, and there's nothing to do.

I shoot off a message to Sophie—omg, remember the Domino's car? Jase and I found a new car to stalk, I thought you'd appreciate it.

She immediately writes back, So not bailing you guys out of jail.

I read it aloud to Jason and we snicker. Sometimes when he laughs that way, something inside me revs to life. I look away quickly, burying the feeling; there's no point.

"This is, like, the weirdest adventure we've ever had," Jase says.

"*The* weirdest? That's a pretty high bar." I kind of love how well he's taking all of this. Jason has a personality that's totally contagious—when he's calm, my anxiety melts away. We're having an adventure. And soon, everything will be totally fine and back to normal.

The green Toyota puts its blinker on. "Wait—he's turning. He's getting on the highway."

"Shit." Jason spins the wheel way too fast, and the centrifugal force thrusts me into the car door.

"Who'd you pay to give you that license again?"

"Hey, you can walk home."

The Toyota takes a right and merges onto I-393. We follow, joining a flood of cars. Our target zips forward, weaving between vehicles. A Chevy with a super-old-looking man in the driver's seat cruises past us. The Toyota gets smaller in the distance.

I tap Jason's thigh. "Speed up, speed up! We're losing him."

"I don't wanna get a ticket."

"You're not even going the speed limit."

"Excuse me for not wanting to get us killed."

If we lose this car because Grandma in the driver's seat won't hit the gas, I'm going to kill him. We coast down the highway, being passed by literally everyone.

"Okay, hang on." I scan the cars around us, my heart racing. "Where is he?"

"I'm looking." Jason clicks his blinker and changes lanes, jerking in front of the Chevy. "Is that him?" He points.

"That's a Honda."

"Okay, sorry, it's green."

My gaze bounces frantically between the white, gray, and red cars around us, but there's no green Toyota.

Crap. "I don't see him." My fingers drum against my jeans. "What do we do now? We could take exit two and try to find him."

"Or, we could also go back and get those noodles," he suggests. "I mean, since we don't know where he went. And we don't know for a fact that he was actually doing anything wrong anyway, you know? He's just some random guy who happened to be there."

He's got a point. "Yeah, but—"

My phone buzzes—Patrick.

Hey, your dad just pulled in and the cops are here and they're all pretty mad that you're not.

"Oh shit."

I contemplate ignoring his text. The green Toyota couldn't have gotten far, and there's still a chance we could catch up to it. But I need to talk to the cops.

I tilt my screen toward Jase. He darts his eyes quickly toward it, then back to the road. "They're all there and pissed at us."

Jason's brows lower with determination. "I'll get us back in five."

IVY

Jason wasn't lying. At exactly 3:04 p.m., we careen back into the vacant lot. Two uniformed cops stand beside their crookedly parked cruiser, talking to my dad, whose blue Honda is parked next to Autumn's. Patrick lingers to the side with his arms crossed, nervously watching everything. His face relaxes when he sees us. Everyone stops to watch as Jason's SUV zooms in and screeches to a halt, straddling two parking spaces. Seriously, I'm half terrified the cops are going to give him a ticket for driving like a jackass, but they don't.

I'm so relieved to see the cops, I can't stop smiling. They came. Finally. I just have to tell them what I found and they'll take it from here.

I nearly fall over myself rushing to get out of the car. "Hey, Dad."

My dad hurries over. "Are you all right, sweetie? I was worried when the police called."

"You should've read your texts! I've been trying to get ahold of you for hours."

Dad pulls out his phone and frowns. "You should've called the shop. You know I can't always check my phone at work. Half the time it doesn't beep when you text anyway."

"I told you, like, eight thousand times—you have to keep your ringer on or it won't beep."

"You must be Ivy." One of the cops, a twentysomething guy with stubble and very nice teeth, holds out a hand. I recognize him from somewhere, but I can't place him. "I'm Officer Jensen. This is my partner, Officer O'Riley."

"Oh man. I'm so glad you're here." I shake his hand.

The woman cop comes over, hands on her hips. "Hello there, Ivy. We've been waiting for you."

I fight the urge to tell her that we'd been waiting for two hours for them to grace us with their presence, do they really have to bitch about waiting ten minutes? But I behave because they're cops.

"Sorry. I had to pee, so we drove to Dunkin'." I step back, dragging Jason to my side. "This is Jason."

Jase nods, his hands buried in his pockets. I roll my eyes. He can barely keep his mouth shut 99 percent of the time, but the cops show up and suddenly he's quiet.

"I'm gonna go wait with Patrick." Before I can stop him, he slides away, right in my hour of need.

"We understand your sister's been missing since yesterday, is that correct?" Officer O'Riley asks, while her partner pulls out a notepad and pen.

"Yes. She never came home from school. I found her car here this morning and the keys were in there." I point at the building. "I also found her phone in the console." I dig in my purse and produce Autumn's iPhone. "Look. She had some texts saying she was meeting some guy here, and—"

Officer O'Riley sighs. "Ivy, I'm not sure if you knew this, but we met with Autumn yesterday at school."

I blink at her. "You did?"

"We wanted to ask her some questions about a suspect in a local burglary case." She gives me a sympathetic smile. "We've since

139

apprehended the suspect and he confessed. He offered up his phone records in exchange for a possible plea bargain, and . . . well . . . he had texts with your sister that implicated her in the crime."

I open my mouth, then close it. What the hell? Autumn robbed someone?

Dad pinches the bridge of his nose. "You don't actually have proof she was there."

"We have phone records showing he asked Autumn if she was interested in breaking into the corner store. They made a deal involving stolen pills, and she agreed to join him."

"Okay, but whether she was involved or not, she's still missing," I say.

"She knew we were on to the suspect. It's likely she left town and didn't want anyone tracking her phone or license plate, so she left them behind."

"She's a teenager," Dad says. "Not a fugitive."

"Do you know anything about where she might have gone?" Officer Jensen asks, his pen at the ready. "Anyone who might try to help her out?"

Dad stares blankly at the policeman, that familiar deer-in-headlights look crossing his face. "I'm not sure. She has lots of friends; she's very popular."

"Any names you know offhand? Someone who might know her whereabouts?"

"Wait a second." I narrow my eyes. "Are you trying to find her because she's missing, or because you want to arrest her?"

"I'm going to stop you right there." Officer O'Riley holds up her hand. "We have no reason to believe that your sister is in imminent danger. It hasn't even been twenty-four hours."

I probably look pretty dumbfounded right now, but I can't hide it. What the actual hell? "She's only eighteen. She could be seriously hurt or something!"

"She *is* a legal adult. We've taken a statement from your father, who admitted she's been known to disappear for a night or two."

"That doesn't mean she's okay." I glare at Dad, then at the cops. "I thought you were supposed to protect people, and it's like you're not even trying."

"Ivy." Dad rubs his forehead. "Autumn's been doing this for years. I . . . I can't pretend I'm surprised."

"But . . . Dad. This time seems different."

"You said in your report you didn't know the names of any of her friends. Is that true?" Officer Jensen stares at me, his brown eyes boring into my soul. Holy shit, suddenly I remember where I know him from.

Last year, Ahmed's parents were driving me and Kevin home, and a cop car zipped out of a parking lot and pulled us over when we were stopped at a light. I was playing on my phone, and when I looked up, Ahmed's dad was literally still as a statue in the front seat. His mom rushed to adjust her hijab in the rearview, her eyes wide, muttering under her breath.

"Why are your parents so freaked out?" I whispered. "They didn't do anything wrong."

Ahmed snorted. "Why do you think they pulled us over? They're a couple of brown Pakistanis whose last name is Bashir."

I squirmed in my seat the whole time. When the racist cop left, it was like everyone could breathe again. And now, when my memory kicks in, dread boils inside me. Of all the cops in Concord, they sent this asshole. I don't trust him one bit.

"No," I croak out. "I don't know her friends." I turn to the woman cop, my only hope. "Please. She's in trouble. I wouldn't have called if I didn't really believe it. You have to find her."

"We're on the lookout," Jensen says. "We'll do everything we can to locate her, and we'll notify you the second we do." I don't buy it for a second. He's got it in his mind that she's a criminal, and that's all he wants to believe.

"But—"

Officer O'Riley smiles at me like she's about to castigate a child. "I know it's hard, because you love your sister. But we know what we're doing. You have to trust us."

"Trust you to do nothing?" My voice breaks. "She'd never leave her phone behind. She could've been kidnapped or something. There was a sketchy-looking guy here who was smoking pot in that building and he said something about not wanting to go to jail, and we followed him onto the highway, and . . . and . . ." I realize how ridiculous it sounds the moment I say it.

Officer O'Riley whispers something to Officer Jensen, who scribbles something on his notepad. My face gets hot.

"You know," Officer O'Riley says, "sometimes when we're desperate to believe something, especially about the people we love, our minds can twist events to make them seem connected and relevant."

I shuffle my feet, kind of glad the guys are out of earshot. "Yeah . . ."

"Let us do our jobs." Officer Jensen winks at me. "We've got this."

I pretty much want to curl up on the ground and die. Everyone else knew I was overreacting—why didn't I just listen? "Okay. Sorry."

The cops go back to talking to my dad. I hear, "She should probably lie down and get some rest," and that makes me want to disappear even more. I slip away, over to Jason and Patrick.

"What happened?" Pat asks. "Are you okay?"

I shake my head, not confident that I could start talking without breaking down. I wasted everyone's afternoon, and now I have to admit to Jason and Pat that I was blowing this out of proportion all day.

"Hey." Jason nudges me. "Alexa texted about getting ice cream tonight. What do you think?"

I know he's saying it to change the subject, but it makes me feel worse. Like he knew it was pointless the whole time and just went along with everything to humor me. "Okay, maybe. Are you both going?"

"Nah." Patrick frowns. "I'm supposed to spend Saturday nights at my dad's place, and he just texted me. He's picking me up here in ten."

I try to mask my disappointment. Great. As if this day couldn't get worse, now Patrick won't hang out with us tonight, and I blew a chance at spending the day with him. Maybe this is just his excuse to get away from me. "Oh. That's fun, though."

"Not really. You remember my dad, right?"

"Kind of," I lie. I do remember Patrick's dad. He's one of those guys who will purposely interrupt your "happy holidays" with "Merry Christmas," just to stick it to the man or something. I once overheard him telling Patrick's mom that the school board was mismanaged "because they put a bunch of women in charge." I can't make this stuff up. Given what I know of his dad, his mom, and Will, Patrick's pretty lucky his gene pool was generous. He's just Patrick. And right now, Just Patrick is what I need. "Maybe see you tomorrow, then?"

Jason rolls his eyes, and I ignore it.

"Yeah, sure!" Pat says. "I have youth group in the morning, but maybe at night?" Okay, his enthusiasm cheers me up a bit.

"Sounds good."

"Hey." Pat holds his arms out awkwardly, as if considering it, then opens them for a hug. I let myself get absorbed by his warmth. "It's gonna be all right."

I inhale deeply, savoring his scent. His fleece feels warm against my skin.

Jason clears his throat, and it makes me hug Patrick closer.

"Ivy," my dad calls across the parking lot. I begrudgingly untangle myself from Patrick's arms. "C'mon. It's almost four. Let's go home."

"All right. I gotta go. See you tonight?"

Jason nods. "I'll text you when I know what time."

I follow my dad to his Honda.

As the police climb back into their cruiser, a soft breeze brushes my shoulder like a hand. I swear I hear the wind whispering through the trees, telling me not to give up.

Dad is silent for a good five minutes of driving. His Honda always has that brand-new-car smell, even though it's at least seven years old and has suffered multiple food spills over the years. I go back and forth between fidgeting with my purse straps and playing with the radio. After flicking between eight thousand stations of commercials, I turn it off and say what I've been thinking this whole ride.

"Are you mad at me?"

"What?" A hint of emotion flickers across my dad's face. "Of course not. I'm glad you called the cops when you felt like you were in trouble." He doesn't have to finish the sentence for me to catch the *even though you weren't really* at the end.

I look out the window, watching the trees and houses sail past.

"Look, Ivy. I'm sorry that happened."

I don't know exactly what he's apologizing for. Is he sorry my sister ran away and got me upset? Is he sorry I freaked out and called the cops for no reason? Or is he sorry he did literally nothing to back me up?

"It's okay." I don't know if it's actually okay, but it seems like something I should say. "I don't want to talk about it anymore."

Dad's still wearing his uniform from the auto shop. He left work early for this, which means he'll have to work overtime at some point to make up for it.

He stares straight ahead at the road. "I saw Patrick Perkins moved back. It's been, what, three years?"

"Four."

"Wow. You guys always got along really well."

"Yeah." I fiddle with the zipper on my jacket. I wonder if Dad remembers the time he chaperoned our school field trip to the Boston Museum of Science and Patrick's shoelace got caught in the escalator. I think he made a dad joke about it that made Patrick laugh and made me want to take the opposite escalator straight back downstairs and out of the room. Dad used to do stuff like that with me all the time. The year after Mom died, he went through this phase of almost overcompensating for her loss—like he wanted to parent us twice as much to make up for her being gone. It was short-lived and stopped when he started working overtime. Sometimes I miss him, even though he's still here.

"Look, Ivy, I want you to know . . . you can always talk to me. I realize I work a lot, but you can come to me with anything. I mean that."

"Yeah. I know." It's hard to feel like a priority when work gets all his time and I'm scrounging up the scraps. I hate that I'm even thinking that. I know Dad works hard because someone has to buy groceries and health insurance and all that stuff. But still. Sometimes the house feels lonely.

"I think we should spend more time together," he says. "You, me, and Autumn. And Kathy. As a family."

I'm pretty sure Autumn won't agree to that, but it's a nice thought. "Okay." I don't add that spending more time together would require him actually being around, but that's another story.

He's silent for a while, then veers off onto the highway at the last minute, two exits from home.

"Where are you going?"

"You want to get a donut? Like the good old days?"

The good old days. It's so weird referring to three years ago as "the good old days," but I guess that's how fast everything can change.

Honestly, all I want to do is go home and swan-dive onto my bed and pretend this whole day never happened. I force a smile. "Sure."

When we were kids, Dad would pick me and Autumn up from school on Fridays and we'd go to Dunkin's and get donuts and hot chocolate. After he started working those ridiculous hours, I craved Fridays so bad, because it was the one time every week I got to hang out with him. We stopped when Autumn started high school and cut off all her hair and decided she didn't want to be part of our family anymore. When Autumn stopped wanting donuts with me, I guess Dad did, too.

Dad pulls into the Dunkin' Donuts lot and puts the car in Park. He opens his mouth like he's about to say something, but his phone beeps. I clench my jaw. Of course, *now* he figures out how to turn the ringer on.

"Oh, Kathy's across the street. She asked if we want anything from Wendy's." He doesn't meet my eyes as he writes back. "I'll tell her to meet us over here instead."

I press my lips together. Right now, I just want to go home and ignore everybody. "Okay. Sure."

We head inside, and of course, there's a long line. I survey the donut selection, even though I already know what I'm getting. I've gotten the same donut here for forever—chocolate glazed.

"Well, look who's here."

I stiffen. Usually, Kathy doesn't bother me, but I don't feel like seeing her right now. I guess part of me was hoping to hang out with just my dad for a little while, like the old days. But I guess that's the thing about "old days"—they're long gone. Sometimes I feel like hanging out with Kathy is a betrayal to Autumn, since she hates our stepmom so much.

I shake it off. Technically, *Autumn* betrayed *me* by disappearing and putting me through all this shit.

Dad and Kathy hug and chitchat behind me, dredging up my awful afternoon at the vacant lot.

I slap my hands on the counter. "A chocolate glazed donut and a medium hot chocolate with whipped cream, please."

Dad and Kathy order after me, and Dad pays the bill. I grab my food, keeping my eyes down.

A skinny thirtysomething woman waiting for her order won't stop watching me. I fidget, her stare hot against my skin. I can't stop feeling like she's judging me because I got a donut. Like because I'm fat, I should do anything I possibly can to lose weight, and how dare I even think about touching something that's not a salad? Sometimes I hate eating junk food in public. I'm not usually self-conscious about my size, but often I feel like I'm supposed to be. My weight doesn't bother me, so why does it seem to bother everyone else?

I grab a table outside her line of vision before pulling my donut out of the bag.

Kathy takes a seat across from me, hanging her purse over the back of her chair.

Dad runs to the bathroom, leaving Kathy and me alone. I'd rather not rehash this afternoon, so I take a giant chug from my hot chocolate instead and immediately regret it. Holy shit. Bad life choice. Oh my God, it feels like swallowing Mordor.

"Are you okay?" Kathy's eyebrows draw together.

I cough into my elbow. I'm pretty sure my entire mouth is on fire. "Yep."

Okay, fine. I need to let it cool. I blow on the surface, not meeting Kathy's eyes.

"I'm worried about your sister," she says.

"She's probably fine." I don't know if I believe the words as I say them, but I don't want to talk about it. Especially not with her.

We sit in silence for a few minutes. Ugh. Why does Dad have to pick today to take forever in the bathroom?

"Hey, Ivy?" Kathy swirls her straw through her iced tea. "I've been . . . meaning to talk to you about something."

Oh God, I hope she's not going to ask about bringing Chris home for Thanksgiving again. "Yeah?"

She takes a shaky breath, her eyes fixed on something outside. "Do you . . . think I handle her wrong?"

"Handle who wrong?"

"You know. Autumn."

I'm taken aback. Could Kathy do more for Autumn? I guess. I mean, maybe she could set some boundaries—the whole smoking-weed-in-the-driveway thing would be a good start.

If Kathy feels guilty for the way Autumn turned out, she's never said anything about it to me before. She's too needy sometimes, always digging around for reassurance.

I shrug. "I don't think so, no."

Something about the way her body relaxes makes me wonder if we're actually talking about the same thing.

But before I can ask, or Kathy can clarify, Dad comes back to the table, and we both pretend the conversation never happened.

Autumn

The scream rockets out of my mouth, draining my invisible lungs of air. I kick the trash can at Dunkin', kick Dad's tire, kick the wall. I shout obscenities at the police station window, stand in the middle of the road and scream, cursing out the cars that drive straight through me. I curse out every member of my family, every guy who ambushed me at that damn warehouse—literally any person I can think of, I curse them out.

And. It. All. Does. Nothing.

By the time Ivy, Dad, and Kathy get home, I can barely see straight. I storm through the front door, plowing through everyone, and they don't even notice. I don't know what pisses me off more: that the cops didn't listen, that Ivy didn't push, that Dad did nothing, or that Kathy had the nerve to ask Ivy that question.

I turn my back to the wall and try to heave the TV off the stand; obviously my hands go right through it, but I picture it shattering against the hardwood and sprinkling glass all over the room.

Kathy flicks a couple lights on. Dad promptly shuts one off, mumbling about giving money to the electric company.

Pumpernickel slips past me and gives a happy bark before leaping onto the armchair. My heart cinches. I wish I could pet him, hold him, feel his soft fur beneath my fingertips. I didn't pet him enough. I should have held him more. He probably thinks I abandoned him, and the thought makes fresh tears spring to my eyes.

Kathy collapses on the couch, her legs strewn over Dad's lap. They're talking about dinner. They're literally talking about what to make for dinner.

I squeeze my eyes shut, forcing back the tears.

This isn't happening.

I never wanted to die. Not seriously, at least. Sometimes, driving on the highway, I'd picture running my car off the road and plunging into the Merrimack. It got so vivid, I could almost feel the water sluicing over me, consuming me. I'd drown in the blackness, floating and airy and peaceful.

In my imagination, Jaclyn and Abby would go on a rampage at school, screaming at everyone who messed with me. Riddled with guilt, Dad would dump Kathy. They'd all come to my funeral and cry, thinking about how they should've treated me better.

But now, all I feel is terror as I listen to Dad and Kathy talk about whether they want chicken noodle soup or eggplant Parmesan, and what food would comfort Ivy after her *ordeal,* and oh no, we have to make stuffed mushrooms because Ivy fucking *loves* stuffed mushrooms.

"We could order pizza," Kathy says mischievously, like she just suggested eating candy for dinner. I hear the hidden thought hanging at the end of her suggestion—*because Autumn's not here.*

Dad ponders a moment. "Yeah. We could do that. Papa Gino's? I think I've got a coupon."

"Sure." Kathy shakes her head. "Still can't believe that girl won't touch pizza. What kind of teenager doesn't like pizza?"

This is what it would be like if I never came home. Everything would move on. Everyone would live and exist and not care that I don't anymore.

Ivy drapes her coat over the rack in the den and comes back into the living room. "I'm gonna lie down."

"Yes, by all means, please go lie down and rest," I shout. "It's not like I'm dying out in the cold somewhere."

"Okay, honey," Kathy calls. "Let us know if you need anything."

"Fuck you," I reply.

Ivy trudges up the stairs. I follow, stomping my feet without making a sound. The silence makes me stomp harder.

Ivy pauses at the top of the stairs.

"That's right, Ivy, go lie down. You're good at that. Lying down and forgetting your problems, pretending they'll just go away." I know she can't hear me, but it feels good to say it, so I do. "Just like you did with the cops this afternoon, huh? They tell you it's no big deal, so sure! You stop trying!" I throw my hands up and let them clap back down at my sides. "Because it's not like it's *your* life on the line, am I right?"

Ivy slogs down the hall to her room. I follow, shouting in her ears.

"You can't stand up for anyone. You can't even stand up for yourself." It's extra cruel and I don't care. "You're just gonna let everyone walk all over you forever. Hell, you're totally in love with that Jason kid. It's so obvious, and you don't even try."

Ivy stops outside her doorway and looks right at me. I go still. Holy shit. Can she . . . can she *see* me?

"I-Ivy?"

But my sister isn't looking at me; she's looking through me. Ivy tiptoes toward my bedroom door. That's not what I was expecting.

Her hand hesitates over my doorknob.

I never let anyone into my room. But I want her to look for me. I need her to find me.

"It's okay. You can go in."

Ivy twists the knob. The hinges squeak as she pushes it open, carefully, like a wild animal might be waiting behind the door. I hold my breath and follow Ivy inside.

A layer of stillness coats the room, like we're walking into a place untouched by time, even though it's only been a day. Ivy brushes her hand along my dresser, leaving streaks in the dust.

She takes a seat on my air mattress and fluffs my pillow. Then she grabs the nest of sheets hanging off the end and tucks them neatly around the bed. I roll my eyes. My sister is seriously making my bed, because of course she is.

"What happened to you, Autumn?" Her words come out softer than a whisper, but I hear them anyway. "Where did you go?"

Ivy stands. She rips open my top drawer and riffles through my underwear.

"I'm not in there," I snap.

She opens the next drawer, and the next, pulling out my clothes piece by piece, as if a clue will be hidden in the linings.

Ivy huffs and slams the drawers shut. A purple shirtsleeve hangs out of one of them. She gets down on the floor and pulls my laptop out of its hiding place, in the crevice beneath my dresser. This is pointless; there's nothing important on there. Still not thrilled my sister's snooping around in my private shit.

Ivy opens the screen and sets it on her lap.

"Okay, let's keep moving." I snap my fingers. "C'mon."

She keeps staring at the locked screen, her fingers poised over the keyboard.

"Really?" I groan. She's obviously not going anywhere until she gets on my computer. I can't let her give up. "Pumpernickel—no capitalizations."

As if on cue, Ivy types in my password. Her eyes grow wide when it works.

"All right, hurry up. Come on."

She opens Chrome. Of course I left, like, a bajillion tabs open. I never remember to close anything.

Ivy clicks on the first one—University of Virginia Veterinary Medicine. I rub my forehead. This is so embarrassing.

Her brow creases. She clicks the second tab—Colorado State.

"Jeez," she mutters. I kind of see her thought process, because it's so obvious. No one expects a girl like me to care about the future. Sometimes it pisses me off that everyone assumes that about me. A badass reputation is a double-edged sword.

I cross my arms. "Happy?"

She clicks the next tab and winds up on Facebook. I never update my profile; I just use it to stalk people. Ivy must notice the lack of information, because she clicks to the next tab, going through Tumblr, then a random Wikipedia page I forgot I had open. Finally, she gets to the last one—my Gmail.

Ivy scrolls through my recent messages. My skin is crawling because she's going way too slow and I need her to stop screwing around.

Ivy scans my emails, finding nothing but spam, and her shoulders slump.

"Told you," I mumble.

She tabs into my Instagram account and starts looking through my photos. I don't post very much—mostly selfies when my makeup is cute (sometimes) and pictures of Pumpernickel when he's cute (always), but she pores over each image like they hold some secret code to my whereabouts. I zero in on the photos and it brings back a memory.

Chris had passed me in the hall on the way back from econ. He smiled and nodded, and it felt weirdly distant, considering the past weekend. I kept wondering if this was how everyone felt after their first time. None of my friends had lost their virginity yet, so I had no one to ask.

I slammed my locker shut, grabbing my phone. I sent a quick text to my friends in the group chat.

`Me: you guys wanna blow off last period English later? I'm falling asleep`

I wasn't really tired, but I couldn't focus. I knew skipping class was bad, but I'd cut Spanish before and the world didn't end. The message went out to Kristin, Dani, Crystal, and Radha—surely one of them would cut with me. Maybe grab some snacks at the Irving station or walk downtown. I felt kind of bad because I'd avoided their texts and hadn't opened their Snapchats all week and kept dodging them in the hall. I guess I'd needed time to process everything, but in that moment, I just wanted someone to tell me I was normal and everything I was feeling was just a regular part of having sex. Maybe they were mad at me because they'd all gone to the pottery-painting place Saturday night; I'd lied and told them my dad wouldn't let me go out because I wanted to go to the party instead.

I stuffed my phone in my pocket, waiting for a reply as I ambled to geometry, when I noticed Warren Marden and Kurt Corriveau from the football team staring at me. I hadn't even known their names until the party, which was at Warren's house, so it was weird they were creeping near my locker. I brushed past them.

"Hey, Autumn," Warren called. "You feeling okay? You were pretty trashed last weekend."

Kurt snickered. "Chris had to practically carry you to his car."

This was so embarrassing. Chris had promised to keep an eye on me at the party, but he'd gotten trashed and subsequently let me get very, very drunk. Which, okay, was my choice, but still. Now I felt like a giant joke.

"I'm fine," I muttered.

"I bet you are."

I rolled my eyes and kept walking.

"We've been looking for a team bus, if you're interested," Kurt added.

Team bus? I didn't get the joke, but I had a feeling it was probably gross. I stopped and whirled around. "What do you mean?" I asked coldly. They were seniors, and I was only a freshman, but they were pissing me off.

"You know, the team bus." Kurt's eyes raked up and down my body. "Everyone gets a ride."

Warren burst out laughing.

I blinked at him. What the fuck?

"I mean, you already did Chris," Warren added. "When is it our turn?"

He might as well have stabbed me in the chest. I stood there, gaping, as they walked away. What the actual fuck? He'd told them? After swearing me to secrecy?

What exactly had he told them?

Who else knew?

My heart thudded like a drum in my chest. I pulled my phone out to find a flood of messages parading across my screen.

Radha: wow hello Autumn long time no see *eyeroll*

Dani: oh ok so now you're talking to us again . . . that's cool

Crystal: um, Christina said you went partying over the weekend? Guess that's why you were too busy for us.

Radha: I heard you slept with your brother . . .

Kristin: Is that real??

Crystal: apparently she was alllll over him at the party.

Radha: gross . . .

Dani: my mom even heard about it.

Kristin: if you didn't want to hang out with us you could've just said so.

Crystal: cutting class, sleeping around, drink-ing?? what happened to you, Autumn, it's like we don't even know you anymore

Kristin: I mean, if there was a party, you could've invited us—just saying

Radha: why didn't you text us afterward??

Dani: I gotta be honest, I'm a little mad that my best friend lost her virginity and I heard about it from someone else . . .

A wave of silence followed, then another text from Dani popped up on my screen in a new window.

Dani: lmao can you believe Autumn right now

I stared at the message, clearly not intended for me. They hadn't stopped responding in the group chat; they had formed another chat—one without me in it.

Water blurred my vision. What was happening?

My phone vibrated with a new notification—some anonymous account tagged me in an Instagram post. Pulse racing, I clicked the image.

My own face filled the screen. There I was, Saturday night, practically passed out drunk on Warren's navy-blue couch. My mouth was hanging open and makeup was smudged beneath my half-closed eyes. A red plastic cup was clenched in my right hand, and I gave a halfhearted middle finger with my left. Black bra straps were poking out beneath my discombobulated silver tank top, which had scrunched up, exposing my stomach. Several upperclassmen sat around me, giving middle fingers and peace signs to the camera, like I was some hilarious piece of art to pose with. I don't even remember having that picture taken.

I scrolled down to the caption.

`Autumn Casterly had fun this weekend #Drunkslut #Takeitoff #skankpatrol`

91 likes, 24 comments, growing by the second. I scrolled to the first one.

`wow, nice outfit—guess we know what she was after`

My face heated. I'd thought I looked hot in that outfit, with my boobs hanging out, but now, seeing it on the screen, I felt like a slut. No wonder everyone said I was throwing myself at Chris—I clearly had been.

`she was practically giving Chris a lap dance on the couch lol`

Holy shit. I didn't. I couldn't have. What was wrong with me?

`wow real classy! Was that pic before or after the drunk sex? I can't tell`

Anger seared hot and red inside me.

Fuck my friends. If they didn't want me, I didn't want them, either.

It was three years ago, but it may as well have been a lifetime. I shake off the memory and return my attention to my sister. I need to focus.

Ivy studies the screen for a minute before clicking out of Chrome, and it's like I've been holding my breath for an hour when I finally let it all out.

My sister starts scrolling through my documents file. Annoyance buzzes through me like a fly I can't swat.

"Yes, by all means, *please* keep reading my homework, this is *so* helpful."

I sigh, watching her examine last year's AP history final, that awful Faulkner paper, and my SAT prep test.

"Satisfied?"

Ivy must sense my irritation, because she starts humming that

"Satisfied" song from *Hamilton*. She cocks her head and clicks the file labeled *Pervert In Chief.*

My muscles tense. I totally forgot about that. I could kick myself for not deleting it from my hard drive last year. *Coach Crespo is a perv who should be fired. He purposely spies on girls in the workout room. Everyone knows he does this shit. Do something about it.*

Ivy claps a hand over her mouth.

Well, this is something I'd hoped would never be traced back to me. And yet, here we are.

Our school takes gym class way too seriously. If you miss class, you have to make it up by coming in before school and using the exercise bikes for forty-five minutes. Honestly, their priorities are screwed up, because they don't give a shit about literally any other class this much. But some people love it because riding the bikes alone is less objectionable than team flag football or whatever other nightmare they subject us to. So some people skip on purpose. Jaclyn is one of those people.

"Let me explain," I say, even though I know she can't hear me. "My friend Jac cut gym and went to the morning makeup class on the exercise bikes. No one else was there, so she just wore her sports bra and shorts. It's like a free gym membership, you know? Then after pedaling and getting all sweaty for twenty minutes, she looks up, and bam! There's Creepo, staring through the glass in the door." She didn't know how long he'd been watching her, but it was sketchy as hell. "So I left the note. That's it." No one would've known about the note if Connor Gardner hadn't seen it on the principal's desk and told everyone. "Greenwich didn't even do anything about it, and no one knows it was me. Case closed."

I don't even know why I did it. Leaving an anonymous note was just shouting into the void, but sometimes shouting into the void can be cathartic. For a moment, you can pretend someone's listening.

Ivy stares at the Word doc for a good five minutes. I can almost see the cogs in her brain working. Finally, she slams my laptop shut and buries it back beneath my dresser.

She tries the closet next.

Hangers rain from her hands as she tugs them out one by one. She takes my gray hoodie and hugs it to her chest for half a second before continuing her raid on my closet.

"Why are you doing this?" My heart sinks. *Why are you looking for me when I've been such an ass to you?*

Ivy doesn't respond, obviously. When the rack is empty, she starts tearing through the shelf above it. I've got all kinds of crap wedged up there—old school projects, crafts, random junk.

Ivy takes out an old drawing I did of our former guinea pig, Roger. He looks like a fat potato—but to be fair, he looked like a fat potato in real life, too.

Ivy unfolds it. "Oh man. Roger."

Roger was our first pet. Everyone said guinea pigs wouldn't live longer than five years, but he lasted almost eight. Probably because Dad fed him organic veggies and Poland Spring water. What a spoiled little piggy.

"You probably don't remember this," I say. "But when you were eight and I was ten, we built him an obstacle course out of foam blocks and laid carrot sticks all through it so he'd actually do it. We called it—"

"Feeding Frenzy." The moment Ivy says it, she glances around the room before returning to my closet.

Ivy grabs my box of tampons and peels it open, revealing cash and plastic baggies full of pills. Everyone knows I deal, so I'm not sure why I suddenly feel so bad about it.

"Oh, Autumn." She shakes her head, setting the box back where she found it. "I don't even know you anymore."

I scratch the tattoo on my wrist. I don't know her much anymore, either, I guess. I used to.

When did we become strangers?

Ivy sits cross-legged on the carpet and starts digging through the boxes on the closet floor.

"What are you looking for?"

Ivy finds a bedraggled old box in the back corner. She gently peels open the lid, and the smell of mothballs fills the space. My sister pulls out the most recent pair of those old reindeer pajamas and slippers. I totally forgot those were in there. I used to get so excited opening new ones every Christmas Eve.

The smallest hint of a smile twitches at the edges of Ivy's mouth. "I thought you threw these away."

I sit down beside her and tap an old shoebox. "Check this one."

Ivy reaches for the box. She coughs into her elbow at the thick layer of dust floating up from the cardboard. I haven't touched it since we moved into this house a couple years ago.

She takes a stack of old photos from the box.

On top is my ninth birthday party. I'm sitting in a deck chair in my pink-and-yellow bathing suit, surrounded by a bunch of other girls in their swimwear. I'd wanted a pool party, but we didn't have a pool, so Mom set up a Slip 'n Slide in the backyard. Ivy's got her arm wrapped around me, and we're making silly faces at the camera. Mom was so sick at that point but still tried to make everything nice for us.

Mom had kind of a crappy childhood. She and her sister went back and forth between living with their young mother, who was an alcoholic, and their grandparents, who were extremely uptight;

they were "spare the rod, spoil the child" kind of people. I'm pretty sure she went out of her way to make sure we would have better childhoods than she did. I don't wonder if she'd be proud of who I've become, because I already know the answer.

I miss my mom a lot. Sometimes it hits me harder than others. Random things trigger memories that bring waves of sadness with them. A line from a movie Mom loved. The smell of cooked celery, which used to make me gag and now makes me think of Mom's Thanksgiving stuffing. She used to doodle a lot; after she died, I found an old notebook she'd used in group therapy, and the margins were filled with drawings of dogs and flowers and my and Ivy's names. I cried for like an hour when I found it, making sure I stowed it away and dried my tears before anyone else got home.

"Remember when Mom and Dad used to grill?" I ask Ivy now, brushing my finger down the photo. "And we'd make s'mores on the charcoal?"

I swear my sister's head dips into a slight nod. Ivy flips to the next photo. It's our church's Christmas pageant, back in the day. Ivy's clamped around my waist, looking like she's about ready to faint, dressed like a donkey, and I'm wearing a set of angel wings and a halo headband. I'm missing both front teeth. That was the year everyone kept quoting that ridiculous "All I Want for Christmas Is My Two Front Teeth" song at me. I still hate that song.

"You had the worst stage fright." I touch the photo. "I had to read that line about the angel Gabriel visiting Mary, and you wouldn't let go of my arm."

"I remember this pageant," Ivy whispers. "You made a joke to the entire congregation about having a clingy ass and got in trouble. But everyone laughed." She's not saying it to me, not really. Still, somehow, I feel like she can sense my presence.

Ivy flips through a few more photos. There's one of Mom, Ivy, and me putting our hands on that electricity ball at the Boston Museum of Science. Then there's preteen Ivy casting a spell on me with a plastic wand our uncle brought her from Harry Potter World. Finally, there's a shot of Ivy and me in our soccer uniforms in elementary school. We used to go to each other's games, and sometimes made giant colorful posters to wave from the sidelines, cheering each other on. The memories feel sweet and prickly at the same time.

Sometimes I think of feelings as giant tidal waves capable of completely overwhelming me and throwing me off my guard. A burst of anger can rage as quickly as a surge of joy. But this feeling seeps in slowly, softer than a whisper: I miss my sister.

Ivy tugs out a crisp photo from the back. I knew it was coming, but my stomach still lurches when I see it.

Dad and Kathy's wedding day. I force myself to focus on Ivy, me, and Dad. The people who matter.

Ivy and I are standing there in our bridesmaid dresses beside the happy couple, smiling. Kathy let us pick the dresses. I chose pink and Ivy picked blue. I still can't believe I wanted to wear that horrible poufy thing. I look like a pastry.

The first day I met Kathy, I thought she was Dad's way of rebounding from Mom. He had driven us down to Bedford for free pancake night at IHOP and randomly struck up a conversation with her on the benches by the door while we were waiting for a table. By the time our buzzer went off at the end of the forty-minute wait, Dad had asked them to seat us as a party of five rather than three. Ivy, Chris, and I sat and colored the menu while they chatted. My first impression was that she was nice—maybe a little overbearing, and she wore too much perfume—but she made Dad smile. It was the first time I'd seen him happy since Mom died, two years earlier. I honestly never thought she'd stick around. But eight months later, they were married.

Sometimes I hate myself for suggesting pancakes. If I hadn't begged to go, Dad never would've met her. Maybe things would've been different.

I look away from the photo.

As if Ivy can sense it, she puts the picture away, slides the box back into my closet, and leaves the room.

Ivy

Dad keeps sneaking glimpses of me out of the corner of his eye at the dinner table. It's like he's scared I'm going to spontaneously combust or something. He never looks at Autumn this way. It's like he knows I'm the weaker child, the one who needs protecting. Autumn doesn't need anybody.

I slide a piece of pizza onto my plate, shifting away from Dad's gaze. But then I'm stuck facing Autumn's empty chair, and that's worse. I hate this.

As always, Kathy sits next to Dad, directly across from me. Muffled sounds from her iPad broadcast a replay of this afternoon's Michigan State game. Apparently, Chris scored a touchdown and it was a big deal. Kathy's been watching the same clip on repeat for the past twenty minutes between bites. I can tell it's the same one, because some frat guy who was probably sitting right next to the camera shouts, "Purdue's getting raped!" the moment the touchdown hits. Every. Single. Time. The crowd explodes in cheers, then the announcer says, "Touchdown scored by Spartans junior Chris Pike," followed by Kathy whispering, "That's my boy." I've heard the trifecta a dozen times now, to the point where I've started mentally saying it the moment they do.

I know nothing about football, and I don't care about Chris, so I try tuning it out. My stomach won't stop wrestling with itself. The last thing I feel like doing is eating, so I pick at my pizza instead. I pull a pepperoni off my slice and pop it in my mouth.

"You okay, Ivy?" Dad's brow creases. "You're not eating."

I shrug. "I'm not really hungry."

I keep ruminating over everything I found in Autumn's room. The college sites. The anonymous letter.

Then there's that photo in Autumn's closet. Why'd she keep it all these years? I guess I didn't expect her to be sentimental. About anything, but especially about Dad and Kathy's wedding.

It was a super-casual ceremony. We went to City Hall. Dad wore his Sox tie over a blue button-down, and Kathy wore a silky purple evening gown. Chris was the lone groomsman. Dad's brother was supposed to drive up from New York, but he got caught in a snowstorm, so the only guests were us and Kathy's huge family. After the ceremony, we all drove down to Texas Roadhouse for dinner, where we clinked our glasses every five seconds to get them to kiss.

Everyone was happy. Dad beamed ear to ear the whole day. You see stories about blended families where the weddings include drunken vengeance toasts and brawls, but not here. Kathy's sisters kept hugging Dad; her brother made a toast, at which the whole restaurant clapped; I danced with Dad, Chris danced with Autumn, and Kathy danced with her elderly stepfather, and she even got him to sit on the infamous Texas Roadhouse saddle.

But that's not what I remember the clearest. What I remember most of all were their wedding vows.

Kathy had written the usual spiel—how Dad was her best friend, how she'd thought she'd never find love again, how he changed her life. But then, halfway through the vows, she turned around to face Autumn and me, standing there at the altar beside them.

"When people ask about my children, I've gotten so used to

saying I have a son. Not anymore. Now I'll tell them I have three beautiful children: a son and two daughters. Girls, I know I'll never replace your mother, and I never want to. But I want to make a vow to you both today. I promise to always be there for you, just like I am for Chris."

The problem with wedding vows is, they aren't different from any other promises. They're only as good as the person making them.

"Are you feeling sick?" Dad's still watching me. "She'll turn up, sweetie."

"I'm fine."

I can't take his third degree, so I text Patrick instead—how's it going at your dad's?

Usually, Dad yells at me for playing with my phone at the table, but I guess he can't tonight since Kathy's been watching that stupid football clip on repeat the whole meal.

"Purdue's getting raped!" the guy says again.

The announcer's deep voice proclaims, "Touchdown scored by Spartans junior Chris Pike."

And of course, "That's my boy."

A V indents itself in Dad's forehead, and I can tell he's contemplating saying something, but he doesn't. So I do.

"Can you turn that down?"

Kathy startles, like she's just remembered there are other people sitting at the dinner table. "Oh, sorry, Ivy." She clicks the volume buttons on the side. "Just watching your brother's game."

"He's not my brother," I mutter.

Dad rubs his forehead.

My phone buzzes.

Patrick: It's all right. You know what's weird?

He's talking to my mom again. He follows it up with a second text, of the boy-shrugging emoji.

Whoa, I write back. Must be the apocalypse or something.

He responds, It's clearly the only explanation.

"Purdue's getting raped!"

"Touchdown scored by Spartans junior Chris Pike."

Kathy sniffles. "That's my boy."

I swear my ears are twitching.

"We hired a new mechanic this week," Dad says, in a futile attempt to break the tension.

"Oh, that's cool." I pull another pepperoni off my pizza.

"We're hoping he can take on some of the work so I won't have to stay late as much."

"That'd be good."

"I'm hoping after this weekend, I won't have to work Saturday nights anymore."

"You're working tonight? Seriously?"

"We've got bills, Ivy. Think about that when you take those half-hour showers. All that hot water someone's got to pay for."

I roll my eyes. I do *not* take half-hour showers. Maybe twenty minutes, when I shave my legs.

Well, that was short lived, Patrick says. They're arguing about Will now. Just saw Dad kick Mom's car tire in the driveway. He sends me an eye-roll face.

Yes, I am so, *so* glad Patrick didn't take after his parents. I text him the wide-eyed-face emoji. Sorry. That sucks. I'm here if you wanna talk.

Not gonna lie, I kind of love how easily we've fallen back into our friendship. It always felt effortless when we were kids. I'm glad some things never change.

"Purdue's getting raped!"

"Touchdown scored by Spartans junior Chris Pike."

"That's my—"

I slam my hand on the table. "Okay, can you not?"

Kathy and Dad both jerk their heads up at my outburst.

"Purdue's getting *raped?*" It's even more vile when I say it out loud. "Does he even know what rape is?"

Kathy's mouth hangs open for a moment. "I know, it's vulgar. Those college boys just don't understand the—"

"No. That's a shitty excuse. If they're old enough to vote, they're old enough to know what rape is. They can't just throw that word around like it's nothing."

A veil of silence descends over the room. I blink. Holy shit. I've never yelled at Kathy before. Guilt tunnels through me.

Dad pushes his chair back from the table. "I have to get ready for work." His footsteps thump into the living room, getting softer as he clomps up the stairs. With a light thud, his bedroom door shuts. Shit. I probably shouldn't have done that. Dad hates conflict between Kathy and us, and I'm pretty sure it's because he doesn't want to take sides. Sometimes I can't help wishing he'd take mine. Ever since Mom died, it's like the floors are made of eggshells rather than carpet and wood.

I prop my forehead up with my hands. "I'm sorry."

Kathy gives me a guilty look. "No, I'm sorry, honey. I didn't mean to upset you. I'll watch the game in the other room."

"It's fine." I force a smile. "I'm going out anyway." And I can't get out of this kitchen fast enough.

The moment I'm out of the room, the cheering football crowd recommences. I clench my teeth and go upstairs to touch up my mascara.

Dad's bedroom door is still closed. I swallow the guilty lump in my throat and tiptoe past his room to the bathroom.

I can't stop thinking about that douche at Chris's football game. And Autumn. And yelling at Kathy. And Dad avoiding everything.

And the cops, and reindeer pajamas, and . . . I don't even know. I rub my temples, wishing she would just come home or call us or something so I could stop freaking out.

I dig into my purse and find Autumn's phone, entering Mom's birthday to unlock it. I open my sister's texts, but this time I go straight past the ones about meeting in the lot.

Okay, here's something. Before Autumn met that guy, she was texting with "Abby N." I scroll through their messages, and of course, they're talking about some guy they know who went to jail. Autumn's friends with some real winners.

I pull out last year's yearbook and flip to the juniors' *N*s. Abigail Nelson stares back at me, a fan of wavy brown hair framing her pale face. She looks about my size, with a nose stud, dimples, and a nice smile. I think I've seen her walking around with Autumn at school before.

Screw it.

I text her from Autumn's phone, `Hey is this Abby Nelson? This is Autumn Casterly's sister, Ivy. I'm worried about her. Can you text me back?`

I stare at the screen for a good two minutes waiting for those little dots to appear, but they don't. My resolve deflates slightly.

There has to be someone else I can message. I click back into her main texts and scroll past Abby N. I do a double take at the name directly beneath hers—Hailey Waters. That's weird. Autumn texted Hailey on Thursday evening, several hours after she asked me if I knew her in the driveway. I swallow hard and click the message.

Autumn: How's Owen?

I read it once, twice, three times. That's it. That's the only message between Hailey and Autumn. My brow creases. Who's Owen? It's weird Hailey didn't respond, especially since it's marked as Seen. Mr. Warner has taken her phone away, like, four different times during band in the past month. She replies to everything. Except, apparently, this.

Hailey's so sweet, I can't imagine her having beef with Autumn. I mean, she goes out of her way to keep cough drops and tampons in her bag, just in case someone needs them. The low-brass line calls her their "section mom," and it's a fitting nickname.

The pepperonis turn to rocks in my stomach. I really, really hope Hailey has nothing to do with this.

I need answers. But I'm not getting any until Abby responds to me—if she ever does.

I watch the screen, waiting, while doing my makeup. I'm not the best at makeup, but I've watched a bunch of YouTube tutorials, and I can do a really awesome smoky eye now. It makes my blue eyes pop. Whenever I take the time to do it properly, I take a bunch of selfies but then get too scared to post them. Sometimes I Snapchat them to Soph and Alexa. One time I accidentally sent a duckface selfie with a silly Halloween filter to Jason's mom, and I pretty much wanted to die. She was cool about it, though.

My phone buzzes, and I nearly impale myself with my mascara wand. Holy shit. Not cool.

What are you wearing tonight? Alexa asks the group chat.

Black jeggings and that blue top you like, Sophie responds, with a wink face.

Oh, that's hot, Alexa replies.

TMI. Omg, my eyes. Open a separate chat before you start full-on sexting, please.

Sorry, Ivy! Sophie replies with the embarrassed face. Forgot this was the group chat.

I roll my eyes and quickly add, I'm wearing jeans and that sweater with the anchor on it.

It's weird when two people in a friend group start dating each other. It throws off the whole balance. Sophie, Alexa, and I always had our little group separate from the Nerd Herd, and now it's like they've got their own group, and then there's good ol' tricycle wheel Ivy, clinging on. Which is apparently my role in the dating world these days. Next time, it'll be Jason who gets a girlfriend.

No. If he got a girlfriend, nothing would change. We'd still be best friends; we just wouldn't go to homecoming together.

I huff, throwing the mascara back into my makeup bag.

He'd start bringing her to Nerd Herd meetings, and that'd be weird.

He wouldn't text me in the middle of the night anymore, because he'd text her instead.

It wouldn't all be bad. Maybe I'd start dating Patrick, and we could go on double dates.

A surge of jealousy revs to life inside me, and it's so petty and ridiculous, I can't stand it. I make an annoyed face at myself in the mirror. His so-called girlfriend doesn't even exist. And besides, I have a crush on Patrick.

I put on my silver eyeliner a little too aggressively and totally screw it up and get it all under my eye. I sigh, pulling out my box of makeup remover wipes.

I have to get used to the idea. He's already hooked up with a bunch of girls. There was one at camp two summers ago, one at church last year, another he met at the Y. And probably loads more I don't know about. It really sucks when guys always tell you about their hookups but never want to hook up with you.

I finally bat the thoughts out of my head and go downstairs to wait for Jason to pick me up, sliding Autumn's phone into my back pocket. Kathy left the pizza box on the counter. I stuff the two remaining slices into Tupperware and pretty much play Tetris trying to fit them in the fridge.

I'm outside, Jason texts.

Then the other phone in my pocket buzzes and I nearly jump a foot in the air.

Abby: Is Autumn ok?? What happened?

I bite my lip. What should I tell her? How do I know I can even trust her? Okay, it's risky, but Alexander Hamilton told me not to throw away my shot, so here I go.

Me: I haven't heard from her since yesterday morning. Do you have any idea where she went?

Abby: Not a clue. She hasn't told me anything.

Me: She goes away overnight sometimes. Do you know where she goes?

Abby: She does?? I didn't know that

Shit. I always assumed Autumn was partying with her friends or sleeping with guys when she ran away. Obviously, she wouldn't tell me, but I'd have thought she'd tell her friends. But if this girl Abby doesn't know, maybe she and Autumn aren't actually that close after all.

Abby: Have you messaged Liam?

Me: Who's Liam?

Abby: Um. This creep Autumn hangs out with.

Okay, this definitely does not sound promising.

Me: Who is he though?

I rotate the phone in my hands, praying she won't think I'm being too nosy.

Abby: Idk how to describe him. Autumn's . . . friend? Dealer? Supplier?

I love how casually she admits he's a dealer. It's like she's announcing he's a dermatologist or the guy who cuts her hair.

Abby: He just got arrested for breaking into the corner store though and last I heard Autumn was pretty pissed at him.

The cops mentioned a burglary, and said Autumn had been texting the thief. It has to be him.

Me: She never came home and I'm super worried. Can you help me find her?

Abby: I ALWAYS thought Liam was sketchy. I'll do anything you need.

Me: Any idea where to start?

Abby: She goes to Liam's house a lot, and that place is a cesspool. I'd look there.

That doesn't give me much confidence.

Me: Where's the house?

Abby: Fisherville Road. That place is seriously shady.

Me: Do you think she's there?

Abby: Maybe?

The cops told me to butt out. But last time I spoke with them, it got me nowhere.

I hope Abby's not lying about the *I'll do anything* part, because I'm getting a terrible idea.

Against my better judgment, I reopen the group chat with Alexa and Sophie.

`Remember when we tried to dress as ninja turtles for costume day in eighth grade and they wouldn't let us wear the masks in school?`

I anxiously pass the phone back and forth between my hands, ignoring Jason's texts rushing me and immediately regretting this plan.

`LOL,` of course, Sophie says. `I'm still mad they wouldn't let us wear them.`

I take a deep breath and type back. `Well good, because we now have the perfect opportunity! Bring the masks. We have a top secret mission to complete tonight.`

Autumn

My knee bounces against my hand. With each passing second, I'm closer to slipping into darkness. And I'm stuck sitting in a diner with Ivy and her annoying friends.

All six of them are crammed into this tiny Friendly's booth meant for four people. The guys are on one side and the girls are on the other like they're in middle school.

This place smells like french fries and grilled cheese and it's making my stomach growl. There're so many weird things that pop into your head when you're dying. Like, what if I never eat another grilled cheese?

"I don't know what I want." The girl with the short black hair and glasses has spent the last century staring at the menu. She's half sitting in her girlfriend's lap.

"Hurry *up*," I groan. The sooner we order, the sooner we leave, and the sooner Ivy can get over to Liam's house, and that's one step closer to finding me. I hope.

I keep trying to convince myself that Ivy's plan is a good one, that just because Liam is in jail doesn't mean his friends weren't involved. I mean, maybe there *is* a clue at his house. But it feels like we're grasping at straws. Liam's friends are like stoned sheep, following their shepherd—and currently their shepherd is behind bars. Plus, I've seen every corner of Liam's house, and there's no tiny wooden room anywhere. I really hope this whole thing is worthwhile and Ivy doesn't end up arrested.

"Alexa," Ahmed says, "what should Sophie get to eat?"

The purple-haired girl shrugs, midtext. "I don't know. Whatever she feels like."

Jason and Kevin snicker.

Sophie ignores them. "I can't decide between the strawberry sundae and the Reese's Pieces sundae."

"Alexa," Ahmed says again. "Should Sophie order the strawberry sundae or the Reese's Pieces sundae?"

Alexa lowers her brows. "Why are you talking to me like that?"

"Oh, for fuck's sake. It's that Amazon thing," I mutter, even though no one can hear me.

Jason and Kevin fall over themselves laughing.

Ivy rolls her eyes and slaps down her menu. "Wow, did you make that joke up all by yourselves?"

"Are you guys seriously making an Amazon joke at me?" Alexa says. "You're, like, five hundred bajillion years late to that party."

Jason laughs. "Alexa, explain the joke."

"Okay," Ivy says. "You're so not as funny as you think you are."

Sophie deadpans, "How about, 'Alexa, let's go find a different table, because our friends are idiots'?"

"My parents got an Amazon Echo," Ahmed says. "Every time they address it as Alexa and tell her to do something, I can't stop laughing."

"I wanna come play with it," Jason says.

"That's what she said," Alexa adds.

I cross my arms. It feels like I crashed a party and now everyone's ignoring me. It's like I'm on the brink of sitting at this table, being part of this group, but not. I hang out with people all the time, but it never feels like this. I'm always on guard, always thinking about how I'll be perceived. No one here seems to be worried about that.

My foot jitters against the carpet. I hate that it's dark outside. That means Saturday is almost over. Every passing moment feels like a too-fast clock, ticking down the last seconds of my life.

The waitress comes over and doesn't even try to hide her scowl. "All right, you kids decide what you're having?"

Ivy is getting a cone-head sundae. I'm taken aback by my own thought. We haven't been to Friendly's together in years, so why do I remember that?

Ivy beams. "Can I get a cone-head sundae, please?"

Sometimes we would come to Friendly's for brunch after church when we were kids. Ivy always got that ridiculous sundae, shaped like a face with a cone for a hat. In a weird way, it comforts me that she hasn't changed.

I wish I had come to Friendly's more when I was alive. I wish I had gotten more sundaes.

"Those are for kids under twelve."

Ivy frowns. "I'm only fifteen, can I get it anyway? I'll pay extra."

"Sorry, company policy."

Ahmed and Jason both roll their eyes.

"It's not, though," Sophie says. "I've gotten cone-head sundaes."

The waitress shrugs. "Sorry. You gotta get something else."

I glower at her.

"Okay." Ivy sighs. "It's no big deal. I'll have—"

Jason cuts her off. "She'll have two scoops of vanilla ice cream."

Ivy's brows draw together, and I can tell she's just as pissed with Jason ordering for her as I am.

Jason continues, "Add three M&M's onto the front scoop, two on top and one directly below, like two eyes and a mouth."

A smile creeps across my face. I know where this is going. "And hot fudge," I practically shout. No one can hear me, but I'm bouncing in my invisible seat. "And a cone on top."

Ivy must catch on, too, because the corners of her mouth slowly tug into a grin.

"Add hot fudge," Jason says. "And a ring of whipped cream around the top. And add on a cone, please, placed upside down on the whipped cream."

Technically they didn't order a cone-head sundae; they made one. The waitress huffs, but writes it down. I'm pretty sure she hates everyone here. Ivy catches Jason's eye across the table, and he winks. She smiles at him but quickly darts her gaze back to the table.

After the lady takes everyone's orders and leaves, the table nearly dies laughing. I laugh along with them, but it fades into this weird, uncomfortable sense of loneliness.

I've never had friends like this. Abby, Jaclyn, and I don't go to the movies or try on clothes at the mall together like girlfriends on TV. All we really do is sell shit and show up at parties just to be seen there. I don't know anything about their families or their crushes or their hopes and dreams, and they definitely don't know anything about mine. We don't have inside jokes that aren't related to the people we sell to.

Maybe in another world, if things had been different, I would've had friends. I would've been sitting with my sister, stealing a spoonful of fudge off her sundae.

I picture that economics class with the trickle-down tree full of toucans. The bird at the top had the most fruit. The most power. But he was also all alone on the highest branch, with nothing but the clouds for company.

Within a few minutes, the waitress returns with a teetering tray of sundaes. Ivy and her group immediately dig in, taking a moment to Snapchat the unofficial cone-head to almost everyone at our high school. Alexa steals a bite of Sophie's sundae (in the eleventh hour, she chose the Reese's Pieces). Ahmed and Kevin start ribbing Ivy about Patrick Perkins, specifically asking if she's sleeping at his place tonight, at which point Jason becomes really interested in his phone.

I should be freaking the fuck out because the day is almost over, and I probably don't have many left. But I can't stop watching them.

Popularity is weird. I'd never consider my sister to be popular. She's a band geek who dresses up for cons and sees midnight show-ings of *Star Wars*, complete with a glowing plastic lightsaber. But she has a ton of friends. Way more than I do. So why am I popular and she's not?

She ended up at a table surrounded by people who love her—and I'm somewhere on the ground, dying.

A bell chimes, and with a gust of fall air, the door swings open. My heart jumps—*Abby*.

"Hey!" I jump to my feet. "Abby!" It takes me half a second to remember she can't see me.

Abby's eyes dart around the restaurant before settling on Ivy, who waves. She cautiously approaches the crowded table with her head down. It's weird seeing Abby like this. Shy. Smiling. Cautious. She's not the same girl who pinned Tyler Fenton behind the Irving station last year, or who ripped Kaitlyn Kennedy's towel off two days ago.

I don't know this version of her at all.

"Hey." Abby pulls up a chair and sits at the head of the booth, halfway into the aisle. Ivy's friends pass suspicious glances between them, and from Ivy's face it's clear she wasn't ready to fess up to her little plan quite yet.

"This is Abby," Ivy says. "She's joining us on a top secret mission tonight."

Jason and Ahmed nod at her. "Hey."

Alexa gives her a friendly smile before twirling a lock of purple hair around her finger and looking away. Kevin doesn't acknowledge her, but his face burns bright red.

Abby darts her eyes down. "Hey, Sophie."

Sophie nods. "Hey."

What the hell? From the look on Ivy's face, she wasn't expecting that, either.

"You know, I'm gonna run to the bathroom." Abby springs to her feet so quickly, she nearly knocks her chair over. "I'll be right back."

The moment she's out of earshot, everyone turns on Ivy.

"Who's that?"

"Isn't she a senior?"

"Don't you know who that is?"

"What's this secret mission? Is this why you wanted me to bring the masks?"

But it's Ivy who whirls on Sophie. "How do *you* know Abby?"

Everyone goes quiet. I lean in, also curious. Abby's never mentioned knowing a sophomore who's friends with my little sister.

Sophie shrugs. "You know. From around."

When every single person simultaneously glares at her, she throws her head back. "From horseback-riding camp years ago, okay? I don't wanna talk about it."

Ahmed raises his brows. "I didn't know you did horseback-riding camp."

"Just one summer after sixth grade. I wasn't very good."

Alexa giggles. "Did you have a crush on her?"

"Oh my God, no!" Sophie fake-shoves Alexa. "It's not like that.

It's just . . ." She bites her lip. "I don't know. I feel bad saying it."

"Well, now you have to tell us," Jason says.

"Fine. Okay? Fine." Sophie puts her hands up, glancing quickly at the bathroom hallway, which is still empty. "The instructor . . . said Abby needed a bigger horse, because she's, you know . . . bigger." She casts a glance at Ivy, who doesn't seem to notice. "The other kids were really mean about it. They called her Flabby Abby and bullied her until she dropped out, like, two weeks after camp started. Someone snuck a picture of her when she was changing and passed it around. It was horrible." She takes a bite of her sundae. "She was a really good rider, too. Way better than me."

I blink, absorbing. *What?* I never knew Abby did horseback riding. If she loved it so much, why doesn't she ride anymore? My stomach sinks when I answer my own question. They ruined it for her. Once something good is tainted by something bad, it can never be that good thing again. It carries a shadow. A ghost.

It hits me that I've been the person on the other end of that. People have called me a bully, but I guess I never associated that word with what I am. I hope I never did to them what they did to Abby.

I'm grasping back at every encounter we had, every person we threatened. It was Abby's idea to rip the towel off Kaitlyn and take a picture. I swallow hard. Maybe if you're the one with the power, it's harder for people to hurt you. No one bullies you when you're on top.

Abby saunters back to the table, which abruptly goes quiet. She takes her seat. "Sorry about that."

I rest my hand on her shoulder, even though she can't feel it.

"Okay, so, now that I have all of you here." Ivy clears her throat. "How much do you love me?"

"Buckets," Alexa says.

"Well, good. Because I need help breaking into someone's house."

I brace myself. Way to be blunt, Ivy.

Ahmed barks out a laugh.

Sophie looks at Ivy like she just grew a spare arm. "What the actual hell . . ."

"Whoa, Ivy, you turning into your sister?" Alexa gently elbows Ivy in the side. I fidget, hating that she's got a point.

"I know, *I know* it sounds messed up. But I have to do it. And I'll be the one doing all the illegal stuff, I swear."

"I'll be helping," says Abby. "I know Liam's house."

"Who's Liam?" Alexa asks.

Ivy fills them all in on my disappearance, the car, the police, the empty lot, and Abby's tip on Liam. I hold my breath, waiting for everyone to freak out, but no one does. They're taken aback, for sure. But no one runs away screaming. The more she talks, the more intrigued everyone seems to get. They listen. Slowly, they come up with a plan.

I've got to be honest, this is the last thing I'd expect my little sister to do. And she's doing it for me.

Would I do the same for her?

Mom used to make us chocolate chip pancakes on Saturday mornings. Sundays were for church and Sunday school, so we had to wake up early; Saturdays we were allowed to sleep in, and always woke up to the smell of pancakes on the griddle. On holidays, Mom put food coloring in the pancakes—red and green for Christmas, orange on Halloween, favorite colors on our respective birthdays.

Three weeks after she died, I tried to make blue pancakes for Ivy's birthday, but it didn't go so well. I got batter all over the stove and the floor. The pancakes came out lumpy and gross. It was a giant mess. Honestly I'm surprised nothing caught fire. Dad came downstairs to find me on the kitchen floor, covered in flour, sobbing. He cleaned up the mess and sent me upstairs to take a shower. Ivy was still sleeping when I got out of the shower, and the kitchen was sparkling clean, thanks to Dad. I felt like I'd failed her—and I'd failed Mom. I was supposed to take care of my sister, and I couldn't even do something as basic as make her breakfast. So when Ivy rolled out of bed and came downstairs, asking if Dad could make her birthday pancakes, I flipped out.

"Why don't you make them yourself?" I snapped. "You're so helpless. You can't do anything."

It was the first time I'd lost my temper at my sister. She blinked at me in disbelief as I turned on my heel and stormed upstairs. Guilt clawed through me, but I never brought it up again. Ivy had a shitty birthday that year, and I can't help feeling like it was my fault.

I try not to think about it.

Ivy's friends piss off the waitress even more by demanding separate checks. The lady practically slams the checks down on the table before storming back into the kitchen.

Everyone leaves their money on the table and heads for the door. Ivy hesitates, examining her four-dollar sundae charge. She pulls out the ten-dollar bill Dad gave her before she left and lays it on the receipt.

Jason's brows shoot up. "You're leaving her a giant tip? She was super rude."

"She gave me my cone-head." Ivy shrugs. "She's probably having a bad day."

"Ivy, Ivy, Ivy." Jason wraps his arm around her shoulders. "You're too good and pure for this world."

She knocks his arm off and scowls. "Shut up. It's just six bucks."

That's not true. Six bucks is a lot to Ivy. She rarely has more than a couple dollars in her wallet, and Dad almost never gives her money. We stopped getting allowances when we were little kids.

I'm struck with a pang of sadness as they walk outside, trying to trip each other. Ivy is such a perfect little do-gooder.

What have I gotten her into?

IVY

Oh my God, we are so getting arrested for this. And I'm not even talking about breaking into Liam's house—I'm talking about this car.

Abby, Alexa, Sophie, and I piled into the back seat of Jason's SUV with Ahmed strewn across our laps. Kevin won the shotgun lottery because he announced he'd get carsick in the back and no one wanted a lapful of puke. I've spent the last ten minutes sandwiched against this freezing window, with Sophie's butt bone digging into my thigh and Ahmed's dirty sneakers in my lap.

With luck, Liam's roommate will be out, the house will be empty, and I can get in and out super quick. Abby says she knows where they hide their spare key. But if someone's home, we'll need to go with Plan B—which involves all my friends. I'm really, really hoping it's the former.

Jason's headlights prowl the darkened road. "If I get pulled over for this, our friendship is over, Ivy."

"Well, maybe if you weren't going twenty in a forty zone, you wouldn't be drawing so much attention to yourself," Alexa counters.

A line of cars has formed behind us, and judging by the guy who keeps flashing his brights into our window, I'm guessing they're not thrilled.

"You know, they'll still pull you over for going too slow." I just want to get there before I have a giant bruise from Sophie's ass.

Abby tells Jason where to turn, and he does. Okay, this is a weird direction—we're, like, dangerously close to the prison. She said we were going to *Liam's house*. What house? A halfway house?

"Okay, we're here," Abby says.

Jason pulls over to the side of the road, idling ambiguously between Liam's house and the neighbors'. The other cars zip by us, including the brights-flashing guy, who rolls down his window and flips us off.

Gravel rumbles beneath the tires when Jason urges the car into a slight ditch and puts it in Park. We all simultaneously release a breath. This was a terrible strategy, but one car makes us look way less sketchy than arriving in a caravan.

"Okay, there's a light on," Abby says. "Someone's home."

My stomach sinks. I knew it was a possibility, but I was hoping it wouldn't come to this. "Plan B, then?"

Everyone agrees, a little too enthusiastically.

We climb out of the car, thankfully concealed by darkness and the trees. I stretch to one side, then the other, working out the kinks from being crammed into the back seat.

"Soph, you have a *really* bony butt."

"Yeah she does." Alexa winks.

Sophie scoffs. "At least you didn't have Ahmed's crotch in your lap."

"What's wrong with my crotch?" Ahmed stretches his arms out in front of him, wincing. "Remind me never to let you guys do that to me again."

Alexa flicks his shoulder. "We still have the ride home, buddy."

"No way. One of you can take on the role of human seat belt."

When we bought these masks, Alexa insisted on going full-on

turtle, rather than the color-coded eye bands also offered by the costume store. They look like they could terrify young children, they ruin my hair, and they stink. I complained about them incessantly at the time. But right now, I'm loving the green, scaly, full-head-concealing monstrosities.

I pull on my Michelangelo mask and it envelops my head like a hot, rubbery motorcycle helmet. The two eyeholes are a little too round; it's like looking through a pair of green binoculars.

Abby twiddles her fingers. I always assumed Autumn's friends would be jerks, but Abby seems cool. We definitely couldn't pull this off without her; she knows this house and knows the roommate—who's probably responsible for that light in the window.

"So, who's home right now?" I ask Abby.

"I'm guessing it's Liam's roommate, Chad."

Everyone snickers, probably because Alexa's cat is also called Chad, but I hate that they're not taking this seriously.

"Okay. Anyone else?"

"I'm not sure. They've got neighbors, but I think they went away this weekend. Liam's friends usually hang out in Manchester on Saturdays, because they've got a friend who's the bouncer at some bar and lets them in without IDs. But I guess there could be other people home. It's a crapshoot. And sometimes they let random people sleep on their couch."

"These guys sound like creeps," Sophie says.

"Oh, you have no idea." Abby flares her fingers out. "But it might be a good thing if Chad's home. He could tell us something useful."

"Okay." I'm pretty sure my heart is on the verge of rocketing out of my chest. This was such a bad idea. I'm not sure why I thought this would work. But I'm pulling at threads, and I don't have any other clues.

I gently push the car door shut, but still stiffen at the sound when it slams. Focus. I can't be jumpy for this. "Okay, you guys know the plan?"

Everyone nods in unison, and it's kind of disconcerting. Also, seeing my reflection in the car window, I'm glad the teachers wouldn't let us wear these to school, because I look ridiculous.

"Let's run through it again," Kevin says, wringing his hands. "Just to make sure."

"You guys are going to ring the doorbell with Abby. She tells Chad she's got some people who want to buy fake IDs, and you'll go inside the house. Once you're in, Abby will drop a few casual questions about the last time he saw Autumn—try to find out if he knows where she is. After a few minutes, Sophie says she has to pee, and when she goes to the bathroom, she unlocks the back door, where I'll be waiting outside in the mask. I come in, do a quick sweep of the house to make sure Autumn isn't there. I'll sneak out within five minutes and then you guys wrap up and meet me back at the car."

Ahmed taps his finger to his lips. "Why don't you come in with us and say *you* have to pee? Then instead of the bathroom, you go walking through the rooms, looking?"

"Nope." Abby shakes her head. "Chad would know something's up if she was gone too long. This way, he doesn't know Ivy's there. Sophie can come back right away."

"What if Autumn isn't there?" Sophie asks.

"Then we try and find a clue about where she might be."

"What if Liam's there?" Alexa asks.

"He's definitely in jail," Abby says. "No one's posted his bail."

"Wait, who am I playing?" Jason holds up the remaining two masks. "What do you think? Am I more of a Donatello or a Raphael?"

"*You* aren't going." I rip the masks out of his hands.

"What do you mean? Of course I am."

"Nope." I jab him in the chest. "You're on doorbell duty. I need you distracting the roommate. If we screw up, I'm not having your arrest on my conscience."

"Who said anything about getting arrested? We're too sneaky to get caught."

"Sneaky? You walk like a water buffalo."

"What's that supposed to mean?"

"Okay, can we just do this?" Alexa bobs up and down on the balls of her feet. "It's freezing and I did not dress for this."

"Yeah, my curfew's in forty minutes," Sophie says.

Jason crosses his arms. "So can I come or not?"

"Seriously? This isn't a joke. You know we're"—I drop my voice to a whisper— "breaking and entering here, right? It's illegal."

"I told you I'd help find Autumn, and I meant it." His eyes lock on mine, and I hate that stubborn Jason Daly-Cruz resolve that makes me want to rip my hair out and hug him at the same time.

"Okay, fine. Whatever."

Jason grins and buries his face in the Donatello mask.

I shake my head. "You look ridiculous."

"I'd say it's an improvement," Ahmed offers. Jason goes to kick him, and Ahmed quickly dodges the attack.

"Can we focus, please?" I'm glad I'm wearing a mask so they can't see how pale I am right now. Seriously, it's like I can *feel* the color draining from my face.

"Go, team!" Alexa puts her hand into the middle and everyone follows her lead. I begrudgingly add my hand to the mix. "Operation Find Autumn." Abby joins in, and is the loudest person to whisper-yell "Woo!" when we all throw our hands up at the end. She's absolutely a nerd. She just doesn't know it yet.

Jason and I creep around the back of the house while the others head for the front door. An upturned wheelbarrow sits in the middle of the backyard beside a rusty old swing set, which creaks every time the wind blows. A circle of rocks marks what's either a fire pit or a tomb, and I'd rather not think about which. My hot breath blows back against my face, trapped by the rubber. I'm beginning to regret these costumes. I'm 99 percent sure whoever lives here would be more likely to shoot a couple of freaks in Ninja Turtle masks than a couple of kids. Being recognized is preferable to being dead.

"What if they don't let Abby and the others in?" The mask muffles Jason's voice, but it's still way too loud for my liking.

"Then we're screwed," I hiss over my shoulder. "And can you not talk so loud, please?" Cars whir by on the main road, thankfully blocking out most of our bumbling around in the dark. A branch cracks beneath my foot and I nearly jump a foot in the air.

"Jeez, Ivy, what happened to not being so loud?"

"Shut it."

Just like Abby told us, three stairs lead up to a small deck and the back door. A flickering porch light illuminates chipping paint that looks like it used to be white. The door has a square glass window near the top, obscured by a white curtain.

I crouch in the shadows beside the stairs, and Jason sinks down behind me. Our breaths cut through the silence, amplified by the stupid turtle masks.

"Hey," Jason whispers. "You all right?"

I nod, not daring to talk because my voice would probably give away the fact that I'm about ready to pass out. Before I can stop it, my hand creeps over and squeezes his; he squeezes right back.

"Do you think Abby and the others got in yet?"

As if on cue, the back door opens and my heart jumps into my throat. But Sophie's face pokes out. *All clear,* she mouths before disappearing back into the house and leaving the door open a crack.

A guy's voice echoes from inside, talking to the others.

I tiptoe up the back porch stairs, cringing when they creak under my boots. The door squeaks when I push it. I can feel Jason's warm body barely an inch behind mine, and I'm really hoping he doesn't slam into me because I'll fall flat on my face.

I'm not sure what to expect inside. What do criminals' houses look like?

The odor of burnt food and cigarette smoke permeates the small kitchen. An old-school clock with a ticking pendulum hangs beside the fridge, which is plastered with coupons and calendars hung up by promotional magnets. It strikes me that this house is perfectly normal. Whoever lives in this *perfectly normal* house could have hurt my sister.

A toilet flushes, then I hear Sophie's voice as she returns to the living room with the others.

I tiptoe ahead, staying close to the wall, careful not to trip over the mound of boots thrown on the doormat.

Jason gently creaks open the pantry door, revealing shelves of opened pasta and cereal boxes, but no Autumn.

"Where do we look first?" he whispers.

The house doesn't seem very big. And it's definitely not like places in movies where people hide hostages in secret rooms behind bookshelves.

"Abby said Liam's room, Chad's room, and the basement are the only places she could think of. Otherwise it's just the living room, kitchen, and bathroom." I don't even know what I'm hoping to find—my sister, held hostage here? My sister, ready to murder me because she ran away and I found her anyway? Proof she's in trouble? Proof she's not? I don't know what would be worse: finding something that proves I've been overreacting and risked my friends for nothing, or something that proves I've been right all along and she's in trouble. Even if I can find something to make the police believe me, I'm not sure how to explain where I got it.

A guy's—I'm assuming Chad's—muffled voice drifts through the thin walls, and I can pick out words like *plastic* and *fail-safe*. Alexa's probably nodding dramatically at everything he says, while Kevin's likely sitting in silence, trying not to puke. I owe my friends, like, a zillion favors for this.

According to Abby, the first door should be the . . .

Basement, Jason mouths, pointing at a cracked-open door leading into darkness.

I cast a glance into what I can see of the living room, where I can just make out the tip of someone's shoe. The distraction seems to be working. I slide through the basement doorway. A loud shudder emits from the stair the moment my foot hits it, and I full-on cringe. We both freeze for a moment, but the only noise coming from the living room is the steady hum of conversation.

"Go." Jason prods me in the back.

I take the stairs two at a time, creeping through the darkness until I reach the concrete floor.

"Autumn," I whisper-yell into the darkness. "Are you here?"

"Shut up," Jason grumbles softly, somewhere behind me. "Are you *trying* to get caught?"

I click the flashlight button on my phone, illuminating the tiny cellar. A musty old refrigerator buzzes softly in the corner. Rusty pipes crisscross the ceiling. There's an ancient treadmill in the back that looks like it hasn't been used since the Dark Ages. I run the light beam around the empty room.

"Okay, she's not here." Jason turns toward the stairs. "Next stop."

"Wait." I don't know what compels me to do it. Slowly, I close my fingers around the freezer door handle and tug. It takes a solid yank to get it open, but there's nothing inside except a few old pieces of Tupperware filled with God knows what.

I start back upstairs, Jason right behind me, but stop halfway when I hear voices in the kitchen.

"So I'm kind of annoyed with Autumn." Abby's voice comes from upstairs, with a tinge more drama than her normal tone. "She's been ignoring my texts all weekend."

Chad laughs, followed by the sound of a cabinet closing. "Autumn ghosts people all the time."

I listen closely to catch their conversation, my heart in my throat.

"Yeah, but she usually doesn't ignore *me*. Maybe she's upset or something." When he doesn't respond, Abby adds, "Have you seen her?"

"Nah, not since Thursday when you guys were all here."

I wring my hands, way too close to them for comfort. *Come on. Tell her something.*

"You should text her." Abby is a terrible liar, but Chad doesn't seem to notice. "See if she responds to you."

"She won't even recognize my number." Their voices fade as they return to the living room.

"Okay, go, go, go." Jason shoves me forward and I creep up the remaining stairs, peeking my head out before rushing back into the hallway.

"Chad's room." I point to the next door. Jason nods, and we practically tumble inside.

There's, like, eight different posters of women in bikinis on this guy's walls, but nothing too strange. Jason tears into the closet as I peer under the unmade bed.

"Nothing," we say at the same time.

I check my phone. Shit. We're running out of time.

We rush back into the hall, and I'm somewhat calmed by the distant sound of Abby laughing. "Okay, Liam's room," I whisper. "Last stop, then we're gone."

A small bathroom with blue wallpaper and cracked linoleum tiles greets us behind the kitchen, and sure enough, beside it is a closed door with a real stop sign affixed to it. I touch the sign, brushing the cold metal with my fingertips. Yep. He definitely stole this.

Jason's face scrunches as he points at the tacky sculpture against the wall. "Is this supposed to be an urn?" He peeks into it, pulling out an empty can of raspberry-lime Polar Seltzer. "Nice. Trash."

My muscles turn to lead. I snatch the can out of his hand—it's missing the aluminum tab. "This was Autumn's. She was drinking it Thursday."

"Wait, really? How do you know?"

"She always rips the tabs off. It's hers."

"Lots of people rip the tabs off . . ."

"I'll go grab some." The guy's voice gets louder. "I think I left it in the kitchen."

"Go, go, go." Jason practically shoves me into Liam's room just as a lanky guy with a goatee steps into the kitchen in a T-shirt and jeans.

I hold my breath, slowly closing the door behind us. We press our ears to the wood and wait, but nothing happens. Something rustles, followed by a few light echoing slams, like he's riffling through cabinets. Jason releases a heavy breath.

"Holy shit. That was close."

A cat darts out from under the bed and shoots across the room; I gasp, quickly clapping my hand over my mouth. Jason holds out his hands, and I can almost hear him saying, *Really?*

The cat slips past us and out the door.

"Shit. Was the door closed before?" I wring my hands. "Maybe the cat's not supposed to get out." I picture the cat as a spy, rushing out to alert that guy of our presence. "What if she's like Mrs. Norris? The cat in Harry Potter?"

Jason raises his shoulders in an exaggerated shrug.

Okay, even if Autumn isn't here now, finding the can feels like a sign that we're getting closer. There must be other clues here.

Other than an unmade bed, piles of dirty laundry, a dresser, and a vintage Coors Light poster, there's hardly anything in the room. I point to the closet in the corner and start wading through ankle-deep dirty laundry to get there. Jason heads for the dresser.

My pulse pounds in my ears. We don't have much time. Abby said ten minutes, tops. We have to get out before they do.

Jason tears through Liam's clothes, throwing shirts and jeans to the floor.

"Careful," I snap. "Don't make a mess, they'll know."

"Have you seen this guy's floor? How could he even tell?"

"Oh my God." I rip my hand back. "There's something sticky in here."

Jason's face scrunches. "Gross. Don't touch it."

"Whoa. Look at this lamp." I pull out the bizarre round light. "Some kind of light to grow weed?"

"It's just a heat lamp."

I tug out dirty socks, an empty shoebox, and a package of half-eaten cereal. My hands grow more frantic. There has to be something.

"What about this?"

I whirl around. Jason's holding a Bow High School yearbook from several years ago. I blink at him. "What's that got to do with anything?"

"I dunno. Might have some more info on him?"

I rip open the drawer to his tiny nightstand, revealing packs of gum and old receipts. Sifting through it, I shove a wad of wrappers aside and my fingers meet something cool and metal. I slap my hand over my mouth. "Holy shit." I jump back so fast, I almost trip and fall. "It's a gun."

Jason shoots upward, his eyes wide. The pistol innocuously stares back at me from the drawer. I don't want to be here anymore.

My phone vibrates with a new text, and I startle, nearly knocking over the lamp.

Alexa: This is getting sketchy. We're leaving. Some other guy just arrived.

"Shit." I stumble across the room and grab Jason's hand. "We gotta go."

Somewhere out in the hall, a door closes, followed by the muffled sounds of two guys talking. We hold our breath, our feet glued to the floor.

Footsteps echo in the hallway, getting louder by the moment, until they're right outside the door.

My mind races. "The window."

Jason unclicks the window lock and wrenches it open. He throws his hands up. "There's a screen."

"Get it out!" I charge forward and push the screen as lightly as I can. Nothing happens. My heart pounds against my ribs.

Someone laughs in the hallway. "Yeah, I don't know, man. Where'd you leave it?"

"It's in Liam's room."

My heart stops.

"Go!" Jason pushes me. "C'mon!"

My friends' frantic voices fill the air outside, stampeding across the front lawn.

The doorknob turns.

I shove the screen and it pops out.

"Go! Ivy!"

I clamber onto the ledge, the wood splintering in my palm. With a grunt, I drop to the ground and stumble, slamming into the gravel.

"Hey!" A sharp voice booms from the room. "There's people here!"

Jason drops down beside me, tripping over himself. "Run!"

I take off as fast as my legs can carry me, Jason at my side. My feet pound the spongy grass.

"The car! Start the car!" Alexa shouts. Jason clicks the unlock button twice, and the car beeps. My friends rip open the doors and shove each other to get inside.

The front door flies open behind us. "Hey!"

My friends beckon from the car, their eyes wide and frantic. I'm running so fast, I slam into the side.

Jason leaps into the driver's seat and I practically swan-dive onto Abby's and Ahmed's laps. "Go! Jason!"

The other guy comes charging after us across the lawn, but Jason guns it, still wearing the turtle mask. Chad hollers something in the distance, growing softer as we zip onto the road.

My pulse gallops under my skin, refusing to believe we got away. I rip my mask off with shaking hands. Ahmed, Sophie, Alexa, Abby, and I are all crammed into the back, halfway in one another's laps.

Heaving breaths fill the car. Tears streak down Sophie's face. Alexa bites her fingernails, her cheeks pallid. Ahmed covers his face with his hands. Jason's normally light brown skin goes white. Abby's staring out the window, her eyes wet. Kevin's whole body shakes in the front seat, his distinct groans the only noise cutting through the silence.

"We shouldn't have done this," Jason says finally.

"You didn't . . ." I trail off. He didn't have to come. But it's still my fault.

"I can never go back there," Abby whispers. "Fuck."

No one responds to her.

After an eternity, Jason pulls back into the Friendly's lot. He puts the car in Park and finally tugs off the mask. "Do you . . . do you think he saw my plates?"

No one answers. Everyone's fixated on the floor, or out the window. My fingers tap against my thighs.

"No," I say finally. "It was dark." I don't know if I believe it.

"He saw our faces," Ahmed says. "They can identify us."

Alexa snorts. "And say what? He tried to sell a bunch of kids some fake IDs, and they tricked him? Yeah, right." Her tone is snippy, even for her.

Everyone silently climbs out of Jason's crammed car, bumping and jabbing each other. I keep my head down.

"Did Chad tell you anything?" Alexa asks.

"No." Abby's voice is a monotone. "And I'm pretty sure he was telling the truth. They haven't seen Autumn since Thursday."

"You guys got something, right, Ivy?" Sophie asks. "You found a clue or something?"

"I found a seltzer can," I say, my voice thick with defeat. "Without the tab on."

The car is silent. "A seltzer can," Kevin responds.

"So . . . the answer is no," Alexa says. "You didn't find anything."

I close my eyes and swallow the hot lump in my throat. "No. It was all for nothing."

———

Jason is silent the entire ride back to my dad's house. He doesn't acknowledge the fact that I'm a sniffling, crying hot mess, and I'm grateful for it. Mailboxes and houses sail past, illuminated by streetlamps. It all blends together into one awful, dark soup.

Sweat cements my hair to my face, and the Michelangelo mask lies limp in my lap, a wrinkled, lifeless mess. I never want to look at it again.

My phone buzzes—Patrick. Of course. How was ice cream?

I blink back the curtain of tears clinging to my lashes and type, I don't wanna talk about it. I stare at the message, but I don't send it. It sits on my screen for five minutes before I delete it and stuff my phone back into my purse.

We pull up in front of my dad's house. Jase puts the car in Park, but I don't move to get out. The living room light flicks on. Dad's never given me a curfew, but he always waits up for me. I know he'll still ask where I was. I don't even know what to say.

Jase's fingers drum against the steering wheel. He doesn't look at me. I don't blame him. "Are you okay?"

It takes me aback. "*Me?* I almost got you arrested—or shot—and you're asking if *I'm* okay? I'm the worst friend in existence. You shouldn't even hang out with me."

"Oh, Ivy." He holds his hand inches from my leg, as if considering resting it on my knee, but he pulls it back at the last second.

I wipe my face on my sleeve, leaving a trail of snot and mascara on the fabric. I don't dare flip open the sun visor to see how attractive I look right now.

"At least we checked, right?" he says. "We looked and didn't find Autumn or anything to implicate anyone in that house. More proof she's not in trouble, just like the cops said. Maybe that eases your mind a little?"

I shrug. It doesn't.

"I'm sorry." I tug at a thread hanging off my jacket. "I'll go."

"It was an adventure."

"Yeah, if that's what you want to call it." I ram the back of my head into the seat. "I feel like an idiot."

A weird, almost tangible veil of silence covers the car. I grab the door handle. "Well, good night."

"You're not an idiot, Ivy." Jason keeps his eyes fixed straight ahead. "You're the best person I know."

All my emotions buzz around my brain like a hive of bees. I don't know if he's patronizing me or being sincere, but I can't deal with this right now.

I step out of the car. "See you on Monday."

AUTUMN

My legs dangle off the edge of the roof, hanging limply against the siding. I can't bear to be inside that wretched house right now. Ivy stormed into her bedroom and did the closest thing I've ever seen her do to a door slam, then Dad grumbled something about teenagers with PMS and went to bed. I have no clue what Kathy is doing, nor do I care.

I stretch back, letting the rough rooftop scrape against my palms, and inhale a deep breath of fresh air. Silver stars twinkle down at me, embedded in a blanket of black. When Ivy or I got afraid of the dark, Mom used to say that without the night, we couldn't see the stars.

I never would've been able to sit on the roof when I was alive. We don't have one of those cool houses with an upstairs porch where you can hop the rail to reach it. My regular body would need a long ladder to get up here. But this ghost body doesn't come with the same restrictions.

Nothing about it makes sense. Does everyone end up in this half-living, half-dead muddy middle? Or is it just me?

Why me?

Everyone knows they'll die someday. But now that I'm on the cusp between life and death, faced with my own mortality, I'm terrified.

When I was a kid, it was common knowledge in the Casterly

household that people who die go to either heaven or hell. It was just a fact. There was no death—just a sort of passing on. Moving from one place to the next. When our first dog, Sebastian, died, Mom said he would wait for us on the rainbow bridge. After Mom died, I pictured her and Sebastian reunited. I thought they'd come visit me, maybe fly in through my bedroom window at night to let me know they were okay and watching over me. But they never came, and eventually I realized heaven and hell were just stories they tell kids to make us behave. If there were a God, he wouldn't have let all this shit happen to me. He wouldn't have taken my mom. He wouldn't have left me dying alone.

But now that I'm in this invisible, ghostly form, I don't know what's real anymore. Why am I here? Why aren't I stuck in my body, waiting for the end to come?

They say when you're dying, your life flashes before your eyes. But right now, on the edge of life and death, all the things I'll never get to do again pass through my mind instead. I'll never get chocolate seashells from Granite State Candy Shoppe, or a chocolate turkey on Thanksgiving. I'll never again sip a cappuccino at True Brew, listening to the musician strumming his guitar. I'll never set foot in that crappy mall again—and I wouldn't have predicted that fact would make me as sad as it does. I used to complain about Concord constantly. But now, more than anything, I wish I had more time here. I wish I had more *time*.

I wonder what I'd be doing right now if I wasn't stuck in this weird half life.

On Tuesday, Becca Truman asked what I was up to this weekend. She was throwing a fund-raiser at Uno's tonight for the animal shelter that got robbed last month; 15 percent of every dinner bill will be donated to them. I told her I didn't know. Also, Becca's a weirdo and I didn't want people to see me talking to her. I kind of blew her off.

But I was planning to be there. I even had an attack strategy: I'd pretend I *really* wanted mozzarella sticks so no one could say I was helping Becca.

Looking back, I don't know why I cared so much what other people thought. Everyone always tries to show off how little they care what people think, but it's bullshit. Of course everyone cares.

I wish I'd told Becca I'd go. I wish I hadn't flipped her off in the middle of the hallway and told her to stop bothering me. I wish I could be there right now, eating mozzarella sticks until all the dogs have enough food to last forever.

Something twinges in my chest. Pins and needles shoot through my body, like every inch of skin is going to sleep. My hands fade to translucent right before my eyes, showing the tree leaves rattling in the wind behind them. But as quickly as the color evaporated, it charges back into my skin, and I'm solid again.

I press the heels of my palms into my eyes.

"Why, why, why?" I raise my voice. "Why am I here?"

The night sky doesn't answer me.

"What do you want from me?" I sniffle, wiping my eyes on my sleeve. I'm still here for a reason. Ivy can sort of hear me for a reason.

This isn't over. I still have time.

I want to be in Ivy's room, so when I open my eyes, I'm standing right by her bed.

Ivy slouches against her headboard, her yellow comforter wrapped around her like a cocoon. Her open laptop sits on her legs, casting a blue glow around the otherwise dark room. Even by the light of her screen, I can see her red-rimmed, puffy eyes.

"Okay, Ivy." I crack my knuckles. "We need a plan."

I take a seat on her bed, and it's surreal when the mattress doesn't indent or squeak under my butt. Ivy's eyelids droop heavily, her finger lazily scrolling down her touchpad.

There has to be a clue I'm not seeing. I think through everyone I've ever seen at Liam's house, anyone he could've recruited to do his dirty work. Anyone I've wronged who has an abandoned barn or warehouse or garage. All the people I've threatened for cash.

The people I hang with are shady, but I guess I never thought I'd end up on the wrong side of it.

The weird thing about being a victim is, no one expects it to be them. Victims are always someone else, someone tragically naïve who foolishly trusts the wrong person. I'd *never* make bad decisions like that. I was always careful. And yet, it wasn't enough. A wave of vulnerability washes over me, and there's nothing I can do about it. It's all too familiar.

My insides felt like a bowl of snakes, writhing and wriggling, threatening to burst out of my skin. I couldn't take it anymore. None of my friends were speaking to me. I had to talk to someone.

I slipped into Coach Bratten's office after soccer practice. She'd ridden our asses in scrimmage for the past week, but I liked her. I trusted her.

"Can I talk to you?" My sweaty brown hair stuck to my forehead. I'd played like shit during practice, and I was kind of worried Coach would call it out.

"Of course. You okay, Autumn? Come in, sit down."

I took a seat across the desk, my hands wringing in my lap. I didn't know how to say it. I didn't even know what exactly I wanted to say. "I feel kind of . . . weird. About something that happened last weekend."

She watched me, concern written all over her face.

"I went to a party. With my stepbrother."

I waited for the inevitable gushing, the usual Oh, you're Chris Pike's stepsister! He's so great! *But Coach Bratten didn't speak. She just listened.*

I rubbed my upper arm. "I got drunk. Really drunk. And then we got home and . . . it just kind of happened."

I pull myself out of my memories.

"All right, Ivy." I snap my fingers. "C'mon."

I lean closer to see what she's looking at. A minimized YouTube video is open on her screen, showing a recording of some guy playing a video game. His avatar prowls across the window holding a scythe. A CGI zombie pops out from the side of a building. The avatar chops it down to a sound effect I can only describe as slicing into a melon. Green blood spatters everywhere.

Ivy grabs her phone off the side table. She opens a text with Patrick and types out, hey, I'm really sorry I didn't get back to you earlier, I had a crappy night. Wanna hang out tomorrow? She watches it for a good thirty seconds before deleting it and retyping, hey, sorry, I had the worst night, ugh with a frowny emoji.

When she deletes that one unsent, too, I full-on groan. "Can you send something already so we can figure out a plan?"

Finally, she types out, Ice cream was good! and hits Send.

"What, you can't tell him you had a shitty night?" I snap. "You're allowed to be upset, you know."

An eerie sense of déjà vu falls over me. *You're allowed to be upset, Autumn.* I hear the words in my head, in my old soccer coach's voice.

Ivy opens Google in a new window and starts typing, *what's the punishment for breaking and entering in New Hampshire?* I huff. She's too distracted.

Then she deletes it and types, *What is the sentence for being an accomplice to breaking and entering in New Hampshire?*

My chest tightens. Ivy is the only person I know who'd be facing serious trouble and worry about her friends instead of herself.

Maybe I don't know enough good people.

When prison sentences and felonies show up in the search results, she slams the screen closed, drowning the room in darkness. She shoves the laptop to the side. Something between fear and defeat clouds her features.

Ivy can't get scared and stop looking for me. I need her. I need a way to convince her.

"Okay, they're not going to turn you in. You do not have to worry."

She lies awake, staring at the ceiling. It's weird being here, watching. Like I'm creeping on her through the window. Seeing all those little bursts of emotion she doesn't think anyone witnessed.

I remember when Ivy called the police, she didn't know how to answer any of their questions. I'm learning all about Ivy, but she doesn't know anything about me. I've spent years building a steel cage around my heart, not letting anyone inside. Not even my sister.

"I drive to Sewall's Falls, park my car by the river, recline the driver's seat, and sleep." I twiddle my fingers, not daring to catch her eye even though she can't see me. "Sometimes I go to the big parking garage downtown and drive to the top floor. I sit on the roof of my car and look out at the city—I mean, if you can call it a city." Everyone does, and I've never understood it. "I don't know. I guess it's kind of comforting." I fidget. "Now you know. That's where I go when I run away. It's probably not what you're expecting."

Ivy doesn't react.

It strikes me that I've spoken to my sister more today than in the past three years combined. Weird that dying would be the catalyst to make us talk. Maybe it doesn't count because she can't actually hear me.

I swallow hard. "I'm really scared, Ivy."

She rolls to the fetal position on her right, but her open eyes still twinkle from the moonlight pouring through the window.

I lean back, resting my head against the wall. "Remember the last time we went trick-or-treating? I was a leopard, and you were . . . oh my God, wasn't that the year you went as a bar of soap? You had those giant silver balloons taped all over you, the bubbles." She won best costume at our church Halloween party that year, and used her prize—a gift card to Target—to get me the Advent calendar I'd wanted, with plastic jungle animals inside every box. "It was really cool of you to get me that calendar. I still have all the animals. I should get them out and line them up on my dresser, like I did at our old house." The moment I say it, I mentally take it back. I don't want those in my room.

For some reason, that memory evokes something, and I remember the exact moment we last talked—*really* talked. It was three years ago.

I was sitting in the kitchen, working on my bio homework and tapping my pencil against the table. I couldn't focus. I kept replaying the party, the music, the taste of vomit in my throat.

It wasn't a big deal. It was just sex.

I shouldn't have told Coach Bratten. She probably thought I was overreacting—I was overreacting.

My eyes kept darting to the clock, because I wanted to be in my room with the door closed by five thirty, fifteen minutes after football practice ended. I twisted my short hair around my fingers, still adjusting to the length. My knee bounced against my hand.

Ivy wandered into the room. She was still just a seventh-grader, sheltered by the buffer of middle school. There was no way she would know . . . would she? I'd reported the Instagram post and it was taken down about two hours after it went up. Maybe my sister had heard about it. The thought froze me to my seat, like my feet had grown roots into the floor beneath me.

Before I could open my mouth, the words flew out of hers.

"Leah Breyers's sister is in your grade. She said you hooked up with Chris at that party." Her mouth contorted into disgust. "Is that true?"

Hearing it straight from my sister's mouth was like getting smacked. That meant it was flying through the Concord grapevine faster than the time Jenn Butler got her period onstage during the school's production of Oklahoma!

I don't know what got into me, but before I could stop myself, I sprang off the chair and got right up in her face.

"You don't know anything. Why don't you mind your fucking business?"

Her eyes grew wide. "I was just asking."

"Well, I wish you'd leave me alone. I wish you weren't here. In fact, I wish you weren't even my sister."

Even now, three years later, I can still feel the shock waves passing through our tiny kitchen. After that, I always imagined her looking at me and seeing only that rumor. I hated how everyone coddled her but acted like I was a walking train wreck who couldn't keep my shit together. I hated it. I hated *her*.

"I shouldn't have said that to you." I fix my eyes on the dark floor. "About wishing you weren't my sister." I reach out to grab her hand, but end up retracting it at the last minute. "I'm glad you're my sister."

I look over to see if she's watching me, but Ivy's already fast asleep.

SUNDAY

Ivy

I've never been drunk, but I'm pretty sure this is what a hangover feels like. When morning sunlight seeps through my blinds, a headache is already pounding behind my forehead. I wince, pulling the covers back over my face.

I was half hoping I'd wake up and last night would be a bad dream, but I'm not that lucky.

My eyes burn like I rubbed sand in them. Ugh. I blink at my digital clock on the desk. It takes me a second to register the clear numbers staring back at me, broadcasting 10:25.

Oh shit. I slept in my contacts.

That jars me awake. I roll out of bed, stumbling into the desk, which impales me right in the thigh. This is not my finest moment.

I rip open the door and plow into Autumn's room, my heart in my throat.

The single flame of hope inside me is extinguished like a snuffed candle. Her empty bed looks almost gloomier today, the sheets exactly as I left them yesterday.

She's not here.

After practically scraping the lenses out of my eyes, squirting half a bottle of eye drops into them, and putting on my glasses, it's time to face the inevitable. I grab my phone, mentally preparing myself. For all I know, they've already texted me with restraining orders. Cringing, I unlock the screen. Seventeen texts.

Alexa: Good morning sunshine, you okay?
Alexa: That was some awesome window-diving last night, I'm so proud.

Sophie: IVY! My love. How are you feeling?
Sophie: I'm sooo tired. Need caffeine. Dunkin' later?

Ahmed: Just checking in to make sure you got some sleep! Next time I call one of the masks.

Kevin: I thought we actually did a pretty good job acting last night—they didn't suspect a thing until the very end!

Jason: Gonna spam you with GIFs until you're not frowny anymore.

I find GIFs of otters eating, people tripping, and Darth Vader yelling. He totally knows me, because he was right; it does make me smile.

I open a new window and add the entire Nerd Herd to a group chat.

Hey guys. I just wanted to say I love you and owe you a ton. No sign of Autumn yet, but hoping she'll show up today. Thanks for being awesome. I'm really sorry. Glad you don't hate me. xx

I leave my phone on my side table next to Autumn's and head downstairs in my pajamas. Dad's standing over the kitchen table, his phone pressed to his ear.

"All right. Thanks. I appreciate it." He hangs up.

My ears perk. "Was it Autumn?"

"No." He collapses into the chair. "That was the police."

I jolt.

"I called to see if they had any updates. They don't."

I let out a heavy breath. Okay, I shouldn't be relieved to hear that, but I am glad they weren't calling to say I'm being thrown in jail or that something unspeakable happened to Autumn. "Have they been trying, at least?"

He props his elbows on the table and rests his head in his hands. "I don't know."

Two things I inherited from my dad: his metabolism, and his allergy to confrontation. Really hoping that doesn't mean I'm also doomed to get a giant bald spot.

I open the fridge and pull out a strawberry yogurt. "Well, are they gonna look for her? Call them back. Let's bug them."

"They think she doesn't want to be found."

"She's only eighteen, Dad. She's your *kid*." I peel off the lid and shove a spoonful into my mouth. "They're treating her like a criminal."

Dad doesn't respond, but I can almost hear the unspoken *because she acts like one.*

I finish my breakfast and dump my spoon in the sink. "Can we track her somehow? Does she have a credit card or an account or something?"

Dad's shoulders hunch. He takes a swig of his coffee and sets the mug back down, harder than necessary. "She has a bank card, and I checked it already. Hasn't been used in two weeks. I've also been tracking that emergency Uber account I set up for you girls, and nothing."

"Are you going to—"

The back door swings open, cutting me off. Kathy bustles into the kitchen with a stack of pink paper. "I hung these up all over town." She holds up the top sheet. Autumn's senior portrait smirks back at me in black and pink.

MISSING: AUTUMN NATASHA CASTERLY
AGE: 18
LAST SEEN AT CONCORD HIGH SCHOOL,
FRIDAY, SEPTEMBER 20TH
PLEASE CONTACT KATHERINE OR STEVE CASTERLY.

Our phone number and address are typed below. I'm not sure what would piss off Autumn most: the fact that our stepmom hung her picture on telephone poles like she's a lost cat, the fact that it's printed in Comic Sans on pink paper, or the fact that Kathy listed herself as Autumn's contact.

"Hung them everywhere," Kathy says proudly. "Put some up at Panera, hung them on the bulletin board at Shaw's, and tacked about fifty of these suckers all over the high school."

Yeah. Autumn's going to be pissed.

Dad stands up and heads for the fridge.

"What do you think, Steve?" Kathy waves one of the flyers like a flag. "Got two hundred more waiting in my car."

"I think she's going to be upset."

"And?" Kathy holds up her hand, waiting for an answer. "What, you're afraid she'll be *mad* at you? For caring about her?"

"That's how Autumn works. She wants us to stay out of it."

"You're being awfully blasé. Your daughter is missing."

Dad closes his eyes. "I know."

"You don't seem very concerned. Maybe you should do something productive to find her instead of moping at the table."

"You think I'm not concerned?" Dad raises his voice, and it's the first time I've ever heard him yell at Kathy. "Dammit, Katherine, she's my daughter."

I tug at my sweatshirt hem. Dad and Kathy never fight. I wish they'd wait until I'm out of the room.

"Well, maybe if you'd set some boundaries over the past three years, she wouldn't be like this!"

Dad's grip tightens around the mug handle, his knuckles bleached white. "Don't tell me how to raise my children."

"I can't even believe you right now." Kathy anchors a hand on her hip, crinkling the paper. "It's like Ivy and I are the only ones actually worried about her. Right, Ivy?"

I stare at the floor. She's right, but I'm not thrilled she dragged me into this.

Dad pushes to his feet. "We're not having this discussion right now." He brushes out of the room, leaving his empty mug behind.

I tuck my head into my sweatshirt hood. Sometimes when there's conflict, I pretend I'm in a turtle shell and no one can see me. Even without the Ninja Turtle mask, I'm pretty much always Michelangelo, only without the mad nunchuck skills.

Kathy rips open the fridge, muttering something that sounds like *unbelievable*.

I'm not sure what makes me do it, but I follow him. "Dad. Wait."

He pauses on the third step but doesn't look at me. His whole body deflates, like someone punctured him and let all the air out. "What is it, Ivy? I'm already late for work."

Anger wells up inside me. It's *always* work. You know how people are always worried their parents have a favorite kid, and it's not them? My dad does have a favorite child: his auto shop. "Every time anything happens, you just disappear. Poof." I throw my hands up.

"Someone has to pay for this house, Ivy. I know you don't get that. Someday, when you have a job, you'll—"

"Are you kidding me right now?" I'm shocked at the words flying out of my mouth, but I can't stop myself. "Don't tell me someday I'll understand. I understand perfectly: Autumn's missing, and you're going to work."

"She knows I'm here if she needs me."

"She's *gone*. She needs you to *find* her."

"I don't know how to raise two girls by myself. I don't know what I'm supposed to do when this happens. What do you do when your own daughter hates you?"

"Dad—"

He tilts his head back and closes his eyes. "I'm sorry. I didn't mean to yell."

I start to follow him but end up standing and watching as he takes the remaining stairs. His bedroom door thuds shut.

Maybe Dad's given up on finding Autumn, but I haven't.

Autumn

The smell of moldy cedar envelops me. I already know, before I open my eyes, that I'm back in my broken body.

A groan escapes me, and I feel it everywhere; knives stab into my lungs, pokers press against my sides, and my dry mouth sears. Exhaustion and a dull ache pin me to the cold floor.

My eyelids crack open and I startle. Someone is crouching over me. A black ski mask covers his face, and a pair of yellow goggles hides his eyes. He tugs the gag out of my mouth.

"Who are you?" I rasp, but it comes out a jumbled mess that leaves my throat searing and raw.

I can't see his eyes, but I can tell they're fixed on me. It sends a shudder rippling through to my core. The man shoves the gag back into my mouth.

He stands and brushes dirt off his jeans; a few flecks sprinkle onto my face. My captor pushes open the wooden door, and the sliver of sun grows into a wedge that burns my retinas. I flinch away from the light. The door slams shut behind him, echoing in the small space and drowning me in darkness. When my eyes adjust, I squint at the strips of light shining through the slats in the walls. They stretch up my body like prison bars.

I try to prop myself up, but my elbow buckles and sends another wave of pain shooting through me. With a metallic grumble, the familiar chain loops back through the door and the padlock clicks shut, sealing me inside.

My eyes frantically scramble to soak up everything they can. A dusty blue tarp covers something that looks like a lawn mower. Rusty tools dangle from hooks in the walls. Old shelves stack high over my head, their contents silhouetted in the dark room. None of this helps me. I could be anywhere.

Footsteps patter outside.

"She's awake." The man's voice seeps through the wood. I strain for a hint of recognition, but I've got nothing. He's a stranger.

"What do you mean?" Another voice—deeper, scratchier. I don't recognize this guy, either. "She wasn't supposed to wake up."

My ears twitch, straining to hear everything.

"We tied her up good. I don't think she can walk."

"It doesn't matter," says the second voice. "We've got to get rid of her."

Their voices fade, and I'm alone again.

I gasp for air like a fish out of water. I have to get out of here. I have to tell Ivy. Now.

IVY

The entire time I'm in the shower, something's pulling at me. It's like there's an invisible fishhook in the back of my head, latching on and prying and begging me to keep looking.

I lather coconut shampoo through my hair, rehashing every moment with Autumn over the past few weeks. She must've said something, let something slip.

I keep coming back to Hailey Waters and the text to her on Autumn's phone. Autumn asked about her on Thursday afternoon. It was the first time she'd said anything to me in a month. Maybe I'm grasping at straws, but I can work with this.

I'm so eager, I almost slip and face-plant over the tub ledge getting out of the shower. Hot steam coats the mirror, but goose bumps still prickle down my skin. Like someone's watching me. It's unsettling. I wrap my hair in a towel, throw on some clothes, and grab Autumn's phone. I read that same text again, the one that Autumn sent Hailey on Thursday night.

Autumn: How's Owen?

I swear I've never heard of any Owen before. Granted, other than band kids and the Nerd Herd, my circle is pretty small. Owen could be someone who doesn't even go to Concord, but if Hailey and Autumn both know him, chances are he does.

I pull out last year's yearbook and start thumbing through names.

It isn't until I get to the juniors that I find the only Owen in our school: Owen Price. He's cute—he's got curly brown hair and dimples, and wore a Godzilla shirt that I want to steal in his school photo. If he was one or two grades younger, he'd be a new recruit for the Nerd Herd. I can tell just by looking at him. Whoever he is, he has something to do with Hailey—and Autumn.

I pull out my phone and scroll through my contacts, stopping on Hailey's name. But my thumb hesitates.

The thing about marching band is, there are over a hundred people in it, but we're all like one giant, nosy family who knows way too much about one another. For example, Luke Hawkins wears red boxers with little foxes on them. I know this because after the freezing-cold Exeter Christmas Parade last year, he shoved a couple of hand warmers into his pants and ran up to people asking them to feel his "hot ass." Then they got too hot, so he ripped his pants off, right there in the middle of the bus back to school. Likewise, Megan Plummer, who's in my grade, hooked up with Kyle Zhang, a senior, in the unisex music-wing bathroom after Tuesday night band camp practice in August. I didn't see it personally, but that stuff gets around. I guess all those hours packed into a sweaty bus together can do that.

So I already know Hailey won't want to tell me why Autumn was looking for her. She's had her heart set on getting into BU for forever, and she just applied early decision. Her boyfriend, Logan Kerch, applied there, too. Pretty sure they're going to get married. If Hailey's into drugs, she wouldn't want anyone to know.

I type, Hey, can we talk? in my text window with Hailey, but my thumb just hovers over Send. I rotate the phone in my hands for a good five minutes. No. This won't work. If she knows anything, she'd never send it over text.

I hop on my bike and head downtown to Red River Theater. Red

River is this awesome artsy theater where they show foreign films and indie movies and serve Polar Seltzer and fine chocolates. It's where all the indie kids and rich old people go. I hope Hailey's working today.

The September sun burns especially strong, and by the time I get to Main Street, a layer of sweat has plastered my hair to my head beneath my helmet. I lock my bike to the rack by the entrance and plow through the door.

The buttery smell of popcorn floats through the air, and movie posters from films I don't recognize line the hallway on either side of me. I stay close to the wall and pretend to be interested in the giant ad for a French movie now playing in Theater Two while inching toward the concessions desk.

This must be, like, field trip day at the local nursing home, because there are at least twenty old people in front of me in line. I can see the top of Hailey's reddish-brown ponytail at the front, peeking out beneath a lace headband. Only Hailey Waters could make a movie theater uniform look cute. Every few seconds, her bubbly voice tells customers to enjoy the show.

A twentysomething guy with a face full of acne leans against the counter. Probably hitting on Hailey—he should know better, because she's practically got Logan Kerch's name tattooed on her forehead. He better leave by the time I get up there; I don't need an audience for this.

My hands get clammy around my phone. I know I'm supposed to be embracing my inner Neville Longbottom, but honestly, I feel like I'm going to vomit before I get the chance to try. What do I even say to her? *Hey, are you responsible for kidnapping my sister?*

The cute old guy in front of me keeps his fingers laced with his wife's, and my heart practically melts. I love older couples. They're goals, for sure.

Hailey smiles at the couple, sending them down the hall to Theater Two with the rest of their friends, leaving us and the random guy alone in the lobby. "Can I help whoever's—" Her eyes land on me and a veil of panic flits across her face. It's super weird, considering she greets me with a giant smile literally 100 percent of the time. Not gonna lie, her sudden aversion to me kind of sucks. "Ivy. Hi." She blinks. "This is my brother, Dave."

"Hi."

"Sup." He nods, pulling out his phone.

I close my eyes and take a deep breath, wondering how the hell I'm going to word this. I wish Dave would go somewhere else. Why is he even here? I have to act natural. Play it cool.

"I have a really awkward question about my sister, Autumn," I blurt out instead.

The moment I say it, I realize I'm not playing it cool at all. Seriously. Most people can communicate like human beings, but I always manage to make everything weird.

She opens her mouth, then closes it. "I'd rather not talk about it."

Holy shit. I was definitely not expecting that response. It's Hailey. My band friend Hailey, the designated mother of the low-brass line. "You've gotta tell me what's going on. Please. I'm really worried."

"I said I don't wanna talk about it." All the color drains from her face. "If you don't leave, I'll get my manager."

"Hailey—"

"I mean it, Ivy. Leave me alone."

Dave lowers his phone, not hiding his interest in the conversation.

"Come on—"

"I said leave me alone!"

I can't believe it. She's involved. "Shit," I whisper. "Oh my God. You did it. I can't believe it."

"Can you wait outside?" Hailey snaps at Dave. "My shift's done in fifteen. I'll meet you by the car." Her brother begrudgingly skulks away, clearly not wanting to miss the gossip. The moment he's gone, Hailey holds her fist to her mouth and her face scrunches. "Yes, okay?" Her voice squeaks out like a mouse's. "Please don't tell anyone. Especially Logan."

"Don't *tell* anyone?" Rage burns hot and sudden inside me. "I'm going to tell *everyone*!"

"Please, Ivy." Her voice cracks. "I thought you were my friend."

"I thought you were a normal person, and you hurt my sister!" I fumble with my iPhone. "I'm calling the cops right now."

Hailey snaps out of it. "What are you talking about?"

"What are *you* talking about?"

"Owen." Her brow creases. "Owen Price. Isn't that why you're here?"

"Wait, what?"

"Autumn. She texted me out of the blue the other day to mess with me, and I think it's pretty shitty that she sent you here to threaten me. What do you want? I don't have any money."

What the actual hell? "I'm here because Autumn's missing."

Hailey gasps. "What?"

"That's . . . that's not what you're confessing to?"

Her jaw drops. "Oh my God, no! What? You thought I . . . I was . . . oh my God. No! Autumn's missing? Where do you think she is?"

"I don't know. I've been looking for her all weekend."

"Oh God, I'm so sorry, Ivy. I had no idea." She leans against the counter. "I swear, if I hear anything, I'll tell you right away. Did you call the police?"

"Yeah. They didn't do anything." My words are thick with defeat. I don't know if I'm relieved Hailey isn't involved, or dejected by the dead end. "Wait, what does Owen have to do with anything?"

"Nothing." She picks at her fingernail. "Don't worry about it."

I give her a serious eye-roll. "Okay, you can't just leave it like that. You have to tell me."

Hailey clamps her lips together, and for half a second I think she's going to burst into tears. But then the truth comes spilling out. "It only happened once, and I'm never going to do it again. Logan and I are soul mates. I don't even know how Autumn found out, but she's holding it over my head."

How did Autumn find out? By knowing everything about everyone—Autumn's worse than the band. But wait a second . . .

"Holy shit—you *cheated* on Logan Kerch?"

She covers her face with her hands. "My parents are friends with Owen's parents and we all went on this camping trip in August and we got a little tipsy after our parents went to sleep and he was really hot and I fucked up. I hate it. Logan's saving himself for marriage, and he'd dump me immediately if he found out. Please, Ivy. *Please* don't tell him."

I can't even believe it. "Why don't you just end it with Logan if you want to be with Owen?"

"I don't *want* to be with Owen. It was a mistake."

Well, shit. So much for their perfect relationship. "I won't tell."

I guess that explains Autumn's cryptic text to Hailey, although I don't get why my sister cares who Hailey's sleeping with.

A lady comes in to ask about a theater event, so I step to the side to let Hailey do her job. My brain won't stop buzzing. Liam's house gave us nothing, Hailey's got nothing, and I've got nowhere else to look.

The lady pockets the manager's phone number, which Hailey'd scrawled out on a Post-it for her. "Thanks so much for this. I'll be in touch."

"Have a great day!" Hailey grins widely until the woman disappears out the door, then her smile fades. She grabs a Twizzler from a pack of movie candy and takes a bite. "Seriously, though, I feel terrible about Autumn. Let me know if there's anything I can do. Jeez, missing person is . . . yikes."

I fidget my hands. It's obvious that she's rushing to change the subject, but it works. I'm still not used to *missing person* referring to anyone in my family. It's surreal.

This whole thing still feels strange to me. I can't see Autumn even giving Hailey Waters the time of day. Autumn's known for threatening and blackmailing people, but never without cause. "Actually, I do have a question. The day before she disappeared, my sister asked about you. Any idea why?"

Hailey bites her lip. "Well, uh. For starters, I accidentally, uh . . . Don't hate me, okay?"

I watch her expectantly. "Okay . . ."

"I told Mr. Browne she was dealing."

She might as well have confessed to snitching on Whitey Bulger. I clap my hand over my mouth. I'm not sure whose safety I'm more afraid for right now—Autumn's or Hailey's. "You ratted her out?"

"*I know,* I know." Hailey rubs her forehead.

"Why would you do that? You know she's not going to forget about it."

Hailey props her elbows on the counter and rests her forehead in her hands. "I don't know. Remember Kasey Muller?"

I think for a second. Wasn't that the girl who moved to Maine? "Vaguely."

"She was my best friend. Autumn started bullying her and it got really bad. Her family moved away in July and she, like, cut ties with everyone in Concord, including me. It sucked, you know?"

She scrubs her hands down her face. "I was pissed at Autumn, and having a bad day, so I did it. I didn't know the police would search her locker. I'm sorry. Okay?"

My sister causes fallout everywhere she goes. "It's okay."

"I felt like shit afterward." She shakes her head. "I've never even talked to Autumn before. I wouldn't have known about the drugs if my friend Kaitlyn didn't buy from her."

I grind my shoe into the carpet, doing my best to look innocent. "Oh yeah? Kaitlyn who?"

"Kaitlyn Kennedy—she's in my grade. Apparently Kaitlyn had a run-in with Autumn on Thursday, right after the police ransacked her locker. I wouldn't have told if I'd known the cops would find out, and now everything's a mess and Autumn hates me and she's messing with me about O—" Blush creeps across her face and she looks down. "About Owen."

Something happened between Autumn and this Kaitlyn person the day before she vanished. Okay, I can work with this. Right now, I need a lead, and Hailey might've accidentally provided it. "Any ideas where I can find Kaitlyn?"

"Uhhh . . . I'm not sure. She plays varsity field hockey. I think they're having a cookout tonight?" I can see in her wide grin that she's milking this Kaitlyn thing for all it's worth to placate me so I don't spill her dirty little Owen secret. I don't care. I'll take it.

"Where?"

"No idea. Someone's house."

Dave saunters back into the lobby, and I'm pretty sure he was hiding somewhere eavesdropping on the whole thing. "Shit, you're Autumn Casterly's sister?" He leans back against the counter and takes one of Hailey's Twizzlers.

I tense. "Yeah. Why?"

Hailey scoffs. "Were you listening to our conversation?"

"I remember her. She was a freshman when I was a senior." He blows out an exaggerated gust of air. "She was . . . wow. Something. Chris was a lucky guy."

I don't even try to suppress my groan. Seriously?

Hailey slaps her brother's arm. "Don't be gross."

It's so weird to me that the whole school knew Autumn when she was just a freshman. Hardly anyone knows me, and I'm a *sophomore*. Guess that's what happens when you're the school pill-pusher. How the hell am I supposed to find out who knows something about her disappearance when literally everybody knows Autumn? Where am I even supposed to start?

"I was just saying I knew her. Stop freaking out."

"Can you please not stalk my friends? I'm gonna tell Mom."

"I'm not stalking anybody." Dave rolls his eyes. "I told Mom I didn't wanna shuttle you around all week."

Hailey slips him a middle finger and a fake smile, then turns to me. "My darling brother here borrowed our spare car—the one *I* usually use—while his was in the shop. He backed it into a parking meter and destroyed the bumper." I'm trying to process the idea of having a *spare* car. Like it's an extra pencil or jacket or something that's just lying around. "So Mom said he has to drive me places until it comes out of the shop."

"Oh." I need to leave. I have no idea where that field hockey party is, and it's already getting late.

Dave rolls his eyes. "It's like I had nothing better to do today."

"Oh please, you never have plans. Whatever." Hailey shrugs. "I'm glad you're driving me. I have a dentist appointment in Manchester on Monday after school and I *hate* walking on that sketchy side street alone. Gross older guys always catcall me.

One time, one of them followed me back to my car." She shudders.

"Ugh," I say. "Men are so gross."

Dave snorts. "Actually, not *all* men do that. You shouldn't generalize."

I can't help it; I burst out a laugh. Coupling this with the fact that he's so pasty it looks like he hasn't left his parents' basement in a month, it's like he's a walking, talking internet troll.

"What the hell?" Hailey crosses her arms. "I just told you some pig stalked me to my car, and your response isn't *Wow, Hailey, I'm glad you're safe*, or, *Wow, Hailey, I'm sorry that happened to you*." She deepens her voice in a near spot-on impression of her brother. "Or even, *Hmm, that's a real problem, maybe guys should stop doing that*. Nope, your response was *Not. All. Men*."

"Yeah, seriously, did you, like, fall out of Reddit?"

Dave rolls his eyes. "I was just saying."

I check the time on my phone. "Okay. I've got to run."

"See you tomorrow." Hailey waves, very obviously wanting to get rid of me.

"Hey, what's Autumn doing these days?" Dave asks. "I haven't seen her since I graduated, but I've heard . . . things."

"Um." How do I say that I have no idea? That I barely know my own sister anymore, and now she's gone? "She's fine. She's a senior." I start to leave, but hesitate. Autumn started cutting class and stuff in eighth grade. But freshman year really messed her up. She changed. Cut off all her hair. Stopped speaking to me. Suddenly I'm overcome with curiosity. "What was Autumn like when you were in high school?"

Dave thinks for a minute. "Um. I'm not sure. I didn't know her very well."

"Oh."

"I mean, I saw the Instagram photo, obviously."

My forehead creases. "Instagram photo?"

"Yeah, there was some party where she got drunk and passed out and they got a picture. It went around the whole school. I saw her in the principal's office with Chris Pike and a bunch of other adults the week after. Probably had something to do with it."

What the hell? She was in the principal's office with Chris? I mean, Autumn gets in trouble all the time, but not Christopher "wow, your stepbrother's really going places" Pike. That seems so off.

"Okay. Thanks. I gotta run." I turn and race back down the theater hall. "See you in band," I call over my shoulder.

Hailey shoots me another wave before I'm out the door. Dave doesn't say goodbye, but that's fine. I have a mission.

Step one: crash the field hockey party. Step two: find Kaitlyn Kennedy and see what she knows. Step three: learn about this alleged Instagram photo.

I didn't want to involve my friends in this mess again, but I don't have any other choice. The moment I'm back in the sun with my bike, I shoot off a quick text to the group chat:

Me: Hey, Kevin—isn't one of your sisters on the field hockey team?

I drum my fingers against the handlebars, waiting for the little dots to turn into a response.

Kevin: Yeah, Nicole. Why?

Me: Is she going to the team barbecue tonight?

Alexa: Wow, way to be creepy, Ivy.

Kevin sends the blushing emoji. How'd you know about that? Here goes nothing.

Me: I want to crash it and I don't know where it is.

There's a long pause. I can practically see all my friends staring at the message and wondering who's stolen my phone.

Of course, Jason is the first one to break the silence.

Jason: Jeez—first a home invasion, now party crashing, who are you and what have you done with Ivy? with a wink face at the end.

Kevin: . . . Why?

Me: There's a girl on the team named Kaitlyn who may know something about Autumn.

Ahmed: Kaitlyn Kennedy? She sat next to me in German last year.

Me: Yeah. I need to talk to her.

Me: None of you have to come, I just want to know where it is. I won't tell anyone you told me.

I hesitate before hitting Send. I'm not going to lie, the thought of crashing a party by myself has already made my palms sweaty. But I can't ask anyone to come, not after yesterday.

The second I send it, a text from Patrick pops up: Hey! I'm at my dad's house, and super bored. Wanna hang out?

My heart jumps. This kid has only been back in my life for four days, but my stomach still flutters every time his name flashes across my screen. Okay, hanging out alone, that could definitely be a date.

A pit drops in my chest. I have to say no. Autumn has to be my first priority right now. So why can't I make my fingers type the damn message?

Kevin: Just checked the flyer the coach sent out to everyone. Here:

He sends a picture of the invite with the time, place, and RSVP instructions. It's at a senior's house—someone named Laura Morton. Everyone's supposed to bring something, but there's no sign-up form. I know how this works. They'll end up with eight thousand brownie platters and bottles of knock-off Coke from the dollar store but no plates or napkins.

Me: You're a lifesaver. Thanks!

Kevin: NP. I guess all the parents are going, too. Nicole said I could come, so if you wanna tag along, that's cool. Less sketchy that way.

I will never *not* owe these people everything in the world.

Me: That would be amazing. So I don't look like a creep crashing a party by myself.

Jason: You'll still look like a creep. Can I come?

Me: Only if you drive.

Jason: Never mind.

Jason: JK obviously I will drive you, freeloader.

Sophie: I wanna go! My parents say I have to stay home for dinner, ugh

Alexa: Yeah, I have this massive English paper I've been putting off . . . if you really need me there I'll go but I should probably work on it . . .

Ahmed: I thought I was the only one who put that paper off until today

Alexa: Don't challenge me in the procrastination Olympics, Bashir. I will win 100% of the time.

Jason: Ivy, when should I pick you up?

I think for a second, then type back: Actually, are you free now? I'm downtown with my bike. I can meet you at your place. And I need to make a stop before the party.

It's probably better if I don't tell him where we're stopping.

I text Patrick back: Hey! You wanna go to a party tonight?

Ivy

The thing about Jason's family is, sometimes I wish they were my family. I'm not sure how long I can get away with making excuses to come over and hang out with them, but Jason hasn't said anything about it.

His mom runs over and hugs me the second I walk in the door. "So good to see you, dear! Are you hungry? You look famished." She pats my cheek. "I can heat something up for you."

"I already ate, but thank you."

"Is that Ivy?" Jason's dad pops his head around the corner. He's a skinny white guy who towers over his five-foot-one Filipino wife. "How's it going? Long time no see."

"Yeah, what's it been, like, six whole days at this point?" I say.

Jason's mom takes a seat at the kitchen table, gesturing for me to sit opposite her. "I want to hear all about your weekend."

"You want some tea or anything?" His dad wraps his arm around his wife's shoulders. "Cookies?"

Coming to Jason's house always leaves a bittersweet aftertaste. His parents are one of those couples who are always smiling at each other, always laughing. Portraits of Jason, his little brother, and their parents on various vacations are tacked up all over their massive house. I make fun of the ones where Jase still had those beaver buckteeth. But sometimes it feels like I'm looking through a window into someone's perfect home; I can see it, feel it, *almost* experience it myself, but it's not mine.

"I'm good, thanks. What've you guys been up to?"

"I've been thinking of getting this for Jase, what do you think?" She slides a catalog across the table, the page bent at the corner. A fancy, heavy-duty saxophone case that looks like it could survive a nuclear blast fills the page, under the word *Indestructible*. "He throws his sax around constantly. At least this way it won't get damaged."

"Jeez. I need one of these for my trumpet."

Jason's dad waves his hand dismissively through the air. "We'll order two. I'm sure they make a trumpet one."

My face gets hot. "Oh, you don't have to." They'd never say it, but the implication is there—*We'll buy you one because we know you could never afford it.*

"Eh, it can be your payment for hanging out with this kid." He loops his arm around Jason's shoulders as he lumbers into the room.

"Dad, really?" Jason knocks his dad's arm off. "Leave Ivy alone."

I scoff. "Just because your parents are cooler than you doesn't mean you need to be so jealous."

"*Cooler* isn't the right word."

"You didn't know we pay her to hang out with you?" Jason's dad winks at me.

"Not nearly enough," I say.

"What is this, open season?"

"Are you going to be home for dinner?" his mom asks. "You're welcome to stay for dinner, Ivy. Nothing fancy, just going to pop some leftovers into the oven."

"We're crashing this cookout for the girls' field hockey team," Jase says. "Free food."

Jeez, way to be a little too honest about it. I rib him in the side. "Not crashing. Kevin's sister Nicole is on the team."

"Sounds fun." His mom hugs Jason and kisses his cheek, then mine. "Call if you need anything."

Jason grumbles at his mom's hugs, but I always hold on to her a little longer than necessary. "Will do."

"Love you both."

"Ugh, Mom. Don't be weird."

Sometimes I feel defensive when people are snarky to their moms. Like, you *have* a mom to *be* snarky with; not all of us do. "It's all right. I love your parents."

"See, *some people* don't think we're weird." His mom grins at me, which makes Jason groan.

"Don't get arrested," his dad says. "I don't want to have to bail you out tonight. *Shark Tank* is on." It's always a running joke here, but the comment hits a little too close to home today.

Jason rolls his eyes and tugs my hand. "C'mon, before they rope you into staying."

"Not that," his dad calls sarcastically after us. "Anything but that."

There's a difference between a house and a home. Jason's place is a *home*, full of love and warmth. Home is where my mom is, where Autumn and I shoot hoops in the driveway, where everyone loves everyone else. Now the place I live is just a structure made of wood and plaster with no beating heart inside.

We leave and I climb into Jason's car. He starts the ignition and wiggles his brows at me. "Okay, where are we going first?"

"Gotta head toward 89."

"The boonies?" His eyebrows shoot up. "What're we doing there?"

"Picking up Patrick."

"Oh. Cool."

I ignore the fact that his tone sounds anything but cool.

"Yeah. He's gonna help us at the party, to find more clues about Autumn."

"Oh."

"What do you mean, *oh*?"

"Nothing." He shrugs. We sit in silence for a minute. "Hey, after the party, do you wanna go catch the new Avengers movie?"

"I can't."

He rolls his eyes. "Big date with Patrick?"

"Um, no." I clench my jaw. "I have to keep looking for Autumn."

"Aren't the police doing that?"

"Not well enough."

"Sorry, I just didn't realize we were going to spend the *whole* day looking for clues."

I bristle. "Well, my sister's still missing, so."

There's a long uncomfortable pause. Jason finally breaks the silence.

"Can I ask you something?"

There's an edge to his tone I don't like. It's like a game of Jenga, where you know the next brick someone pulls off the tower will make the whole thing collapse. And you're just sitting there, holding your breath, as someone's fingers brush the wooden piece that's the inevitable end of the game.

I brace myself. "What."

"Well, you're spending all this time and energy searching for Autumn when you don't even know something's wrong with her. I thought you two weren't even that close."

His words pierce me right in the heart. My sister flashes through my mind, scowling at me, yelling at me, slamming the bathroom door in my face, calling me useless, calling me stupid, telling me to eff off because I asked her for a ride to school that one day Jason stayed home sick.

I look out the window, watching the pine trees get thicker the farther we get from downtown. "We're not."

We don't talk the rest of the way there.

A chill rustles through the tree branches towering over our heads. I ring the doorbell while Jason stands beside me with his arms crossed.

Patrick's head pops out. "Oh, hey, guys. I just gotta grab my coat."

"Ivy has to pee," Jason says.

I shoot him the deadliest of my death glares. "If it's *okay*, can I come in and use the bathroom?"

"Uh, yeah. I guess." He steps aside and holds the door open for us.

I haven't been to this house in years, but my nose gets déjà vu the second we walk through the door. I'm still not used to calling it "Patrick's dad's house." It was always just "Patrick's house," back when his parents were still married.

It's been four years, but it might as well be yesterday. The same high wooden ceiling stretches over our heads, and the familiar picture of Will and Patrick as toddlers eating Popsicles greets me on the wall.

A pink tinge spreads across Patrick's face the moment we step inside. "We weren't really expecting company."

Everything's the same, except for one thing: the place is a total sty. Uneven stacks of papers litter every surface, a heap of clothes festers on the couch, and I can't even see the kitchen table beneath the piles of junk. Patrick's mom never would've let it get this bad. Or maybe it got this bad, and that's why she left.

Who am I kidding. I've met Patrick's dad before; obviously I know why she left.

"Wow. This is awesome." Jason runs to the back window and stares at the endless pine trees. "Is this all your backyard?"

Patrick shrugs. "Kind of. I don't know where the property border is."

Looking into Pat's backyard brings on an overwhelming sense of nostalgia. Pat and I used to spend hours exploring these woods. We'd play on the winding forest path behind his house, and bounce balls off the shed, pretending they were missiles. One time we set up the hose and tried to build a river, and then dam it up with sticks. Seriously, we could make a game out of anything. But the path looks completely overgrown with weeds and debris now. It's kind of a bummer seeing it like this.

"We're absolutely playing flashlight tag in the woods here next summer," Jason says. I knew from the moment he saw it that he'd mention flashlight tag. Anytime there're woods, that's his first thought.

"I guess." Patrick fidgets. "It's kind of useless for a lawn when you don't have any grass."

"Woods are cooler than grass." Jason presses his hands to the glass. "Your yard is huge."

I jab him in the ribs. "You live in a mansion, don't even."

"It's not a mansion."

"It's on Pill Hill." That's what everyone calls the rich area because it's full of doctors—like Jason's mom, the head cardiologist at Concord Hospital.

"Excuse me, it's *next* to Pill Hill."

"I love how you think the rich section has a border line."

Patrick clears his throat. "Um, did you need to go to the bathroom? I'm not sure I'm supposed to have people over."

"Oh yeah. Sure." I shrink down, kind of wishing we hadn't come inside.

At Pat's request, I use the upstairs bathroom—thankfully, it's cleaner than the rest of the house—wash my hands, and rip open the door a little too quickly. Before I realize he's walking down the hallway, I slam into Patrick's dad, getting a faceful of sweaty undershirt. This guy is a tank; it's like hitting a solid wall.

"Shit." I immediately slap my hand over my mouth. "I mean, shoot."

It takes him a second to recognize me. "Ivy Casterly." He brushes a hand through his dusty brown hair. "It's been a minute."

"Wow, yeah. Hey."

Mr. Perkins looks a lot older than he did four years ago. Bags hang under his eyes like he hasn't slept in days, and the wrinkles around his mouth have gotten deeper.

He scratches the back of his neck. "So, what've you been up to?"

I shrug. "Not much. School."

It seems to dawn on him that he's wearing an undershirt, and he quickly throws on the red hoodie hanging over the banister. "Sorry about that, wasn't expecting company."

"Yeah, sorry. Just wanted to use your bathroom. We're heading out."

"Okay. Well, have fun." His mouth stretches into a smile that's obviously forced. "See you around. You're always welcome here." I can tell from his tone he doesn't mean it. Part of me doesn't even think he wants Patrick here.

He clomps back down the hall to his room, his boots leaving

bumpy indents in the tan carpet. I'm struck with a pang of affection for my dad. He's not perfect, but he tries. Sometimes.

I feel bad for Patrick. It must suck to grow up with parents practically tearing each other's throats out all the time. Maybe that's why Will's so screwed up.

I used to love how warm and cozy Patrick's house was. His mom has issues, but she kept the place looking nice. Now it just feels dreary. It's funny how one person can change the mood of an entire house.

Our house has definitely been different without Autumn. What would happen if she never came home? The thought starts as a seed and takes root, spreading through my brain until I can't think of anything else.

Her room would be empty. Maybe Kathy would turn it into a guest room or a shrine to Michigan State Football, with a life-size cutout of Chris in his Spartans jersey. I'd walk by Autumn's room every day, but it wouldn't be hers anymore. I'd never see her car in the driveway. Her chair would be empty at every meal. I'd be the one feeding Pumpernickel.

Dad would either spiral out of control or bury her disappearance and pretend it never happened. I'm not sure what would be worse.

Chris would come home for Thanksgiving. He'd probably still make it to the NFL, and Kathy would still watch his games on her iPad. Their lives would be business as usual.

It hits me: nothing would really change for me, either.

I'd get up and go to school. Hang out with the Nerd Herd. Come home and be semi-ignored by Dad. Stay up late stalking people online.

There was a time when Autumn and I were two threads knitted into the same cloth. Now we're strangers. Our lives are two circles in a Venn diagram where the only intersection point is our last name and legal address.

But I would miss her.

If nothing else, my life would not be the same, because I would miss her.

I wish I'd told her that when she was here.

Ivy

My head bobs up and down to the music blaring from Jason's radio. Patrick pokes his head in from the back seat. "Where's the party?"

"Wilson Street," Jason says. "We've gotta meet Kevin and his family at the top of the driveway in ten so it's not totally obvious when we crash."

"Wait . . ." Pat's forehead wrinkles. "We weren't invited?"

I bite my lip. "Not technically?"

I throw on some mascara in the visor mirror. I wish I had time to do my smoky eye. My stomach has gotten all fluttery ever since we left Pat's house.

I hear about senior parties through the grapevine—which is usually band—but I've never been to one. She'll probably have a keg, and maybe a deejay and the type of music that you can feel through your shoes and up your whole body. All the seniors will be there, wasted and hooking up in bedrooms. They must have a separate area for the parents or something.

I meet Patrick's eyes through the visor mirror and he smiles at me. My heart does a full-on backflip. Okay, it's a tiny chance, but maybe this will be the first of many parties, and Patrick and I will end up in one of those bedrooms. We wouldn't have sex, but I'd definitely make out with him.

We pull up to Laura's house, a small split-level with a long, winding driveway. A crimson CONCORD FIELD HOCKEY balloon is tied to the mailbox, wafting in the light fall breeze. I can hear laughter and chatter the moment we step out of the car.

"Must be in the backyard," Pat says.

Nervousness spikes through me. Something tells me this party is my last chance.

I kind of stare for a moment.

Adults lounge in folding camping chairs on the wooden deck, sipping cans of Heineken and Diet Coke. A cloud of smoke drifts up from the surface of a grill, accompanied by the aroma of char-grilled burgers and sizzling hot dogs. A bunch of people crowd around a badminton net in the backyard—five girls on one side, six guys on the other. They scream and laugh, pelting three different birdies back and forth over the net.

"What a beautiful rock garden." Kevin's mom carries a bowl of macaroni salad. "This is so nice."

Nice is definitely not the type of party I was anticipating.

She sets her bowl on a long, tarp-covered table, which is already overflowing with an assortment of desserts, dips, and sodas.

Coach Bratten talks with a group of parents, holding a hot dog in one hand and a bottle of water in the other. Every few minutes, they erupt with laughter.

The four of us stand side by side, surveying the party. Not gonna lie, it's a little bit like watching from behind glass; we're here, but not really.

"So this is cool," Jase says.

I squint at the girls' side of the badminton pitch, trying to match faces to the Facebook profiles I searched earlier. None of them look quite right. "Which one do you think is Kaitlyn?"

"Kaitlyn's not here yet."

I startle at the voice behind me. A tall girl with amazing rainbow hair spoons pickle spears onto her plate.

"Oh." My heart sinks. "Is she coming?"

The girl shrugs. "Probably, yeah. She's usually late." That's both promising and not—what if she doesn't show up? Can I bug one of these people to give me her number? "Haven't seen you guys at one of these barbecues before. You have friends on the team?"

Jason's "My girlfriend's on varsity" intersects with my "I'm thinking of trying out next fall," which runs into Kevin's truthful "My sister Nicole's on the team."

Oops.

Her eyes light up. "Oh, you're Nikki's brother?"

"Yep," Kevin says.

"She's great. Saved us in the championships against Nashua last year. I'm Becca, Becca Truman. I'm on the team."

"Becks! You wanna play?" One of the girls at the badminton game cups her hand around her mouth. "We need an extra."

Becca sets her plate down. "Sure! Nice meeting you guys."

We all release a heavy breath. That was way too close for comfort.

"Okay, so, plan." I hold up my hand. "We hang out, get food, and stay under the radar until Kaitlyn shows up."

Kevin nods. "Got it."

Patrick is the first to sidle over to the food table, and the rest of us follow. Someone's already loaded cheeseburgers, hamburgers, veggie burgers, and hot dogs onto paper plates, all in labeled lines. I take one of the burger plates and pile a handful of chips, some baby carrots, and a brownie on top.

Jason snaps the tongs at me, then uses them to grab a roll. "This is like those band camp parties."

"Not cool enough for that. Oh my God, you do *not* need three hot dogs." I pretend to slap his arm. "Seriously, this is like that first band camp cookout when I met you, and you're still incapable of controlling yourself around free food."

"And yet, you befriended me anyway. You have no one to blame but yourself."

"This is true. What was I thinking?"

Our eyes lock, and I quickly look away.

The four of us take seats on the grass, trying to stay out of the way. I keep glancing up at the driveway, waiting for Kaitlyn to come walking in.

I check the time on my phone.

She'll show. She has to show.

An hour later, the mood of the party has shifted.

Kevin took off with his parents about ten minutes ago, leaving Jason, Patrick, and me to our own devices.

The sun has mostly sunk beyond the horizon, leaving an orange-and-pink glow in the sky. The adults who hadn't filtered out have all left the deck and taken up residence around the fire pit. Embers crackle and pop, filling the air with a woodsy scent that reminds me of summer. Empty beer cans litter the grass. Okay, of all the people I expected to get drunk tonight, the parents were at the bottom of the list. But their laughter fills the air, and I'm 99 percent sure it's not sober laughter.

That was surprise number one.

Surprise number two is that the field hockey players and their boyfriends and friends joined our little circle on the grass, out of earshot of the tipsy parents. Jason, Patrick, and I have spent the last twenty minutes embroiled in their conversation.

Or rather, we smile and laugh when it seems like everyone else is.

One girl leans into the guy behind her, who keeps an arm wrapped around her and his hand clenched around a can of Sprite. I'm still not over the fact that they're not drinking beer.

I tap my fingers against my thighs. I wish Kaitlyn would hurry up and get here.

"Okay, so you know Mr. Brightman, right?" The girl flares out her hands for dramatic emphasis. "I got my AP history paper back from him last week and it *reeked* of pot."

Everyone cracks up. I pretend to laugh, even though I have no idea who Mr. Brightman is.

"I'm not surprised," another girl adds. "Didn't Kayla run into him at the movies last year and say his eyes were completely bloodshot, or was that someone else?"

"It was Kayla, I remember that story."

"Definitely Kayla," Jason whispers in my ear. Neither of us knows who any of these people are, but whatever. I'm kind of pissed he's not taking this situation as seriously as he should be. Then there's Patrick, who's been playing on his phone the whole time.

"Oh shit." One of the guys lowers his gaze, obviously reining back a laugh. "Look who's here."

I jerk my head up so quickly, I nearly get whiplash. But it's not Kaitlyn.

It's Coach Crespo.

"Great," I mumble to myself, picking at a blade of grass. So far, I'm no closer to finding Autumn than I was two hours ago. But the moment I see Creepo, I remember the letter on Autumn's computer, and suddenly I can't think about anything else.

"Creepo's looking for some action," a guy says.

Everyone watches Creepo crack open a can of beer and wander over to the group of adults. The girl next to me hides her mouth behind her hand to block the giggle.

"Oh shit, he's going for it." The first guy pretends to scratch his neck while very obviously watching the coach slink over to Coach Bratten's chair with his back to us.

Coach Bratten had been Autumn's soccer coach. I didn't know her very well, because Autumn only played high school soccer for, like, a month, and I stopped playing after middle school. But I'm struck with sympathy for her. I can't imagine dealing with this guy every single day.

Creepo wraps his arm around Coach Bratten's shoulder, leaning against her chair. She stiffens and slides closer to the opposite arm-rest. It's so cringeworthy, I don't even want to look. But everyone around me snickers.

"Do you guys know Lydia Taylor?" one of the girls asks. "She's a junior."

No. "Yeah," I say, even though no one else responds.

"Well, her mom's the Commons D secretary, right?" The girl leans in, holding everyone hostage with her eyes. "She had to deliver a memo to Creepo's office last year, and he asked her for a blow job."

Laughter explodes around me.

"Creepo's getting bold," someone says. "Like, even for him."

"How does he do it?" Another guy presses his hands together like he's praying. "Teach me your ways, Coach Creepo."

More laughter. Patrick shifts in place, his forehead crinkling. He probably has no idea who Coach Creepo is, and I'm a little embarrassed this is one of his first impressions of our otherwise decent school.

"He asked me to come to his office after class one day last year, so I brought Michelle with me," another girl says, with a dramatic shiver.

"Aw, you missed out," says another guy. "He would've offered to show you his bat."

Another guy chimes in. "Please, he's the pitcher."

"Gross," says a girl.

"Why do you joke about that?"

Everyone's eyes settle on me. All the heat in my body floods into my face. I should've spoken up last time. I should've, and I didn't. Before I can stop the words, they're pouring out of my mouth. "It's like this gross public secret everyone knows and no one does anything about."

They're all gaping at me, but I can't stop.

"He's a predator, and he's harassing people. They probably don't even feel safe coming to work—*you* didn't want to be in his office alone." I point at the girl. "It's disgusting, and I'm sick of everyone treating it like this hilarious joke."

I dart my eyes to the ground. Silence descends over the group.

Becca Truman clears her throat. "She's right, you know. I'm gonna get a snack." She pushes to her feet. A couple of other people mumble about joining her and get up.

Well, great. I finally get into a senior party and I drive everyone away. I keep my head down. That's not like me. But I can't make myself regret saying it.

I'm so distracted, I barely notice the two pinpricks of light pulling into the driveway.

"Oh hey, Kaitlyn's here!"

A bunch of people stand and rush to greet her.

I jump up so fast, I stumble, steadying myself against Patrick's arm. A cloud of seniors flocks around Kaitlyn as she climbs out of her Volkswagen. I've never seen her in person before, but I recognize her dirty-blond hair and round face from the Facebook picture.

What do I say? What if Hailey was lying and Kaitlyn doesn't even know Autumn?

"I'm going to find the bathroom," Pat says.

"Fine." I wave him off.

Patrick disappears into the house.

Jason digs his sneaker into the dirt, keeping his eyes down. "Hey, I'm really sorry about Thursday."

I don't have the energy for this. "What happened Thursday?"

"I made a joke about Coach Creepo. You're right. It wasn't cool."

"I'm always right, about everything," I say. "You should know by now."

"You wanna go check out what's going on inside? I think they're setting up the PS4."

Laughter roars from the group of girls surrounding Kaitlyn.

"I have to find Kaitlyn first." I shove past him, elbowing through the mob of people. "Kaitlyn!" She turns around. "Hey! I need to talk to you." The people crowding around her slowly dissipate, their interests turning back to the party.

Kaitlyn's wearing skinny jeans, boots, and a black North Face fleece. It's pretty much the unofficial uniform of the senior class. "What's up?"

I nod toward the shadowy side of the house for some privacy, stepping between some leafy bushes. Kaitlyn narrows her eyes, and I realize how bizarre this looks, but I can't just bring it up out in the open. I push through the bushes until my back is flat against the house. Kaitlyn follows, but doesn't step into the shrubs. She keeps several feet of distance, with a leafy barrier between us.

"Come over here, it's quieter."

"In the bushes? No." She folds her arms. "Who are you?"

Jeez, nice girl. "Ivy Casterly. I was wondering if—"

Recognition crosses her face. "I'm gonna stop you right there."

"Wh—"

"I have no interest in talking to you, or your bitch sister."

I blink at her, uncomprehending. "What?"

"You heard me. Why are you even here?"

"I need to talk to you about Autumn."

"Just leave me alone, okay?" She turns around and walks away.

"Wait!" I claw my way out of the bushes, scraping the crap out of my arms. I wince, stumbling back onto the lawn. Kaitlyn's already joined the group of field hockey players who are now toasting marshmallows around the fire.

I clench my jaw and make my way back toward Jason, who's standing by the snack table, playing on his phone. He'll know what to do. This can't be a dead end.

I pull out my phone. 8:02. It's been hours since I last spoke to the cops. I'll try again.

"Concord PD, this is Doug."

"Hey, this is Ivy Casterly. I filed a report on my sister, Autumn Casterly, yesterday afternoon?"

"Casterly . . . Casterly . . ." Some pages crinkle over the phone speaker. "Yep, right here."

I'm pacing back and forth beside a red car parked at the edge of the driveway. "I was wondering if you had any updates on the case?"

"You'll have to call back during normal business hours. I'm not at liberty to discuss sensitive information over the phone."

"Sensitive information?" My stomach lurches. "So, did you find her? Do you know something?"

The man sighs, sending a wave of static over the receiver. "Not that I know of. But you're going to have to call back in the morning. I'm just here to answer emergencies."

"This is an emergency."

"If it's a missing persons report, I promise they're doing the best they can."

Why does no one take me seriously? "Can I speak to someone else?"

"During normal business hours, call this line, and someone can help you out, okay?"

I hesitate, trying to think of something to say, but the line goes dead.

He hung up on me. He actually hung up on me.

I screw my eyes shut. I have no clues left. No more leads.

"I don't know if I believe any of the shit people say about Crespo." A guy I recognize from the circle earlier takes a swig from his Coke Zero, ambling past me with his friend. "I mean, you can't just accuse someone of something without proof. That's not how this country works."

I bite my tongue, wondering why they instantly believed that girl's drug accusation against Mr. Brightman, but find sexual harassment to be such an unbelievable concept. If Coach Crespo was a suspected thief, or stoner, or murderer, somehow I doubt they'd be so skeptical.

His friend shrugs. "He seems like a nice guy to me. And he's a great coach. My dad said the baseball team sucked before Crespo took over."

"Football team, too," the other guy adds.

I bristle. It's like being good at sports gives you immunity from doing anything wrong.

"Yeah, I mean if they were serious, why wouldn't someone just come forward and, like, press charges or something?"

Screw it. I jump in front of them. "Have you ever thought that maybe the other coaches don't come forward because, I don't know, he's the *head coach*?" I snap. "They'd have to put their jobs on the line, and for what? For people to call them liars and sluts? They tell each other in whispers so when he calls people like that girl into his office, she knows to bring a friend."

"Wow, okay." One of the guys makes a face at me like he just witnessed a toddler throwing a tantrum. "You don't need to flip out about it."

I clench my hands. They say *girls* are the sensitive gender, but call out the shit their friends do, and all of a sudden guys think you're *flipping out*.

I have a right to lose my temper because it's infuriating. God forbid I raise my voice to anything louder than a whisper, oh no, can't have that.

One of the douchebros heads toward the snack table, but the other lingers behind.

"Wait . . ." He cocks his head.

I sigh, because I've dealt with more than enough toxic masculinity today. "What?"

"Aren't you Chris Pike's sister?"

"Stepsister." I narrow my eyes, waiting for the inevitable ribbing about that gross Chris-Autumn rumor. "Why?"

"I played on the team with him when I was a freshman. He was great—single-handedly got us into the Northeast championships."

Yes, please tell me more about how utterly great my stepbrother is. "Mm-hmm. Yep."

"Doesn't he play for the Spartans now? Always thought he was gonna hit the NFL someday."

I don't try to scowl, but I feel it stretching across my face anyway. "Yeah. Maybe."

"See, you should be happy Coach Crespo's here," he says.

"What do you mean?"

"You don't know? He saved Chris's ass back when your drug-dealer sister tried ruining his reputation. That bitch is *crazy*."

It's like he ripped the asphalt right out from under my feet. "Wait, *what?*"

"She got wasted at Warren Marden's party, then went home and fucked Chris. Afterward she regretted it and said he forced her." He shakes his head. "Imagine if they'd believed her? Chris's whole life. Destroyed."

My mouth hangs open. "Autumn told Crespo that?"

"No, she told Coach Bratten. Of course Bratten believed her." He rolls his eyes.

I remember Dave's comment about the meeting in Principal Greenwich's office. My stomach sours.

Douchebro laughs. "Thank God Crespo was there to attest to Chris's character. Chris would never do anything like that—he's so careful, he won't even get behind the wheel after a single beer. He's a good guy. And he hugged his mom after every game—the guys used to give him shit for it. Plus, he's got tons of female friends."

"What the hell does that have to do with anything? That's like saying Ted Bundy didn't kill people because he had some friends who were also people."

"Autumn obviously just wanted attention, or revenge, or something."

All I can do is stare, absorbing.

"It was such a mess," he continues. "The school called both their parents and everything. Glad it's over."

What the hell? Kathy and Dad knew about this?

Douchebro drifts back into the party without giving me another glance.

I remember Autumn throwing her mattress into the dumpster, chopping off all her hair, how much it freaked me out. How things got so weird with Chris, and with Kathy.

If Chris did something to Autumn—if their hookup wasn't the giant drunken mistake I always assumed—then what the hell really happened at that party?

My feet auto-pilot me back to the snack table, where Jason's still playing on his phone.

"Brownie?" He holds out a plate, his eyes on his screen.

I frown at him. "No, I don't want a brownie. I'm trying to find my sister."

He puts the plate back on the snack table and nods at the douchebro, who's currently hitting on one of the senior girls. "Who's that guy?"

"Some jerk, I don't know. I was talking to the police and he came over to start gushing over my stepbrother."

"Oh, you spoke to the cops?" His attention's back on Twitter. "What'd they say?"

"They keep telling me to trust them and I am so sick of it."

"Okay, well, let's think." He finally puts the phone down. "You checked her room, right? Her computer?"

"Yes."

"Her search history?"

I blink. "No. That's a good idea. I can look at home."

"See? Cheer up." He pretends to punch me in the arm. "You've got another lead already. Probably better than randomly interrogating people here, you know?"

I grit my teeth. "I'm not *randomly*—"

Becca saunters over and skewers a marshmallow on the end of a roasting stick. "You guys are in band, right?"

"Yep," Jason answers, halfheartedly checking Twitter again. "Living the dream."

"I used to really want to play the snare drum," she continues.

"You should learn. Hang out with us cool kids."

"Hey, *I* think it's cool. I only come to the football games for the field show. And the fries."

"You know what they say." Jason wiggles his eyebrows. "Without the band, football's just a game."

"Well, I hate to interrupt this little party," I snap, "but I have to find my sister." I start walking away.

Jason runs after me. "Hey! Wait up."

The second we're out of Becca's earshot, I stop and whirl on him. "You know, you could at least pretend to take me seriously."

"What are you talking about?"

I continue walking. "You've been on your phone and stuffing your face and having a grand old time. You could humor me and *act* concerned."

"I am concerned!"

"Funny way of showing it."

"I've been following you around all weekend while you play detective—"

I stop. "Is that what you think this is? Playing?"

"I checked Twitter for, like, half a second! Becca came over, I was being nice!"

"My *sister* is *missing*. Sorry if you can't understand that with your perfect little family."

"*What?* What the hell does that even mean?"

"You know what it means."

"My family's not perfect. Why would you even—"

"If you're gonna argue with me, just go away." I put my hand up. "Seriously. Turn around and leave."

"I didn't have to come tonight."

"Maybe you should've stayed home, then."

"Maybe I should've." He turns to go, but stops, and I can see it, right there, about to spill out of his mouth—the last Jenga block. "You know, if *you* were missing, she'd never do this for you."

Jason's words sink into my skin, settling deep down in my heart. He's right. A zillion percent right. Autumn doesn't care about me, Dad only cares about me sometimes, and Jason only wants me as a friend. The backs of my eyes burn, threatening to spill tears.

"Fuck you." I sweep away from him. He doesn't follow.

I storm into Laura's house and let the door slam behind me. A burst of warm air envelops me, along with the smell of cat food, but thankfully I'm alone. I hold my fist to my mouth to stop myself from crying, but let the waves shudder through me.

Jason was supposed to be here for me, and he doesn't give a shit. He's not even trying. He's given up. I'm used to people ditching me when it matters, but for some reason, this one really hurts.

This might be my last chance, and I'm not wasting it, whether Jason's with me or not.

I peek out the back window onto the deck, where Kaitlyn sits in one of the camping chairs, talking to some of the field hockey players.

I rip open the door and stomp onto the deck. They startle, watching me with curiosity—except Kaitlyn, who looks like she's ready to punch me.

"Hey." I level a glare at her. "What do you know about Autumn Casterly?"

The other girls look at me like I just told Kaitlyn I'm her biological mother.

She crosses her arms, daring me. "I'm not talking to you." A twinge of fear twitches across her face.

"Yeah you are." I have no clue where all this is coming from, but I can't shut up. "Because she's been gone since Friday, and I need to know what you know."

One of the girls slaps a hand over her mouth.

Kaitlyn shrugs. "Good."

I blink at her. "What did you say?"

"I said, good. I'm glad she's gone." She smirks, getting to her feet. She's got a good five inches on me, along with a ton of muscle, but I don't back down. "I don't know where she is. And if I did, I wouldn't say a word. Autumn Casterly is a bully, and a druggie, and a slut, and I hope she never comes back."

My vision flashes red. Before I can stop myself, I fling my hand back and slap her across the face. The clap echoes in the night air. A couple of the girls gasp.

I glance from Kaitlyn to my hand, disbelieving. I hit someone. A senior. What the hell?

Kaitlyn presses a hand to her reddening cheek. Before I know what's happening, she's charging at me. I shield my face, but she grabs my hair, so I take a swipe at her, sinking my fingernails into her cheek.

"Stop it!"

The other girl jumps between us, shoving us apart. Kaitlyn touches the scratch on her cheek, and her finger comes back stained with blood. Wincing, I massage my scalp, pretty sure she yanked out a clump of my hair.

Holy shit. I've never gotten into a fight before.

The girl whirls on Kaitlyn. "You wanna get kicked off the team? She's just some random sophomore, she's not worth it."

Kaitlyn scowls, examining her scratched face in her phone camera. "Bitch." She spits a wad of saliva at my feet. "You're as bad as your sister."

For some reason, that makes me feel smug.

She shoves past me, clomping down the wooden steps and back into the yard. The other girls follow, leaving me alone on the deck.

As soon as they're gone, I collapse into the folding chair with my head in my hands. This is so messed up.

Something thumps and I jerk up. Patrick sits in the chair next to me with a plate of pretzels, sipping from a red Solo cup.

Patrick. My Patrick.

The adult cooler lies on the floor beside us, with a label that says "21+ only" in black Sharpie.

"I'm glad I found you," Patrick says. "I don't know anyone here." He holds up his cup. "I found ginger ale, though, if you want any."

Old Ivy would've taken this crap lying down. Old Ivy's the one who gets abandoned and shit on. Old Ivy definitely wouldn't drink.

I don't want to be Old Ivy. Not anymore.

I grab a bottle of Budweiser from the cooler and wipe the excess water off the sides. "I'm having this instead." It takes me three tries to remove the top using the frog bottle opener before I realize it's a twist-off.

Patrick raises his brows. "I didn't know you drank."

"I don't. I'm a beer virgin. Popping the ol' cherry right now." Patrick clears his throat, his cheeks pinkening. I hold it up to him in a toast. "Cheers."

This is it. My first beer. I slug back a hearty gulp and almost gag it right back up. Oh my God, it's the grossest thing I've ever tasted. How can people enjoy this? I'm pretty sure this is what sewer water tastes like. I feel like I've been lied to for years.

I take another gulp.

"Jeez, Ivy. You can sip it." Patrick laughs.

I glance into the yard. Jason's standing by the almost extinguished fire pit, talking to Becca Truman and some guy I don't recognize. Screw him. I knock back half my beer in a single slug.

"You must be thirsty."

"Something like that." I swallow down the last swig of my beer. That 5 percent alcohol content hits me like a freight train. I crack another and chug it. The second one doesn't taste so bad. Maybe that's the trick.

I've spent this whole weekend looking for Autumn, running around Concord, breaking laws for a sister who hates me. Maybe it's time I did something just for me. That familiar Patrick-induced lightness swarms my chest—or maybe it's the alcohol. I need this. I need *him*.

"You know what?" I sling my arm around Patrick's shoulders, tugging his chair closer to mine; the legs scrape against the wood. "We should date. You should be my boyfriend." Well, I guess I've hit the famous honesty portion of being drunk.

He gives me an amused look. "Are you drunk? After two beers?"

"Yeah." I think for a second, leaning my elbow against the plastic arm of the chair. "No." Maybe? I don't even know what drunk is supposed to feel like. Fed up? Sick of everyone's shit? They all feel the same. "I don't know." I pluck a third beer from the cooler and pop the top. Honest Ivy's raging hormones are out in full force. "I mean it, though. We should date."

Patrick laughs and shrugs out of my arm. "Ivy, I . . . That's so nice of you."

My shoulders hunch. He doesn't need to say anything for me to read his face. That's the *it's not me, it's you, I'm definitely not interested* look. I made a huge mistake.

"Holy shit." Why did I drink so much? "Oh my God. I ruined everything."

"No!" Patrick rests his hand on my shoulder. My face scrunches. I can't look at him. "No. I swear you didn't. I just . . . I like you as a friend."

I'll never be enough. The tears betray me and start full-on leaking from my eyes. "Of course you do. I'm always a friend." My voice breaks. "Never more."

"No, jeez, Ivy." He scratches the back of his neck. "It's not like that. I'm just—I'm not into dating. The whole boyfriend-girlfriend thing. But I'm so, so glad you're here—when I moved back to Concord, I thought I'd be a friendless loser all year."

"I know that excuse. You say you don't want a girlfriend, and then two weeks later you're dating some girl who's not me."

"That's not it, okay? That's not it. I don't want to date . . . any girls."

"You're . . . gay?"

"No." Patrick fists his hands in his hair. "I'm not gay. I just . . . Ugh, this is so hard." He looks at the table, at the floor, at literally anything but me. "I don't . . . like anyone, not like that."

I just kind of stare at him. "What does that mean?"

He closes his eyes and takes a deep, shaky breath. "I haven't even told my mom, I just . . . I don't know what she'll say, she's always asking if I like anyone at school and I never know how to respond. She's already so stressed living here, and I'm stressed, it's like I'm in this town I know, but it doesn't know me, and I . . . I want to tell you. I do." His words all jumble together in a heap. "Please don't tell anyone, all right?"

I don't know what I'm agreeing to, but I nod. "All right."

"I'm ace." The moment the word leaves his mouth, it's like he'd been holding his breath for an hour and finally let it out.

I keep staring at him, and I realize I'm being rude, but I have no idea what I'm supposed to say. "A-ace?"

"Technically ace-aro. Asexual. Aromantic."

My lip warbles. "Oh . . . I don't know what that means."

"I don't want to date anyone, I don't want to sleep with anyone, I'm just not . . . attracted to anyone. Not in that way." He shrugs. "The whole kissing, sex thing? I've just never really understood it or been interested in it. I'm not ready to tell everyone yet, you know? Please don't tell anyone."

I'm still absorbing. Patrick won't date me—he won't date anyone. It's like my mouth moves before my brain can catch up. "I won't," I say. "I promise."

My mind races. I'm still sober enough to realize he's coming out to me, and the thoughts all kind of stew together in my brain. I think back to when Alexa came out, and I Googled all those articles on what to say. "That's totally cool. I support you. And I'm here for you if you want to talk about it." I mean every word, but it comes out stiff and robotic. It's like all the energy has been sucked from my limbs. "Really, Patrick. You're one of my best friends."

He smiles and squeezes my shoulder. "You're one of mine, too, Ivy."

It doesn't hurt, not really. Maybe I didn't even want to date him. Maybe I just wanted someone to want to date me.

I hate myself for making this about me. "Hey, I'm tired. I think I'm gonna head out."

"Yeah, I already texted my mom. She's coming to get me. You want a ride?"

I shake my head. "Nah. It's the other side of town." This isn't about me and I need to stop being such a shitty friend. "Thanks for telling me. I'm sorry I acted so weird." I bury my face in my hands.

"I'm really glad you're here, Ivy. I don't know what I'd do without you." He stands to leave. I smile after him, trying to show my support, but he's already disappeared back around the front of the house.

I definitely wasn't expecting that.

What am I supposed to do now?

I'll find her. No matter what else happens, I'll find her. I *have* to find her. I'm at the end of my rope, hanging by a thread, and I can't let go.

Jason is standing by his car when I get back to the driveway. "Ivy—"

"Nope." I brush right past him, onto the empty street. "Don't wanna talk to you."

"Can I drive you home? Look, I didn't mean it. I was being a jackass."

Anger boils white-hot inside me. "I don't care what you think. I'm looking for my sister because she's *my sister* and it's the right thing to do. And that's me—good ol' pathetic Ivy, always looking out for everyone else."

"I'm sorry, okay?"

"Sorry?" I whirl around. "You're not sorry. You meant everything you said."

"No, I didn't. C'mon, Ivy. You know I don't think that."

"I don't want to talk to you right now. Go back to the party and hang out with Becca—you're probably waiting for me to leave so you can anyway." It's petty, and a low blow, but I don't care.

"What the hell?" He gently grabs my wrist. "What are you even talking about?"

"You wanna talk about it?" I twist out of his grip. "It's been floating invisibly between us ever since Sophie's movie night last summer, so we might as well just get it out in the open."

He visibly swallows. "Ivy . . ."

"You broke my heart." Deep down, I know I should shut up. I'm making a fool of myself, and I don't think I can blame it on three beers. But I feel like a soda bottle that's spent the last two months being shaken, and now that the cap's been blown off, the rest of it comes spilling out, too. "I liked you, Jason. *Really* liked you. And you broke my heart."

"C'mon, Ivy, you're—"

"No." I hold up my hand, cutting him off. "Do *not* say I'm your best friend."

His mouth opens, then closes.

"I don't have time for this." I close my eyes, fighting back the tears. "I need to find my sister."

Before he can stop me, I walk away.

Autumn

I follow Ivy on her long walk home. It's only about two miles, but the September wind chills the air, and it isn't long before her cheeks turn red. Maybe it's from the cold, or maybe it's because she's spent the last hour crying.

I still can't get the image out of my head. Ivy slapped Kaitlyn Kennedy in the face, for me. She doesn't even kill spiders.

I never saw that coming.

Her footsteps patter against the sidewalk, barely audible over the rushing car engines that zip past on the main road, but I hear them.

"You didn't need to hit her." I try and kick a pebble, but of course, my foot goes right through it. "But thank you for standing up for me."

Ivy says nothing and plows ahead, hands buried deep in her coat pockets.

My skin fades to translucent before my eyes, flickering for a moment. When I finally inhale, the color returns, but it's muted. A ghost of my usual skin tone.

The color doesn't come back.

I screw my eyes shut. I can still hear that bastard's deep voice—*We've got to get rid of her.* I wish he'd said when they're going to do it. I'm almost glad he didn't. I don't know what's worse—knowing or not knowing.

The cold air is raw against my skin, even though I can't feel it. "You should've taken the ride home. You must be freezing."

Ivy presses onward, her eyes glassy and determined. I never knew my sister had a stubborn streak. Then again, there are lots of things I didn't know about her.

Something that random douchebro said to Ivy is bothering me, about my stepbrother never drinking and driving. I don't know why I can't shake it out of my mind.

Chris was drunk that night. Really drunk. I remember it; he was trashed. Although, the more I think about it, that doesn't seem right. He drove us home. A DUI would have killed his chance at a football scholarship. I was the one puking my guts out in the bathroom the next morning, not Chris. Maybe he wasn't as drunk as I remembered. I don't know.

With every footstep, a second ticks away. I feel each one draw another breath of life from my dying lungs.

When Mom was still alive, we had this New Year's Eve tradition where we all ate junk food and watched the *Twilight Zone* marathon on TV. Ivy and I would try to guess the big twist in every episode, and we'd practically hold our breaths during the last five minutes, waiting for it.

There's one episode where this guy finds a stopwatch that can freeze time. After Ivy and I saw it, we'd pretend to click our watches at each other, and the other person would have to freeze right in the middle of whatever they were doing.

Of course, to a little kid, the concept of freezing time absolutely sucks. Everyone wants to get older, because the older you are, the more cool stuff you get to do. No one wants to stay a kid forever. Everything good happens later.

No one warns you about death.

When you're a kid, death is something that happens to old people and betta fish and plants you forget to water. Not to you, never to you—not for years and years and years. Unlimited years.

I find myself subconsciously pressing the bone on my left wrist, even though I haven't worn a watch in years. Maybe if I press it hard enough, time will stop.

It's happening too fast. It's all going way too fast.

It's after ten by the time Ivy takes a right onto Church Street and our tiny home comes into view. Dark puddles dapple the crappy road, reflected by streetlights high over our heads.

She wipes her muddy boots on the mat by the front door and pauses with her hand over the knob. Her lips press together.

She twists the knob and bursts through the front door, all traces of emotion wiped from her face. Dad and Kathy startle from where they'd been sitting on the couch.

Dad's brow creases. "You okay, sweetie?"

"Hey," Ivy mumbles before disappearing straight upstairs, still wearing her boots and jacket. Dad makes a move to stand and go after her, but Kathy rests her hand on his elbow and gently shakes her head.

I follow Ivy back into my room. She goes right for my laptop, powering it up and typing in the familiar password. My hands subconsciously clench at my sides. I watch, holding my breath over my sister's shoulder, while she clicks into Chrome and delves into my browser history. There's nothing relevant in there. She's wasting her time.

Ivy scrolls through random things I've searched over the past couple months—music on YouTube, random wiki links for school papers, that time my intestines felt like someone was hitting me with a baseball bat and WebMD convinced me I was dying before the culprit revealed itself as my period. She gets through all my internet history from the past year . . . two years . . . three years. Her cursor pauses on a series of old Google searches from ages ago. I tense.

```
sex while drunk
sex consent intoxicated
is it still consensual if you don't say
no but don't say yes either
had sex drunk feel weird afterward what
should I do
```

My eyes are glued to the screen. I forgot I Googled this shit. That same unease that spread through my body the day I searched it comes back. It's like a thousand caterpillars are crawling on my skin. Why'd I look that stuff up, anyway? I'd already made a fool of myself over that whole situation, and now my sister knows it, too.

Ivy stares at the screen for a moment, then slams my laptop screen shut. She plows back down the stairs with me following close behind.

"Ivy? What's wrong?" Dad rushes over. He sniffs the air and recoils. "Have you been drinking?"

Kathy hoists herself up. "Honey, what happened?"

Ivy takes a deep breath. "We need to talk."

Something heavy settles in my chest.

Dad and Kathy watch her, unblinking.

"What do you know about Autumn and Chris?" Ivy visibly tries to keep her resolve, but the moment she speaks, her voice cracks. "What happened three years ago?"

"What do you mean, sweetie?" Kathy's brow furrows.

"I think there's something you've never told me."

I stare, unable to look away.

Dad glances from Ivy to Kathy. "Sweetheart, what are you talking about?"

"Did they call you in to the school?"

"Autumn Casterly, please make your way down to the principal's office." The announcement had chimed into my freshman English classroom.

I wrung my hands, crossing the catwalk and tiptoeing down the stairs to the main office. The week before, I'd cut study hall and geography. I didn't feel like going, so I hung out with Jaclyn in the common room instead—she was a loner, too, and we got along instantly. Surely the school was going to yell at me for skipping. But as I got closer to the office, I could see the back of Chris's head through the window. The principal sat in his swivel chair, along with Coach Bratten, Coach Crespo, and my stepbrother.

Kathy sat beside her son, her hand in his lap. She didn't look at me when I entered the room. A man stood behind her, and I only recognized him from photos—Kathy's ex. He kept his distance, typing on his phone in the corner.

Coach Bratten wasn't supposed to say anything. Anger, fear, betrayal, panic—they all flared to life inside me. I had let my words run away from me in her office. I shouldn't have told her what happened. I was just think-ing aloud. But maybe it was the law and she had *to report it.*

I let them direct me into a chair, not daring to meet my stepbrother's eyes. The room felt hot, too hot. Suffocating me.

"What's this all about?" The ex-husband glowered down at me. "I have a meeting in thirty minutes."

Coach Bratten glanced at the principal. "Is Autumn's father coming?"

"He was supposed to be here." Principal Greenwich checked the time on his phone. Dad was working a double today. They wouldn't start without him. They couldn't.

I scraped my left thumbnail over my right, scratching off the dark blue polish and watching the chips flutter to the stiff gray carpet.

"I don't have all day," Kathy's ex snapped. "Can we get on with it?"

"It's okay, we can start without Steve," Kathy said with a wave of her hand. "I'll update him later."

"Yes, yes." The principal steepled his fingers over his desk. "Autumn, can you tell us what happened two Saturday nights ago?"

My pulse thundered underneath my skin. What happened that Saturday? I wasn't supposed to be at the party, wasn't supposed to be drunk. Definitely wasn't supposed to have done what I did with my stepbrother.

"I . . . I don't know." My voice choked off. It all happened so fast, and then I was confused. And they wanted me to cough up the details of my sex life to the entire room? All those intimate, personal, terrifying details? "Chris . . . Chris and I . . . It just happened."

"We shouldn't have been drinking," Chris said, with more strength in his words than I had in mine. He didn't meet my eyes. "It was all a big mistake."

"Oh for fuck's sake." Kathy's ex whirled on the principal. "You made me leave work for this?"

"Try to remember, Autumn," the principal said. "Just do your best."

The shuddering breath rips into my lungs and tears back out. I remember regurgitating the story to the entire office. Skinny jeans and a T-shirt covered my body, but it was like I was bare, exposed naked to people I barely knew.

I remember the night with vivid clarity now. I was old for my grade, and Chris was young for his, but I'd only been a freshman for a few weeks, and I was already invited to a senior party. I remember the outfit I wore. The top was low-cut and silvery, the type of thing the older girls wore to parties and guys seemed to like—I liked it, too. I looked pretty. I liked what I saw in the mirror. I haven't worn that shirt since.

I remember the drinks he handed me. They burned my throat going down, but I kept drinking. Because he was. And he'd brought me to the party. I owed him that.

I remember the car ride home, and how everything outside blurred together.

He was sober enough to drive.

When he helped me to my room, he pressed his finger to my lips, then his lips to mine. I remember thinking it was wrong, because he was my stepbrother, and I didn't want it, and I should make him stop. But when he shoved his tongue into my mouth, the taste of pepperoni pizza on his breath, I opened up and let him in, because I couldn't tell him no. *No* wasn't fun. *No* was bad. *No* was what the boring girls said. I didn't want to be a boring girl. Boring freshmen didn't get invited to senior parties.

I remember the room spinning around me. How much had I been drinking? I couldn't even remember. The drinks all blurred together and churned in my otherwise empty stomach.

When he laid me on the bed and unzipped my pants, I remember the words forming on my tongue.

No. Stop. I don't want to. I'm not ready.

But everything came out muddy and incoherent, tinged with rum. I didn't say no. I *had* been all over him at the party, leaning on him, laughing with him. I kept telling myself this was supposed to happen. I'd flirted with him all night. This was the next step, the natural progression. I was supposed to be doing it.

I remember the weight of his body, pressing down on my lungs. I remember his lips, fused to my neck, my cheek. I remember the sweat and how his skin stuck to mine. I remember how I scrubbed for hours afterward and never felt clean.

I remember the pain.

I remember the plastic animals on my dresser from Ivy's Advent calendar, and how I focused on each one in turn. How I shut my brain off and refused to think of him. I would only think of the animals on my dresser, standing in a line, watching us.

It was fine. It was just sex. Everyone's first time was supposed to hurt a little. That's just how it worked.

I remember the feel of his hand tugging my long hair that sent a wave of nausea rolling through me. I remember how the first time I brushed my hair after, I felt that same tug on my scalp and that same pit in my stomach. I remember how good it felt to take the scissors to my ponytail and lob the whole thing off. I remember finding the condom wrapper, discarded on the floor under my bed. I remember being grateful that he'd been sober enough to remember a condom.

Mom had raised us in a sex-positive household, and she gave us the condom discussion when we were kids. I'd just started the pill, mostly to regulate my periods. I was fine with the idea of sex. But I couldn't wrap my brain around what I'd done.

I glanced at the office door, waiting for Dad, but he didn't come.

I told the school everything I could remember. The smell of the room. The taste of the rum. The feel of his weight on top of me. When I was done, I squeezed my eyes shut.

"That's not what happened," Chris shouted.

Coach Crespo cleared his throat. "Autumn, do you remember exactly how much you had to drink?"

I blinked at him. "No. A lot, I think."

"And how many people were at the party?"

"I . . . don't know."

The coach sighed. "With all due respect, Autumn, it sounds like maybe you're not remembering the night clearly. You're fifteen years old; you shouldn't have been drinking—either of you."

I opened my mouth, then closed it. Maybe I wasn't remembering it clearly.

"I know, Coach," Chris said. "It was a mistake."

Crespo pulled out his phone, producing a screenshot of that wretched Instagram photo. He showed it to the room, and humiliation burned hot in my throat. "Here's what I'm seeing. You kids had a bit much to drink. Autumn, your clothes were already half off at this point." The principal shot him a warning glance, but he continued. "I'm just saying."

Chris lowered his head. "It was a mistake. But I feel like I'm being attacked here for something I didn't do."

"No one's attacking you," Principal Greenwich added. "We're just trying to find out what happened."

"Autumn, honey." Kathy squeezed Chris's hand and smiled at me. "It's okay. It was a mistake. Lord knows I regret my mistakes." She nodded toward her ex-husband across the room.

A mistake. That's what the night was.

"It seems like you did something you regret. But you can't just say things and expect them not to have consequences." She was talking to me like a little kid who ate the last cookie and then lied about it. "I have to talk to Steve about this, because just last week you cut some classes and told us you didn't. You can't just lie when you don't like the truth."

My face burned. "I'm not." I don't think?

Her ex snorted. "Look, I don't know why we're here. You trying to send your stepbrother to prison? He rejected you and now you're pissed? Is that it?"

I wasn't trying to send Chris anywhere. But he kept going, hurling names at me. I was a liar. I was a slut. I should have said no. He was right—I didn't say no, and I should have. This was all my fault.

"I didn't do anything," Chris said. His face flushed red. *"I'd never sleep with anyone who didn't want to. That's not who I am."*

"We know." Coach Crespo nodded at him. "This is just a formality."

Coach Bratten hesitated, but cut in. "I think we should hear more from Autumn's perspective."

"Oh please. We've already heard her nonsense," Kathy's ex thundered. The man rounded on Kathy. "We all saw the photo. Just because your step-daughter is a little whore who regrets her mistakes in the morning doesn't mean our son should be punished for it." He slammed his fist on the princi-pal's desk. "She lies about cutting class, and you believe her now because she says something might have happened when she was wasted? Chris should flush his life down the toilet because he got ten minutes of action?"

Kathy's face drained of all color. "Flush his life away? No, of course not." She gave Chris a comforting smile, like he was a little child who needed shielding. "Don't worry, honey. It's okay."

"Did you say no?" the principal asked, looking dead into my eyes.

I hesitated. "No."

"I told you!" Chris said, a hint of whine in his voice.

"Aha!" Kathy's ex pounded the desk. "I knew it. You were probably begging him for it and don't want to admit it because he's your stepbrother."

"That's enough." The principal glared at him. "Do you have anything else you want to add, Autumn?"

I'd caused a giant mess; blown everything out of proportion. In that moment, I wanted to be literally anywhere else. I just wanted the meeting to end. I didn't know what to say.

So I said nothing.

Ivy stands in the middle of the room, suspicion in her eyes.

"He raped her, didn't he?" My sister swallows. "Is that what happened?"

It's like the air is sucked from my lungs. There's that word. The word I never dared to say, couldn't bring myself to type. I don't know why I never could.

Dad's brow creases. "Where would you get that idea, Ivy?"

"Tell me the truth," Ivy says. "What happened at the meeting you had at school?"

Kathy's eyes crease. "Ivy—"

"I wasn't there. Kathy handled it." Dad casts a cautious glance at his wife.

"It was a witch hunt." Kathy shakes her head. "That female coach wanted to target Chris."

"I don't believe that. Not Coach Bratten." Ivy looks at the ceiling, then back at Kathy. "Chris should have gone to prison for what he did."

Dad holds his hand up. "Wait. Ivy, are you saying what I think you're saying? Because that's a very serious accusation."

"Yes." Ivy forces the word between gritted teeth. "I am saying exactly what you think I'm saying."

Silence blares around us, louder than shouting. I close my eyes, letting her simple words wash over me.

"Do you really want to talk about this?" Kathy's voice is softer than a whisper.

"Yes," Ivy says. "I want to talk about this."

Another wave of silence follows.

Kathy holds a shaking hand to her face. "He didn't do anything. Autumn made the whole thing up, she regretted their mistake and tried to get him in trouble, or wanted attention, or something."

Ivy's face scrunches. "No. She searched about this on her private computer. She wasn't looking for attention, she was looking for help—and it's clear she wasn't getting it from you."

"She was accusing my son of something he didn't do." Kathy's voice grows more frantic. "It would've ruined his life."

"*His* life? What about Autumn's life?" Ivy raises her voice.

Neither Kathy nor Dad responds.

"Chris's life is *fine*. He's probably going to get drafted into the NFL, and where's Autumn, huh?" She throws her hands up and lets them slap back down against her sides. "Gone."

I remember how we looked side by side on paper: the football star with the bright future, and the troubled ninth-grader with the dead mother who always cut class.

Dad's brows lower. "Kathy, you said everything at the meeting was fine. That everyone agreed it was all . . ." He cringes. "Consensual."

"Autumn makes a lot of . . . bad decisions." Kathy wrings her hands. "But you can't blame it on Chris—"

"Oh yes I can." Ivy points at her. "Because it's his fucking fault. You think it's not his fault she sleeps on an air mattress? Why she turns her head every time she walks through the door? To avoid looking at that wall." Ivy points. I don't follow her finger, but I know where she's pointing. "So she doesn't have to see his face staring back at her from the bookshelf."

Dad slowly turns toward Kathy, narrowing his eyes. "You told me everyone admitted it was just a mistake."

"It was," Kathy insists. "They heard something happened between Chris and Autumn and wanted to make sure it was consensual, and it was. Autumn didn't even deny that. That's what I told you."

"You told me they had sex, you didn't say anything about . . . about *rape*." Dad raises his voice. "They're not the same thing, Katherine."

Dad and Kathy start arguing, getting right in each other's faces. But I barely hear a word they're saying.

I remember Officer O'Riley's words from yesterday—*Sometimes when we're desperate to believe something, especially about the people we love, our minds can twist events.* Kathy will never see her son as anything but her innocent little boy. She won't see it because she doesn't want to.

When I was a kid, Mom told me never to say the R-word. But there's another R-word I never said. Because that would've made it real.

He raped me. He *raped* me. I can't stop thinking those three words. I was raped. I was *raped*. It sounds wrong and accurate at the same time.

I lost my virginity to him, but it didn't feel like something I had lost. It felt like something that was taken from me.

I didn't say no. But I also didn't say yes. And even if I had, I would've been too drunk to mean it.

"You defended him." Ivy keeps her face emotionless, but her words are rich with acid and powerful enough to silence the yelling in the room. "He walks free because of you. She needed you, and you didn't help her." I can't tell if she's talking to Kathy or Dad.

Tears sting my eyes.

I remember how they blamed it on the alcohol, on my outfit, on literally everything but him. How they made me into a monster for being a fifteen-year-old at a senior party. How they decided that I didn't say no because I wanted it.

How they urged me to confess when I hadn't committed a crime. It didn't feel right, because it wasn't.

I was raped.

I remember the weight of my mattress when I heaved it into the dumpster. I remember every detail I tried to bleach out of my mind. I remember the first time I tasted Ativan, and it tasted like nothing and everything, and the bad memories slipped away.

"You know I love your sister," Kathy says. "But she does not have the best track record, Ivy. She lies. She smokes. She deals—"

"No. Stop it." Ivy's hands are balled in fists, shaking at her sides. "She's a person, and she deserves to be listened to and believed. She deserved so much more than what she got."

My hand hovers next to Ivy's, an inch from reaching out and brushing her skin.

Dad stares at the ground. Kathy watches the TV, mute in the background, her eyes glazed over.

People talk about it like it's a moment in time, a blip on the radar. They never mention the ghost that lingers after. The taint on everything that can't be undone. How every touch becomes offensive. How the first time I bit into a slice of pizza afterward, I shoved my finger down my throat and spewed it back out.

I remember how word of the meeting in the principal's office got out, and Chris told everyone at school I was a liar. That I threw myself at him and then changed my story. It was so easy to become a criminal once they already thought I was. I had no reputation left to ruin.

I hate that I don't wear low-cut shirts anymore. I used to love how they looked on me. I hate that he ruined that.

I haven't touched alcohol in three years and haven't dressed up since then, but I wonder if any of those things mattered. It could have happened anyway. Because none of those things caused the rape—Chris did.

And now I am still at the mercy of a monster whose future is valued more highly than mine.

Ivy turns away and takes the stairs, one by one.

"I'm sorry, Ivy." Kathy shakes her head, and calls after her, "I'm so sorry."

Ivy pauses on the top step. "It's not me who needs the apology."

I let the tears streak down my face. There's no point in hiding it anymore. I'm already invisible.

I follow Ivy into her room and sit beside her on the mattress. The solid mass of ice in my chest thaws and melts, leaving behind the raw lump of pain I'd buried there.

I run a finger down the tattoo on my wrist. "Thank you."

Ivy doesn't respond, but I swear she turns her head.

I let my hand hover over her thigh for a moment before resting it gently there. Warmth emanates from her body, bleeding into my lifeless hand. She places hers on top of mine, and it sinks straight through me until she's touching the denim of her jeans instead of me.

I'm here, Ivy. I close my eyes. *I'm right here.*

Something jerks my hands upward, like someone's pulling me away and forcing the air from my lungs. I suck in a breath and inhale the familiar stench of moldy cedar. Pain stabs into me from every angle.

A sliver of light peeks through the bottom of my vision, but something soft covers my eyes—a blindfold.

Cold air pierces my skin, and my body feels stiff and disoriented. Fresh rope burns into my wrists, binding my hands together.

"All right, that should do it," says the grisly voice that sends a chill deep into my core. "She's not going anywhere."

"Good." It's a different voice. It sounds familiar, in a strange way. "Liam's gonna be relieved."

That piece of shit. I knew it.

"It'll be dealt with soon," the first guy says. "Tomorrow morning, this'll all be over."

"Did you come up with a plan?"

"Yeah. First thing in the morning, I'm gonna put her in the truck, weigh her down . . ." Something rustles, like the man stood up. "And throw her in the Merrimack."

AUTUMN

I squeeze my eyes shut. When I open them again, I'm back in Ivy's room, sitting on her bed.

Everything inside me tightens and hardens until I'm sure I'm more rock than human. Oh my God.

That's it. Tomorrow morning. It's so *soon*.

What do I do? There has to be something I can do.

I have no idea where Liam would've put me. He's in jail; he couldn't have done this alone. But still, after two days, I'm no closer to knowing.

What the hell can I do?

Ivy kicks her boots off and throws them against the wall. They thump, leaving black scuff marks on the plaster. She grabs her hair in fists and sinks back onto the bed beside me. "I'm sorry, Autumn," she whispers. "I failed you."

I rest my hand on her leg. "You didn't."

The revelation hits me.

Nothing.

There's nothing I can do.

I close my eyes, letting it wash over me.

Somehow, it's freeing. I don't have to try anymore. It's inevitable. All I can do is wait.

The unknown makes everything churn around inside me. It

seems like forever ago I had that conversation with Liam in his car. What comes after death?

Tomorrow, I'll either be with my mom, or I'll be nowhere.

I hope it's quick. I hope it doesn't hurt.

It hits me that I'm kind of lucky to know it's coming. Most people don't get a warning, so there's no time to tie up their loose ends.

Mom and my aunt Bethany never had a good relationship. I'm not sure why; something happened when they were kids. When they put Mom into hospice, the doctor said she had a week left. Her sister made plans to come and visit her on the weekend. She bought a plane ticket and booked a hotel room, just to say goodbye.

But Mom died on a Friday. By the time Aunt Bethany arrived, she was gone. Bethany never said it, but I always wondered if she'd intended to apologize for whatever happened between them.

I have one night left.

What do I do with it?

I focus on Abby Nelson. The moment she pops into my head, the scenery around me changes, all the colors and edges blurring together.

I'm standing outside Abby's apartment. It's a crappy brick public housing building with brown shutters on every window. Every apartment has its own entrance, and Abby's already has an orange garland strung around the door for Halloween. Flower stickers cover the windows, probably put up there by her little sister.

I can't remember her sister's name. She's probably said it a million times, and I never paid attention.

A few years ago, this complex made the news because a guy hanged himself in the parking lot and a bunch of little kids saw. It crosses my mind that I never asked Abby if she was one of them.

I've dropped her off here a million times but never set foot inside.

I float through the wall, into the cramped apartment. From the living room, I can see straight into the kitchen; piles of dirty dishes are stacked in the sink. Toys litter the living room floor. A TV blares, showing reruns on the Disney Channel. It smells like Kraft Macaroni and Cheese in here—it's a very distinctive smell. Our AP physics textbook lies on the coffee table with a brown ring burnt into the top, like someone left a hot drink on it. Typical Abby. I don't even know why she signed up for AP classes when she never does any work.

I tiptoe inside, careful not to step on anything, even though it wouldn't matter if I did.

A little girl sits cross-legged on the brown crumb-covered couch in her pajamas, her eyes fixed on the TV. I should be looking for Abby, but I'm too distracted by the pictures on the wall. There are portraits of Abby, her sister, and her parents for every year since she was born. I've never actually met any of them before. In the most recent picture, an oxygen tube is linked into her father's nose. Abby's got her arms wrapped around her little sister, and her mom's looking right at her dad instead of the camera.

When a commercial comes on, the little girl shakes out of her trance. "Abby!"

Something thuds in the distance. "Be right there, Cass." A toilet flushes.

Cassie. That's it.

"What time is Mommy coming home?"

"Easy does it, I gotcha," Abby's voice says softly from another room. A clicking sounds in time with footsteps, and her dad comes around the corner, pushing a walker. Abby follows behind, rolling an oxygen tank. Jeez. He can't be more than fifty, but he looks at least twenty years older. It hits me that he's sick—maybe the same disease as Mom, maybe different, but still. He's *sick*. That's something Abby and I always had in common, and I never knew it. She's never mentioned him, and I never talk about my mom.

Abby smiles at her sister. "What is it, sweetie?"

"What time is Mommy coming home?"

"She gets off at one tonight." Abby helps her dad into the velour armchair; he grunts when his butt hits the cushion.

Cassie pouts. "Can I stay up to see her?"

"Nope. In fact . . ." Abby pulls out her phone. "It's almost eleven, and it's a school night. Bedtime."

"But—"

"Nope." Abby shuts off the TV, which is met by a longer groan from Cassie. "Go and brush your teeth. Mom will kiss you good night when she gets home, okay?"

"Do what your sister says," their dad grumbles, his eyelids hanging heavy over his eyes.

Cassie gives an exaggerated huff before slogging down the hall as slowly as humanly possible.

"Can you put on the news?" Abby's dad asks, his voice scratchy.

Abby sinks onto the couch and turns the TV back on, flipping through the channels until she arrives at CNN. The reporter's voice fills the room, but I tune it out.

Abby's eyes glaze over, and I'm pretty sure she's not even paying attention to the TV. Exhaustion covers her face like a mask. Finally, she grabs the physics textbook off the coffee table, flips to the right page, and starts making notes on her phone.

I sit beside her, reading over her shoulder. She's studying Newton's third law.

I never got to this assignment. I'd been planning to read it over the weekend, and look how that turned out.

This is so weird. Abby hardly ever does her homework, and I

always assumed she just didn't care. But by the way she's clearly forcing her eyes to stay open, I realize: she always cared. She just cares about other things more.

"Hey, Abby." I touch the textbook, feeling the smooth paper beneath my fingertips. "I wish I'd gotten to know you better when I had the chance. I'm sorry I wasn't a better friend."

She doesn't look up. I don't know why I never tried to get to know her better. I guess I never wanted to. The closer you get to someone, the more painful it is when they stab you in the back. If you don't trust anyone but yourself, then there's no one there to let you down.

I wish I had done it anyway.

"Take care of yourself." A pit forms in my chest as I stand up. "Bye, Abby."

I think of Jaclyn.

The room disintegrates around me.

Soon I'm in another apartment, standing in a kitchen with cracked tile floors and various posters tacked up on the walls.

I've been inside Jaclyn's parents' house before, once, when I picked her up. This isn't it.

A door at the end of the hallway is cracked open, and hushed voices drift through. I tiptoe over and peek inside.

Jaclyn's lying on her back on the bed in jeans and a bra, texting. Her phone casts a light glow in the otherwise dark room. She's always had resting bitch face, but she looks especially pissy right now.

At the other end of the room, a sleazy-looking guy in a dirty white tank top and boxers slouches in his desk chair, his face slumped against his hand. I recognize him instantly; Jaclyn left with him after we went to Liam's on Thursday.

"You should probably go."

Without a word, Jaclyn sits up and whips on her sweater. It's a different one from the shirt she'd worn to Liam's on Thursday.

"I don't get what the big deal is," the guy continues.

Jaclyn adjusts her shirt. "I told you I wasn't ready."

"You didn't need to lead me on like that. One second we're making out, and the next second you're screaming at me."

I already hate this guy and I don't even know him.

"You kept pushing my head toward your crotch," Jaclyn snaps. "I told you no. I wouldn't call that *screaming* at you."

"Well, then you shouldn't have come over tonight."

"Yeah, you're right." She grabs her purse off the floor. "Clearly that was a mistake."

"I mean, you're all over me, climbing on top of me, what do you think that does to a guy? You can't just stop because you change your mind halfway through—that's so unfair to me."

"She's allowed to change her mind," I snap, even though he can't hear me.

"I mean, you've fucked half the town, but suddenly you're not interested in *me*?" He snorts. "Yeah, okay."

"Just because I've had sex before doesn't mean I'm up for grabs for everyone that wants it."

The guy huffs. "Just get out."

Jaclyn grabs her coat from where it was balled up on the floor and shoves a lock of dyed-blond hair behind her ear. "So, what now?" There's an unspoken plea hidden in her voice. "We still hanging out tomorrow?"

"You wasted my night, what do you mean, 'what now?' Nah, I've got shit to do tomorrow."

Her face falls, and I can see his words had the effect he intended.

Jaclyn sweeps past me and charges out the bedroom door. The guy turns his attention back to his phone.

I wish I could rip the phone out of his dirty fingers and crush it on the ground.

I follow Jaclyn out of the apartment; she slams the door, and the crash reverberates in the narrow hallway. Jaclyn presses her back to the door and closes her eyes, her chest heaving.

"Oh, Jaclyn." I crouch beside her and wrap my arm around her shoulders. "I'm sorry. I'm so sorry. He's not worth it."

I sit beside her for at least ten minutes while she cries into her hands. Finally, when an old guy exits the apartment across the hall and gives Jaclyn the harshest glower ever, she gets up and heads to her car. I stand beside her while she digs through her purse, looking for her keys.

"I think you and Abby are the closest things I had to friends. I wish I'd known that at the time." I squeeze her shoulder before she climbs into her car. "Goodbye, Jaclyn."

She clicks the ignition, and I feel myself slipping away.

There are so many people I owe apologies to, but I don't have time for all of them. So I visit the most recent one—Kaitlyn Kennedy.

She's home now, lying on her bed in a bedroom that looks like a fairy vomited pink shit everywhere.

Kaitlyn's fingers dance across her phone, and I'm not surprised to see Ivy's name make an appearance in the nasty texts she's sending to half a dozen people. I scowl, because really?

"Hey, bitch, looks like you're going to get your wish." I cross my arms, watching her type. "I'll be dead within a few hours."

Kaitlyn's pink-socked feet tap along to the music playing softly from her iHome. Her lips mouth the song lyrics, two beats late. I can't stand her.

Shouts erupt in the hallway outside her closed bedroom door. An angry woman's voice, followed by an angrier man. Kaitlyn's mouth thins to a tight line across her face. She clicks the volume on her iHome, and the music gets louder.

"... don't know why I even stay here," shouts the woman. "You're nothing but a bum."

"So leave!" shouts the man. "Get the hell out."

"I pay the mortgage every month. Why don't *you* leave, you dirty bastard?"

Kaitlyn toggles the volume up some more, until the music pounds so loud, I can feel it in my bones. But it still doesn't drown out the rage outside her door. I've done that before—I've blared my headphones to the precipice of obliterating my eardrums, just to escape.

Maybe Kaitlyn and I aren't so different.

I grind my foot into her pink carpet. "We shouldn't have ganged up on you last week."

She nods her head in time with the music, trying to lose herself in the notes.

"It was a dick move, and I'm sorry. I deleted the picture, which I didn't tell you, obviously, but I did. It's gone. I'm still glad Ivy hit you, because you totally deserved it, but I'm sorry. I hope you have a nice life." The moment I say it, it's like a weight's lifted off me.

Kaitlyn's eyes flick up, and for a moment, I swear they lock with mine. But it's short-lived, and soon, she slides giant headphones over her ears and closes her eyes. I can still hear the music pounding through them.

Looking back, there are lots of other people I should probably visit. But time isn't a luxury I have right now, so I go home instead.

A shroud of silence covers the house, but I already know everyone's still awake. That's how my family is. We can exist in separate rooms, our paths never crossing.

Kathy's sitting at the kitchen table, both hands cradling her phone. Her ringtone fills the air, one of those annoying generic iPhone ringers that everyone has. *His* name flashes across the screen. She stares at it for a good thirty seconds before laying it facedown on the table, unanswered.

I pull up a chair and slump down next to her. "So, you probably realize I hate you. And I don't forgive you." My eyes dart to the crucifix hanging on the wall in the living room. I hope Jesus really *is* as forgiving as they told us in church, because I'm pretty sure he'd frown upon this, and if he exists, I'm like eight hours from meeting him.

Kathy pinches the bridge of her nose.

"But if you're going to be here with Dad and Ivy, I hope you pull it together. They're good people, and they deserve the best— especially my sister. Don't ever hurt them, or I will haunt your ass."

I go into the foyer and turn my back to the wall. I'm about to head upstairs, but I stop. Slowly, I turn to face it. It's Chris's graduation picture, and he's wearing that ugly crimson mortarboard. He's got a wide smile, full of bright, shiny teeth. I think people assume monsters will always look like monsters, but they rarely actually do.

I stand and stare at him. "You don't control my life anymore."

Then I turn around and walk upstairs.

Pumpernickel is curled in a ball at the top, his face pointed so he can see down the stairs, a direct view of the front door. No matter how many times I left, he was always waiting for me when I came home again. I reach down and scratch his ears. "Be a good boy, okay? No stealing socks. I love you." I kiss the top of his fuzzy head, and I swear his tail gives a slight wag.

I visit Dad next. Shocker, he's in his room, sitting up in bed, watching *Pulp Fiction* on his laptop. I roll my eyes; he's seen it a zillion times and can probably recite every line from memory. My dad always sleeps in sweatpants and a T-shirt, regardless of the temperature. I look into his brown eyes, and it's like looking in a mirror. I used to hate that I got my dad's eyes; I wanted pretty blue eyes like my mom and Ivy.

I watch him for a few minutes, not really sure what to say. There are some people you can go months or years without talking to, and when you reconnect, it's like nothing has changed. Then there are other people where regular communication with them is like watering a plant; if you don't talk, the leaves wilt, and the relationship deteriorates until you've got nothing but a dead stem and a handful of dried-up petals. My dad and I are the second one.

Dad pushes his laptop to the side. He gets out of bed and pulls an old school photo of me off his dresser. I was in fourth grade then, with long hair and horrible braces. I'm not sure why he never replaced it with an updated picture. Maybe to him, that's when I was still young and innocent and worth loving.

Dad holds the picture to his chest and closes his eyes. A sob ripples through his body and he buckles, collapsing back to the bed in tears. I haven't seen my dad cry since Mom's funeral.

I feel like death is supposed to be a time for forgiveness. Letting things go.

I want to tell him I forgive him. That it's all okay.

I try to form the words. He didn't know what happened at the meeting, and if he had known what it was about, maybe he would've missed work. But the words won't come. Sometimes I wondered how that meeting would've gone if Dad had shown up. There were so many times after Mom died when Dad would leave for work on a weekend or holiday, and I'd want to look him in the eyes and say "Choose me," but I never did, so he never did, either.

In church, they used to tell us to forgive everybody for everything, because Jesus does. Maybe it would be easier to live like that. Maybe if I were a better person, forgiveness would come easy.

But the truth is, maybe not every sin is forgivable.

"I wish you'd been there," I say instead. "I wish you'd stood up for me. You weren't the father you should've been."

The laptop keeps playing softly in the background.

"I hate how you changed after Mom died. It's like you stopped trying, and we needed you. *I* needed you."

"I'm sorry, Autumn." He swallows hard, his Adam's apple bobbing down, then up. "I'm sorry I let you down."

I close my eyes. It's the first time he's ever apologized to me, and technically I'm not even here.

"I love you, Dad." I reach out to touch him, but my hand just hovers in the air. "Goodbye."

Ivy's still in her room when I get back, but she's managed to change into her pajamas. There's no laptop on her legs tonight. She's just lying there on her side, alone, in the dark.

I glance at the clock on her bedside table. Midnight.

Today is the day I'm going to die.

It doesn't hit me as hard as it should. I'm not ready. But I guess no one ever is.

I climb into bed with Ivy. I curl against her warm body and snuggle underneath her fleece blanket. "Thanks for everything," I whisper in her ear. "I love you, Ivy."

Within a half hour, her light snores fill the room. I stay awake, wrapped around my sister, my eyes fixed on the window.

I know it's coming, but I'm still not ready for the sliver of orange to appear.

But I don't have a magic watch, and before I'm ready to face it, it's nearly sunrise.

MONDAY

Ivy

A high-pitched beep pierces the air, and my eyelids crack open way too early. I groan and reach for my phone, which I forgot to put on silent before bed.

4:17 a.m. A light orange glow shines at the edge of the otherwise black horizon outside my window. If Jason woke me up in the middle of the night to give me shit about yesterday, I'm going to scream.

I click my home button, and a new message pops up, but it's not Jason—it's Abby.

Abby: Hey, just wanted to know if you'd heard from Autumn yet

I deflate slightly. Nope. Nothing.

She responds within seconds. Oh sorry, hope I didn't wake you up. I figured your phone would be on silent.

Me: No worries, I was awake.

At least, I am now.

Abby: Well, I was up writing a paper and I had a thought. There are a few guys we hang out with sometimes. Maybe try Facebook messaging them? I don't have their numbers but search Brendan Hernandez, Derek Foster, and Collin Jameson.

I jump out of bed and fire up my laptop. The thing is a fossil that usually hates loading, but it seems to sense my urgency, because Chrome pops up immediately.

Abby told me to look on Facebook. But something inside me hesitates.

Facebook won't tell me where Autumn is. If she left on her own, she's not in danger—if someone took her, they'd need a place to keep her. That's what I need to find.

I pull up Google Maps instead and open the white pages in another window.

I type in *Brendan Hernandez*. It takes me a few minutes to find the right guy, because he lives in Goffstown, not Concord. He lives with his parents in a nice house with a tiny yard. That doesn't feel right.

I type in *Derek Foster*. He's the only Derek Foster in Concord, and lives with someone who I assume is his mom, because they have the same last name. He lives on Warren Street, right near the high school, in a tiny apartment three floors up.

I type in *Collin Jameson*. He lives alone on Mountain Road—with a giant sketchy-looking barn in his backyard.

Holy shit. This could be the guy.

I quickly jot down the address and rip off my pajamas, throwing on the first clothes I can find and practically flying down the stairs.

Darkness envelops the abandoned living room. The pendulum clock cuts through the silence, ticking in time with my heart. I shoot a quick glance up the darkened stairway. No one's up yet. I've never snuck out before. I gulp. I have to do this.

I'm coming for you, Autumn.

AUTUMN

My heart jumps into my throat. Oh my God. A shred of hope.

No. I can't get ahead of myself.

It seems a little too random. I've never even been to Collin's house, and Liam hardly knows him. He's just this loser twenty-five-year-old who grows his own weed.

But this is our last chance. *My* last chance.

"C'mon, Ivy!" I shake her shoulders, pushing her faster into the foyer. "I believe in you. You gotta find me. Let's do this."

Adrenaline spikes inside me. It's almost sunrise. We've got an hour, maybe two, tops.

"Go, Ivy! Go, go, go!"

Something yanks at my wrists, and I'm swept off my feet and thrust through a cold, dark tunnel. I blink, those familiar shards cutting into my ribs, that same cloth blacking out my eyes.

Oh my God. No. Not yet. It can't be time.

Fear turns my veins to ice. My heart slams against my ribs.

Come on, Ivy. Come on.

Someone's clammy hand latches around my wrist. I lurch at the touch. I hate not seeing what's happening.

I squint, desperate to soak up anything through the fabric, any final detail that could delay it and save my life.

"She's awake." A hand brushes my forehead. My muscles tense, and with one swift tug, my blindfold is yanked off.

It's Nick—or whatever his real name is.

I jerk away from him. He strokes that shitty attempt at a goatee. "How're you feeling, sweetheart?" A click echoes in the room, a bolt sliding into place. He's got a pistol, locked and loaded, clenched between his hands.

Ivy can't take on a gun by herself. She needs the police.

Hollow breaths rip through me. This is the end.

Nick bends over, and I catch another glimmer of silver from his holster.

Guns. So many guns. I clamp my eyes shut, waiting for it to come.

"Put the damn blindfold back on," a deep voice growls. It strikes me with a pang of familiarity again. "Mark's coming with the truck in an hour. We've gotta do this before the whole town wakes up. I'm not dumping a body in broad daylight."

I whip my head toward the familiar voice.

The revelation smashes into me.

I know where I am.

I'm thrust back out of my body as quickly as I was pushed into it. It takes me a second to catch my breath, back in the hallway at home. A spark of hope explodes in my chest.

"I know where I am." I whirl toward my sister. "I know where I am!"

Ivy sits on the bottom step, putting her boots on.

Her phone lies open on the ground, with Google Maps pointing toward the Mountain Road address she found online.

It's the wrong way.

"You're going the wrong way." I rip my hands through my hair. "Ivy. Listen to me. Don't go to that address. That's the wrong place. You'll be too late."

Another tug wrenches the breath from my lungs, throwing me back through a long tube of darkness.

I'm in my body. A man stands with his back to me, a long rifle clenched in his grip. Another gun. They've left the blindfold off after all. My captors file out of the small wooden prison, their heavy boots clomping against the cedar, and bolt the door. That chain rattles through the hole, sealing me inside.

They'll be back with the truck in an hour.

I close my eyes, forcing myself back to Ivy. The familiar tunnel encapsulates me, spitting me back out at home.

I steady myself against the banister.

Ivy buttons her coat, her face rigid with determination.

Ivy. My sister, Ivy. The only sister I have. She can find me. All I have to do is send her there. It's so easy. I know how to do it; if I focus hard enough, if I grab on to that invisible connection binding us together, she'll hear me.

I swallow hard as it hits me.

She'll go without question. She'll charge right into the lions' den, unarmed and unaware.

I hesitate as she slides her purse strap over her shoulder. She's risked everything for me this weekend. She could've lost her best friends, could've gotten arrested, could've ruined her reputation at school. All for me.

I press my hand to her cheek and close my eyes, feeling her warmth beneath my palm. That familiar connection thrums to life between us.

"You're going the right way." The words gum up in my throat. "You did it. You found me. I'm in the barn on Mountain Road. And I'll see you . . . soon." My voice breaks.

Ivy's brows lower. She takes a deep breath and pushes open the front door, cringing when the hinges squeak. I watch as she plows outside, into the soft morning darkness tinged with pink.

A new sense of finality settles deep in my bones. I'll go back to my body. I'll wait for the end.

"Goodbye, Ivy," I say to no one. And then I let myself drift away.

Ivy

Crap, I did not think this through. I need a ride to Mountain Road. I hate not being able to drive. Dad will never take me; he probably wouldn't even believe me. Worse—maybe he wouldn't even let me go.

I stand at the edge of the driveway, shivering. A glimmer of sunlight peeks up from the horizon, casting an orange glow over the star-speckled sky. I check my phone: 5:11 a.m. Dad will wake up for work in twenty minutes. I can't let him catch me. I open up the group chat, bobbing up and down on the balls of my feet.

Me: Can someone pick me up? I think I know where Autumn is.

It's a long shot. Sophie and Jason are the only ones with licenses, and they're probably not even awake yet. And after yesterday's blowout, I doubt Jason wants to see me. Frankly, I'm not so eager to see him, either.

No response.

Shit. Okay. This isn't the worst. If I have to, I'll use the emergency Uber account Dad made for me. Maybe I could even get there and back before school, and I won't have to cut.

My bike. It's a long ride from here, but I'll do it.

Shit. It's still at Jason's. I can take Autumn's—she hasn't used it in years anyway.

I'm about to sneak back into the garage when my phone vibrates—Jason.

`Be right there.`

My heart jumps. Okay. I have a ride.

`Me: You're awake?!`

`Jason: I am now.`

Another Jason text pops up in our private chat. `PS—can we talk about yesterday? I feel really bad.`

This is absolutely the last thing I want to deal with right now.

`Me: Later. We need to hurry.`

`Jason: OK. I'll be there in ten.`

`Me: I'm waiting at the end of my driveway.`

I hug my arms around my torso and jump around to create warmth. Everyone should be waking up for school soon.

As if on cue, a text pops up from Patrick, and I realize I still never added him to the Nerd Herd group chat.

`Hey, just wanted to say thanks for being so cool about everything yesterday.` There's a smile emoji at the end.

I check the time, wishing Jason would hurry the eff up. I type back, `Of course. I'm here if you need anything.`

`Me: Or, you know, if you have any questions about Concord stuff. Four years is a long time! Not that much changes here.`

`Patrick: Actually, can you explain something to me?`

`Patrick: What was that whole Coach Creepo thing? Everyone kept laughing about it, but I don't get the joke.`

I roll my eyes.

`Me: It's gross. He's this pervy coach that has,`

like, immunity from being fired. You should ask Will
about him. Creepo was probably still creeping around
back then.

Seriously, I wish we didn't need the whisper network. Some
dudes need to be put on blast.

Ew, that's not cool, he says, followed by a vomit emoji.

Me: Not in the least.

Patrick: Will probably doesn't know about him
though, he didn't go to Concord High.

Patrick: He went to Bow.

My eyes stutter over the last text. I read the word ten times
before it hits me.

Bow.

There are four things I know about the town of Bow: it's in the
middle of nowhere, Patrick used to live smack dab on the town border, Jason found a Bow yearbook in Liam's room, and the town is
super, super small. Like, their whole high school has a few hundred
kids at most. Assuming Liam's around the same age as Pat's brother,
there's a 99 percent chance they know each other.

I quickly text back. Does your brother know any Bow guys
named Liam?

My heart races as I wait. I open my Facebook app and search for
Will Perkins. I'm not friends with him, but it doesn't take me long
to find his profile. Thankfully, he kept his page public. I'm totally
judging him for the fact that he's on here as William Perkins III.
Wow, he looks so different now. I hope poor Pat isn't doomed to lose
his hair this early. It's hard to believe this is the cool guy we used to
shoot hoops with when we were kids.

I open up his friend list and search for Liam.

No results.

I scroll down Will's profile. It's a small chance, but maybe he was tagged in a photo with Liam back in the day and I can find his profile that way. Their high school isn't that big. But Pat's brother apparently never posts, because the most recent updates on here are an onslaught of birthday messages back in May.

`Happy Birthday, Will! Hope it's a good one.`

`HAPPY B-DAY!!`

`Big L! When did we get so old? Lol`

My nose scrunches. Big L? Is that some sort of dick metaphor? Strange nickname.

There's another one. `Old af big L, happy b-day, man.`

Okay, what the hell?

`Happy Birthday, Liam! Have a great day!`

I read it once, twice, three times.

My eyes zero in on his name—William Perkins III—and only four letters stick out: *LIAM*.

A chill courses through me.

No way. It can't be.

A new text from Patrick pops up. `Some of Will's friends call him Liam, actually! Mom hates it though. Why?`

I swallow. Patrick did say Will was troubled. How troubled are we talking?

My thumbs hover over the keyboard. I need to phrase this right. How do I ask *is your brother a criminal who might be connected to Autumn's disappearance?* and not lose Patrick as a friend? What if I'm wrong?

`Me: What's Will up to right now? He doesn't live with you anymore, right?`

`Patrick: Nope. He lives on Fisherville Road with a roommate. But he stays at Dad's house a lot, because`

```
all his crap is still stored there. He's currently
monopolizing Dad's basement and his shed. Dad won't
even let me go in there—I think he's afraid I'll
mess with Will's stuff or start using his drugs or
something.
```
He adds an eye-roll emoji.

Fisherville Road—the site of Saturday's infamous Ninja Turtle break-in.

```
Patrick: Why are you so curious about my brother
all of a sudden lol . . . please don't date him.
```

I shudder at the thought. I quickly open Safari and type in *William Perkins, Concord Monitor, police log.* The page immediately pops up—and there's Will's mug shot, right along with a report of a break-in at the corner store.

The night before Autumn disappeared.

The cops said some guy broke into the corner store with Autumn, but it wasn't just some guy—it was Will. And Will was trying to get a plea bargain, handing over a bunch of texts implicating Autumn in the crime. If he's throwing Autumn under the bus to save himself, maybe he doesn't *want* Autumn to tell her side of the story.

But Will's in jail. He couldn't have hurt Autumn. It had to be someone who'd care about Will and want to shield him.

Or someone who wants to avenge him.

```
I was jk,
```
Patrick replies, with a wink face.

Low, simmering fear spreads through me. Patrick couldn't be involved. He wouldn't be. He's not like that. But part of me hesitates. How well do I really know him? What would he do to protect his brother? Part of me refuses to believe it.

I think back to when we were kids, running through the woods behind his dad's house.

His dad's house.

If anyone would do something shitty to Autumn to protect Will, it's their dad.

I find Patrick's dad's house on Google Maps—4.2 miles from here. The opposite direction from this Collin Jameson guy's house. I need a way to investigate both—somehow.

Jason.

I open my text with Jason. `Scratch that. I need you to drive to Mountain Road, the big yellow house near that stop sign you ran last month when I spilled coffee all over my pants, and look in the old barn in the backyard. Make sure the mailbox says Jameson. Look for Autumn. Tell me what you find.`

He texts back, `Wait, really? Why aren't you coming?`

`Me: I need to cover all my bases. I'm checking somewhere else.`

`Me: If you crash because you're texting me while driving, I will kill you.`

My pulse thrums in my ears. A sense of urgency whispers over my skin. I jump on Autumn's bike and pedal as fast as I can, my phone clenched between my right hand and the handlebar, with the map on the screen.

The entire ride, my brain is in total freak-out mode. Maybe she won't be there. Or maybe she will. I don't know what would be worse.

I'm getting ahead of myself. I'm just going to check quickly, do a clean sweep of the yard, then pedal straight to school. Pat's dad works weird hours, so he's probably at work now. No one will see me.

The longer I ride, the lighter the sky gets.

I know people assume that fat girls are out of shape, but I have really strong thighs. I can outbike literally anyone. Okay, except maybe Olympians and professional cyclists. But it's a long, up-hill ride, and by the time I reach Mr. Perkins's street, my legs are screaming and my lungs are burning and sweat is dripping down my face.

I pull off the road and catch my breath. If anyone sees me, I'm totally screwed. I check my phone—5:45 a.m. I tense. Dad should be awake by now. Did he notice I'm missing?

I stash Autumn's bike in the patch of trees in the vacant space between Pat's dad's house and the neighbors'. I'm suddenly all too aware of how secluded this house is. Leaves rustle as I pass through the underbrush, creeping toward the house. I tiptoe, but branches still crack beneath my feet. When I can see the house clearly, I crouch behind a rock and peek out.

The driveway's empty, but I can't see the garage from this angle.

It doesn't look like anyone is here. For a good five minutes I sit, and wait, and watch, probably stalling, but I blame it on being care-ful. He must be at work.

Cold gray clouds blanket the lightening morning sky. I shiver, wrapping my arms around my torso.

Now or never.

The small wooden shed comes into view, shielded by trees, a good hundred yards behind the back of the house. I'm struck with a heavy dose of déjà vu. Pat and I spent so many hours in these woods, playing in this shed. I could be killing our friendship if someone sees me here.

But Autumn's life is more important.

The moment I see the heavy silver padlock on the door, a veil of dread cascades over me. This shed was *not* locked when we were kids—why would anyone need a heavy-duty lock to guard some old gardening tools? If the Perkinses were going to hide something, this would be the place to keep it.

"Autumn?" I whisper. My heart pounds against my ribs. "You there?"

I press my ear to the wood, but my pulse thrumming in my ears and the wind whispering through the trees blocks out everything.

A pile of heavy rocks sits beside the shed, marking the graves of countless goldfish and bettas Patrick refused to flush. I grimace, darting a glance up to the quiet house.

Screw it.

I wrap my fingers around the biggest rock I can carry. It's a struggle, but I get it to the shed door. Using all my strength, I heave it against the wood above the lock. The metal crashes, but the wood doesn't crack.

I try again. Sweat beads on my hairline. Gritting my teeth, I throw all my strength into the push. A small crack spiders across the door.

Again.

With a grunt, I plow into the wood. The door cracks, and the padlock falls to the grass with a thump. I yank the chain out of the door, my breath catching.

My phone vibrates.

Jason: I'm here, I don't see anything. There's like eight different pot plants though.

A photo of the barn follows.

Jason: One other thing. I took Fisherville to get here. I did a double take when I drove past the house. And, uh . . . I'll just show you.

Another photo comes through. There's Liam's house, the site of our break-in. Parked right there on the side of the road, a stone's throw from where we parked Saturday night, is a green Toyota covered in bumper stickers, AL HAWKE FOR DELAWARE 2012 clear for all to see. The same car we followed from the vacant lot where I found Autumn's keys—where those sketchy guys were lurking—is parked at Liam's house. They're connected.

Somewhere, deep down, I know what's coming.

I rip open the shed door. My heart plummets.

There, lying on the floor in a heap with her hands bound, is Autumn.

Autumn

When the wooden door opens, my heart practically explodes in my chest. But it's not one of the men returning to kill me. Even through my swollen eyes, I can tell it's Ivy framed in the doorway. My muscles turn to liquid. For the first time in days, I could cry from sheer relief.

Ivy rushes over and drops to her knees. "Autumn. Oh my God." She brushes the blood-caked hair off my forehead and rips the gag out of my mouth.

She found me. She's really here. I almost don't believe it.

"Ivy." The word feels like sandpaper in my throat. Everything is swollen and sore, but oh my God, she found me. *How?*

"Hang on." She pulls out her phone and texts Jason, `Call 911. Patrick's dad's place.`

My relief melts away into stone cold terror.

"They're . . . coming back." I force the raspy words through the desert in my mouth. "Have to . . . leave."

"C'mon." Ivy tucks her phone into her back pocket. She darts her eyes around the small space and grabs a rusty hacksaw off the wall. I cringe as she tears the saw back and forth through the rope binding my hands.

"Hurry," I force out.

With a snap, it breaks, and the frayed rope falls to the floor.

Ivy wraps her arm underneath me. Her fingers bite into my

broken ribs and I grind my teeth together, forcing my throbbing muscles to work.

It takes every ounce of strength for my stiff legs to push me up, but between the two of us, we manage to hoist me to my feet. White-hot knives stab into my sides. Pain shoots up my left leg. Dizziness swarms my brain the moment I'm upright, and the room spins around me. I latch on to my sister's waist to keep from spilling back to the ground. She puts my arm over her shoulders and we hobble toward the door. I can't. Every step drains the energy from my limbs like water through a sieve. My knees buckle and Ivy staggers, struggling to support my weight.

Nick's low voice penetrates the wood. "Yeah, man. I— Oh shit. I'm gonna have to call you back."

The color drains from Ivy's face. Our frantic eyes meet each other's. I try to tell her she should run, she should save herself and get out of here, but my mouth is too dry with dehydration and Nick's footsteps get louder and I know it's too late.

She sets me back on the wood floor, my back pressed against the wall facing the door. I hold my breath.

Ivy's gaze bounces around the small space. She grabs an old metal hammer off a hook. I nod. She tiptoes backward until she hits the wall by the door, her knuckles white around the wooden handle. Shadows conceal her from the light.

Nick charges over the threshold and his eyes lock with mine. My blood runs cold. His upper lip curls into a sneer. "You're still here."

I force my eyes to stay trained on his, not daring to blink.

He pulls out his gun and cocks it. "Not waiting around for the—"

Ivy lunges from the shadows and slams the hammer into the back of his head with a sickening crunch. Blood spurts from the wound. He crumples to the ground like a rag doll.

I brace myself. Is he dead? Or just knocked out?

Ivy drops her weapon to the ground with a clang and slaps her hand over her mouth. "Holy shit." Her feet stumble backward in quick, jerky steps.

"Ivy," I whisper, pleading with my eyes.

She nods and steps around Nick's body. My clammy fingers fumble with the weapon in his still fingers. It's a Colt .45. Liam taught me how to shoot a gun once. Fuck. Why didn't I pay better attention?

The room swims. I can't even see straight, let alone aim a weapon, and I doubt Ivy could do it, either. I slide the gun under the tarp-covered lawn mower. At least they can't use it against us. I lean into my sister and let her help me up, my arm slung over her shoulders. We slowly stumble out of the shed, into the dusky morning.

They say when adrenaline hits, a person can lift a car by themselves. Walking outside, forcing my broken body to keep going, feels a lot like lifting a car. But dammit, I lift the car.

Everything looks different out here. The tiny shed sits at the back of the property among the trees. The outline of a tan house peeks through the thick trunks and pine needles.

"This way." Ivy steers us toward the side of the house, half carrying me. "I've got your bike."

Shallow breaths tear through my lungs, each gulp of air like swallowing razors. A hacking cough tears my body in half, and blood sprays from my mouth, coloring the dirt red.

Branches crack beneath our feet. Too loud. We're being too loud.

A door slams, stealing the breath from my lungs. Patrick's father stands between us and the road, a handgun clutched in his hands.

"C'mon!" Ivy steers us back the way we came.

The man charges toward us and we hobble to the cover of the thick trees, Ivy struggling under my weight.

He follows, his footsteps slow and deliberate, and cocks his weapon. A gunshot cracks through the air. Ivy screams, nearly dropping me.

I push myself, my muscles screaming, but my broken body can't go any faster. I won't make it. My foot hooks on a tree root protruding from the ground and I lose my footing, nearly taking Ivy down with me.

"Go." I shove Ivy away from me as I hit the ground, gasping for air.

Indecision crosses Ivy's face.

Pain clouds my vision. I can barely force the breath out of my broken lungs. "Go!"

Ivy drops to the ground, hooks her hands under my arms, and pulls, but the movement slices into my body. Pain splinters through my core. Finally she releases me and I fall back to the earth.

I pant on all fours, focusing on the wet grass and dirt beneath me. His footsteps thump, louder and louder, in time with my heart, until they stop and I can see the tips of his brown boots in the dirt, twenty feet away. I slowly raise my head.

"Will's already in jail. I can't let him blow his life in prison." Patrick's father raises his gun, trained on me. "I'm sorry."

I close my eyes.

The Lord is my shepherd; I shall not want.

He maketh me to lie down in green pastures. He leadeth me beside the still waters . . .

Yea, though I walk through the valley of the shadow of death . . .

A crack of thunder breaks the silence. I wrench my eyes open.

My ears ring. A flock of birds bursts from the tree overhead. I flinch, waiting for the pain, waiting for the darkness to consume me. For a moment, everything goes still.

Ivy stands in front of me, shielding my body.

She falls to the cold earth at my feet, a spot of red blooming from her chest. It takes me a second to process. Her face blanches.

Oh my God.

The world grinds to a halt in slow motion around me. It's not happening. She didn't get shot. I don't. I can't. She didn't. No.

The wind roars, bitter with the stench of blood. A scream rips from my core, stabbing into my lungs like a thousand knives.

Patrick's dad lowers his weapon, his eyes wide, as if it's just dawning on him that he shot someone.

"Fuck." He drops his gun and stumbles backward, his hands behind his head. "Oh fuck." His face scrunches. "Shit. Ivy. I didn't . . ." He holds a fist in front of his mouth. "I'm so . . . fuck." He turns around and charges into the woods, his footsteps pounding softer and softer until they disappear.

"Ivy." I crawl toward her, my body suddenly numb. Her blood leaks across my tremoring hands. "Ivy. Ivy!"

Her eyelids droop low over her eyes, seeing something or someone far away. "Autumn."

Tears cloud my vision. The pain overwhelms me, and I feel myself fading.

Sirens wail somewhere, getting louder.

I collapse beside my sister, the ground cold and hard against my back. My fingers entwine with Ivy's as the world dims. Pine trees tower high over our heads, but the sunlight still cracks in between the needles.

I squeeze my sister's sweaty hand and pretend we're somewhere far away.

The last thing I see are blue and red lights flashing in the distance, before everything fades to black.

THURSDAY

THREE DAYS LATER

IVY

The smell hits me first. It's like a large bottle of disinfectant erupted in a tiny space. My eyelids flutter open. A groggy haze wraps my whole body in a blanket, distorting everything. Like the whole world was painted by soft watercolors that bleed into each other. It takes my eyes a second to adjust.

A soft pillow cushions my head, and there's a warm blanket wrapped around my lower half. My forehead creases.

"There she is, there's Ms. Ivy. You've been drifting in and out of consciousness all week." A young woman in polka-dotted nurses' scrubs smiles down at me. She grabs my left wrist and presses two fingers to it. "Just taking your vitals. I'm Nurse Emma, by the way, but feel free to call me Emma."

A heart-rate monitor beeps steadily beside me.

I try to sit up, and a sharp pain slices through my chest. I grimace, sinking back to the pillow.

Emma's eyes grow wide. "Oh, don't do that, sweetie. You took a bullet to the chest, and it's probably best you just lie there for a while."

I did *what*?

It takes me a second. My memory kicks in way slower than my body, like a jigsaw puzzle with half the pieces missing.

"What . . . happened?" Pushing out the words feels like talking with a mouthful of cotton balls laced in barbed wire. "How am I . . . here?"

Emma raises her brows. "You got real lucky. The bullet missed vital organs by this much." She holds up her thumb and forefinger really close together. "You got a punctured lung and severe internal bleeding. You're lucky it was only a .22 handgun. But you would've died if the ambulance had been about ten minutes later."

"Holy shit." My words come out raspy and thick. "I mean, holy crap."

She smiles. "You saved your sister's life."

"I did?" It all slowly trickles back into place. Patrick's dad. The gun. *Autumn.* "Is Autumn okay? Where is she?"

"She's right down the hall. Unfortunately we didn't have the right space to put you two in a room together, so your poor dad's been going back and forth between them for the last three days." She thrusts her thumb over her shoulder, and it's the first time I notice my dad, passed out in a chair. "He's barely slept since you girls got in."

"Oh." I don't know why that surprises me so much, but it does.

I glance down at my right hand and immediately wish I hadn't, because there's a giant tube stuck into it. I hate needles even more than I hate spiders, and that is a very high bar. "Can you take that out?"

"Soon, dear. You've gotta get your fluids. But the doctor says you both might be ready to discharge in a few days, although you might take a little longer." She clicks her tongue. "Can't just take a bullet to the chest and walk right out."

"They took the bullet out, though, right?" I rasp. "Can I keep it?" I mean, seriously, the least I deserve from this ordeal is a souvenir to prove that once in my life, I did something totally badass.

Emma looks at me like I just asked to rip the divider curtain off the wall and use it as a cape. "Um. I can talk to the doctor and see what we can do. You still sound pretty dehydrated, though—drink up." She points to the swivel table next to the bed.

Three giant vases of flowers are on it, along with a Styrofoam cup with a straw poking out. I grab the cup and take a long swig, relishing the cool water washing over my dry mouth. Emma must catch me looking at the flowers, because she says, "You're very popular."

"Who are they from?"

She checks the tag on the biggest one. "This one's from Sean, Anna, Micah, and Jason?"

Of course Jason's parents would send me an enormous bouquet of flowers. I love how they signed it from everyone, even though I'm pretty sure Micah and Jason weren't involved. My heart sinks. *Jason.* I wish I could erase that awful fight at the party. I wonder if I can just stay in the hospital for a few months until he forgets about it.

"Your father brought these daisies, and this last one is from"— she checks the tag—"Ms. Fournier and Patrick?"

I'm taken aback. "Oh." Wasn't expecting that at all. I mean, deep down I knew he wasn't involved. But still. His dad took my sister hostage in a shed. What friendship can withstand that?

I swallow hard. I hope ours can.

"You also got a bunch of cards. One of your teachers dropped them off yesterday." She points to the stack of cards sitting on the chair. Getting shot gets people to notice you, I guess.

There's a small TV screen embedded in the wall, playing *Harry Potter and the Goblet of Fire*. It's right before the hedge-maze scene, which is my favorite scene in the book, and probably in my top five scenes from the movies, even though they cut all the best parts.

"Can you turn it up?" I rasp.

Emma smiles, ticking the volume up a few notches. "Your dad thought you'd like this movie. You've got to drink more of that water, though, okay?"

I nod and take another sip. "Can I see my sister?"

She gives me a sympathetic smile. "Soon. When one of you is healthy enough to walk."

The next few hours pass in a blur. Dad wakes up; I convince him to go home and take a shower now that he knows I'm not dead. I talk to the doctor, who does, in fact, let me keep the bullet—or at least, the shard they pulled from my lung. They give me my phone, and I get a good kick in the feels at all the messages from my friends. There are over a hundred just in the Nerd Herd group chat, plus texts from Abby, Hailey, random band kids, and even Becca Truman—although I have no idea how she got my number.

At 3:05, footsteps trample in the hallway outside like a stampede of buffalo. Alexa, Sophie, Ahmed, and Kevin pile into my room, out of breath. Kevin's pushing Sophie, with Alexa in her lap, on an old wheelchair I'm pretty sure they stole from the nurses' station. I'm so excited to see them, I almost rip my body in half from how fast I sit up; I immediately regret this decision when a burst of pain slices through my abdomen. I press my hands to my middle, trying really hard not to shout the F-word at the top of my lungs. When the pain subsides, I soak up my friends, huddled around the foot of my bed. I keep waiting for Jason to walk into the room, but he doesn't. Something knots in my chest. I guess that fight did royally screw our friendship.

"Oh my God, I am so happy to see you guys."

Sophie climbs out of the wheelchair and takes my hand—the one without the tube in it. "You have no idea how happy we are to see you. We stopped by on Monday and they wouldn't let us in."

It crosses my mind that I should probably be embarrassed of how I look right now. I haven't showered or brushed my teeth in four days and I literally have a pee tube shoved up my crotch. But I'm so happy to see them, I don't even care.

"Oh, we brought contraband." Ahmed dramatically pulls a *Game of Thrones* coloring book, some colored pencils, a Miyazaki DVD, and a little stuffed alligator out of a Target bag and places them on my side table.

"How did everyone find out what happened?" I ask. "I mean, I've been passed out since Monday, so."

"Jason told us," Kevin says.

"And I have a hard time keeping my mouth shut when my friends do really cool heroic things." Alexa picks up the stuffed alligator and chomps Sophie's arm with it. "If you're wondering why the whole school knows."

"How'd you guys get in here?" I croak out, then clear my throat and take another sip of water. "I thought Emma said only two visitors at a time."

Alexa smirks. "We snuck in."

"Pretty sure we've only got until they see the names on the sign-in sheet," Sophie adds. "Mike Rotch and family have overtaken this hospital."

I laugh. "It was totally you guys who pranked Jason at the bagel place. I knew it."

"Oh, of course," Alexa says. "Was that even in question?"

I fidget my fingers. "Where *is* Jason, anyway?" I'm not going to lie, the fact that he's not here really sucks.

"Detention, all week," Ahmed says. "For blowing off school on Monday."

Great, another reason for him to be pissed at me. Although, it's kind of douchey they won't excuse him cutting for a pretty valid reason. "Oh. That sucks."

"I'm surprised you haven't seen him, though," Ahmed says. "He's been here every day."

I wrinkle my nose. "Really? I just woke up, like, four hours ago."

"Yep. Every day after school, until they kick him out."

For some reason, that makes my chest all fluttery. "That's cool."

"He and your dad have been having some heart-to-hearts, I bet."

There is no part of that sentence that doesn't make me feel super awkward.

Alexa shrugs. "To be honest, I'm pretty shocked you two aren't together."

She doesn't mean it like a low blow, but it still feels that way. "Well, you know." I look away. "Being together requires both people actually wanting a relationship. It doesn't count if it's just me."

Everyone shares uncomfortable glances, and I realize it's the first time I've admitted my crush out loud. But when you almost die, it puts things in perspective. I'm going to speak up and say what I really mean from now on.

"So, can we call you Wonder Woman now?" Alexa makes a finger gun. "Bulletproof Ivy to the rescue."

"I think we need a play-by-play," Ahmed adds.

Sophie brushes the hair off my face. "You're basically the town hero now."

"I am not the town hero."

"You saved someone's life," Ahmed adds. "There's nothing more heroic than that."

No one's said it like that before. "I guess that's true. But you guys were my accomplices. I couldn't have made the connection about Liam if we hadn't done our break-in on Saturday."

Alexa grins. "This is true. We will accept credit for that."

"People made fun of us for dressing as superheroes, but now we're actual superheroes, and no one's gonna make fun of that." Kevin flexes his wimpy right biceps. Maybe he's got a point. Maybe anyone has the potential to be a superhero in the right circumstance. Sometimes it takes saving a life; other times it's just speaking your truth.

Emma plows into the room with her hands on her hips. "Okay, troublemakers. Out."

Everyone groans.

"Where did you get this?" She rolls her eyes at the stolen wheelchair. "She's recovering from a major surgery. Out."

I stifle a laugh that burns in my throat as we say our goodbyes.

Another hour passes uneventfully, during which I watch the cheesiest possible hookup show on MTV and color in the book my friends brought me.

My phone vibrates.

Patrick: Hey.

I stare at the text. I'd already started ruminating over what our first interaction would be like after the whole Liam mess. But the moment I see his name on my screen, I relax. He's not the one who hurt Autumn, and he's not the one who shot me in the chest. Being an asshole isn't hereditary. And plus, I'm genuinely happy to talk to Patrick. Maybe I was so worried about getting Patrick to *like* me, I didn't even realize he already did—as a friend. And maybe that's not so bad after all. Maybe that's pretty great.

Me: Hey.

Three dots pop up, then disappear. My anxiety kicks up a notch, waiting. Finally, he sends me, like, a novel.

Patrick: I don't even know what to say. Ivy, I'm so glad you're okay. I've felt like crap all week. I really had no idea—neither did my mom, she's beside herself. We wanted to stop over to see you at the hospital but I was so worried you hate me and don't want to see me and would kick me out and I'm just so sorry. I hope you can someday forgive me.

Usually long texts full of confrontation and drama make me freak out and pretend I never saw it. But this time, I don't even have to think about it. I just type.

Me: There's nothing to forgive.

Patrick: I can't stop thinking about it. She was right there, in his backyard, all weekend, and I didn't even know.

Me: There's no way you could've known. I was there on Sunday too and had no idea. But it's okay now! Autumn's going to be all right! I put a smiley emoji at the end, because I know he likes them.

Patrick: My dad's in jail.

Me: I heard. I'm sorry.

After I hit Send, it strikes me how weird it is to be sympathetic to this, because Mr. Perkins absolutely deserves to go to jail, but in the end, he's still Patrick's father.

Patrick: I'm glad he's in jail.

Patrick: I know he did it to protect Will, but they're both criminals. Everyone wants to act shocked that Will became an asshole, but that's

what Dad taught him. He became Dad. It really pisses
me off.

He's got a point. Maybe if their dad hadn't been a raging
douchebag, all of this would've turned out differently. It's good
they're in jail. But it probably sucks for Patrick, losing a brother
and a dad in the same week.

Me: You okay?

Patrick: I can't believe you got shot, and you're
asking me if I'm okay.

Me: I care about you.

People make fun of me for caring too much, but I don't think it's
a weakness. It's one of my superpowers.

Patrick: I'm not going to turn out like him,
though. Either of them.

Something about the way he phrases it hits me. Maybe there are
some things about our lives, our families, our circumstances, that
we can't control; but the biggest things, the people we choose to
become, we can.

I smile as I type my reply.

Me: I know.

Emma brings my dinner, which is a generous word, considering it's
a bowl of broth and another cup of water.

Dad comes back in around 6:00 p.m., exhaustion trenched all
over his face. "How are you doing, sweetie?"

I put down my coloring book. "I'm fine. How's Autumn?"

"She's awake." He rubs his forehead. "And she's doing better.

Very dehydrated, and almost all her ribs are broken. We spent the last hour watching *Judge Judy* together. She's not really talking, but she smiled at me, so that's a start."

"Definitely a start." I take another sip of water. "So, do they have any idea why he did it? I mean, other than the fact that he's a raging dou—jerk."

Dad sighs. "I guess the son—William, Liam, whoever—thought Autumn might tell the police he broke into a store, even though they'd already identified him from the security footage. He got freaked out when the police started questioning him. So he had his gang beat her up to teach her a lesson and keep her from snitching."

"Jeez."

"Yeah." Dad pinches the bridge of his nose. "William got scared when it went too far—I guess they didn't mean to hurt her—" He clears his throat. "Hurt her that badly. So William called his father begging for help, because he didn't want to go to federal prison for the rest of his life, and his father wanted to protect him."

I shiver, picturing Autumn dying in that freezing old shed for three days. "I hope he's in prison forever."

"He is." Dad's face grows stern. "Both of them, and their accomplices, too. Including that guy you hit with a hammer; he'll be joining his friends in prison the moment the hospital deems him well enough to discharge. Lawyer says most of them should get twenty to life for what they did."

"Good."

Dad tilts his head up, studying the ceiling. A sheen of glass reflects in his eyes. If I didn't know better, I'd say those were tears. It's surreal seeing Dad cry. He rarely shows emotion at all. In a way, it's nice to know he cares.

I rush to change the subject. "Hey, where's Kathy?"

"At her sister's house, where she'll be staying for a while." His voice remains monotone. "She wasn't sure if she'd be . . . welcome here. I think it's a good idea for her to take some time away right now. But she stopped by yesterday to visit you both, and she sends her love."

"Oh. Okay."

"Hey, listen, Ivy. There's something I need to tell you." He pulls up a chair, moves the cards off it, and takes a seat by my bed. "I want you to know, things are going to be different now."

"What do you mean?"

"I know I haven't always been the best father, and you girls deserve better. I'd really like us all to start seeing a therapist, to work through some things. I'd never force you and your sister to come, but I think it'd be a good idea. Kathy and I are going to go through couples counseling, too—we have a lot to figure out."

I'm totally taken aback. I've been wishing Dad would see a therapist for years. "Wow, really?"

"Yep. But I am pulling the dad card to implement a new rule around the house."

"Oh no." I groan. "What?"

"Dunkin' Donuts Fridays. I think we should bring them back. Just you, me, and Autumn." He twiddles his fingers. "I mean, if you want to."

I smile. "I'd like that." Maybe in time, Autumn will, too. I don't think there's going to be a magic Band-Aid we slap over our family to heal all the wounds. But even the deepest wounds can fade to scars over time, if you take care of them properly.

"Me too." He gently squeezes my arm. "So, how are you feeling? Do you need any more meds?"

"What I need is for you to go home and sleep. You look really tired."

"I can't just leave you girls here," he says. "Besides, that chair is more comfortable than it looks."

"That chair looks like a deathtrap, for one, and for two, I'm fine. They've been taking great care of me, I swear."

He gives me a guilty smile. "Are you sure?"

"I don't want to see you again until you've slept for, like, twelve hours."

"All right, then." He kisses my forehead. "If you need anything, no matter how small, you call me, okay?" Dad pulls out his phone and turns the ringer on. "See? Nice and loud, from now on. Even when I'm at work."

"Thanks, Dad." I blow him a kiss. "You're the best."

He hesitates in the doorway. "I'm not the best. But I'm going to be better."

At 9:00 p.m., Emma comes to say goodbye when her shift ends. She flips off the TV and turns off the lights. I lie back in bed, the fluorescent hallway lights casting a glow into the otherwise dim room.

I wish Autumn was here. The moment the thought flits into my head, I realize how weird it is. Autumn hates me. She probably wishes she could trade me in for a different sister, or just get rid of me completely. But still. I wish she was here.

I start nodding off around 9:15, when a soft knock on the doorframe startles me back awake. "Ivy?"

I slide my glasses on. "Jason?"

"Hey." He buries his hands in his pockets. "The gang said you were awake."

The moment I see him, my heart skips, and I really hate my body for betraying me like that. "Are . . . you going to creepily linger in the doorway? Or are you going to come in?"

He plops down in the chair by my bed, but keeps his eyes down. "You look a lot better."

"Well, my organs are no longer bleeding out, so that's a plus. Also I got this." I place the bullet fragment on the side table. "Pretty badass, right?" I'm not sure why I'm talking so fast, but I need to get it together. "I mean, not badass like I'm bragging or anything. Just, like, it's pretty cool."

"Jeez, Ivy." He rests his elbows on his knees, his head in his hands. "You scared the shit out of me."

"Yeah, bullets are pretty terrifying. You should try having one shot into your chest. Or actually, don't, because that would suck. For me. To have to go to school without you, I mean. I'd have to find another ride." Jeez, word vomit much? "By the way, thanks for, you know, calling 911 and checking out that barn and everything. Sorry about all the detentions."

He reaches out, and for a second, his hand brushes mine. Then he pulls it away. "Is Autumn okay?"

"I think so," I say. "I haven't seen her yet. We're both kind of confined to our rooms."

"I'm glad she's all right."

"Me too."

We sit in silence for a moment, looking anywhere but at each other.

"I'm sorry I was a jerk at the field hockey party," he says. "You were right the whole time."

"I usually am."

"I hate that we fought—it's been bothering me all week. I was so scared when they said you got shot. I just . . . It's probably the most scared I've ever been."

"Yeah, well, how do you think I felt?" I say it as a joke, but he cringes, and I hate talking about this, so I quickly add, "Did you see these flowers your parents sent?"

"Oh wow, yeah. They said they were doing that. They wanted to come visit you, but I told them it would be weird."

"It wouldn't be weird!"

"Yeah, I knew you'd say that. You like my parents more than you like me."

"That's true. As always."

We look away from each other. I start fiddling with my IV tube, which is probably a horrible idea, because I can imagine myself accidentally ripping it out of my skin.

There're a million things I want to ask him.

Did you really come to see me every day?

Is it because I'm your best friend?

What's going on with us?

Why wasn't I good enough for you?

I open my mouth to blurt it out, when he beats me to it.

"Do you still like Patrick in that way?"

Well, that's nosy. And totally none of his business. But I don't mind. "No. He's one of my best friends, though. Probably will be forever."

"Really? I thought you were in love with that kid."

"Yeah, well. *Love* doesn't always have to be romantic love, you know? I do love him. As a friend."

"That's cool."

My heart monitor beats a little too quickly beside me, and I kind of want to smash it against the wall.

Jason's knee bounces against his hand. "I have to tell you something. I probably should've told you forever ago, and I didn't, and when you got . . . you know . . . I kept thinking that I should've just sucked it up and said it, and ugh, it's driving me nuts."

"Just say it."

"Remember last summer at Sophie's house, when . . . you know."

All the heat in my body floods my face. Sometimes I really hate this kid. "When I asked you to kiss me, and you did, and then you got all awkward about it and rejected me?" I keep my expression neutral, trying to mask the fact that inside I'm totally freaking out right now. "Yeah, I remember."

"Okay, so. Do you remember last year on the band bus when we were all playing truth or dare, and Maura Williams dared you to kiss Brandon Myers?"

"How could I forget? It was my first kiss."

"Yeah, well, then do you remember when it was my turn, and I picked truth, and drummer Jon asked me how far I'd gone with a girl?"

"Yeah." I roll my eyes. "You had a long list. The girl from camp, the girl from church, the two girls from that Battle of the Bands at the Y, that girl—"

"I made it all up."

I give him a weird look. "What? Why?"

"I was embarrassed, okay? I was almost sixteen and still hadn't kissed a girl. I had a huge crush on you and I was a sophomore and you were a freshman and you already had more experience than I did."

"I wouldn't call a dare-kiss 'experience,' but okay. Wait—you had a crush on me?"

"And after I blurted it out, I couldn't just take it back, you know?" His words all cram together into one long sentence. "When you wanted to kiss me last summer, I thought you liked me back, but then I felt awful that we were being, you know, kind of physical and I hadn't told you the truth. And then because I'm a huge loser, I didn't know how to tell you, and you didn't mention it again, so I thought I could just let it go."

"That's the most ridiculous thing I ever heard. What, because you're the guy, that means you're supposed to be more experienced? Who made that rule?"

My heart beats faster. Jason *wanted* to kiss me?

"I know. It was stupid. And anyway, now you know your best friend is a buffoon who was like an inch away from ruining our friendship forever." He raises his shoulders like he's a turtle retreating into his shell. "Please don't hate me."

It takes a second for it to sink in. Jason liked me. All this time I thought *I* was the one who almost ruined our friendship, and he was worried it was him.

Jason's fingers drum against his thighs. It strikes me how jittery he's being. Like he's super nervous. Jason. The guy who's always cool and collected and giving me attitude. *I'm* making him nervous?

"Please," I say. "First of all, I knew you were a buffoon way before now. And second of all, it would take a lot more than that for you to get rid of me, Jason Daly-Cruz."

We share a smile that quickly turns into both of us looking away as fast as humanly possible.

I want to know what he's thinking. I want to know everything he thinks about me. And I'm pretty tired of staying quiet. Didn't I say that was Old Ivy? New Ivy speaks her mind. New Ivy says her feelings. So what if I get rejected? Knowing is better. I need to stop dicking around and tell him how I feel. Tomorrow's not guaranteed—who'd have thought, this time last week, that I'd be in the hospital for a gunshot wound? Not me, that's for sure. I can't keep living my life this way, tiptoeing around the edges, peeking in from the outside.

"Oh jeez, it's late." Jason stands up. "I think visiting hours technically ended like two hours ago, and I kind of snuck in. You'd be proud, I did this whole duck-and-dodge move to get past the nurses' station." His smile falls. "I guess I should go before they kick me out."

"Do you still like me like that?"

The heart monitor beeps steadily beside me, the only noise breaking through the silence.

"Yeah." He blinks. "I never stopped."

"Really?"

"Really."

A soft silence fills the room.

"I was gonna tell you," Jason whispers. "But then Patrick showed up and I . . . I didn't want to get in your way, because you liked him so much. But man, seeing the way you looked at him just . . . killed me."

"Now you know how I felt every time you mentioned one of those imaginary girls you hooked up with."

I don't know what gets into me, but I reach out and take his hand. He laces his fingers with mine, and my breath catches. This feels right. It's a pretty cool thing, when you like someone and they like you back.

"So, are we really doing this? You know." He nods at our joined hands.

I can't stop the smile bursting across my face. "I mean, if you want to. Do you? Want to, I mean?"

"How about this." He takes a deep breath. "Do you want to go to homecoming together?"

"I thought we were."

"You know. Not as friends. Do you want to go as my date? Or . . . as my girlfriend?"

My heart full-on somersaults. "Yeah. That'd be cool." I don't know where this nerve comes from—maybe it's the painkillers—but I can't stop myself from saying it. "Took you long enough to ask."

Jason smirks. "You know, you could've asked me."

"How about I ask you this, for the second time." I bite my lip. "Kiss me, maybe?"

"Okay, now *that* is long overdue."

He leans down and kisses me super gently, and my heart goes so wild, I'm shocked that little monitor doesn't full-on explode. And it's real, and right, and everything I ever thought kissing Jason would be. I let myself get swept away, and for a few moments, all I feel is him. The best part is, this time, he doesn't pull away.

I can't stop smiling the whole rest of the night—when he's sitting by my bed, brushing the hair out of my eyes, when we're laughing our heads off and then quickly shutting up when we don't want to get caught, and even when it gets to be midnight and the night nurse comes in and throws a hissy fit and makes Jason leave.

I don't have a lot, but tonight, it feels like I have everything in the world.

First thing in the morning, a new nurse brings my breakfast. I get oatmeal today, which is an improvement on the all-liquid diet. Jason's coming over after school, and I get this giddy flutter every time I remember that. Dad texts that he'll be here in an hour, and I guess that makes me happy, too.

I wish they'd let me see Autumn.

I'm spooning the last bite of oatmeal into my mouth when Emma knocks on the doorframe. "You up for a visitor, Ivy? There's someone here to see you."

I suck another mouthful of lukewarm water up the straw. "I'm pretty sure half the universe has visited me over the last twenty-four hours, so I'm not sure who could be left, but sure."

The nurse steps out into the hallway, speaking in hushed tones to someone I can't see. She comes back in, rolling Autumn in a wheelchair. My sister drags an IV pole behind her. A bag of clear liquid hangs off the hook, attached to her hand by a long tube. A purple ring encircles her left eye, and bruises dapple her arms. The moment I see her, it's like my heart could burst.

"Well, I'll give you two some privacy. Press the call button when you're ready to go back to your room." Emma pats Autumn lightly on the back and disappears into the hallway.

We stare at each other for a good thirty seconds.

Autumn scratches her neck. "Can I come hang out for a bit?"

"Hey." I blink. "You're back."

In some ways it's like I'm looking at a stranger, or someone who's been gone a long time—three days, three years. But then, somehow, it's like she's been here the whole time.

Autumn smiles, and it's the first time I've seen her smile in years. "I never left."

EPILOGUE

11 MONTHS AND 15 DAYS LATER

AUTUMN

This cardboard box is killing the circulation in my fingers. I let it fall onto the rubbery dorm mattress with a thud, then catch my breath, wiping a lock of sweaty hair off my forehead.

Somewhere in the building, a stereo pounds, vibrating through the thin walls. I take a seat on the edge of the bed and survey the room. I'm usually not lucky, but I won the room-lottery jackpot and wound up with a single. Sweet, sweet privacy.

Various boxes and garbage bags stuffed with my clothes and knickknacks litter the floor. The wooden desk looks like it's been around since the seventies, and the tiny dresser probably won't hold half my clothes.

White walls with chipping paint surround me, and there's only one window in the back of the room. My therapist has gotten me into painting. I'm not very good, but I like it. These walls are begging for some artwork.

"So this is college, huh?" Ivy shuffles into the room hugging my giant purple body pillow with one arm and a garbage bag full of my clothes with the other. "Where are all the raging parties?"

"Going to wager a wild guess that they're not in the chem-free dorm."

She gasps in mock offense. "Hey, us sober kids can have pretty cool parties, too."

It's good to see Ivy smiling. Things at home have been rough lately. Dad and Kathy sleep in separate rooms now, and I wonder how long their marriage will last. I still can barely stand the sight of that woman, and I'm pissed Dad's still with her. But the gem in all of this is that I've found my sister again.

Dad strides into the room carrying my shiny new microwave, still in its box. "Where do you want this?"

"Um. Put it on the dresser for now."

He sets it down and stretches out his arms. "Okay, I think I've got one more load from the car, and then we're done! Be right back."

Dad heads out into the hallway. He starts chatting loudly with someone, and Ivy and I both roll our eyes.

"So, are you excited?" Ivy asks.

"I guess. I didn't know pre-vet came with all these math and science classes right off the bat." I stroke the tattoo on my wrist. "I'll miss you guys." I never in a million years thought I'd end up going to school only forty minutes from home. I used to think that was way too close for comfort. Now it feels like I might as well be going to college in another country.

"You can come home every weekend." Ivy smiles, but it doesn't reach her eyes. "And I'll come visit you now that I'm a licensed driver. I mean, when Dad lets me borrow the car."

"You better."

Every time I see my sister, I remember how she looked in that hospital room, all those months ago. I can picture it with perfect clarity, like it's tattooed on my brain. But I don't want to forget any of it, not a single moment.

I can spend every second of every day thanking her, and it will never be enough. That's a debt I'll never be able to repay.

But she's my sister. She'll always have a chunk of my soul, no matter how many miles separate us.

I never told Ivy about those two and a half days I followed her around as a ghost. I don't even know if she'd believe me. But in a way, I didn't have to tell her. It's like this unspoken understanding passed between us, a connection that doesn't need words to be kept alive.

"Oh, before I forget. I made you something." Ivy digs in one of the boxes and pulls out a picture frame, the kind with three photo slots. On the left, there's Ivy and me as kids, in that ridiculous photo with the Harry Potter wands. In the middle, we've got our arms wrapped around each other at my graduation a few months ago. I cock my head. "Why is the last frame empty?"

Ivy shrugs. "For future memories?"

"I like that." I set the frame on my dresser by the microwave. The room looks better already.

Dad comes back in with the last load—my laundry basket, filled with endless packages of Easy Mac and ramen. He sets it on the floor.

"That's the last of it."

I wring my hands. I guess I never thought this moment would actually come. Now that it's here—independence, adulthood, all that shit—it's kind of overwhelming. I feel like I have no idea what I'm doing. But maybe no one does.

Dad puts his hand on my shoulder. "Are you sure you're going to be okay?"

"I'm sure." I'm not sure, really. But I'll do my best. It's bittersweet when they head to the door. "I'll see you guys Friday? My last class is . . ." I quickly scan my schedule. "Chem at two. I can be in Concord for games by four?"

"Five on Friday," Ivy corrects. "Patrick, Alexa, and Sophie have Pride Club on Fridays after school now, so we moved it."

"Maybe I can come a little early, then? Hang out with you guys? See Pumpernickel?"

"Dunkin' Donuts Friday?" Dad and Ivy say at the same time.

"Oh my God." I roll my eyes. "You guys are so cheesy."

"Can I invite Jason?" Ivy asks.

"No, Ivy, your boyfriend is totally unwelcome." I make a face at her. "Yes, obviously. I think we're all more than used to his presence by now."

Dad squirms, and it's kind of hilarious that he still hasn't gotten used to Ivy dating.

I hug my dad and Ivy in turn. "You'll take care of my dog, right?"

"You mean *my* dog?" Ivy wiggles her brows.

I deadpan glare at her, and Ivy cracks up laughing.

"Yes, of course I'll take care of *your dog*, jeez."

Ivy and Dad walk out, leaving me alone in my new dorm room. I watch them through my window, heading down the steps and into the parking lot, where various cars and trucks wait in the loading zone, packed with boxes, wide-eyed freshmen, and nervous parents.

I don't know what hits me, but I turn around and charge out the door after them, through the hall and outside to the parking lot. My flip-flops clap against the pavement.

"Ivy! Wait!"

She spins around. "What's wrong?"

I run up and throw my arms around her. "I'm just going to miss you."

We hold on for at least a minute. Finally, she climbs into the front seat of Dad's Honda and they pull out, giving a few short honks back to me.

I wave, watching until their taillights disappear onto the main road. In some ways, I guess this is an ending. It's the end of my childhood, the end of living at home, the end of my old life. But in other ways, it feels like the whole world is spread out at my feet, like a million new beginnings.

AUTHOR'S NOTE

Autumn's disappearance in *The Last Confession of Autumn Casterly* is a metaphor for rape culture. We live in a world where abusers' futures are often prioritized over their victims' lives. Just like Liam's father was willing to harm Autumn to protect his son from facing consequences for his violent actions, far too frequently, convicted rapists are given egregiously light sentences for their crime(s), many times due to the desire not to damage their futures and careers, with little or no regard to the damage done to the victim's future and career.

Much like Autumn shouting into the void in her out-of-body experience, many assault victims are gaslighted, accused of lying, and forced to watch their abusers walk free. When Ivy reports the very real danger she fears her sister is facing, Autumn's situation is disregarded due to her history of substance use, misbehavior, and crime; this is similar to when sexual assault victims' pasts, intoxication, outfit choice, and sexual history are unfairly scrutinized and used as reasoning to justify what happened.

I wrote *The Last Confession of Autumn Casterly* from a place of frustration, sadness, and anger. While Autumn Casterly's story is fictional, her circumstances are all too real. According to the Rape, Abuse & Incest National Network's website (rainn.org), one in six American women has been the victim of an attempted or completed rape in her lifetime (https://www.rainn.org/statistics/scope-problem); however, out of 1,000 rapes, 995 rapists will walk free and never serve a day in jail (https://www.rainn.org/statistics/criminal-justice-system). We have a serious problem in this country, and it's not okay. Change starts with listening to and believing victims. If you were a victim of rape or sexual assault, I'm so sorry that happened to you. Please know that you're not alone and it wasn't your fault. I see you, and I believe you. You matter. Never stop fighting.

National Sexual Assault Hotline: 1-800-656-4673

—M

ACKNOWLEDGMENTS

The Last Confession of Autumn Casterly would not be here today without the help and support of many wonderful people.

First of all, I would like to thank my phenomenal agent, Sarah Landis, who supported me and this story from the beginning. I am forever grateful to you for everything you've done for me, my career, and this book. I'm so lucky to have such an amazing agent! And thank you to everyone at Sterling Lord Literistic.

Ari Lewin, my fabulous editor—thank you for taking a chance on me and for bringing this book to the next level. You've been so supportive of Autumn, Ivy, and me, and I'm so lucky to have had an editor who really understood the story.

Elise LeMassena—thank you for all your support and spot-on editorial work on this book. I am so grateful to have had such a great team working on Autumn and Ivy's story!

To my copy editor, Cindy Howle—I am still in awe of your copyediting skills. I am so grateful and lucky that I had someone with such a keen eye for detail working on my book. Thank you!

Thank you to Jennifer Klonsky for believing in this book and for all your support, to amazing cover designer Dana Li, and to publicist extraordinaire Tessa Meischeid for everything you've done for my work! And to everyone at Putnam, Penguin Teen, and Penguin Random House—working with you has been a dream come true, and

I'm honored you chose to publish my book. And thank you to Susie Albert for helping me get my college football facts straight!

I would also like to thank the wonderful literary agents who saw something in this book. I am so grateful to have had the chance to speak with you, and I took all your feedback to heart and used it to improve the story. Thank you for believing in this story.

Jamie Howard—who'd have thought when we started chatting on #CPMatch back in 2014 that you would become one of my best friends and lifelong critique partner? I'm so grateful for your friendship and for all your notes and critiques over the years, especially with this book.

Jennifer Stolzer—thank you for your epic plot-whispering and CPing over the years. I'm so lucky to have you as a CP and friend!

Ron Walters—thank you for continually supporting me over the years, for your beta reading, and for everything you did for this book!

A big thank-you to my beta reader friends who helped make this book shine—Kirsten Cowan, Monica Craver, Julie Abe, Erica Cameron, and of course, my fabulous husband and eternal beta reader, Vincent Servello.

I'd like to thank all the wonder authors of #TeamLandis for all your support, wisdom, and guidance. Erin Craig, Shelby Mahurin, Jess Rubinkowski, Leah Johnson, Julie Abe, Ron Walters, Elisabeth Funk, Jen Adam, Isabel Ibanez, Lyudmyla Hoffman, Jennie Brown, and Mindy Thompson, I'm so grateful to have you all in my corner!

To all my writer friends who supported this book: Amanda Heger, Marie Meyer, Annika Sharma, Joanna Ruth Meyer, Erin Callahan, Diana Pinguicha, Jamie Krakover, Emily Hall, Zoulfa Katouh, Rosaria Munda, Lisa Hood, everyone in the NAC, the Electric Eighteens, my Twitter buddies, the entire Write Pack, and everyone else—your support and friendship mean the world to me.

I'm lucky to be surrounded by such wonderful, talented people. Thank you.

And thank you to the fabulous teachers Jon Kelly and Jackie Catcher for answering my high school teaching questions!

Vincent—I could list you as my husband, or my best friend, or my beta reader, or my biggest supporter, and they would all be true. I love you so much. Thank you for everything you are, and everything you do.

Dad—thank you for all your support and love over the years. I am so lucky to have such a supportive father! I love you.

Thank you to my mother, Jessica Ross Tate, who is no longer here but inspires me every day. I carry you in my heart. I love you.

Thank you to Vincent F. and Michele Servello, all the Tates, Rosses, Siegels, Servellos, Murrays, Bombardiers, and Pions—I'm very grateful to have such supportive family and in-laws!

To all my friends not mentioned above who have supported me and my writing from the beginning—Caitlin Clark, Rebekah Mar-Tang, Kristina Rieger, Sarah Winters, Caitlin Stevenson, Joanna Wolbert, Corey Landsman, Caity Bean, Alexis Carr, Audrey Desbiens, Katie Levesque, Brendan Bly, Molly Hyant, Amy Debevoise, Eric and Amy Lousararian, Lauren Vanderslice, Jill Schaffer, Brett Roell, Paige Donaldson, Katie Gill, Ashley Taylor Ward, Jess Taylor, Barbara and Ed, all the Dizzy Dames, all my wonderful teachers, and everyone else—you know who you are—thank you from the bottom of my heart!

And thank you to my cousin Jon Siegel for taking my author photos!

Wonder Waffel, Plusch Cafe, True Brew, Kaldi's Coffee, and others—thanks for letting me take up a table and write/edit this book for hours, and for feeding me lots of delicious food and coffee.

Shout-out to Friendly's, Red River Theater, Szechuan Gardens, Dunkin' Donuts, Polar Seltzer, Granite State Candies, Midnight Merriment, True Brew Barista, Concord High School, White Park, and every other real Concord location, event, or local product referenced in this book—you're all wonderful, and are all featured because you hold special meaning for me. I hope you don't mind that I named you in my book. The name-dropping came from a place of love and respect, and I hope that shows!

To my lovely hometown of Concord, New Hampshire: I would not be who I am without all those wonderful years and memories that went on to inspire this book. I wrote about Concord, a town of extreme importance to me, from a place of fondness and admiration, and I hope that comes through in the text. Please forgive the playful jabs, which I promise were made with love!

I took some liberties on some aspects of the town, which were exaggerated or added from my imagination for the story's sake, and I hope you understand. This book is not autobiographical and does not reflect my experience attending Concord High School.